PENGUIN BOOKS

MY DREAM OF YOU

'Nuala O'Faolain's tale of passion, independence and loneliness set in contemporary and nineteenth-century Ireland is a real page turner' *Daily Express*

'A big, generous, essentially old-fashioned novel … affecting and entirely believable' *The New York Times*

'This is above all a story about living life with zest. What is truly delightful is the book's warmth and generosity … a considerable fictional talent' *Image Magazine*

'*My Dream of You* is mesmerizing and lyrical, a welcome departure from the formulaic tedium of so many romantic novels' *The Times*

'O'Faolain's debut is impressive … she controls an elaborate plot with confidence. A multi-layered and sensuous book' *Sunday Tribune*

'An intelligent, energetic and absorbing read' *Mail on Sunday*

'There are plenty of fantastically entertaining opinion columnists who can't write novels for toffee, but O'Faolain, a veteran of the *Irish Times*, makes for a wonderfully good exception' *Guardian*

'If novels can be said to be machines for accumulating meaning, the journalist and memoirist Nuala O'Faolain's extraordinary first novel is all meaning. This is true from the start, and meaning grows, so that the ending is more devastating than anything I've read since *The Mill on the Floss*' *Observer*

'A grand achievement of storytelling. A lovely heartbreaker of a novel that asks the hard questions' *USA Today*

My Dream of You

NUALA O'FAOLAIN

PENGUIN BOOKS

PENGUIN BOOKS

Published by the Penguin Group
Penguin Books Ltd, 80 Strand, London WC2R 0RL, England
Penguin Putnam Inc., 375 Hudson Street, New York, New York 10014, USA
Penguin Books Australia Ltd, 250 Camberwell Road, Camberwell, Victoria 3124, Australia
Penguin Books Canada Ltd, 10 Alcorn Avenue, Toronto, Ontario, Canada M4V 3B2
Penguin Books India (P) Ltd, 11 Community Centre, Panchsheel Park, New Delhi – 110 017, India
Penguin Books (NZ) Ltd, Cnr Rosedale and Airborne Roads, Albany, Auckland, New Zealand
Penguin Books (South Africa) (Pty) Ltd, 24 Sturdee Avenue, Rosebank 2196, South Africa

Penguin Books Ltd, Registered Offices: 80 Strand, London WC2R 0RL, England

www.penguin.com

First published by Michael Joseph 2001
Published in Penguin Books 2001

13

Grateful acknowledgement is made for permission to quote from the works of others: Lyric
excerpt of 'If I Loved You' by Richard Rogers and Oscar Hammerstein II, Copyright 1945
by Williamson Music. Copyright Renewed. WILLIAMSON MUSIC owner of publication and allied
rights throughout the world. International Copyright Secured. Reprinted by Permission.
All Rights Reserved. From *The Complete Poems of Walter de la Mare*, copyright 1969. Reprinted
by permission of The Literary Trustees of Walter de la Mare, and the Society of Authors. 'Love
Again' from *Collected Poems* by Philip Larkin (Faber and Faber). Reprinted by Permission of
Faber and Faber Ltd and Farrar, Straus & Giroux. Lyric excerpt of 'Friends in Low Places' by
Garth Brooks, Copyright 1990 by Hal Leonard Corporation. All Rights Reserved. Lyric excerpt
of 'All the Things You Are' by Jerome Kern & Oscar Hammerstein II, Copyright 1941 by
Universal Music Group. Reprinted by Permission. All Rights Reserved. Lyric excerpt of 'Tea
For Two' by Youmans, Caesar & Harbach, Copyright 1925 by Universal Music Group.
Reprinted by Permission. All Rights Reserved. Grateful acknowledgement of Estate of Padraic
Colum and Dolmen Press for 'An Old Woman of the Roads', copyright 1921 by Padraic Colum.
While every effort has been made to obtain permission from the owners of copyright
material, the publisher would like to apologize for any omissions or inaccuracies and will be
pleased to correct the acknowledgements in any future edition.

The moral right of the author has been asserted

Set in Monotype Garamond
Printed in England by Clays Ltd, St Ives plc

The passages in italics in this book are verbatim quotations from original source material relating to the Talbot divorce case, which is an actual event.

Prologue

We used to stay in bed most of the weekend, Hugo and I, when we lived in the attic of a rambling house with pinnacles and gables, among chestnut trees, on the edge of a park in south London. We had a wide mattress on the floor in front of tall, warped windows that could be pushed and dragged open onto a dank balcony. That spring, a pigeon nested in a bower of branches on a level with our pillows. Its nest used to rock in the breeze, and spangles of green light would spill through the canopy of leaves and across our bodies. On weekdays we worked. I got up early to clean two pubs; I had to pay the fees for my journalism diploma as well as make enough to live on. Hugo got up to study, at a desk in a little tower off the end of the room; he was doing law in the daytime and the journalism diploma at night. But at weekends we played.

We lived on the mattress as on a raft. We gathered everything we needed or wanted around us on the floorboards, reaching out for things from under the quilt when it was cold, and in summer, sprawling across the sunlit sheets. Hugo used to bring coffee and toast up from the kitchen. He kept the bread for the toast in the room, because the other students who lived in the house ate like locusts when they came in from pubs and discos on Friday night. His mother had given him a real coffee-maker. Hardly anyone had one of those in the early seventies – even in London. His mother had brought it back from somewhere abroad – I don't know exactly where, because he told me very little about her, and I never met her. She always gave him some expensive thing, when he had supper with her.

That's what he called it. I'd only just got used to the meal in the evening being called dinner and it embarrassed me when Hugo said 'supper'. In the Ireland I grew up in, there was no such meal, any more than there was real coffee. You got your dinner when you came in from school – or, in our house, you did if Mammy had made any. There was the tea, later on. The only time we ever used the word 'supper' was in The Last Supper. But why what I secretly felt was *embarrassment* at Hugo using a humble word like supper about dinners in expensive restaurants, I do not know.

I watched him all the time, though he didn't watch me. Yet he was mad about me. He hardly ever got through an hour of study without stopping to stroke a flank again, or to pull my slack mouth onto his, or to guide my hand into a caress he wanted. He showed me that he needed me. Well, wanted me. I had noticed, soon after we started to live together, that though he praised my body and my hair, he never said anything about my face. So I was a lot more confident rolling around with him in the dark than when he was looking at me.

When we lived in the room full of the liquid cooing and gobbling of the pigeons, he was in his last year of studying for an LLB. The degree required some legal history, including an hour or so on the history of divorce law, which is how he came to toss onto the bed one day a photocopy of the proceedings in the House of Lords of *Talbot v. Talbot (1856)*. It was a Sunday evening, when we were getting ready for the coming week. I loved those times. Criss-crossing the big room purposefully. The crumpled newspapers tidied away and the bed shaken free of crumbs. Hugo was usually a bit tetchy – tired of me, really – and mentally turned towards work. But I'd be sated, and content. The darkness outside, and we so safe.

I lived in the house among the chestnut trees for only a while. I was expelled from that Eden when I was twenty-three, and I'm almost fifty now. Once, years ago, I was in the gym of a hotel in Madeira, or maybe Malta – some place that was hot, anyway, and dull in a British way – taking notes for an article, when I glanced up at the mute television sets. For some reason they were all showing a debate from the Canadian Parliament. Behind the portly man who was speaking, there was a thin, absent-minded one, with his head sunk on crossed fingers, and I think that man was Hugo. My skin flushed for a second. Those fingers . . .

Now, it is for a document he once – carelessly – gave me that I am grateful to him. He was the one boy I knew who was ambitious enough to be studying law, and who was scrupulous enough to bring home the lecturer's xeroxed pages to study, and who would have thought of clipping them together and turning to me, instead of throwing them out with the other reading material he was finished with.

You'd be interested in this, Kathleen, he said. Real women's lib stuff. And it's Irish. Or, at least, it happened in Ireland.

Ahrash, he made it sound like. Ahland.

You had to go to Parliament to get a divorce then, he said. That's what this is – the *Judgment* on –

the petition presented by one Mr Talbot of Mount Talbot in Ireland, praying that your Lordships would pass the Bill for divorcing him, as it is called, from his wife, her having or having not been guilty of adultery.

The English in other people's countries, I said. Committing adultery. Sure that's what they did all the time in Kenya, too, and in India – anywhere they hadn't enough to do, kicking the natives around.

This was with a native, Hugo said. He read out:

My Lords, the adultery alleged against Mrs Talbot is an adultery alleged to have taken place commencing in the year 1849 with one of the domestic servants in Mount Talbot, a man of the name of William Mullan. Though it does not appear that Mr and Mrs Talbot ever kept what is ordinarily called a carriage, they had an Irish car, as most families have in Ireland; and when they went out in that car, Mullan drove them, as well as took care of the horse –

I like that bit about most families, I remember saying. 1849, you said? 'Most families' were either dead in the Famine or getting the hell out of Ireland.

Oh for Chrissake, Hugo said, mildly enough.

I looked through the *Judgment* for a minute or two.

God! They were bold lovers! I said, and read out to him:

The witnesses both say they saw Mullan and Mrs Talbot lying down together in the straw in one of the stalls. You have it that he was in his stable clothes, and a witness calls him a dirty, filthy-looking person; and that — that does not alarm her. Now, when you talk of the impossibility of a lady allowing an act of sexual intercourse in a stable, where, as it is said, the beasts copulate, that may sound very well, but you are to recollect that if a grovelling passion of this kind engrosses a woman towards a menial servant, how is it to be gratified? Opportunities will not always occur: they must be sought.

Come here, Hugo interrupted me. They must put something in the water in Ireland.

He'd sat down in the big wooden rocking chair and patted his lap. My hair was halfway down my back then. He bent and wound a long lock around his hand and pulled me towards him.

I was interested, always, in any story about passion, so I was interested in Mrs Talbot and William Mullan. I believed in passion the way other people believed in God: everything fell into place around it. Even before I started mooching around after boys when I was fourteen, I'd understood, watching my mother, that passion was the name of the thing she was pursuing, as she trawled through novel after novel. And it was extraordinary to me that the Talbot affair began when it did — just after the very worst year of the potato famine. The Famine was the one thing in Irish history that I sometimes tried to imagine. When I was about nine or ten, I was playing one day on the seaweedy rocks across the road when a man came past, pushing a bicycle, and stopped to talk to me. He was a historian, from England. He told me that the Famine had happened even there, in Shore Road, where I thought nothing had ever happened. He told me that there had been people, when the Famine came, who lived, unimaginably ragged and poor, in the holes and crevices that were still there above the beach — the ones where we played house ourselves. And that those people had been wiped out and had left no trace, unless a heap of stones near the tideline was the cairn above a mass grave. I asked at home — what happened to our own family in the Famine? How was it that we didn't die? No reply, as usual.

4

But I found a way to link the pictures the scholar put in my head to my real life. My father was angry nearly all the time and my mother just went around in a silent bubble of her own. I didn't know why they bothered to have children. So I put the two things together, home and the Famine, and I used to wonder whether something that had happened more than a hundred years ago, and that was almost forgotten, could have been so terrible that it knocked all the happiness out of people.

For those two reasons – because it was about passion, and because it happened during a time I had brooded about since I was a child – I kept the pages of the Talbot *Judgment* safe, and even before I read the whole thing properly, I could always have put my hand on it in the dark.

By the time I was middle-aged I was well defended against crisis, if it came from outside. I had kept my life even and dry for a long time. I'd been the tenant of a dim basement, half buried at the back of the Euston Road, for more than twenty years. I didn't like London particularly, except for the *TravelWrite* office, but I didn't see much of it. Jimmy and I, who were the main writers for the travel section of the NewsWrite syndicate, were on the move all the time. We were never what you'd call explorers, we never went anywhere near war or hunger or even discomfort. And we wrote about every place we went to in a cheerful way: that was the house rule. But we had a good boss. Even if it was the fifth 'Paris in Springtime' or the third 'Sri Lanka: Isle of Spices', Alex wouldn't let us get away with tired writing. Sometimes Jimmy accused him of foolish perfectionism, because every *TravelWrite* piece was bought immediately anyway. But having to please Alex was good for us. And then, people do read travel material in a cheerful frame of mind, imagining themselves at leisure and the world at its best. It's an intrinsically optimistic thing, travel. Partly because of that, but mostly because Alex went on caring, I liked my work.

I even liked the basement, in a way, in the end. I don't suppose more than a handful of people ever visited it more than once, in all the time I was there. Jimmy was my close friend and since he'd come to *TravelWrite* from America he'd lived twenty minutes away, in Soho, but we'd never been inside each other's places. It was understood that if one of us said they were going home, the other didn't ask any questions. Once, early on, he said he was going home, and I happened to see, from the top of the bus, that he had stopped a taxi and was in fact going in the opposite direction. After that, I deliberately didn't look round when we parted. Anyway, my silent rooms were never sweetened by the babble the two of us had perfected over the years.

And for a long time, there hadn't been anyone there in the morning when I woke up. Sex was a hotel thing. I don't think I'd have liked to disturb the perfect nothingness of where I lived.

Then a time came when I began to lose control of the evenness and the dryness.

I was waiting for my bag in the Arrivals hall at Harare airport when I fell into conversation with the businessman in the exquisite suit who was waiting beside me. Favourite airlines, we were chatting about.

Royal Thai Executive Class is first-rate, he said.

Ah, don't tell me you fall for all that I-am-your-dusky-handmaiden stuff, I laughed at him.

Those girls really know how to please, he went on earnestly, as if I hadn't spoken at all. And there was a porter with gnarled bare feet asleep on the baggage belt, and when it started with a jolt the poor old man fell off in front of us, and all the businessman did was step back in distaste and then take out a handkerchief and flick it across the glossy toecaps of his shoes. But I accepted his offer of a lift into town, all the same. We were stopped for a moment at traffic lights beside a bar that was rocking with laughter and drumming.

They're very musical, the Africans, he said. Great sense of rhythm.

Just what are you doing, I asked myself, with Mr Dull here?

I half knew: no, quarter knew. But if nothing more had happened I would never have given it a conscious thought.

Men can't allow themselves that vagueness. At his hotel he said, Would you like to come in for a drink? Or would you like to come up to the room while I freshen up? I've rather a good single malt in my bag.

I propped myself against the headrest of his big bed and sipped the scotch and watched him deploy his neat things – his papers, his radio, his toiletries. When he came out of the bathroom with his shirt off and the top of his trousers open, I was perfectly ready to kiss and embrace. I was dead tired. I'd had a drink. I was completely alone in a foreign country. I was more than willing to hand myself over to someone else.

But very soon I was frowning behind his corpse-white back.

If only I knew how to take charge of this myself, I thought. If I could be the real thing myself, I could bring him with me . . .

I honestly don't know how any person could make as little of the living body as that man did. Even the best I could do hardly made him exclaim. But he seemed to be delighted with the two of us, afterwards. At least I thought he was. He invited me to have dinner with him the next night, and I accepted though I didn't much want to struggle through hours of trying to make conversation. And I was in a great humour when he saw me into a taxi. It had been human contact, hadn't it? I was a generous woman, wasn't I, if nothing else? I hummed as I hung my clothes in the wardrobe of my mock-Tudor guest-house, under huge jacaranda trees that in the streetlights looked as if their swathes of blossom were black. My favourite thing: a hotel bedroom in a new place.

The phone rang. It was Alex to say that he needed Zimbabwe wildlife copy within forty-eight hours.

I suppose you think that elephants and giraffes just walk around downtown Harare like people do in London? I shouted sarcastically down the phone. I suppose you think they have a game park in this guest-house *where I have just arrived*. Then I hung up.

When the phone rang again I picked it up, ready to do a deal about the deadline. But it was the businessman.

How are you, my little Irish kitten? he said. I am thinking of you.

Oh, really? I said, embarrassed. Kitten. I was forty-nine.

Unfortunately, he said, I must go out of town.

One hour after I'd been with him! He hadn't even waited till the next day.

And that's what I learned from him – that my heart was still ridiculously alive. I was sincerely hurt. What had I done wrong? I actually swallowed back tears.

And then, he continued, I must go directly back to my office.

There was nothing between the man and me – nothing, not even liking. But because of the memory of some wholeness, or the hope of some regeneration, I would have dropped whatever I'd planned, just to go back to scratching around on his bed.

I cannot go on like this, I said to myself. *Tears*!

I went on to the East a few days later to do a quick piece about a hot springs resort in the Philippines. I walked up to the famous waterfall, and though the humid, greyish air smelled like weeds rotting in mud and there were boys everywhere along the paths between the flowering trees, begging, or offering themselves as guides, it was possible to see that this was a marvellous spot, with hummingbirds sipping from the green pools that trembled under each fall before silently overflowing and sliding down the smooth rock to the next terrace. It was going to be easy to put a positive spin on the place. I made notes and took photos of the birds for identification, and then I got a bus to Manila. It arrived in the sweltering heat and dust of the evening rush. My hotel was on the far side of a busy dual carriageway. I started across the road, and reached the central reservation where there was a bit of a dust-covered low hedge. A small hand came out of the hedge. I bent down. Two dirty-faced girls of seven or eight had a box under the hedge with an infant sleeping in it.

Dollar! the girl said. Then she stood on the central reservation with the traffic going past on both sides and lifted the skirt of her ragged frock and pushed her delicate pelvis in threadbare panties forward. I didn't know what she meant, and maybe she didn't, either.

What money I had in my pocket I gave her, and then, instead of checking into the hotel I got a taxi to the airport, looking neither left nor right.

There are children living in the middle of the road, I said.

Yes, the driver said. The country people come to town and they live in the street.

There was silence. He flicked on a Petula Clark tape.

After he took my money, outside Departures, he said, We don't need no fuckin' grief from some old bitch.

The flight back to Europe was very long. I sat in the dark with my eyes open and grainy while the other passengers slept. The man beside me had slumped to one side, the napkin from the meal still tucked into his collar, like a baby's bib.

9

I was ashamed of myself at first for the egotistic way I reacted to the children in the middle of the road. They made me think about myself – me, me, me as usual – instead of the injustice of the world or anything like that. But then I thought, isn't it some kind of good, that a person can be shocked into truthfulness, even if it's only for a few hours and only with herself? I sat in the thick night air of the plane and I thought, if anyone had said to you, all these years, Are you interested in sex? you'd have said, haughtily, No. I'm interested in passion. *Passion.* I murmured the word half out loud. What passion? It was never real excitement that got you into bed; it was hope, like some stubborn underground weed. Look at the way you've believed every time, at the first brush of a hand across a breast, that the roof over your life was sliding back and a dazzling, starry firmament was just coming into view. When it never happened! When a one-night stand has never, in all the years, done what you wanted it to do. What's more, the whole thing is getting more and more pathetic. The truth is, I said to myself, that the older you get, the more grateful you are for being wanted on any terms, by anybody.

But if I stopped all that, how would I ever meet anyone? If I didn't have this kind of sex life, bad and all as it is, I'd have none. Then I thought, But should it even be called sex? Look at the businessman in Harare. You're not even giving them pleasure anymore, never mind getting any for yourself.

Then I started to smile, remembering Harare, at something else that had happened there. I'd got talking to a big, warm woman who was hanging out the guest-house laundry while I was sitting on a back porch, working on my laptop. I helped her with the flapping sheets. Later I walked across town with her to see the room in a township that she'd raised her family in. We sat on the bed telling each other our life stories while she leaned across to the cooking ledge and made a stew. She took down a plastic carrier bag from a nail on the wall and showed me her treasures. Her radio that got two stations. Her conical pink bra, for best occasions. I went with her when she poured the stew into a bucket to sell around the big, bare beer halls. She made a wonderful sexy comedy out of offering it, and after a while I stopped being shy and joined in the spree. The men laughed their heads off at the sight of us two women and scooped the stew into tin bowls beside their bottles of beer. We danced around and shrugged and rubbed ourselves in a parody of excitement, and wiggled our bosoms at the fellas. By the time the whole pot of stew was sold we had a band of children following us and we were weak with laughter.

I do still know how to live, I said to myself.

On the plane, the man in the seat beside me had let his head somehow fall onto his plump fists – a wide band on one finger gleaming in the dark – and he was making grumbling noises in his sleep at the discomfort. I eased him into a better position as carefully as I could. Then I slept, too.

In London I tried to raise Jimmy on his mobile. We'll have to face up someday to all the awful things in the world, I wanted to say to him. If he'd allow me. He hated me getting serious.

Jimmy really does want things kept cool, I once said to Roxy, the office secretary.

Well, you're a bit too emotional by any standards, she said to me.

Roxy was so exceptionally stolid that I didn't have to take this remark very seriously. But I had squirreled it away to examine it. No one in my life told me anything about myself except Roxy and Jimmy and, occasionally, usually crossly, Alex. In that way the three of them were my family.

Jimmy wasn't answering his mobile. It occurred to me that he was in New York. I sent him an e-mail.

I need to talk to you, Jimmy, it said. I think I've had it with *TravelWrite*. I'm getting old, sweetheart. The good has gone out of the job.

I sent another one half a minute later.

Not just out of the job, Jimmy – the good has gone out of *me*.

Jimmy had been at the Mercer but he'd checked out. When I finally got to talk to him he said the place was so fashionably young that it made him feel old. He was coming back a roundabout route via Miami but we arranged to get together after work a few days later in a wine bar near the office – a place that had once been a cavernous Victorian pub and now had a split personality, with mean little chrome chairs looking all wrong in the heavy pitch-pine booths. I thought, watching Jimmy go up to the bar, about him saying that he felt old. When he was so slender and vivid! Had I ever really tried to understand the ways in which a gay man's ageing might hurt differently from my own? The boy in fake Prada behind the counter was laughing up at him. Everyone liked Jim because he had an open face and a quiff of straw-coloured hair, just like Tintin's. Of course, he didn't want to look like Tintin – he wanted to look like James Dean in *Rebel Without a Cause*.

I think you *are* looking a bit Dean-ish this evening, I said to him when we were settled. Those narrow, hot eyes, you know? Eyelids bruised from nights of excess?

Jet lag, he said. And what has you being so nice to me, Dame Freya darling? If this is a symptom of your mid-life crisis, I hope you're going to go on having it.

What were you doing in Miami, dearest Mr Chatwin? I said. You were hardly there for the fine wines.

You can't get a decent bottle of Sancerre south of the Mason–Dixon Line, Jimmy said. Or even a good Chinese meal.

The best Chinese food in the world is in Seattle, I said, where the Chinese draughtsmen from Boeing open restaurants with their severance pay. They've got American raw materials there. That's what Chinese food needs.

You know the problem with Seattle? Jimmy said. It's too far away.

It's only too far away if you start from here.

I disagree, he said seriously. There are some places that are too far away even when you're in them. Seattle is one.

We talked this kind of nonsense a lot of the time. Roxy said it drove her crazy. But after twenty years together, Jimmy and I didn't listen to ourselves. We told each other everything through smiles or frowns or whether we cut a date short or lingered, or whether we looked down at the table or into each other's eyes, or whether we took a sip of the wine with gusto or flatly. Once, when I was upset at a meeting, Jimmy said, What's up, love? and Alex got really cross.

How do you *know* there's something up with her? he said, frustrated. *How*? The two of you always seem much the same to me.

There were ways in which we did acknowledge, in the wine bar, that something was happening but that we had confidence in each other and would deal with it in time. That Jim ordered a bottle of wine, for example, instead of starting with a glass each, said to me that if I insisted on having a serious talk, he was there for me. And my mock petulance when we were hugging goodbye told him that I wasn't going to be difficult about whatever he was up to in Miami.

Why can't I have a rendezvous with you? I said. Why can't I lie on a mattress in the pool of the Delano while a hunky waiter brings me a Cuba Libre and a slice of key lime pie?

Later, sweetie, Jimmy said. When we're old we'll move to South Beach for our arthritis.

I'll be jealous of all your geriatric rough trade, I said, rubbing his springy hair.

That was the last time I ever touched him.

There'll be no rough trade left, he said. The boys will all be dead.

I had a funny story to tell him the next morning when I went in to work. Well, not all that funny, maybe. I'd been coming out of Euston Road station, going home from the wine bar, when a pair of feet seemed to run towards me across the dirty pavement and stop, and a girl's voice said, Hi! I looked up and saw that behind her madly smiling face a video camera was pointed into mine. Fashion Channel Plus! the girl carolled, coming around shoulder-to-shoulder with me and beaming into the camera. It's the Vox Pop Shop! Hi! We're coming to you live from the streets of London to tell you what the happening people are wearing!

The camera with a man's legs walked backward and framed me. I'd looked to see what I was wearing. It was a charcoal wool trouser suit that had fitted when I was still smoking, but the pounds I'd put on since I stopped poked out between the edges of the jacket now. I'd remembered that when I put it on, but I'd said to myself, Sure what of it, I'm only going to the office. Then I'd thought, That's a depressed woman's way of thinking.

I don't know why you're asking me, I said to the camera, smiling pleasantly and pulling my stomach in. I'm afraid I don't know the first thing about fashion.

I expected to be contradicted, of course.

Leave it! the girl stunned me by shouting at the cameraman. This one's a no-no. She turned back to me for a moment. Sorry about that, she said over her shoulder. We're only talking to people who live here. Londoners.

That was all. No big deal. But I'd gone back to the basement stinging with chagrin. I live here! I protested in my head. I've lived in London since I was twenty years old! And that's a designer trouser suit – that cost a lot of money, so it did!

And there and then I'd picked a psychiatrist from the Yellow Pages and left a request for an appointment on his answering machine.

I was going to tell Jim all that.

It was the monthly planning meeting that morning. Alex and Roxy and I waited and waited. The phone rang. Alex put the phone down and said to us from lips gone chalk white: Jimmy is dead. He had died, during the night, of a heart attack.

I never cried. My sister, Nora, who has managed to misunderstand me consistently from the hour I was born, rang me not long afterwards and said, You're getting over Jimmy very quickly, aren't you? I thought he was your big pal.

She'd taken against him, early on, because once when we stayed with her in New York, he thanked her by giving her a subscription to a Beethoven sonata cycle at Carnegie Hall with a little joke about showing the world she was not just a moneyed Mick. Nora is a big-deal personal assistant and earns a fortune and she's confident to a fault, but even she couldn't say what she wanted to, which was, What's wrong with being a moneyed Mick?

But the reason I did not cry was that I dared not.

I didn't know what to do. The first three or four days after he died I spent in the basement. I heard Alex calling down through the letterbox in the hall door, and my friend Caroline called a couple of days later. But I shouted up to her that I was busy – that I was reading. I didn't come out till I had nothing left to read. I read all the paperbacks on the top shelf of the bookcase, from left to right, and then I read the whole of the Talbot *Judgment* because it was on the next shelf and then I read the guidebooks on the bottom shelves. After the funeral, I stopped reading and instead I wrote as much as I could. I wrote the pieces Jimmy had been scheduled to do as well as my own. I didn't stop moving and writing until I realized, in a crumbling spa in the Tatras foothills, that nothing was helping. Not the oxen dragging the old ploughs up to the small fields that survived on the hillsides, or the smell of woodsmoke and stabled animals along the muddy roads of the low villages as the cold evenings came down. It was no good being there without Jimmy to call to say that I had yet to see a vegetable, or that I was reading the new Theroux and I disliked the man more than ever. Hello, it's only me. Hello, Only You. Where are you? I'm waiting outside the Minister's private office in a gilded villa. I'm having breakfast in a milk bar in a place I can't pronounce. Are you well? Do you have anyone there to talk to? I went to a god-awful folk-dance thing last night. The tourism bloke kept the penthouses for our group. How's Alex looking? The plane was diverted. I forgot to pack sunglasses. Did you have the duck with redcurrants? The maize crop has failed and they're trying to get a World Bank loan. I have a toothache.

But back in London, I did not say that I was finished with the job. I didn't want to disturb the quiet we had pulled around ourselves. Alex sat in his boss's cubicle, and Roxy sat at her secretary's desk, and Betty the administration lady sat down the corridor in her room. I made as little noise as possible, working in the corner. We were gentle with each other. We tried not to mention Jimmy. One of his trainers lay on the floor under his desk. None of us put it away.

De Burca, I said to the psychiatrist's receptionist, when my appointment came around. Kathleen de Burca.

She looked at me as if my not being called Smith or Jones was the very last straw, and put down her pen. Then she picked it up again, wearily.

Could you spell that? she said, as if it were entirely possible that I couldn't.

And what did I do? I said, that's Burke, in English, if that would be easier for you.

Then I complimented her on the New Age flower arrangement on her desk – fawning on her, because I was so afraid. The flesh on my cheeks was actually quivering with fear. By the time I went in to the psychiatrist's office with its antique furniture gleaming in the low light, I was not so much crying as snivelling. I thought everything might unravel then and there and I wouldn't be able to go on. I had let things be. I did my work, and let the rest pile up behind me. I was afraid he would move one little thing in my head, and the whole lot would crash.

There are tissues just beside the chair, he murmured.

I tried to tell him how desolate the nights had been for as long as I could remember. Yes, he murmured. Yes. I told him my best friend was a gay American man and he dropped dead and now I have nobody. Yes. My body slackened with the force of my crying. I howled. I'm getting old! I have made nothing out of my life! Yes, he said. Siblings? he said. A brother at home, and his wife and child, I said. And Nora in New York, the eldest. And my little brother Sean died when he was six and a half and if I'd stayed at home I might have been able to save him! More howling. And there were three or four babies who died soon after they were born. Why do you mention them? he said. I don't know, I said. Except – my poor mother! I moaned and hiccuped, but then the storm of crying began to pass. I tried to explain to him: I'm too depressed even to dress properly. I was wearing a jacket the other day that doesn't even fit me! Units of alcohol? he was saying. I luxuriated in the safety of the exquisite room and his hands lying quietly on the desk, reflected in the polished surface. I did not pull myself up and sit properly, though now only the occasional sob shook me. If you could get it down on paper, he was saying, just the general picture – ages of the children at your mother's death, that kind of thing. Next time we meet I'll ask you –

And then I heard it. I wouldn't have, but that I had stopped crying.

Someone made a furtive movement behind a screen in the dim corner behind him.

I sprang upright like a hare in the grass, and searched his face.

It is quite common! he said. Our trainees are allowed to monitor first consultations on exactly the same basis of absolute confidentiality as the primary relationship.

My legs were shaky as I walked to the door.

They do it in your country, too! he called after me. I can assure you!

That's how I know, I said to Nora when I phoned her, that he took the chance because I was Irish.

Nora was silent. She passionately believed in her own shrink. She'd been trying to get me to go into therapy for years. She'd even sent me a blank cheque once.

Maybe they do it to everybody, she began.

They don't, I said. You know they don't. If that was one of his own kind – if I'd been a university lecturer from Hampstead . . .

Come to me! she said. Come here! Or go home! I don't know how you stuck snobby old England all these years.

But I'd tried that before. The last time there'd been an upheaval in my life, I went to New York to stay with Nora, with the idea of maybe settling down near her. It lasted a week. And Ireland – well, I certainly wasn't going to live in Ireland. Though Ireland was on my mind, in a way it had never been before. Maybe it was going to the psychiatrist that had stirred up the murk. Or maybe it was reading the Talbot *Judgment* again, even though I hadn't realized at the time – so soon after Jimmy died – that I was taking it in.

Something had started moving inside me. I realized it standing in a private zoo near London, taking notes for a piece Alex wanted on animals as tourist attractions. It wasn't a zoo, exactly, as much as a species rescue place where they were running a breeding programme to save the miniature lion tamarin monkey. The reddish-gold colour of spaniels, the monkeys were, with ruffs like the MGM lion around each tiny, melancholy face. I leaned my forehead against the glass to watch them go about their business. I loved looking at them. They

17

hung from branches by one arm, swinging slightly to and fro, pensive, or they crouched under the fleshy leaves of the habitat, or they scratched their heads, completely indifferent to scrutiny. I followed the busy little doings of a lionheaded monkey about the size of my hand with an even smaller one clinging to its stomach. Mother and baby. Poignant little eyes, they had.

It struck me suddenly: I have never looked at my family the way I look at animals. I have never taken an unhurried look at the people by whom I was formed, wanting nothing but to see clearly, the way I look at animals or birds – appreciating them, without having any designs on them. My family has been the same size and shape in my head since I ran out of Ireland. Mother? Victim. Nora and me and Danny and poor little Sean? Neglected victims of her victimhood. Villain? Father. Old-style Irish Catholic patriarch; unkind to wife, unloving to children, harsh to young Kathleen when she tried to talk to him.

Then I lifted my head as if I could smell something odd.

What was I being bitter about, nearly thirty years after I'd seen my father last, and when he'd been dead five or six years? I couldn't *not* have changed. I could not be the same person now that I was when I left home. It just wasn't possible. Although I had lived for a long time, during the basement years, in a state of suspended animation, I had been alive. And everything that is alive changes all the time.

The mother and baby monkey had disappeared. I think they'd gone in behind the big leaves of a tropical tree.

Where are you? I whispered. I tapped lightly on the glass.

The lines of a poem we learned at school came into my head and they pulled at me as I came away.

'Is there anybody there?' said the Traveller, knocking on the moonlit door –

There was a man knocking on the door of a deserted house deep in a forest. And there were ghosts inside on the stairs, weren't there? Listening to him.

'Tell them I came and no one answered – that I kept my word,' he said . . .

I tried to remember it properly.

'Is there anybody there?' said the Traveller, knocking on the moonlit door,

And his horse in the silence of the – something – *champed the grasses of the forest's ferny floor,*

And a bird flew up out of a turret above the Traveller's head,

And he smote upon the door again a second time. 'Is there anybody there?' he said.

A picture formed at the back of my mind, of silent ghosts waiting and listening, and me, the Traveller, riding up and calling to them. Whether these were the ghosts of Marianne Talbot and William Mullan, watching each other on the lamplit stairs of Mount Talbot, or of my father and mother – his watch chain gleaming, her face a pale patch over his shoulder – I didn't bother to decide. It wasn't people I was thinking of. It was a *shape*, a blurred image – me outside somewhere, calling, and tragic ghosts listening to me and waiting for me to free them – that settled itself inside me.

2

I knocked on the door of Alex's cubicle.

Boss darling? I said. Are you busy?

And I told him I was leaving *TravelWrite*.

You can't leave, was the first thing he said.

I thought for one second that he was going to make some kind of personal plea.

But what he said was, The travel trade are giving you the Lifetime Achievement Award at the lunch next week. I wasn't supposed to tell you.

Why me? I said. Why not Jimmy and me? We did the same work.

Yes. Well, initially the award was to Jimmy and you.

There was a sorrowful pause, and then he said, I only wish I'd told him, surprise or no surprise.

After a while I burst out, Lifetime! The Travel Writing Lifetime Achievement Award! Have you ever heard a sadder accolade, Alex? That 'lifetime' was my *life*! My one and only *life* slipped past and I never even noticed! And now I'm nearly fifty and what am I going to do?

It's useful, at least, that you're fifty, Kathleen, he began cautiously. The syndicate does a remarkably good pension arrangement at fifty –

I'm only forty-nine and six and a half months! I snapped at him. Pension! As if I'm interested in *pensions*.

I know, he said. You seem young to me, too. And you've far too much energy to do nothing.

There was a silence.

You're a born writer, you know, he said. You should go on writing. A book, maybe. Something historical.

I don't know any history, I began, gloomily.

If you don't, he said, you're the first Irish person I ever met who doesn't.

Alex, I said, I don't know if I have the energy to try something new. The truth is that I feel I have nothing, now that Jimmy's gone.

You *do* have something, he said earnestly. Really, Kathleen. There is no such thing as having nothing. Jimmy loved you. But God loves you, too. God loves you *more* –

Ah, for sweet Jesus' sake! I yelled at him. You and your *God*!

And I slammed out of the office.

The day of the lunch, in the foyer of the hotel, I came up behind him and watched him for a moment. I knew the anxious angle of his head. Being around smart people did that to him. He was wearing his best lounge suit, the one that Jimmy could hardly bear the sight of, and he had his hands clasped behind his back and was rocking slightly on his heels. He was going very thin on top but his black hair was still beautifully silky. He was wearing lace-up shoes when I was willing to bet that all the other men would be in loafers. If Jimmy were here he'd say, At least they're not those unspeakable brown things.

You look stunning, he said to me – sincerely – when anyone else would have seen that even crushed into a girdle for the occasion, I had a distinct tummy. And the hairdresser had given me weird purple highlights. And I was wearing black tights that were slightly too heavy for my frock. But Alex was as innocent as a baby about things like that.

Now, don't be nervous, Kath, he whispered to me as we walked to the top table. We didn't know most of the people sitting there.

I'm not nervous in public, I said.

This was an invitation to ask me what I meant, and for me to tell him about being afraid of the people I knew, not the people I didn't know, and for him to tell me what he felt, and so on. But he didn't know how to talk that kind of talk.

The chairman introduced me as the doyenne of travel writers. I winced. The oldest, in other words. He said it was the first time the jury had given this coveted award to a syndicate writer, but that the late Jimmy Beck and Kathleen de Burca had, over more than twenty years, given *TravelWrite* a reputation for material of a consistently high standard, blah blah. I could see Alex's face, pale with emotion. Then I went up and made a short speech and ended by accepting the award on behalf of dear Jimmy, who many of those present would remember with affection, and also Alex, our boss at *TravelWrite* – an editor of genius. Then the chairman presented me with a Waterford bowl. And Alex, who I'd noticed was knocking back the wine, gave a raucous football supporter's yell when everyone else was applauding politely, and he shouted, Hold it up high there, Kathleen! Show them what little *TravelWrite* can do!

Everybody turned to look at him. He sat back onto his chair, blushing painfully.

So, to divert attention from him, I said to the people at the top table when I got back from the podium, That's it! I'm going to go out at the top. I'm retiring. I'm going to do some new kind of writing.

Writing about what? someone said.

The woman on the other side of Alex must have been drinking as fast as he.

You're Irish, aren't you? she said. And then she leaned over to an uncleared plate and with one crimson-nailed finger flicked a small potato across the table to me. The yellowish, imperfectly oval potato rolled towards me down the damask tablecloth.

Potatoes, probably, she said. That's what the Irish know about. Potatoes.

Everyone at the table froze.

You're so right, I said to her, smiling angelically. How extraordinarily insightful of you!

And I announced to the table, as if I were totally confident about it, an idea that had just that moment come into my head.

I'm going to write something, I said, about a scandal that happened in a remote part of Ireland, when the lady of the Big House – an Englishwoman – had a torrid fling with one of the coachmen. Marianne Talbot, her name was. I don't know exactly what happened, but I'm going to go off and try to find out.

When was this? someone at the table said.

Around the middle of the last century, I said, when Ireland was in a terrible state after the years of the potato famine. An event with which this lady – I nodded at the red-fingernailed woman – is evidently familiar. That's the most interesting thing about the scandal, in fact. The time it happened.

Oh, I don't know, Alex said, still dismal at having made a display of himself. I don't know whether there'd be any takers for that kind of thing. You can get a bit sick of the Irish going on about their woes.

I glared at him but couldn't say anything, because I had to be loyal to him when there were other people around.

That very afternoon, back in my basement, the minute I'd peeled the crucifying girdle off, I rang Caroline at her big house up the hill.

I must get out of this cellar, I said to her. I'm going to give in my notice to the landlord today. I don't know where I'll live next, but out of here I must get, Caro. It's not a place I can bear to be in any more. In the short term I'm heading over to Ireland, to do a bit of research. And what I want to know is – may I leave a couple of boxes with you when I pack up here? And can I stay with you for a while when I come back from Ireland while I'm sorting things out?

Of course! she said. It'll be lovely having you. And the timing's great – I'll have just finished the BEd exams. Oh, we'll have such fun! It'll be just like old times.

This was a typical Caroline remark, blandly airbrushing out those aspects of the old times that weren't fun at all. Still. There had been a good stretch when we were in our early twenties and I lived in a room in her sunny mews. Maybe I was too quick to patronize her altogether. Maybe I was in need of being near to someone I had been happy with, now that Jimmy was gone.

Jimmy. I crawled into bed, though there was still light in the patch of distant sky.

All day I'd been listening to myself announcing plans for the future, as if I were interested in it. When all I want, I said to myself, is to survive the present.

The next day I got moving. It was a relief. I took a taxi to Fleet Street and followed the Library signs past the Law Courts to the Inner

Temple. The man at the desk said that unfortunately outsiders were not permitted to use the library, except in cases where it held the only copy in existence of the book or document in question.

But I don't know what material there is! I said. For all I know there *is* something about the Talbot divorce that only your library has.

He smiled at my ingenuity.

Wait here, he said, and I'll have a look through our catalogues.

I sat at a table beside the window in an alcove between high bookshelves, and watched the barristers in their gowns hurry back and forth across the cobbled yard below me. It had been years since I'd sat in a library – not since I was a student, and not very often, then. I'd forgotten how much I liked it. Calm stole over me at the thought of sitting there all day, making notes in my new Talbot notebook. Thank God I'd managed to stop smoking.

The man was carrying only one book when he came back to me. And it turned out to be bound copies of the judgements in private Divorce Bills, including the *Judgment* in the Talbot case. The original of the xerox I already had. Hugo's law lecturer, in fact, must have got it here.

There might be something in Ireland, the man said. The husband would have had to take separation proceedings in the Ecclesiastical Court there. The evidence given in those might have been preserved in Ireland. But I did a computer check and there's nothing in any of the legal libraries.

I didn't give up. I took the Underground all the way out to Colindale and I went in and got a reader's ticket for the newspaper section of the British Library. The law might not be interested in the scandal, but surely the readers of newspapers were. There weren't many Irish newspapers listed for the period, but there was one that might have something.

I'd barely started reading the microfilm of the *Northwestern Herald* when I caught my breath. There was the name – her husband's name!

1850, September. On Monday last John O'Hara, sub-sheriff, passed through Ballygall to the lands at Mount Talbot, the property of

Mr Richard Talbot, and being accompanied by the police of the contiguous stations evicted 83 families and levelled 75 of the houses, making upwards of 600 levelled houses besides dilapidated ones in the different outlets of the town. On the 7th inst. more than 100 human beings were thrown upon the world houseless and destitute. Many of the unfortunate creatures who could get no lodgings from the neighbours, are obliged to live under the arches of the old bridge . . .

The next time Richard was mentioned was the following winter:

1851. November. 16 brace of woodcock, three hares, a brace of rabbit and some snipe were bagged by Mr Richard Talbot and another gentleman. The cover was not drawn until late in the day and the cocks, notwithstanding the severity of the weather, were in first-class condition.

Then, in a column about workhouse admissions, there was a hint of criticism:

. . . The wretched creatures before the Board of the Union were once in comfortable circumstances and were tenants of Mr Talbot's but Mr Talbot's men ruined them, as they did hundreds whose houses were thrown down and their lands given to a more favoured class. The management of the tenantry robbed the ratepayers in consequence of the number of paupers they created.

Was the *Herald* anti-landlord, then? If it was, it would surely report the Talbot divorce proceedings. I started reading the editorials to see where the paper's sympathies lay. But I soon realized that while the paper might express the resentment of the merchants of the towns whose rates kept the workhouses going, that didn't mean it had anything against the landlords. Or against workhouses for the Irish. Or even against the extermination of the Irish.

May 1st, 1852. The Irish cottier, the man with his half-dozen acres, his bit of common right, his hut without floor, without chimney, without window, without furniture and without a separation between the human and the brute occupants, was a mere savage. Calamitous as are the events by which it has come to pass, we now thank Heaven that we have lived to speak of the class as a class that has been . . .

Talk about a pro-establishment paper! There'd be nothing here disrespectful to the Talbot family. And sure enough, I spent two hours going through the *Herald* and there was no reference at all to the private life of the gentry. There was nothing but obsequiousness towards them, except on the subject of who should pay to – grudgingly – keep the destitute homeless alive.

I looked up the directory of libraries in the UK and Ireland and got the number for the Ballygall library – Ballygall being, according to the Ordnance Survey map of 1842, the name of the small town at the gates of the Mount Talbot estate. But when I got through to Ireland later, I was told that the person I needed to speak to was the retired head librarian, a Miss Leech, who was now building up their local history section. And Miss Leech was not available. Try again in a week.

I rang Alex that evening and told him about the day's work.

Nothing's turned up so far, I said. But could you put me down for two or three weeks' leave anyway? I'm going over to Ballygall to have a look around. I'll let you know when I find a base there; I'm not taking my mobile with me, because this isn't that kind of trip. I'm moving out of here before I go, but I can always be reached care of Caroline. And Boss, ask Administration, will you, to start the pension paperwork? I really am finished with *TravelWrite*, Alex. I've just discovered how much I love libraries.

I didn't add that a library was the one place where my mother was always confident. But I'd thought it. I remembered how she used to walk into the public library in Kilcrennan with that brisk, focused, self-forgetful air that other women have in clothes shops. It was a pleasure to me, to remember her like that.

I waited in the empty basement on the day I went back to Ireland. I put a clean tea towel on the seat of the low armchair beside the table and sat down. I was wearing my Mani suit for going home. Well, not going home – going back. It didn't quite fasten at the waist anymore, but you couldn't see that under the jacket.

I reached up and turned the kitchen light off. The room settled into a silent darkness.

The only times I could think of that I'd liked this place were the long mornings, after a trip, when I moved around slowly in the silence and plucked my eyebrows and did my legs and finished my airport paperback and made piles of clothes for the washing and the cleaner's and sorted out my handbag and put my passport away. I'd savoured the little actions because they were necessary. They didn't feel as selfish as nearly everything else I did.

Jimmy used to claim that he could tell, when I walked into the office, whether I had come from the basement or not. He said darkness clung to me if I had.

A goddess like you, Kathleen, he said once, should *descend* on London, not climb up into it.

He always treated me as if I were beautiful. He informed me, the day he came to *TravelWrite*, that grey eyes and black hair were the most elegant of all the colour combinations. And when he came back from doing his first Irish piece he said that on top of my colouring, I was just about the only tall Irishwoman in the world.

So why do you bury yourself in a cellar, like your squat peasant sisters? he said.

His face was troubled when he said it. He meant that I evidently didn't care where I lived, and that I should care. But I felt suited to the dim rooms. I'd only lived in three places in London in my whole thirty years there, if you didn't count the floating student years. I'd lived with Hugo in south London. Then I'd lived in Caroline's mews. Then this. Now that I thought of it – up in an attic with Hugo; then in Caro's ground-floor place; then half underground, here. Downhill all the way.

See? Caroline had her finger on the doorbell. Rich-kid as ever, she'd parked up on the path.

See? She was grinning at me. Now perhaps you'll stop sneering at my four-wheel-drive, now that it's useful to you.

27

You don't need an all-terrain vehicle, Caro, I said, to move two boxes a mile across London.

Is that all you have? She stopped at the door to the kitchen. The first sun of the year spilling down the stairs from the hallway above her edged her fair head with light. We were exactly the same height, which used to please me, secretly, when we were young and we went round together. I loved being with a beauty.

She said to me once, You have such distinctive looks, Kath. A colleen's looks. And those wild curls!

I cherished the remark for years, even after I knew that she said something extravagantly nice to everyone she met. Like Browning's Last Duchess, *she smiled, no doubt, whene'er I passed her; but who passed without much the same smile?*

I wish you were coming to me straight away, she said. The exams begin next week and it would have made me cleverer if a clever person like you was around the house. It's a bit much, you suddenly getting interested in Ireland. And I don't know whether to put you in the guest room or to redecorate the top floor –

Don't put me anywhere, I said. Just shove these things somewhere out of the way. We'll talk about it when I'm back from home. And you're a great woman anyway to have gone back to college –

Since when is Ireland home? she said. The time we went to Belfast and drank all the champagne – you never said anything about home then.

Belfast's nothing to do with me, I said. Belfast is yours. Your lot have made rather a point of that –

Oh, don't start! she said. You know I don't understand politics.

Don't you start, I said. Pretending to be a dumb blonde.

She came back into the hall from storing the boxes.

I'm heading for the airport as soon as the landlord has a look around this place, I said. But I'll give you a call, Caro, when I've settled somewhere. There's a hotel in Ballygall called The Talbot Arms and I'll try that, but I don't know whether I'll stay there – it might be awful. Small-town Ireland – who knows?

Promise you will! she said. She was bending down to drop a kiss somewhere near my cheek.

You *confer* your kisses, I said. Like the Queen Mother or somebody. It's ridiculous. We're only forty-nine –

What's only about that? she said, getting into the driver's seat. What's the next one after forty-nine? Fifty! We're nearly fifty!

Nel mezzo del cammin, I began.

Stop showing off! She was smiling at me through the window. You think you're so clever.

But I am clever! I was dancing along beside the jeep as she bumped off the pavement.

I ran the few steps to the corner.

I'm clever, and you're beautiful! I called after her, and she was laughing as she pulled out all the way and drove off up the street.

I'd noticed a thoughtful shadow on her face when I was clowning around. But what could she do? She had always been too polite, if someone else signalled a tone, to challenge it, even when she suspected it of being fraudulent. She reminded me of one of those English tennis players who never get to the final. Not blank, exactly, but definitely not cunning.

I went back down into the kitchen to wait for Mr Vestey. Next door's cat was sitting on the sill outside looking in at me, intent and perfectly still. I fell once, when I was balancing on a chair, trying to lift a suitcase down from the top of the wardrobe. The cat came into the flat for the first time and settled on its haunches beside my contorted face, and put out one plush paw and touched my cheek. Then it waited beside me until I could get up. I never told anyone, even Jimmy, that I thought about that cat when I was away, and I tried to get back from trips in daylight, so that I could hope to see it. It had never allowed me to touch it, and sometimes I wanted to so badly that it was a pain in my chest. I didn't know whether it was male or female and I called it different names. Beth, I called it for a while. Ferdy. Inigo. Pangur, I called it most often, after the Irish monk's cat in the poem. I never meant to love a cat; it created my love for it. Maybe I was betraying the little thing by leaving.

Get a grip! I said to myself coldly.

I'd thanked heaven for this basement once. When Caroline was getting married and I had to move, I had a hard time finding somewhere to live. I'd begun the search full of confidence – I wanted to live in Bayswater because in *The Wings of the Dove* Kate Croy met her lover in Hyde Park. I didn't know enough about London to know that you couldn't just walk into the district you liked and expect to find a place. I didn't know that within a day of being turned down everywhere, I'd be using a false English accent when I talked to estate agents. I will never forgive this city, I said to myself on the fourth morning of my search, for making me demean myself like this.

I forgot that I'd been saved from Ireland by England. Instead, I was fortified as I tramped around by the memory of my father's outrage every time he told us his story about going to England to look for work. He came out with it at the Sunday dinner whenever something said at the lunchtime session in the pub had reminded him.

I went over to England, he'd begin, when I was waiting to be called to the civil service, to earn an honest shilling . . .

The climax of the story was a notice he saw in a boarding-house window: NO BLACKS NO IRISH NO DOGS. He used to bellow those words.

I didn't know what blacks were, the first time I heard the story, but I knew it was not right to be put on the level of dogs. I asked Nora when we were clearing up after the dinner, and Mammy and Daddy had gone into the bedroom.

What's a black?

They're people that live in hot countries and the sun turned them black.

What's an honest shilling?

Stop annoying me.

It had been like a miracle when Mr Vestey of Vestey Bloomsbury Estates interviewed me.

Sit down, young lady, he'd said. You're an Irish lady, I gather from the name?

He was a big man, with a florid, shiny face – a tavern-keeper's face.

That's right, I said, leaning forward earnestly. But I did a diploma here at the London City Poly. And, of course, I've been working here, for *The English Traveller*, for the last year.

When he spoke to me pleasantly the relief brought tears to my eyes.

This area should suit you, then, he said. Very convenient for the mainline stations.

Can I have the place, then?

That was when he paused. It was so quiet that I actually heard the weightless tick, tick from the watch on his big wrist.

Of course you can! A lovely young lady like you!

The compliment didn't go unnoticed. Who forgets compliments? I always smiled at him when I saw him, over the years, as he came and went to the offices above me. I smiled at him before I remembered why I was smiling, as if the relief of tension when he gave me the flat had left an imprint of pleasure on me. I was at ease with him, anyway. He was such a caricature – buttoned importantly into his pinstriped suit, under his purple face. Wet enough for you, Mr Vestey? I'd call to him if it was raining, or, Gorgeous weather, Mr Vestey! And he'd give me a lordly nod. Miss Burke, he'd murmur.

Now I could hear him tramp down the hallway above me.

The woman in your office, I said as I went ahead of him into the kitchen, could do with a stint at charm school. She's really rude. She said you had to see the condition I've left the place in personally because you've had so-called career women before, and pigs would have left their places in better order. It's not often you hear pigs praised.

That's my wife, actually, Mr Vestey said.

I whirled around to look at him. Oh, I'm so sorry! I said. I didn't mean –

That's all right, he said. I'm used to it.

He stood in the small room. He was as high-coloured as when I'd met him first, but he was much heavier now. An elderly man.

I was bewildered by him standing there looking at me.

How much? he said.

What?

How much would you say you owe me?

I haven't a clue, I said. There's a crack in the wash-hand basin. Forty pounds, maybe? Fifty?

You're a very attractive woman, Mr Vestey said. I always thought so.

I gaped at him.

I usually never let to Irish, he went on. I've had very bad experiences with your compatriots. To put it mildly. But you were different. I had a nice little look at you when you came in to see me the first time.

You what? I said.

I wouldn't be interested in the money you owe me if you were nice to me.

How do you mean . . .?

Now that you're leaving the flat. And you said you were leaving England, too, didn't you?

Well, no. I'm going to Ireland, but just for a while.

Silence. The fridge suddenly began to hum, as if it had been startled.

You could be nice to me, he said. That's why I came here today. No one will know how long I'm in this flat today. We could forget business. Part as friends.

The air in the kitchen stood still.

Full circle. He was me now – trying to hide his need, and waiting to hear what I'd say, in painful suspense. But then again, this wasn't about me, at all. This was about buying sex. I didn't have to do anything except lie down.

A small lick of excitement, at that thought.

And even while my mind hunted for ideas, I bowed my head and turned, and walked into the bedroom. I think I did it because, across the inches of air between Mr Vestey and myself, I could feel his trembling, and I couldn't think of any reason for saying no to someone who was in that state.

He stood close behind me, not touching me, as I drew the curtains against the mild light. I could feel a disturbance in the air of the darkened room. Ah! He put a splayed hand on each buttock. Rested them there. I could feel his tremble go through me – delicate at first, then more like a shudder.

We took off our clothes without looking at each other. He lay awkwardly beside me, his eyes shut tight. His ragged breathing was the same as an excited boy's. His big fingers fumbled when they touched me between my legs. Then he heaved himself on top of me and started poking around down there. Like a blind man with a stick. He pinched my nipples. I hated that more than anything. I hated lying on my back, as a matter of fact, helpless, with my chest flattened. The weight of him was squashing me. I thought as busily as I could while he snuffled around. Splinters of thought; not thoughts. Of course, this would confirm him in thinking the Irish were basically scrubbers. He'd ask the next Irishwoman tenant, too. She'd probably slap his face. If the nuns from school were standing around invisibly, that's what they'd be waiting for me to do. But it hadn't occurred to me, and you either slap someone's face immediately or never. This was quite a good way, now that it was happening, of saying goodbye to England. I'd escaped from being named. You couldn't call him English, at that moment, or me Irish. This person and I were just slabs of flesh held in by skin, one sandwiched on top of the other. The first time in my life, this, that I'd been offered money. I could have owed him hundreds of pounds. How high would he have gone? But still, he'd done me a kindness back then – no, not quite, but he'd chosen not to do me an unkindness . . .

I knew, underneath the chatter in my head, that it was an awful thing that I'd stripped the bed when I was tidying up, so that we were exposed on the bare mattress with nothing to cover us. People our age! I peeped from my clenched eyes and saw the outline of him. His eyes were closed, too. He had a big round bald head like a baby.

He was beginning to go soft. I couldn't lie there without helping him. Whatever it was I was doing, it would be no good unless he got something out of it. Anyway, if I was doing it I was doing it, and there was no point in half measures. So I pushed him onto his side and rested my forehead against his damp forehead and began to caress him with my hands. And after not very long, I heard his little gasps and then his cry.

I made an attempt, holding him to me for a moment, to feel generous and motherly. But it didn't work. At the end we lay beside each other looking up at the ceiling, like strangers sunning themselves stiffly on deck chairs that are too close together.

I turned away onto my side. I hid my stomach automatically, even from him.

He got out of bed and I could hear him slowly putting on his clothes.

I'll pull the door shut when I go out, he said.

Okay.

Leave the keys on the table, please.

Okay.

Every good wish in your new life.

Thanks, Mr Vestey. Same to you.

I got up when I heard the front door bang above, and went out to the bathroom and washed myself. I had to use Flash because I'd thrown out the last bit of soap. When I pulled my tights back on they stuck to me uncomfortably.

Then I went back to the kitchen and rang for a minicab.

I sat again in the armchair. My body was shaking as it began to relax after the tension. Next door's cat was still watching me from the sill. I should say a prayer now, I thought, like Russians always did when they set off on a journey, in thanks for the past and to ask a blessing on the future. Even Tolstoy, running away from the home he hated, would have paused to say a prayer. As for the journey I was going on . . .

Make it not be too late! I prayed to nobody. Look what age Tolstoy was, and still he set out! Make it not be too late for me!

That man did understand, didn't he, I said to myself, that I allowed him to do what he wanted because otherwise I would have had to discuss it with him? Because lying down for him in silence was the only way to tell him absolutely nothing about myself –

The bell rang. The taxi. I got my bag and my coat and gave one last look around. I moved towards the stairs, but then I stopped.

I dropped my things and scribbled a cheque for fifty pounds to

Vestey Estates and pushed it under the keys I'd left on the kitchen table.

Then I walked out of the room carefully so as not to have to look for a last time at the cat. I climbed the stairs to the hallway. I closed the front door behind me without – it occurred to me as I did it – checking that I had my key to get back in with. I would never go in or out of this door again. I had thrown myself out of the nest.

I hung back in the doorway, frightened. Then the warm spring sun washed over me, because the porch blocked off the wind. I turned my face up to the bright day – the first one, after a long winter. There was a single cloud, like a dab from a white paintbrush, at the very highest point of the sky. In the instant I glanced at it, the cloud melted into nothing, and the wide arc became perfectly, intensely blue.

Orpheus ascending, I said to myself. Here I go.

3

At the baggage carousel in Shannon I was behind two huge men. You'd think they were gun-dogs, I thought, getting ready to jump forward to take their bags in their teeth. When I couldn't get past them and muttered, Bloody *men*, they smiled at me and one of them said, You're not supposed to say that. We're visitors. You have to be nice to us. This is our first time here.

I beamed at them and gushed, Oh I'm *sorry*. You're very, very welcome to Ireland!

I walked away smiling to myself. Me, the ambassador! Me – who'd never even seen Irish decimal currency before!

I was always careful in Arrivals halls because the things you see can hurt. A child calling Dada! Dada! to an ordinary-looking businessman, and the businessman hurrying forward, his whole self forgotten, his arms wide, his face transformed by the smile of an angel . . . But I raised my head here. My native soil. The hall was tinged with green from the low hills outside. Sun and air poured in with the opening and closing of the glass doors to the roadway, and a woman ran down a shaft of light, the silhouette of her open coat flying around her, into the arms of a man. The two stood immobile, face laid against face. When I turned away, I caught the eye of the woman at the car-hire desk, also looking at the ecstatic lovers, and we smiled at the same time as we shrugged.

TravelWrite Syndicated Features, she said, looking at my card. Smashing job to have.

I've just packed it in –

I wouldn't mind packing in work myself, she said. The lunatics I have to cope with – you wouldn't believe! I'd a fella in here this morning –

She settled into a comfortable leaning position on the counter to talk to me, like one housewife to another over a back-garden wall.

Giving out. Don't know where he was from. Anyway he said that everywhere he went on his trip he saw this sign, Full Irish Breakfast. What did they think I was expecting in Ireland? he said to me – and he was really cross – a full *Norwegian* breakfast?

You're welcome to Shannon, anyway! she said, when I stopped laughing. Are you back for a holiday? Or do you still have family here?

I remembered this about Ireland – the way people asked each other personal questions, and did it with so much charm that there was nothing for it but to be charming in return. Both parties perfectly conscious of being charming, but appreciating the effort put into it all the same. All the same, I wished I'd brought the Ray Bans I'd deliberately left behind with the mobile phone.

I have family, I said. But I'm not here to go visiting. It's complicated. Anyway – have you a car for me?

I have of course, she said. What kind of thing were you looking for?

Well, what are the roads around Ballygall like? I said.

Ballygall! she said. I'm working here ten years and I never heard anyone ask for Ballygall before.

West of Ballygall is where a story I'm looking into happened, I said. Near there. The husband was a big gentry landlord and he accused the wife of adultery with a groom.

When?

A few years after the worst of the Famine.

You never think of them having sex during the Famine, the woman said.

People have to have sex, I said. No matter what. Even in Auschwitz, probably.

You can live without it, the woman said drily, tapping the keyboard in front of her with sudden sternness. If you have to. Lots of us have to.

She craned her head efficiently to scan the screen.

Any chance you could get Flanagan's Car Hire into a story about the potato famine? My boss is so thick that if I told him I'd given you a reduction for that, he'd believe me. A brand-new Audi, I have. If you're going to Ballygall you'll need a good car. Is it Roscommon or Mayo or Galway, that bit of the bog? I'd say they eat their dead there, anyway.

You're wasted in this job, you know, I said. You could have been a stand-up comedian.

The car is on its way round, she said. Sign this. Enjoy your trip. Be good to yourself –

I *am* good to myself, I said.

No. She smiled at me. I don't think you are.

I stole a look at myself in the reflecting wall as I turned away. My hair was pinned up with the amber slides I got in Korea and I was wearing the good Italian suit. Above the clothes my face was bare of make-up and there were lines and grooves and a softening jawline. But all the same! Surely I was still in the game? Surely misery didn't sit on me the way it did on the drunk woman who made the crack about the potatoes at the awards lunch? I wouldn't have it! I slung the coat I was carrying over my shoulder and straightened my back and kept my legs together so I could feel the brush of thigh against thigh, and I walked with careful pride towards the exit.

The evening was darkening as I drove away, except that a dramatic slash at the horizon showed a delicate pink far beyond, as though there were a world with its own sun on the reverse side of the cloud.

The road signs brought a sting to my eyes. *Aerphort. Lár na Cathrach. An Tuaisceart.*

Now, wait a minute! You can't even speak Irish.

Yes, I can, a little bit. I know a lot of words. I know songs.

I began to sing – *Anois teacht an Earraigh* –

Daddy tried to use Irish at home but we children sat there sullenly and wouldn't let it into our heads. But the nuns were different. Nothing the nuns taught us was ever forgotten. Nora and I could chant all the questions and answers in the Maynooth Catechism, and give the causes of the Thirty Years War. I could give an example of a resolved anapaest. I could recite every poem we'd ever done, especially the Romantic poets that Sister Pius dinned into us. And as for songs!

Anois teacht an Earraigh – And so it has! Spring has come! *Ó chuir mé in mo cheann é, ní stopfaidh mé choíche, go seasfaidh mé thíos i lár Chontae Mhaigh Eo* –

Since I got it into my head nothing will stop me till I sit myself down in the County Mayo –

I tried to fit the words to the jaunty tune. Even alone in the dark car, pronouncing the Irish words made me shy.

A junction with traffic lights. I was on the outskirts of a town. From long habit, I'd put my handbag under the driving seat, and my notebook on the seat beside me.

Shannon airp. cheerful, I jotted down, in the pause at the lights. Local driving X. True about Ir. talkers (woman). Ir. air soft, feel of rain –

And then – I threw the pen down.

I wanted to throw the busyness away from me – the singing and thinking and making notes. I was back! I wanted to take that in . . .

I pulled in to a hotel.

What's the name of this place? I said to the young girl with a face like a flower when she was swiping my credit card.

What place? she said.

This hotel.

Oh, she said. The Half-Way Hotel.

What's it halfway between, then?

I don't know, she said timidly. I think they said, when we were doing our training, but I don't remember.

A beige room with a big bed and a window onto an empty car park. My kind of room.

Before I let myself talk myself out of it, I called Nora. It would be four o'clock in New York – she'd be back at her desk after the afternoon meeting with her CEO. I never told her anything about my feelings if I could help it. But there had to be someone who knew what I was doing today. I couldn't bear to be back after twenty-nine years – more than half my whole life – and nobody know it but myself.

Guess where I am, Nora?

Ireland.

I was astonished. How did you guess?

Where else would you ring me from and ask me to guess?

I'm doing a bit of work, I began.

Are you going home? she said.

I might head over there if my work goes well, I said lightly. But I'm nowhere near Kilcrennan. I flew into Shannon, not Dublin.

That doesn't make any difference, she said. If you're in Ireland you have to go home. You know that. Suppose they hear you're there, and you haven't been to see them? And they will hear. Someone is bound to see you –

Who are *you*, Miss Bossyboots, I flared up, to tell me how to treat Danny and Annie? Since when did you become an expert on that? You haven't even been back to see them once. You didn't even come back to say goodbye to Mammy. You didn't even go to Uncle Ned's funeral –

Neither did you!

I was in China, working! I didn't even know –

Uncle Ned could have *bought* Kilcrennan with the money I offered him over the years!

Since when was Ned interested in money? Anyway, Nora, it's ridiculous to be talking about that now! The whole thing's ancient history. And I'm here to work, not see family –

What kind of work?

It's sort of history –

Forget Irish history! she said. When was the last time in Irish history anyone ever got laid?

Charles Stewart Parnell? I said.

Well –

Charles J. Haughey?

You know perfectly well what I mean! she began.

Gotta go! I said. I'll be in touch. Here's looking at you, kid –

Kathleen! I could hear her calling, Kath!

But I hung up.

I was furious with myself for letting her get to me.

Whoever vacuumed this carpet didn't try very hard, I said to myself, wandering around the room, trying to regain my good humour. But I was still seething. Money! Her and her money! When even now, the word Thursday felt warm to me, because that was the day Uncle Ned cycled out to our place at Shore Road, rain or shine, after he collected his dole, and, first thing he did, he lit the range. He was supposed to be inferior to Daddy because he was left on the farm when Daddy got into the civil service, and the farm made no money, but he'd cycle out to our place, with his grey plastic shoes on that his neighbour had brought him home from England, and his good striped suit, even though it was only us he was coming to visit. Don't disturb your mother, he'd say, when he came quietly in the back door and bent to take off his bicycle clips. Your poor mother is not in the best of health. He'd send Nora to Bates's to get stuff for the tea. He'd start raking out the range. We'd have fried eggs, and Swiss roll. He showed us how to put it nicely on the tray and then he'd take it in to Mammy and we'd hear him say, How are you today, Eileen? and he'd come back out, and have his tea with us. It wasn't just the money. He'd show us how to do up shoelaces. He taught us to read the clock. He'd write notes for us for school, taking ages to inscribe them into our jotters. Sometimes he'd go down to the shop and bring a cylinder of Calor gas home on the crossbar of his bike.

Years later, when Mammy and I had a day in Dublin when I won the essay competition on the subject 'The Beauty of this World Hath Made Me Sad', I asked her, coming home on the bus – because I was thinking about love all the time then –

Was Uncle Ned ever in love?

Love, she said bitterly. Nobody around here was ever in love.

I had a shower and wrapped myself in a big towel, and I plugged in the laptop and worked. When I was accepting my Achievement Award I read out the itinerary for the first day of the first travel-trade freebie I ever went on. Morning: Milan to Garda 140km, boat trip to Malecesine, climb to castle, visit grappa distillery, five-course local speciality lunch. P.m.: cable car to Mount Baldo, visit Bolla vineyard, to Verona and amphitheatre, to Vicenza – tour of Palladian buildings, reception by Minister for Tourism, seven-course dinner, overnight in Venice . . . The audience laughed knowingly. I used to stay up drinking with the others after a day like that, or maybe go back to someone's room. But when Jimmy came to *TravelWrite* I saw how carefully he worked. And I taught myself the discipline of making notes or writing drafts for maybe an hour every evening when I was travelling, no matter where, no matter how late.

And so, I opened the Talbot file and spread out the *Talbot* xerox, leaning against the pile of pillows. I didn't need to do any thinking. I was too tired to think. I just copied a bit more of the Lord Chancellor's introduction into the narrative I was constructing.

> *. . . Mr Talbot married his present wife, Miss Marianne McCausland, in January 1845 and in that same year, some nine or ten months after the marriage, Mrs Talbot gave birth to a daughter. Towards the middle of the year 1846, Mr and Mrs Talbot with their infant child I presume went abroad. They remained abroad for one or two years. Shortly thereafter, Mr Talbot lost his uncle Mr Talbot who was the owner of Mount Talbot in a remote part of western Ireland, a large mansion apparently, and Mr Talbot and Mrs Talbot as she was then called took possession of the property.*

'One or two years.' The Talbots then might easily have come to Ireland in 1847. The Year of the Big Hunger. That was what the tableau I was in when I was sixteen was called. The nuns put on a pageant to celebrate the fiftieth anniversary of the Easter Rising, and I was one of the barefoot starving girls in shawls on the back of Murphy's coal lorry that had been lined with crêpe paper. It had a big sign on it: 1847 The Year of the Big Hunger. We were all holding buckets of potatoes and crying and wailing, in case anyone didn't get the point, and a man sitting on the cab of the lorry played sad airs on his fiddle. The fiddle was nearly drowned out by the next lorry, which had Canon Murray reading out the Proclamation of the Republic through a loudspeaker. But even so, when I bumped into Uncle Ned in the car park afterwards, I could see the marks of tears on his cheeks.

I lay back on the pillows. I said it to myself, *You are in Ireland.* But I was only an hour from London.

Marianne Talbot would have had to get a horse-drawn cab to Euston, and then spread the skirts of her crinoline on a wooden bench in a train where the carriages were full of smoky, cindery air and juddered on iron wheels, and it would have taken half a day to cross England and Wales. And the shock of coming into Ireland must have been extreme. She would never have seen anything like the chaotic quayside at Kingstown. Crowds and confusion, yes, she would know from her travels on the Continent. But Ireland was a place exhausted by three years of famine, and a place gripped with fear – a place that did not know that the Big Hunger was over. Its people were pouring out through the ports, not travellers but emigrants, hordes of them, hauling everything they still possessed up into the boats, calling to each other in Irish, crying and lamenting, not leaving but fleeing. And she would have followed her husband as he pushed his way through the crowd, head down, assailed by strange smells and noises, assaulted by beggars . . .

I was falling asleep. I leafed through the *Judgment* to find one of the bits I liked. It had a touch of Uncle Ned about it.

Mrs Talbot gave Mullan, it has been testified, articles of more delicate food than was commonly enjoyed by the servants. The witness mentioned bread and butter and wine among other things, jams, and delicacies of that sort.

Mrs Talbot also insisted on his shirts being washed twice over, and having herself gone to look at the shirts, she sent one of her maids to see that they were all well got up, a course of transactions which is not to be accounted for except by long familiarity leading to criminal intercourse between the parties. Then what took place afterwards? She had new buttons put on three or four of her husband's shirts for Mullan . . .

That was affection. It wasn't just a physical affair . . .

I could stay awake no longer. I pushed my scattered things to the side of the big bed and folded myself in, and sleep came to me like an interruption, not an ending.

As I drove up through Ireland next day they remembered Jimmy, by accident, on the car radio. They played a poignant melody, and then a variation on it, and then another, and when it ended the announcer said, And that was the orchestral suite, *Jimín mo mhíle stór*, and I could do the simple translation – *mo stór*, my beloved, *mhíle*, a thousand – Jimeen, little Jimmy, my thousand-times beloved. I missed him so much. But wherever he was, he didn't care. All the missing was within me.

It is Kathleen you mourn for, I said to myself.

When he came to London he took an apartment – three rooms, and a door out onto the leads of the roof – at the top of an eighteenth-century house in Soho.

The water pressure's terrible, he said, but the floorboards are the original oak. And there's a club on the corner if ever I need a roll in the hay.

He was usually as insouciant as that about himself. But when we talked obliquely – lying around the office arguing about things like whether Arthur Miller really loved Marilyn Monroe – longings in him much like my own revealed themselves. I said to him, the night of the day he came to *TravelWrite*, that travel writing is the ideal job for someone who wants to forget the past, because it pivots you into the present.

Then I'm in the wrong job, Jimmy said. I had a very happy childhood.

Didn't your parents mind you being gay? I asked.

Being gay in Scottsbluff, Nebraska, was nothing, he laughed, compared to not being a jock in Scottsbluff, Nebraska.

I liked it there, he went on. I like places that really are the way they are.

I could hear the practised note. He'd said that sentence often before.

You didn't like it well enough to stay there, I notice, I said. You're a fair few thousands of miles from Nebraska now.

Tell me about where you grew up, he said.

That's the difference, I said to Nora when I told her about him, between Jimmy and the other men I've known. He's as interested in me as I am in him.

It was true. He often asked me about Kilcrennan. I saw that he sometimes did it to deflect me from asking him about himself. But it didn't make me cherish him less, that there were things he wanted to hide. And I needed so badly to talk about home that I wasn't scrupulous about how sincerely he wanted to listen. Late that first night, in a Greek café – I know that's what it was because I can still see my tense hand on the red plastic table rolling and crumbling a piece of pitta bread – I described to him the last time I saw my mother. He cried.

Don't forget, I said to Nora, I never actually saw anyone up to this point shed a single tear for Mammy. I didn't go to the funeral. Nobody ever cried for her, as far as I'm concerned, till Jimmy did. He went out to a phone box and rang his own mother to tell her he loved her –

Huh! Nora snorted. Another drama queen like yourself.

I hung up on her.

It was during that drive up through Ireland that the first pain about Jimmy began to fade. Ireland distracted me. I was shocked by its plainness. A road sign would give the name of the next village which would turn out, when I'd managed to translate the Irish words into their meanings, to be a lovely name. The Mill of the Stranger. The Fort of the Dun Cow. The Bright Swans. And then would come the dull reality – a wide street of two-storey houses of grey plaster and grey brick and a single big grey church and a couple of plain pubs. All the history of the place was in the language. There was hardly a building or artefact from centuries of social life to be seen on the ground. Ruins of medieval abbeys and castles. Then nothing. Then the buildings from my grandparents' time.

I kept going back in my mind to my days on *The English Traveller*, when I used to marvel at the villages of England. Villages tucked away at the end of hedge-lined roads into valleys, with low-windowed cottages and mossy stone paths between cottage gardens, and streams running down to the ponds in the village greens. Low stone villages up on moors. Villages with little ancient churches, obdurate as barnacles. The paths to villages that led through beechwoods hidden in the ravines between sloping meadows. And the plain Queen Anne rectories, and the roofs of the squires' fine places through the trees, and the schools of golden stone that the squire built. The rose-covered dispensaries, the gift of Lady So-and-so ... I used to read the names on the war memorials. I used to imagine it – the landlord and the labourer carried in their coffins through the same lych-gate. And the gleaming, mellow pubs – The Plumed Feathers, The Coach and Horses. I couldn't get over being in a country where all the different classes lived in villages together. Those villages are jewels, I said to myself now. But Ireland was robbed. Ireland was stripped and left bare.

I turned north-east. There weren't even any villages by afternoon, when the car began to climb in wide curves across low hillsides of coarse grass. I felt a shift, as if Jimmy's death moved from inside me out into the landscape. Its bleakness was taking physical form all around. There was a long straight stretch between plantations of conifers, immobile and black, and then a descent into a shallow valley, empty of human habitation as far as the eye could see. Sheep idled down the wet road. When I slowed for them I heard the rustling of water in the ditch. The brightness had gone out of the day. The grey sky was very low. In the hotel car park there'd been vivid dandelions in the grass, and a forsythia bush trailing yellow branches in a hedge of bone-white ash saplings. But there was no spring in this valley.

Poor Marianne, I thought involuntarily. Poor thing! Imagine being brought to this dreadfully lonely spot when she wasn't much more than a girl – a fashionable London miss. Well, I had no evidence that she was particularly fashionable. The Lords *Judgment* said that Marianne's father, Mr McCausland,

> *was a gentleman of property. He appears to have been a man of family, and in the habit of constantly or frequently passing some months of the spring in this metropolis . . .*

But she surely read Jane Austen, and the girls there have their husbands' estates to look forward to. Emma will cherish Mr Knightley's place, and Elizabeth is going to love Mr Darcy's Derbyshire estate. For a young London woman to be brought across the sea to this desolation!

Ballygall. Four miles.

I was at the bottom of a valley now, passing through a wood. Old trees, behind half-tumbled, lichened, cut-stone walls.

This must be it! This must be the edge of the woods of Mount Talbot! These were Talbot trees! This tarred road surely followed the line of the dirt road along which Mullan the coachman would have driven young Mrs Talbot . . . I looked up at the low, heathery ridges that closed off the horizon in every direction. I was looking at what she had looked at. And what Richard had looked at, and William Mullan, and all the men and women and children and animals who endured, as best they could, the various anguishes of that time in this corner of this country.

God, I wish I could have a cigarette, I thought.

Fine rain had begun to drift down when I pulled up on the gravel in front of The Talbot Arms. It was a small, square place, with long sash windows and a handsome portico, with daffodils in a golden scatter under the thick ilex trees. A fat blackbird with an orange beak landed on the worn stone of the steps. It stalked about importantly on its twig legs. An old dog slept on the bottom step, oblivious to the wet turning the pale stone to black. Now that I was in Ballygall, I could start making Talbot notes. Sm. mkt. town on hill, I scribbled. Grey. Dog. Peace. Then I said to myself, Well, the dog and the peace are hardly relevant, are they? You're not writing travel features now.

The hallway of the hotel was wonderfully pleasing. A faded Turkey rug had lain on the floor of wide flagstones for so long that it was shaped to them and followed their dips and ridges. There were sprays of pussy willow, with buds of grey velvet, in the jug from an old bedroom set on the reception counter. Behind, a tall casement window was half-covered with evergreen creeper, and beyond there were trees and a church spire. Staircases led up and down, back there, and an open door showed the corner of a dark wooden bar and shelves of gleaming bottles.

There was no one about. Then I realized that a low noise was coming from behind the heavy curtain at the back of the reception desk.

Hello? I called.

No rooms! a muffled man's voice said. Sorry! Full up!

But there are no cars outside! I said before I could stop myself.

I know there's no cars, the voice said. We've umpteen rooms tonight and tomorrow night. But we've a wedding coming in on Friday and they'll be here a week.

I looked around the hallway again. The wood panelling was as fine as pleated cloth.

I'd like to stay till they come, I called. Please.

I'll be out in a minute, the voice said. Meg is after telling Bobby she's pregnant and Cheryl is getting anorexia. Do you follow the soap operas yourself?

I don't, actually.

The dog waddled in and collapsed at my feet.

I'm coming! the voice said.

And then he came out, while theme music swelled.

Bloody rubbish, he said. He was an elderly man in a tweed jacket and a flannel shirt, with a shock of white hair and round brown eyes. His face was still credulous and soft from looking at the television.

You're a sight for sore eyes, he said, whoever you are. But we've this wedding to do. There's grand rooms in the pub in the square.

No, I said firmly. This is The Talbot Arms. I want to stay here if you'll have me.

There was another family around here one time, he said, a bit grander than the Talbots – the Cobys of Castle Coby – and an English girl who's a dot.com millionaire, if you follow me, who's a distant one of them, is coming over here for her wedding. We have the dining room and the bar done up already. But sure, we could look after you till Friday anyway if you don't mind coming down to the kitchen for your meals? And we've a little place out on the coast if you're stuck, when we have to throw you out. But nobody calls it The Talbot Arms – it's Bertie's place. We bought it with the money I won on a horse. Actually, my late wife Lord have mercy on her picked the horse. I'm Bertie.

He leaned across the counter and shook my hand.

Are there any Talbots left? I asked, feeling real tension as I said it.

Not in these parts, he said. I've lived in Ballygall all my life – sixty-three years – and I've never met a person from the Talbot family once. And the funny thing is – I often think about them. They had a walled garden on their estate, and I cleared a corner of it long ago and I grow a few things in it for the dining room here. I often wonder if some oul Talbot is going to turn up from the back of beyond and ask me for rent. Like Lord Lucan. That boyo's solicitors were looking for ground rent from Castlebar long after he'd disappeared into thin air. I'd give any lord who asked me for rent what for, I can tell you! We're a republic now, me boy, I'd say. You may feck off!

I came across the story of the Talbot divorce, I said tentatively. The one back long ago? Where Mrs Talbot had the – well, I suppose you could call it the *relationship* with a groom? I'm a journalist myself, or I was. I was thinking of maybe seeing whether there was a book to be written about all that.

You need Nan Leech! he said. That's who you need.

Yes! I said. Miss Leech. But when I rang the library here they said she was unavailable.

She was away in Dublin, he said, but she's back. I know she went up to the library this morning . . . He dialled a number and I could hear it ring somewhere.

I'd say she's gone home, but – Ella!

A young woman in a white shirt and a black skirt was slipping along the back of the hallway.

I see you, Ella! That's my daughter Ella, he said to me in a loud whisper. She's helping me out while she's living with me. The husband, between yourself and myself – Hello! he said into the phone. It's Bertie here! Is Nan there? I have a visitor here in the hotel that's looking for Miss Leech.

She is there, he said, nodding to me. You're steeped. You couldn't ring Nan Leech at home, she'd eat you. Here – he passed the phone across to me. They've gone looking for her. I'll send Ella up to give you a hand.

And he shuffled down the hall, in big felt slippers. He smiled at me peacefully while he waited at the back for the dog, who limped after him.

I couldn't leave here after the wife died, he said. This old thing wouldn't have liked it. Would you, darling? he bent down and said lovingly to the dog. Six thousand pounds, that dog cost me last year.

The *dog* did?

Yes. Some fella from the food hygiene people caught us cooking the guests' breakfasts in our own kitchen with this old lad waiting to lick out the pots. We had to build on a kitchen extension to the dining room. But you'll come down and muck in with us while you're here, won't you? You don't mind a few oul hairs?

Oh, no, I said.

The dog pushed its curly grey muzzle into Bertie's hand.

Sixty thousand, and he'd still be worth it, Bertie announced, and ambled off.

Miss Leech here. A gruff voice.

I began to explain myself.

Silence.

I tried again, but my voice trailed away.

You're a travel writer, you say? she said.

Yes.

But you wish to become a historian?

Well, no, not exactly. No – not at all. I'm just doing some research at this stage – just generally informing myself. I'm retiring soon, and I thought I might try to write something telling the tale, more or less, of what happened to the Talbots of Mount Talbot at the end of the 1840s. Setting it in some kind of context . . .

And how do you propose doing that, she said, if your chief skill is writing travel articles of a popular nature?

I've been to university! I said. As a matter of fact, I got the top county scholarship to Trinity College. I did English Literature there. I don't have a degree, but that's only because I had to leave after two years. Literature is full of history. And anyway, lots of journalists write – they know how to organize material, for one thing, which is more than you can say for a whole lot of academics. I've already done a certain amount of reading about conditions in Ireland immediately after the worst of the Famine, and I would have done more research but I was impatient to come here and get a sense of the place first. That's what you do in travel writing – you go to the place, and take it from there. And I thought that if any more documentation on the divorce episode itself exists you'd have it here –

We have had better things to do in this library, Miss Leech cut across me, I can assure you, than turn a prurient eye on the bedroom antics of so-called lords and ladies who should not have been in our country in the first place –

Listen, Miss Leech, I interrupted her in my turn, don't get upset. I can always just have a look around and go up to Dublin to the National Library. Or back to London. All I have so far is the House of Lords *Judgment*, but it has a lot of detail. If there are no other documents, then it will do perfectly well –

Nonsense! Miss Leech cried. That is not a responsible attitude! Indeed, though I have not myself come across print material on the Talbots, we do have the *Judgment* here, and it has occasionally been borrowed. The older women used to talk behind closed doors about the scandal. Where you are speaking from now played a part in the story, as a matter of fact. Bertie's place was a vicarage until sometime shortly after the Famine, and the vicar was mixed up in the whole sordid thing. A worldly lot, the Church of Ireland clergy –

But Miss Leech –

What did you say your name is?

Kathleen de Burca is what I use, I said nervously. Caitlín de Búrca, on my birth cert –

A fine native name! she said warmly.

I could give you a few notes on the general outline of the relationship, as it came out in court, I began.

Send them to me from Bertie's, she said. And come and see me tomorrow afternoon at two. I am not available in the mornings at present.

But Miss Leech –

Tomorrow, she said. Two p.m. sharp, and hung up.

*

Ella hopped ahead of me up the stairs like a young girl, though she told me in the first minute that her husband was working in Saudi Arabia and she had two children and he'd be home soon.

God! Isn't that a lovely coat! she said, gazing yearningly at my coat as she hung it in the wardrobe. It was a fabulous coat – black suede lined with black cashmere. I'd bought it with the entire fee for a script for French TV on *L'Angleterre Profonde*.

How much would a coat like that be? she said.

A lot, I said. Try it on.

It was so long on her that it draped around her feet like the train of a wedding dress. Her perky face and bobbed hair decorated with plastic slides stuck out from the black collar incongruously. She had round brown eyes just like Bertie's. The coat looked immensely sophisticated. I stood there, struck by the thought that when I left Ireland, I was a girl with a bright face and nothing else, and that I had become the kind of woman who could wear a coat as formidable as that . . .

She could hardly bring herself to close the wardrobe door. She peered at me.

Were you never married at all? she said. Or do you just not wear your ring?

Never, I said. I'm a working woman.

That's what I wish I was sometimes! she cried. A working woman!

But you are a working woman. I smiled at her. You do two jobs.

Tell my da that, will you? she said. Maybe he'll believe it coming from you.

I arranged my work things on the worn leather top of the desk in the window niche. My laptop. My trashy paperback. Two histories of the Great Irish Famine. An anthology of poems in the languages I was always trying to learn that I'd kept out when I was packing the rest of my books.

I opened the anthology at random, and the pages fell back at Eugenio Montale.

L'attesa lunga,
Il mio sogno di te non finito.

The wait is long, I translated to myself. *My dream of you has not ended.*

I worked with my notebook and the xerox of the *Judgment*. I made the précis as neat as I could, so the volatile Miss Leech would not be displeased.

1. *Purcell being rather a free and easy workman, and working at the house not as a labourer, but on his own account, went down to the entrance door, and began smoking his pipe, and turning round he saw through the window Mrs Talbot and William Mullan in his stable dress having their arms around each other's necks. They were sitting on the sofa, as he has described . . .*

2. *Mary Anne Benn says that while Mr Talbot was absent at his sister-in-law's funeral she saw Mrs Talbot and Mullan in Mr Talbot's dressing room, there being a bed in that dressing room, at three o'clock in the day.*

(NB ask Miss Leech about the furniture and other artefacts the wealthy planters brought in to poverty-stricken parts of Ireland. What did the things mean to the native people? Ornamental ferns in brass pots. Rococo ironwork conservatories. Plush footstools. Low-cut satin gowns with huge flounced skirts. What would Mullan make of the idea of separate beds for husband and wife? Would a man of his background know himself how to use shoe trees, or what a piqué evening waistcoat is, or how to wax a moustache? Who was the anthropologist: Talbot or Mullan?)

3. *Bridget Queeny tells that Mrs Talbot frequently was in Mullan's room, and*

53

she heard them talking and laughing together. Then, upon one particular occasion, Mrs Talbot upon going into that room, sent her away with the child to the carpenter's shop, and so she was left alone with Mullan in his room. That is corroborated by Michael Fallon, the carpenter, in the strongest possible way. He states that the child was brought down; he says he saw Mullan in the room with Mrs Talbot; and that the child afterwards came back to the room, and called out, 'Mamma, are you here?'

(Mullan would have spoken English as an employee of a landlord, but would he have been able to say complex things? Wasn't the Ballygall area so remote that it would have been Irish-speaking in 1848/9 – so the only English he could have known was servants' English – Musha, yer Honour, the blessins' o' God on ye, etc. NB – is this correct, Miss Leech? Marianne would have spoken the high-flown, exaggerated English of an English girl of the early Victorian era. How did they know the nuance of what the other meant?)

4. *The witness also saw the two many times go into the orchard together which was situated at some distance from the house.*

5. *The sawyers both say they saw Mullan and Mrs Talbot lying down together in the straw in one of the stalls.*

6. *Maria Mooney says that on opening the door of Mrs Talbot's bedroom she saw there Mullan and Mrs Talbot on the bed together – to use her own expression – 'in the very fact'.*

7. *'They were sitting by the fire in the drawing room. She desired me to bring her a cup of milk and I went out and did not go in again.'*

   That is a very strange thing for a groom, especially for a groom who is described by all the witnesses as being a man ordinarily of rather dirty appearance, and not a smart-looking person.

(Why did she send for only one drink of milk? Did she not think to ask him whether he wanted some, too? Or was he drinking something better – his master's whisky, perhaps?)

Thank you. Caitlín de Búrca.

I asked Ella, when she brought up a toasted sandwich, to fax the notes to Miss Leech.

Ella's little boy carried the saltcellar.

Joe is my name, he said. *Cad is ainm duit?*

I blushed like a girl, but I got the words out: *Caitlín is ainm dom.*
Seosamh is ainm dom, he said. We're learning names at school.

Then he told me he had a budgie downstairs in a cage. Had I ever seen a budgie? Did I want to come and see it now?

And a little brother, Ella said to him with a persuasive smile. You have a little brother downstairs, too, don't you?

Joe ignored her.

My daddy's in South Arabia, he said.

Ella gave me a helpless smile. He's a carpenter, she said. Da got him a job in a hospital there, so we can put a few pounds together for a house.

Yes, Joe said. We're going to have our own house. You can see the budgie tomorrow.

In the silence after they went a gust of wind whipped rain against the window. I drew the old velvet curtains. Thank God to be warm and safe. If Jimmy were here he'd say, First thing tomorrow, let's locate the wine shop and the Indian restaurant in this neck of the woods.

I told Roxy and him the outline of the Talbot story on one of the days we lolled around the office. The three of us were always telling each other stories. If one of us saw a movie, we'd tell the others the plot. Or if we read something exciting. Not Alex – Alex was always in his cubicle, working away. But I liked that: I wouldn't have been happy, when we idled, if I hadn't known that he was keeping everything going. Jimmy wasn't as excited as I thought he would be by the Marianne Talbot and William Mullan story. He said he'd need to know more, before he could be sure one of them wasn't exploiting the other.

But Kath, he said, it sure makes your face light up.

I heard the rain again on the window. I would miss the *TravelWrite* office more than anywhere on earth. I loved it physically, the feeling of being tucked away where no one could get at us, up on the attic floor above the warren of offices in the solid Victorian building – right up under the slates, looking down on a roofscape of brick and stone and copper and one patch of green that was the top of the linden trees in the dark little square below. Roxy kept a row of busy

Lizzies and geraniums in tins and pots pressing against the glass at the front of the sill. I used to watch the showers approach over the roofs. The rain would hit our big window, and the view would disappear for a moment, and the magenta of the flowers would get brighter against the curtain of grey, and we would be locked into our eyrie, with the cast-iron radiators clanking and groaning as though there were hundreds of tiny Vulcans in there.

Once, I went to the office straight from the airport, late at night. I got a taxi through the deserted city, and waved my pass at Erroll the porter, and crossed the entrance rotunda of liver-coloured marble, and took the slow lift up through the dark building and let myself into the silent room, stripping the mystery from the shapes that inhabited it when I flicked the switch and light stuttered along the fluorescent tube and steadied into illumination. I spent the whole night there – wandering the attic like Grace Poole, I laughed at myself – until I fell asleep in the big leather chair. When I half woke, resettling myself, I'd hear the delicate sound of rain on the steep skylight over my head. I washed my face in the washbasin in the morning and ran down through the building and out to the deli for a coffee and a currant bun, as if from my own house . . .

The rustling of the creeper against the window panes of my green bedroom said, All gone now.

Would Jimmy have been suspicious of my Talbot project – wondering if I wasn't attracted by the melancholy in it? Would he have said, You're *where*? You're in the north-west boglands of Ireland? I thought you told me you were never going back to Ireland? I thought you said to me, last time I was enthusing about your country, 'Why don't you count the terrified women at the check-ins in Dublin Airport on their way to England for secret abortions?'

But I could show him another way of looking at it.

There could hardly have been two people less likely to be drawn to each other than an Anglo-Irish landlord's wife and an Irish servant. Each of them came from a powerful culture which had at its very core the defining of the other as alien. But they sloughed off those cultures to reach out to each other. They didn't even have a native language in common, yet they pierced through layers of custom and dared every sanction, impelled by the need within desire to express itself.

I knew all about the act of love as a non-event, but I still believed it was the act in which one person can truly learn another, and build on what they learn. It seemed to me that William Mullan and Mrs Talbot had been builders – had made love in the literal sense of 'made' – had manufactured love. Their passion led to love. The *Judgment* was full of her gestures of care for him. And he – the three years he was with her were the years in which his own world convulsed and expelled its people, but he stayed on with her when there could be nothing in it for him but punishment. All the more because it was a journey I had failed to make, I believed that the body was the way to the heart, and the heart was the way to the soul. When I told the story of William Mullan and Marianne Talbot, I would be preaching that belief.

And Jimmy – you believed that, too! You should be glad . . .

Oh, catch yourself on, Kathleen! I cried, and I stood up and began to move, agitated, around the room. Jimmy won't be either sorry or glad. He is nothing! His body is ash and bone fragment and dust!

We went on a trip in a microplane over Manhattan, once, he and I. We were squashed in together behind the pilot in the little Perspex bubble, and Jimmy's arm was hooked around my neck and the weight of him pressed on me as we rose above the skyscrapers and swooped out across the boisterous bay. I could bring back the feeling of his side against my side in our thick winter coats as we circled the Statue of Liberty, and I could recall the sensual rhythm of him falling away, falling back onto me, falling away, falling back, as we dipped and banked over the great harbour. And that's what being alive is – being there in the body. Being there to be felt. There was no Jimmy, now that that palpable body was no more.

I came up to the old mirror on the wall opposite the window. Behind my reflection the room was a cave, with mysterious lights and shadows moving in its milky depths.

He has gone away for ever.

Then I turned on the table lamp and the light over the bed and the ceiling light. The shadows disappeared in the brightness. I looked at myself in the mirror, and I said goodbye to Jimmy.

4

I didn't know whether to make my own bed in the morning.

I'll assume I'm more a friend than a guest, I thought. Everything seems to be so personal in this country.

So I made it, and tidied the room.

I tiptoed downstairs to go out through the back door. But when I went into the kitchen, I stopped, struck. A soft morning light came into the room from two high windows. The air smelled of the cloths that had dried overnight along the front of the big cream Aga. A brightly laden dresser covered one wall and a wooden table – the grain coarse, like sand – filled the middle of the room. On the table, two cakes of home-made bread sat on wire trays. Below the windows there was a long, sagging sofa, and someone had gathered newspapers and toys onto one end of it, and roughly tidied the things on the two window sills behind it – jars, books, a big alarm clock, a frame of honeycombs half wrapped in newspaper, a wine bottle with one thin branch of pussy-willow stuck in it, a sheaf of bills and letters on a spike. The room was full of tiny noises. The budgie moved discreetly behind the cover over its cage. Something inside the Aga made a small, plopping noise. The tin clock vibrated every time the hands clicked forward.

A footstep. Bertie came into the room carrying a small child, with Joe in pyjamas behind him.

Well, look at you, my dear! he said. Standing there like a ghost! This is Joe's little brother, Oliver.

Lolver, the child said.

Kitchens . . . I said. I've been in more museums than kitchens. I've probably been in more rococo chapels than kitchens –

Lady Muck! he said, but pleasantly.

He propped the infant on the sofa and turned on the picture of the television. Chorus dancers in purple cavorted mutely.

We'll have a cup of tea, he said.

Gggh! the child wailed.

Ollie wants his spoon, Joe said, with the manner of a weary interpreter.

Bertie gave Ollie a wooden spoon and the infant waved it happily at the dancers.

Let poor Spot in, there, he said to me. The fella that owns her lets her sleep beside his bed but when she's staying with us I put her in the shed.

The terrier burst in with such exuberance that we both started to laugh. The old dog, over on his blanket, lifted his grizzled head for a moment and went back to sleep with a loud sigh. I left the back door open. A gleam of sunlight lay on the stone of the sill of the door, and lit up a corner of the red woollen rug in front of the sofa. We had tea, and slices of the new bread with Ella's blackberry jam. The news came on the radio in Irish, and then it played Van Morrison singing 'The Star of the County Down'.

Van the Man, Bertie said musingly. I remember when I first bought a Van Morrison LP. *Astral Weeks*. It was the year I got married. I used to drive my poor wife mad playing 'Madame George'.

I did a quick sum in my head.

You married late enough, I said.

Yes, he said. I wanted nothing but the best – you know? Till I saw I was getting to the age where no one at all would have me if I didn't hurry. But where would I be now without Ella and her little fellas? Did you ever take the plunge yourself, may I be so bold as to ask?

Not me, I said. I was never in the same place long enough.

I was never any other place than here, he said. Ballygall is the world to me.

Joe was fidgeting beside my chair, waiting for me to notice him.

Guess the name of the budgie, he said. Go on – guess!

Pope John Paul the Twenty-second? I said.

No! he said. *No.* It's Spice! Budgie Spice!

I was *nearly* right, I said. But here – I'd better get going. I want to have a look around.

You're a hard-working woman, Kathleen, Bertie said. Like myself! There's no justice. I'd have loved to train horses.

Sure it's not too late, I said, laughing at him. Isn't the oul fella that trains for the Queen in his nineties?

Get out! Bertie said, and Spot thought he meant it, and did his best to menace me. I started moving, laughing, towards the door.

Bye, Kathleen! Joe said.

Bye, Attly! Oliver copied him.

I was shaken by a memory. My little brother Sean once, sitting up at the table banging his mug and chortling, and calling after me as I hurried out the door – Attly! Attly! It sounded the same. Almost exactly the same.

I sheltered outside the back door for a minute from the end of a shower of rain. Yes. That had happened on my last day in Shore Road – the day I left home and went away to Dublin, to college. Sean was three. I saw him again a couple of years later for ten minutes or so, when I called out to the house. But he'd forgotten me by then. He didn't know my name. I saw him waving to me from Mrs Bates's front window that day, as I began my flight from Ireland on the bus into Kilcrennan from Shore Road. But I never heard him say my name or anything else again. He died when he was about six and a half. There had been something wrong with his blood, Danny said when he phoned me. He was dead before I even knew he was sick.

The rain moved on, and a watery sun came out and laid a sparkling filigree on the wet grass of the garden. I waited a moment before I started the car to hear the birds begin their tentative calls – more as if they were talking, than singing.

The weather never seemed to settle. I smiled, as I drove away from the town, remembering a conversation with Jimmy, once, in a big, rough north London pub. We were sitting having a glass of beer on a summer evening when a massive Irishman came over to us, and for no reason at all stood in front of Jim in a threatening manner. Well, it would have been threatening if he hadn't been so unsteady on his feet.

Come outside and fight like a man, he growled at Jimmy.

61

Jimmy was the most peaceable man in the world.

Certainly not, he said to the man.

C'mon, ya fucker! the man roared at poor Jimmy.

No, Jimmy said. I don't want to.

Come out and I'll murder ya! the man said.

No, Jimmy said.

Aw, please, the man said. He said it not just politely but abjectly. *Please*.

Jesus! Jimmy said when the man wandered off disconsolately. What was all that about?

He just wanted a fight, I said.

But why did he want a fight? What is it about the Irish that they want to fight?

He wanted a fight because he was drunk.

Okay, Jimmy said. Okay – push it back a bit. Why do the Irish get drunk?

Odd you should ask me that, I said impressively. Because it just so happens I can tell you the answer. I read in a book – a perfectly reputable book – that Ireland has a very narrow range of weather. Nothing like the extremes of heat and cold you get in other places. But within that range, it is extremely variable! So, if you were an Irish farmer and you decided to do such-and-such a job one day and you got yourself all psyched up to do it, next thing you'd look out the window and the weather wouldn't be suitable and the whole thing would get to you and you'd have to go down to the shebeen instead.

Jimmy looked at me. This is a reputable book, you say?

Definitely, I said.

So the reason Godzilla there wanted to take me outside and flatten me is because the weather upsets him?

That's right, I said. Or, it's more that the weather upset his ancestors.

Kathleen, Jimmy said, do me a favour. If ever I ask you a question about the Irish again, don't answer it . . .

From a wide road that went along a ridge a couple of miles from Ballygall, I looked down on a landscape of low hills and small lakes in marshy valleys. There wasn't a house to be seen, and no fields, no woods, no farm buildings. I clambered up to a rocky outcrop, and I looked around, trying to see the detail of things. As I stood there I felt, in spite of the fitful spring sunlight, a hostility rise up from the place. The grasses were either a blackish-green or an acid green, and the rushes that ringed the blue-grey lakes were pallid.

The emptiness was a positive presence. There were exact figures for how many tens of thousands had died in the workhouses in this county, but no one knew, apparently, how many people had died unknown to officialdom. They knew how many families had been formally evicted, with an eviction order nailed to the door of the home and its execution duly notified to the authorities, but they didn't know how many families had been hunted from their cabins by hunger and fever. The landlords and their agents had taken the opportunity the Famine gave them to clear the land of people – throwing them out as they fell into hopeless arrears with the rent. But how many thousands had never been counted in the first place? The cabins of the pauper Irish were made of the materials ready to hand – sand and straw and grass and sods of turf and sallies and boulders and bits of wood. Their dwellings had melted back into the fabric of landscapes like the one before me.

I stood there and closed my eyes and tried to remember the feel of an earth floor under my own bare feet. I tried to remember the worst attacks of dysentery I'd had – the shiver of cold flesh and cold bone, the whole of me so sick and feverish that my head lolled on its stem and my knees buckled. But it would have been more awful than that. To lie on wet earth, under rain-sodden straw, your face greasy and grey with sweat, while hot, yellow, poisoned stuff trickles out from between your dirt-encrusted buttocks and streams down your legs . . . Did the dying people writhe and call on God? *A Dhia! A Dhia!* Or were they dumb? In one of my books a traveller was quoted as saying that the ones who caught the cholera swelled up and turned black – their faces turned black – and they died lying on the roads heading into town, because they came out of places like the valleys before me and tried to crawl towards the workhouse. But they all knew that the death rate in the workhouse was terribly high, too. They must have wanted not to die alone. Or wanted to die fed.

Does dying of hunger stop hurting at some point? Like dying in snow? *First – Chill – then Stupor – then the letting go . . .*

My father told us that Queen Victoria wrote a cheque for Battersea Dogs' Home for ten pounds and then she wrote one for five pounds for the relief of the suffering Irish. The only feeling he showed about the Famine was rage against England. There was no pity in him. He didn't imagine to himself the people who stumbled out of this watery, secretive landscape, squelching along the edge of the marsh, mud bubbling up between their thin toes. Old men's feet with blackened nails. Soft children's feet. Brown feet, white, purple and misshapen . . . The people who would have come up out of these places to walk the stony road to Ballygall had stick limbs and sunken faces. Were they silent, or would I have heard, up on this rock above the road, the murmuring of the slow-moving, ragged bands, or the voices of mothers calling to children? What did they call the children? Máire? Pádraig? They would not have been pretty children in red flannel. The convent schoolgirls in the tableau '1847, The Year of the Big Hunger' on the back of Murphy's lorry, in the pageant, were spotless – my friend Sharon even gave me colourless nail varnish for my toenails. But the real famine children would have been like the ones that come running towards the camera from napalm bombs and strafing and earthquakes – children with runnels of snot and sores at the corners of their lips, on faces tense with fear and hatred . . .

I turned away, and drove back to Bertie's.

I was uneasy with myself. Who was I to say what my father felt or not? Imagination of others doesn't go very far even when you're trying, and I had never tried for him. Yet here I was, attempting to imagine a whole nation in the time of an unimaginable catastrophe! For what? Could I move beyond some momentary imagining of the past towards finding a meaning for it? Not an explanation, but a meaning? And not a meaning in history but in my own life?

In Shore Road, beyond the circle of tarmacadam where the bus turned around, there was a stretch of short turf above the strand, grass as dense as suede and pitted with bunker-like holes. You jumped down onto the sand at the bottom of them and then up again if you were playing chasing. Nora and her girlfriends and the big boys went into them after dark.

People used to live in those holes, I told Nora, after the Englishman on the bike told me. When the Famine came, that's where they were living. They had hardly any clothes or anything. There were hundreds of them. He's writing a history book.

Nora said, How do you mean, they had no clothes? Of course they had clothes.

She wasn't interested in the Famine, she was just interested in naked people. How would they go to Mass if they had no clothes?

I don't know, I said. How would I know?

I'd thought about that for a while – what it would have been like to live in those holes, where the sand is silky but bone cold. Babies and children in there under branches, maybe, laid across the top, and the mother out on the grass trying to boil potatoes in a pot in the rain or the wind over a fire of sea-sodden sticks. But picturing a scene wasn't the same as feeling it. Yet the Famine and the destruction of rural Ireland had been experienced only a few generations back. There were people alive whose grandparents had lived through those years. The trauma must be deep in the genetic material of which I was made.

I cannot forget it, I thought, yet I have no memory of it. It is not mine; but who else can own it?

Miss Leech turned out to inhabit a cluttered room, right at the top of a hidden back stairs, in the handsome sandstone building in the square that housed the Ballygall library. She was very small, with a pixie face entirely covered in wrinkles, and soft grey hair, pinned, inefficiently, into a cottage-loaf shape. Her dark eyes were set deep in the wrinkles, but her small mouth had lips so perfectly cut and shaped so prettily that every time I happened to notice them I felt a dart of pleasure.

You're a lively looking woman, was her opening remark to me. And much younger than I expected. I thought you said something about this being a retirement project of yours? I haven't retired yet, though admittedly I only look after the local history side now, and I'm seventy years old.

I'm not exactly retiring, I said. More trying to change direction.

She hadn't asked me to sit down, though she was sitting. I corrected myself –

I'm trying to change in general, I said awkwardly.

There was a long silence.

Sit down, Miss de Burca, she said.

I must have smiled so widely with relief that she smiled back at me.

Have you looked for inspiration to the natural world at all? she said. I must say that for myself, I admire the Creator more every day.

She told me that she'd stopped that morning to watch a wren teaching her fledglings to fly.

The mother bird had them lined up on a branch opposite her, she said. Nine of them. Tiny little things. And she was standing on a twig with flies for them in her beak, and they were standing there looking at her, chirping and squealing, and eventually they all got courage and one by one they jumped off the branch and fell down, and by the time they landed on the lower branches they could fly. But one little fellow wouldn't budge. You should have heard the shrieks out of him! Bawling at her he was, and he just would not jump. And do you know what she did when she ran out of patience? She flew over to him and she knocked him off the branch. Thumped him off it!

She laughed at the memory and I laughed, too, at her delight.

They say, I said, that in winter they sleep in a ball, wrens, and the ones in the middle come out to the edge so that another bird can move in and get warm.

Bees do that, too, Miss Leech said. I've often seen them. Do you believe in the Creator, Miss de Burca?

I believe there is a Creation, I said carefully. I see and hear things every day that make me think there must be a Creator. But . . .

Yes, she said. Exactly. But.

There was another silence.

She looked at me inquiringly. This Talbot business, she said. What interests you in it?

Well . . . I began. The unlikelihood of it, maybe. I mean, she was an upper-class Englishwoman and the man involved was only a minor servant –

He may have been a servant in her eyes! Miss Leech snapped. But the Mullans were a very old family and very respected in this locality. From the seventeenth century – from the sixteenth –

Well, I said. I didn't know that. That's an example of what I came here to learn. And that the affair happened just after the Famine, too. I haven't been back to Ireland for nearly thirty years. I've lived like a kind of stateless person, working in travel writing. I thought that as an Irish person I should know something about the Famine.

It causes a lot of trouble, the Famine, she said. When I was putting an exhibition together here for the hundred-and-fiftieth anniversary I was very careful. But a young instructor in the training centre put the teenagers onto a project to computerize the records of the workhouse – all the workhouse books were found when they demolished it to build the supermarket. He was trying to teach them computer skills. But of course the records caused uproar. Everyone started going into what really happened. How come so-and-so was admitted to the workhouse and their farm taken by their neighbours? Hadn't the big shops in the town made a fortune out of supplying the workhouse and at that, hadn't they cheated on every contract? Didn't so-and-so's great-grandfather get dismissed from supervising the women's ward because of the advantage he was taking of some of the poor women? Oh, I assure you! Our own forebears were part of the system, too, you know. None of the gentry around here died. But you can be sure that our ancestors weren't out among the cabins of the dying any more than the gentry were. If you and I are sitting here in a warm room having a nice talk, we have to ask ourselves how our own people survived. What did our people do at the time, that you and I came to be born? Anyone who had a field of cabbages or turnips put a guard on it to keep off the starving. We were those guards, Miss de Burca.

I need your help, was all I could find to say. Far more than I realized.

Another silence. But it was a warm silence.

I faxed you a few notes, Miss Leech, I said tentatively, from the Talbot *Judgment* –

Oh, I had a quick look at them, she said. It made a change from answering quiz-show questions for the good people of Ballygall. So far the only record of Marianne Talbot I can find, apart from the *Judgment* you already have, is in the ledgers from Hurley's drapery shop that was here in the town at the time. I looked through them last night. Missy, they called her. The account in her name begins in 1848. Mrs Missy Talbot. But I've printed out a couple of pieces of background information. It seemed to me after our telephone conversation that you would not necessarily have come across them while pursuing your truncated studies in literature – forgive me if I am wrong. One is an inventory, made by the local schoolteacher, of the total material possessions of a community of four thousand people in Donegal, in 1837. The other is an inventory of the possessions of an estate comparable to Mount Talbot. Though Mount Talbot had an exceptional amount of land. The estates around here were so big that there were in fact very few landlords.

So who would have been Mrs Talbot's neighbours? I said.

She had no near neighbours.

She had no one to talk to, then, I said.

It is quite a modern thing, Miss Leech said, this talking to people. When I was young, nobody complained if they had no one to talk to.

She stood up and came around the table and handed me the pages. She moved briskly as a bird, and though I half rose, I felt big and clumsy, so I sat down again.

If I am being a bit harsh with you, Miss de Burca, she said, it is partly to impress on you that if you are attempting a historical reconstruction of the Talbot scandal you have a great deal of work to do. *Years* of work. I know this library's holdings and I doubt there is anything here to help you. None of the estate records of Mount Talbot have survived, for instance, as they would have in many other counties. The Talbots were not at all liked, you know. That's putting it as mildly as I am capable of putting it.

Perhaps, then, I could start thinking more about a fiction of some sort? I said. But one based on a *feel* for the place and the people . . .

My voice faded away. I could hear myself how feeble I sounded. She looked at me for a long minute, and then something made her choose to be kind to me.

Well, she said, if it's feelings you want to begin with, I think we should go out to the bog around Mount Talbot. I can manage that for an hour or so. Because when I said a minute ago that Mrs Talbot had no near neighbours, I should have said – none that she would have called neighbours. She had several thousand neighbours, of course. They lived in the bog around her mansion.

She perched on the seat beside me like a little girl, in her grey cap and red jacket, as she directed the car through a scattered estate of large brick houses with conservatories, so new that they rose surreally out of the raw earth of a field with remnants of a thorn hedge around it. Beyond, a lane led down between stone walls towards the brown expanse of a bog.

Stop here, she said. She climbed out of the car. See?

She stood on her tiptoes and picked out with her small, mittened hand a rectangle of cut stones within the uncut stones of the wall.

That's the doorway of a house that once stood here. And see further on where the wall gets high, for no reason? That's the gable end of a house that has vanished. This stretch, from the main road to the bend in the lane – on the Ordnance Survey map of 1842 there are thirty-two houses marked in on this stretch alone, before the Famine. There were maybe ten to a house. Three hundred people, in just this corner. It was as crowded as Bangladesh, you know, anywhere near bogs like the one at the bottom of this lane where there was marginal land that could be squatted.

She pushed the toe of her little boot into the soft verge of the lane.

We used to come out on our bicycles and play along this lane, she said, because we could be sure to dig up pieces of dishes. Girls, of course. Chaneys, we called them. I love thinking about that, now – that we used that word, not knowing that it was the word 'china' pronounced the way our ancestors pronounced it. Bits of brown bowls with a cream glaze on the inside we often found, and once, even, I found a quarter of a plate that had Chinese pictures on it. I kept it under the stairs, in a shoe box that was my dolls' house . . .

We got back into the car and went down to the bog. The sky as far as the eye could see was piled with majestic clouds with flat undersides, and behind them in the pale blue a sliver of young moon showed. From the furthest range of clouds streaks of white and charcoal grey washed down the sky.

There's bad weather over Mount Talbot, she said.

She directed me out onto a causeway, beside a clearing where there were tyre tracks in the impacted brown earth and bright shards of plastic fertilizer sacks caught in the bushes. The harvested bog beyond was chocolate brown, and as flat as a lawn. The surface of this part of the bog had been peeled off, and the stripes the big machines made in the peat stretched away to the horizon.

The delicate complaining of the larks far above us stopped, as a hail shower raced superbly towards us. For a long moment it played, staccato, on the roof. Then I nosed the car forward, the hailstones melting into a silver glare as they were wiped aside, until the causeway ended at the foot of a small rise. Stands of alder and larch guarded the black pools and the silently rippling ditches and the small patches of lush meadow grass that rose from the water. We got out.

She said, We know from the Constabulary records that there were two shebeens here. So there must have been a fair few people living around.

They can't have needed much room, I said.

They dug the potatoes into what soil there was. Nothing else would grow here, because it is too acid. But they had a big, coarse potato at the time that would grow even in a bog.

I was in Africa once, in Mali, I said to her, and the only way to the village I was going to was by river. We were two days on the river, and the boy would pull our boat into the bank or tie up at an island to try to buy a chicken. And I met people completely hidden from the world – naked babies playing in the dust, men and women in rags laughing and waving at us. They owned no things. The boy couldn't even pay them with money, because they were so isolated that they had no use for money. It must have been like that, here, before the Famine. No matter who you were, or how poor, you could link up with someone you liked and find a bit of soil and throw up a bit of a cabin and have babies and live on potatoes . . .

Except for the rain, Miss Leech said. And the cold. But yes – I think they were perhaps the happiest people in Europe, for a while. They had an unbroken heritage of language and music and stories and customs and traditions that went back hundreds and hundreds of years. And the faith. They had the old faith. It was a whole civilization . . .

No one ever thinks of them as civilized, I said. Any more than they do ragged Malians. It's so easy to think of them as if they're childlike, and death and exile don't really hurt them . . .

We stood there. A light, chill wind strayed across the bog and blew on our faces.

The name of this townland where we're standing, Miss Leech said, is Gurteenmullane. *Goirtín Uí Mhulláin* – the little field of the Mullans. That's why I brought you here. When I was preparing my Famine exhibition I got the children to interview their grandparents. And one child wrote down that his grandfather called this part of the bog 'Mullan's bog' and he said there used to be a cottage here that everyone called into on their way in and out of the town, in his own grandfather's time, and that people by the name of Mullan lived here once.

There's nothing now? I said.

Nothing. Though not long ago I saw a strange bush out here, covered in white flowers, and it might have been the last straggler from a garden.

I saw that she was shivering, and I put my hand tentatively under her arm as we picked our way through puddles back to the car. The larks had stopped singing. The whole wide scene was perfectly still in the cold air.

In the car, I turned the heater to high.

This must have seemed a terrible place to the young Talbots, I said, after the Grand Tour. Paris, Naples –

On our money they travelled! Never forget that! Miss Leech said

71

smartly. They left this country in ruins, that lot. Them and their art and antiquities! Thieves! I was a girl in this town in the forties. It wasn't just the poverty and the TB and the way the men poured out of here on the railway we had then to work like serfs in England. It was that this was a stupid place. Dull as ditchwater. It's only beginning to come out of the fog of superstition and ignorance now. The landlords stole *everything*.

But Miss Leech, I said – tentatively – Miss Leech, *you* came from here. You're not ignorant or superstitious. So there were people like you, too –

Do you think I've had much company? she said. Do you? Do you think I've spent my evenings among the wits of the Ballygall *salons*?

And she waved around at the expanse of silent bog.

But that's what I was saying about having someone to talk to, I said. Loneliness is the bad thing. Marianne Talbot would have been so lonely here.

Idle parasite! she said. They could do what they liked, her kind. They made the law and they administered the law. They did nothing for us when times were good and they stood by and let us die when times were bad. And they couldn't even be true to their own code, whatever it was. Look at your friend Marianne. She had nothing on earth to do except be a proper wife and she couldn't even do that.

She was young, I began.

She was a libertine! Miss Leech all but shouted.

It was as if to make up to me for her bad temper that, a few minutes later, she called me by my name for the first time.

There's one last thing I want to show you, Kathleen, she said.

She guided me along a rutted lane to where the expanse of grass and brown water was broken by a line of thin birch trees. A silent wood pigeon drifted across the darkening sky.

Stop. She wound down her window. See there?

She pointed to where, a couple of feet away, there was a rough floor of hard black turf, and behind it, a wall of dry black turf, that was the side of an old trench.

When I was growing up there were two old ladies living there, she said. They'd hollowed out a kind of cave in the turf, and they'd covered the front with sacking, held up by branches of wood. They used to go out around the houses, selling camphor balls and needles – little things. But they weren't pedlars. They were most respectable ladies. Only, they'd been evicted. Like many another poor person in this country of ours. Their names were Biddie and Mollie but no one was so familiar as to call them that. They were always called the Misses Flynn.

They died out here, she said. First Biddie, then Mollie. Sometime in the 1940s. By rights they should have been buried in the paupers' plot, but the priest opened a big grave for the two of them. Still – this is where they lived. They wouldn't go in under a roof, if it wasn't their own roof.

I sat very still.

And now, she said, after you drop me home, I want you to go on into Pat the Pizza in the square and tell Nario to send me up one of my pizzas. It's a kind of tinned-sardine pizza that I don't think anyone else in Ballygall would eat if they were starving. But I share it with my cat. We love it.

I was longing to ring Alex. I wanted something for myself, after the long, intense day. I wanted a bit of comfort. I hurried in to phone him from Bertie's den behind the reception desk.

He sounded miserable.

Oh, he said, the office is very quiet. Roxy says she's going back to St Lucia and I don't know what I'll do without her. And my mother isn't very well. And I really don't know how I'm supposed to run *TravelWrite* without any assistance whatsoever. What about you, Kath? Are you having a ball –

I started to laugh. Then I tried to describe the acid-yellow grass and the grey rushes.

He said, Hold on there, Kathy! Can I get something straight here? I thought it was the love story you went over there to get background on – the *Lady Chatterley's Lover* situation?

Well, yes, Alex, but now that I'm here –

Excuse me, Kathleen – sorry to cut across you, but as I understood it, the love affair happened *after* the potato famine –

Oh, Alex! I said. *They* didn't know it was 'after'. Its effects were still all around. And even if landlords like the Talbots suffered no want, they must still have been terrified, if only that the cost of running the workhouses would ruin them. And, anyway, on a deep level, there was so much horror in the air, that it must have affected everyone –

I'm afraid I think that's a bit fanciful, Kathleen, Alex said firmly.

Well, I don't, I said.

Well, I do, Alex said, but even leaving me out of it – I said to you that I thought a book about an unusual love affair and a sensational Victorian divorce case would do very well, but I certainly don't think that about yet another tome on the sorrows of Ireland.

It wasn't 'sorrows', Alex, I said through gritted teeth. It was our Holocaust. Well, no – it wasn't deliberate like exterminating the Jews. But the British government was glad that we were being exterminated by accident.

There was silence from his end.

Listen, Alex, I said. Just listen with an open mind to one short paragraph from one objective, scholarly book about the Famine. I swear that this is the last time I'll quote anything at you.

From the summer of 1846 on, the potato blight brought immediate and horrible distress, with the countryside 'from sea to sea one mass of unvaried rottenness and decay'. One historian estimates that between 1.1 and 1.5 million people died of starvation and famine-related diseases, and scenes of almost unimaginable mass suffering were witnessed: 'cowering wretches almost naked in the savage weather, prowling in turnip fields and endeavouring to grub up roots'; 'famished and ghastly skeletons, such as no words can describe'; 'little children, their limbs fleshless, their faces bloated yet wrinkled, and of a pale greenish hue'.

All over the country landless labourers died in their tens of thousands, and even shopkeepers, townspeople and relatively comfortable farmers perished from the effects of the diseases spread by the starving and the destitute. Although the blight itself was unavoidable, its impact on Ireland was magnified by the response of the British government, blinkered by free-market dogma and by a profound, almost malevolent indifference to Irish ills . . .

I do see what you mean, Kathleen, Alex said, and he said it quite slowly, as if he'd really been listening. But it'll be the romantic side of the thing that the ordinary reader will relate to. I really think you're going to have to be very careful with the historical stuff . . .

Now I was silent. We heaved huge sighs, simultaneously.

We never had any of this trouble with straight travel features, Alex said wistfully.

Did I ever tell you the one good joke there is in *Lady Chatterley's Lover*, Alex?

No, Kathleen, he said.

Connie is boasting to her sister about the great sex life she has with Mellors and she says that she feels when they're making love that she's in the very middle of creation. And the sister says, I suppose every mosquito feels the same.

I roared with laughter, but Alex didn't.

I went on up to my room, cheered up. I'd once tried to explain to Jimmy what it meant to me that no matter where I was in the world I knew that Alex would be at his desk from early to late, in one of his cheap suits, going through copy meticulously, his hands fine and white on the keyboard, his face self-forgetful as he scanned the screen. The dome of St Paul's behind him. The phone on his right for the rest of the NewsWrite syndicate and his personal network of publicists, editors, publishers, advertising buyers. The phone on the left for Jimmy and me.

He's always *there*, I said.

Yes, Jimmy said sourly. Such as he is.

In the bedroom I practically threw my Famine notes off the desk. I'd had enough. What about this life, now? I plugged in the kettle to make tea and I rang Caroline's in London and left the number of Bertie's place on her machine, with my love. I rang Nora's apartment in New York – knowing she'd be in the office – and left the same. I hooked my feet under the radiator and did thirty sit-ups and then

I put a conditioning treatment on my hair and showered. I pulled a fleece top over my nightdress and lolled in front of the television and painted my toenails while I watched an antique episode of *Dallas*, with Sue Ellen in shoulder pads.

I had a good gossip with Ella when she brought up the tray. I sent her back down for a bottle of wine and two glasses and she sat on the bed and I learned that Bertie had never liked her boyfriend and the night they had to tell him Ella was pregnant was dreadful. But Miss Leech talked to him –

Who?

Miss Leech. Nan Leech. She's Daddy's friend all his life – they used to live next door to each other as kids, the other side of the square. Anyway, she got him round, and we'd a great wedding. And there's Oliver now, as well as Joe, and their granda loves them, he really does. If things go well in Saudi we can put a deposit on a place of our own. I'd love a place of my own, not to be always looking over my shoulder. Worrying if the kids make a mess, you know? There's nothing my fella can throw his wages away on in Saudi. Please God. Only the kids miss their da . . .

It was how she leaned forward towards me, and I sat in my nightdress and munched as I listened to her, and the room smelled of perfumed shampoo, that brought back the time I lodged, when I was a girl, with a whole lot of other girls in a house in London called Joanie's. I hadn't thought about it for years, perhaps because I hadn't sat with my wet hair wrapped in a towel talking to a young woman. And the way I was looking at myself in the mirror while Ella talked and sipped – that reminded me, too. The girls in Joanie's never really looked at each other, either, but fussed with emery boards and nail varnish and curlers while they talked.

Below the hem of my nightdress I could see – and I noticed it with a quick flick of misery – that the skin was blotchy over the knob of my anklebone. And when I lifted the leg and twisted myself to look at it more closely, I saw that the veins at the back of my knees were coarse and blue-black. That was new, wasn't it? Then – because the mirror was in front of me – I experimented with moving my head while I listened to Ella. Yes – the skin of my neck puckered when I bowed my head. I leaned across and peered into the mirror and did it again: lower chin, throat puckers; lift chin, throat smooths out.

And to think that when I was young, I took the fabric of myself for granted! It never occurred to me, no more than it would to Ella now, that someday I would be afraid to look at myself closely.

I miss my husband something shocking, Ella said, and she blushed.

How old are you? I asked.

Twenty-four. He's due home on my birthday, my twenty-fifth. He's dying to get home. He's afraid I might get off with someone else, she said happily, as she collected the things and got ready to go downstairs. But there's no danger of that! I'm a one-man woman!

Marianne would have been that kind of age. Just kids, they are, at twenty-five, in spite of having babies.

How do girls find out about themselves? How do they learn the rules? A well-brought-up miss like Marianne – who would have warned her that forces exist that might lead her to abandon herself to a groom on the floor of a stable? Would she have heard below-stairs talk in her father's house in Harley Street in London? Did her maid escort her to dancing class, and did she and the other decorous misses giggle and gossip behind their fans? What words did they have for their bodies, or for the boys their bodies responded to? Did Marianne have a mother less silent than mine? How did it happen that someone like my sister-in-law Annie had the same boyfriend – my brother Danny – since she was twelve years old, and as far as I know has loved him from then to this, and been loved by him, so that they look at each other full in the face when they talk? I noticed, every time over the years they came to London, that they had perfect confidence in each other. Why couldn't that have been Marianne's fate? Or mine?

I didn't know, when I was fourteen, that what was happening to me was something to do with my body. My friend Sharon and I had never heard of puberty or hormones, and we never called the thing we were after, sex. We called it being mad about this boy or that boy. Not mad about boys – mad about specific ones. We thought our quest came from the heart, even though it was felt on the body. I was clever in school, but cleverness couldn't help with these mysteries. The convent girls went out to roam the main street every day in the lunch break, and the boys from the Christian Brothers burst out of their buildings at the same time, and they'd all queue for chips, jostling each other and giggling while the bad-tempered Scotsman slammed things around behind the counter and shouted at them to wait their turn. But they weren't serious about courting. Not compared to Sharon and me. I lived for boys with the single-mindedness that working-class girls like Sharon did.

We were stretched impatiently towards the future, the two of us. We couldn't wait for it. We were exactly the opposite of famine people, lying down to die.

We found out the main thing about men, together, when we were fifteen. One Saturday, we followed a mad old priest who was back from the missions on his holidays. He turned around in the lane behind the supermarket and threw his overcoat back and his thing was sticking out of his trousers like a torch. He said something in a funny voice – something about a tickle and a lickle baby.

Is that the size they all are? I asked Sharon.

Oh, yes! she said. Because I was doing a slow waltz with the hunk from the vegetable shop last Friday. 'A Whiter Shade Of Pale'. And his was sticking into me and that's the size it was . . .

I got into bed. The room smelled of conditioner and nail varnish – exactly like Joanie's.

I learned a lot in Joanie's. London was the next step in my sentimental education, after the streets of Kilcrennan with Sharon. In Joanie's there were two or three narrow divan beds in every room, pushed almost up against the gas fires. The girls climbed over the beds to get to the clothes they'd hang from hooks on the wall after they ironed them. There were always girls in dressing gowns, with scarves over the rollers in their hair, eating biscuits and drinking tea in the long, narrow kitchen. It was always biscuits and cakes. I brought home fruit that was left by the guests in the hotel where I was a chambermaid, but no one in the house would stop smoking long enough to eat it. They'd take a bite and leave it. There were six older girls there, and me. Joanie had got us all jobs. We were all Irish, working in factory jobs or as maids in hospitals or hotels. We all wore minidresses and little white boots, even the big country girls with thick, weather-beaten legs. And eyeliner and white lipstick. Joanie took our rent out of the pay packets before she passed them on. But she'd give us smokes when our money ran out. She'd let us get calls on the phone in her bedroom, where the window was tight shut, and the heat made the place smell of the pink talc on her satin-skirted dressing table.

On Saturday nights she did herself up and went with the girls to the ballrooms in Kilburn or Camden Town, though she was hard-looking, with her wine-coloured lipstick and the black hair she gave a colour rinse to every few days. She was too old to be giggling with them. She'd be different from them again only the next morning, when she'd be banging on the doors shouting, Youse'll be late for Mass! when their eyes were still stuck together and they were mumbling, Would you ever fuck off, under the sheets.

Joanie was related to Mrs Bates at the shop in Shore Road. Otherwise I'd never have got to London.

I nearly blew it. I asked Daddy if I could go over to London for the summer till I heard whether I'd got a scholarship to Trinity, and he said, What's wrong with Ireland? I said I could earn money. He said, You don't need money to help your poor mother, and I said, Why don't *you* help my poor mother?

I couldn't stop myself, even though I was dying to go to London. Why don't *you* help my poor mother with *your* children?

But I was guilty about leaving Mammy. Nora had jumped ship and disappeared to America the summer before. Even I didn't know that she'd talked Uncle Ned into giving her the fare. Mr Bates came up from the shop when we were having our dinner one Sunday and said there's been a phone call from New York and Nora said to say hello and goodbye. Daddy roared at Mammy that that daughter of hers must have forged his name to get a passport and that he was a civil servant and he should report her and where did she get the money? Mammy said nothing much. Afterwards, she used to wear Nora's coat, because Nora had gone in just the clothes on her back.

We never got anything from her except the odd postcard, though she told me once that she'd repaid Uncle Ned within six weeks. She never even sent Mammy a birthday card. I used to send Mammy a pound a week from London. Me and the Spanish chambermaids would come in the back of the hotel through the bins, and get our cleaning carts and go up in the service lift. We listened to the radios in the rooms all day. On Monday mornings I went to the post office on the way to work and put two ten-shilling notes in a stamped envelope and wrote Mrs de Burca, Shore Road, Kilcrennan, Ireland, with the pen they used to have in post offices then, that you dipped in ink.

All that summer Luisa and Pilar and I got fellas everywhere, especially at the dances for foreign workers the priests used to run in a hall in Soho, so that young Catholics would marry each other. The waiters from the cafés around would grind their pelvises into us and swoop up and down the floor bent backward to the records the priest played. *Bèsame! Bèsame mucho . . .*

After about an hour we'd all start shouting at the priest, Beatles! Beatles! Play the Beatles!

And he'd put on *Sergeant Pepper*, and we'd gyrate . . .

Afterwards, you'd be kissing some fella, and there'd be a warm bulge going nudge, nudge into your thigh, and you'd ignore it. If he tried to make you touch it and you jumped back, he'd say, 'S okay, and kiss harder. I'd run for the Cricklewood bus on shaky legs, back to the girls in their sprigged dressing gowns, in the house that smelled of soap.

In Joanie's, I lay on my bed and read when the other girls were out. The girls knew I wasn't like them. They wouldn't have gone to university if you paid them. But when there was a big white envelope for me from Trinity College, Dublin, one night and I started sniffing with joy when I read it, they were lovely to me. One of them ran out and got a cake from the petrol station.

I rang Bates's shop, and Mrs Bates ran up the road to get my mother, and I hung on and hung on, afraid that Joanie would say I was on the phone too long.

Mrs Bates came back on, out of breath.

Your ma's not well enough to talk to you herself, she panted. But she said to say she's proud of you and you're a great girl . . .

I hunched down further under the bedclothes in my bed in Bertie's place. These were very happy memories. Sharon and I crushed into her little bed side by side, Pond's cold cream slathered on our faces, cigarettes protruding, one of us going into elaborate detail about why such and such a fella was gorgeous . . .

But the atmosphere of the bog crept back around me as I fell slowly towards sleep. I did not fall asleep like the girl I had been remembering. My body grew old and tired, and I lay with the Misses Flynn in their cutting in the bog, and I heard foxes cough in the night, and I heard birds alight on the tarpaulin. I heard frost crackle on the grasses, and rain slide down into the gurgling ditches. I thought I heard people tapping on the roof of the shelter to say that my sister was dead, but that wasn't real. That was the creeper tapping against the window of the bathroom in Sharon's where we put in our rollers, dampening each fat curl – no, tapping on the window of this room, as the wind rose.

5

It often took me ten minutes to brush the tangles out of my hair in the morning, and I usually got bored and tied it back before it was properly done. But today I did it perfectly. I'd nothing else to do. Bertie had been supposed to take me up to Mount Talbot, but rain was streaming down the window.

I rang London from the office to tell Alex that I was moving to the cottage the hotel owned over in Mellary, on the coast, while the wedding party came in.

Oh, Kathleen! Roxy said. I've taken the plunge! I'm going back to St Lucia to see what kind of work's going there. I'm supposed to be training in a new girl but I won't have much time. I've a cheap flight for next week. So goodbye and God Bless . . .

I asked to speak to Alex.

Alex isn't here. He's taking his mother for a check-up. But I'll leave a message. And, Kath – I'm gonna get my cousin who's a pastor to make a beautiful service for Jimmy . . .

I smiled, going back up to my room, thinking about Roxy. She had been the first secretary to stay with *TravelWrite* – the others always found our isolated attic too lonely. But Roxy made friends with prickly Betty down the corridor in Administration, and she settled down with us, and from then on the office always smelled of West Indian food. Every day, she brought in a basket with the lunch her mother had cooked for her. A basket! And her mother would have had her in white ankle socks, too, if Roxy hadn't been so very large. Her mother used to send us in wonderful cakes. There was a winter day, once – I remember the yellow-grey sleet on the skylight – when I came back up from having a smoke in the basement with the messenger boys, and I stood at the door of our office and named it an enchanted playground. That was in honour of the particularly wonderful smell of Jamaican coffee and sugary coconut cake.

I got a call, Roxy said that lunchtime, from the new Human Resources guy to say he wants you two to fill in a questionnaire about prioritizing your goals.

My God! I said. We're expected to have goals?

My goal, Jimmy said earnestly, is to spend every morning at the gym and every afternoon at lunch and to have my paycheque sent round by messenger.

I want a flat stomach and a heart-shaped face, I said. And a perfect love. And my life given back to me, so I can live it again better.

Jimmy looked at me, but he let it pass.

What's your goal, Roxy? he asked.

To see you do some work for a change, she said, and he sprang across to her and began to tickle her.

We were eating the cake and licking our fingers and going mmm! and okaay!

Funny, isn't it? Roxy said musingly. The three of us, sitting here in England. Because none of us are English. Well, I'm a British citizen, of course –

We're ex-English, Jimmy and me, I said. We come from former colonies.

We're lucky, the three of us, Jimmy said. We have England, but we have our own places, too.

We do not 'have' England, I said. Maybe you do, but I don't. Not a day passes but some remark about 'you Irish' is made to me in a condescending tone.

You should try being black, Roxy said.

Well, why are you two here, then? Jimmy said. You're free, white and twenty-one, same as I am. Well, if you stretch a couple of points about the white and the twenty-one.

Because it's better than St Lucia, Roxy said. I'd have three or four little toddlers already and they'd be going to school in bare feet . . .

Kathleen? Would you have toddlers if you'd stayed in Ireland? It's hard to imagine classy Kathleen with toddlers.

If there's one thing, Jimmy Beck, I said, that I do not have, it is class.

Natural class, I meant, he said.

You can't have natural class, I said. The whole thing about class is that it's a social measurement.

Oh, don't be picky, Kathleen! And you're trying to distract me, too. Why are you in England if you don't like it here?

It's not that I like it here, I said with a vehemence I hadn't expected. I didn't like it there!

My eyes had filled with tears. I was astonished to feel them. The other two looked at me with shocked faces.

It's no good in Ireland! I cried. I never want to see it again! It's no place for a woman.

Jimmy came over and tried to hold me, but I did not want to be touched.

You didn't finish your slice of cake, he said after a minute. He doubled a sheet of typing paper and put the cake neatly on it, and drew up a chair beside me.

Open up! he said, and popped a corner of the piece of cake into my mouth as if I were a fledgling.

I'm *sorry*, Kathleen, he said. I'm *sorry*, sweetheart. I didn't mean to upset you.

Roxy just looked at the two of us sceptically, as if we were actors.

I put on the ancient pair of jeans and old boots I'd been wise enough to pack. My sweater was Comme des Garçons, not that anybody in Ballygall would know. I'd walk around the town, later on. There was nothing I liked better than walking around a strange town. I had a transparent plastic pouch for my notebook, and I slipped in my copy of the *Judgment*, too – there were bound to be marks of the Talbot dynasty everywhere.

I sat back down on the bed with surprise when it occurred to me that this would be the first Irish town I had ever in my life walked around. I didn't even know Kilcrennan well, because where we lived in Shore Road was three or four miles outside it. I knew the centre of Dublin from my two years at Trinity. But that was all. That was the sum total of my Ireland. Yet I knew tens of English towns! I couldn't drive, when I began working on *The English Traveller*, so

I criss-crossed the country on my gentle little assignments by train, getting down from compartments where the beige cut-moquette cloth on the seats smelled of dust, dawdling along platforms past intricate sheds of brick and tile and doors that said LAMPMEN No. 2, passing refreshment rooms with wooden benches made slippery by use where thin tea was splashed straight from the kettle onto trayfuls of thick cups, and going out into station yards, my head craning around in happy anticipation. I'd navigate my way to the market square by the spire of the cathedral. I'd pause here and there, and take my notebook out of its pouch. And that contented me – that kind of belonging. Just to look, and make notes –

Kathleen! Kathleen! Ella was shouting up from the hall. Daddy says the rain is easing off and he'll go up to the demesne with you in an hour.

Great!

On the desk, I had a blurry photograph of the Mount Talbot house that I'd found in a book about Ireland's stately homes. The place looked like a Scottish hotel – all Gothic windows and ivy-covered castellation, and chimneys, and a massive bell tower like a keep. I pored over it. There had been a photo of our family at home, standing out on Shore Road, everyone's hair blowing the same way in the wind that I could tell had been coming off the sea. The baby Sean in the pram in front. Mammy behind Danny in the middle in his confirmation suit with a big rosette in his lapel. Nora and I in our school uniforms. One photo, all people and no house: one, all house and no people. In the other photographs in the book there were ladies in long skirts and great hats on front steps, and a boy holding a pony sideways-on to the camera, and a pug in someone's lap, and a Labrador sprawled on the gravel, and a girl in a pinafore who had moved at the wrong moment and would for ever have a blur for a head. But this view was just of part of a large building, with black trees beyond.

I've come to put the people back into the picture, I said to myself – conscious of being fanciful.

The house, lit up by lamps and candles and sconces, must have been like a landed spaceship in the dark silence of the bog. Marianne

Talbot and William Mullan moved around in it, and the servants crept after them. Seven places where they'd been seen together had been described in court. I liked that. There were always seven stopping places, and seven prayers to be said, in an Irish pilgrimage. The first station – the sitting room where Marianne rang the bell and asked for milk – would have been the daytime room of the lady of the house, feminine, softly carpeted and dressed with delicate, gilded furniture hauled across half Europe to this outpost. Yet an under-groom was seen standing in it!

The Lord Chancellor commented:

That is a very strange thing for a groom, especially for a groom who is described by all the witnesses as being a man ordinarily of rather dirty appearance, and not a smart-looking person.

But what does appearance matter to lovers? Or place? Hugo and I made love everywhere on the way back from Paros. On the ferry. In the train from Bari to Rome. Against the wall in the lowest level of the Basilica of San Clemente – the level of the Mithraic temple – when the other tourists climbed back up to the chapel. I remember the dank smell of underground, and our breaths, quickening, in the silence.

The second station was the dressing room where Mullan had stood. The third, the drawing room, where the two were seen sitting together on a sofa with their arms around each other. Then Marianne's bedroom, where Maria Mooney saw them 'in the very fact'. The stables where the sawyers from the carpenter's shop saw them on the floor. Mullan's room, upstairs over a yard, where they talked and laughed. The orchard into which they were seen to go.

They must have seemed like luscious fruit, to each other. Their bodies must have ripened on each other.

I'd had a half-hour or so in the juicy grass on the edge of a sweet-smelling orchard once myself, at someone's wedding, on a hot autumn evening, somewhere in Kent. I remembered the orange moon through branches with black apple shapes on them, and I remember the man putting a gold sandal back on my foot – I even remember the tickle of the blades of grass on my sole and then the firmness of his fingers. That wasn't making real love, of course, it was just a party thing. His wife watched us coming back up the lawn to the lights of the terrace.

The memory made me stand up, uncomfortable.

I thought of something useful to do. I'd type the inventory of an estate comparable to Mount Talbot, that Miss Leech had given me, into the 'Background' file on my PC. That would help me to make sense of what I'd see when I got to the house.

Mount Talbot, her note read

was by no means a grand place – a Rockingham or a Carton. It was merely, in terms of Anglo-Irish big houses, a lodge. An estate of that kind, although commanding – of largely boggy and hilly land – perhaps 80,000 acres, would typically consist of a 25–30-room mansion, a village at the gates, and dependent houses and cottages in the vicinity in considerable number. The following features of a comparable estate would have been present within the demesne itself:

Walled gardens and orchards, lawns and gatehouses and at least one fishpond, a kennels, a deer park, a bull-paddock, a piggery, a harness-room, a vegetable garden, calf sheds, various stables including one for hunters, duckponds, lofts for the storage of grain, etc., beehives, a heated brick wall behind greenhouses for the cultivation of exotic fruits such as peaches, and flowers such as camellias for the house. A fernery. An inner walled garden for vegetables and soft fruit. Sheds with wooden shelves put up by the estate carpenters for the storage of estate produce. A dairy. A varying but very large number of pedigree cattle and sheep. Breeding sows and their bonhams. A lumber mill and one or two cornmills. A mock hermitage or ruined castle. An icehouse. Staff, comprising at the least, cooks, house-maids, kitchenmaids, parlourmaids, gardeners, stewards, yardmen, farm-hands. And furniture, silver, paintings, plate, rugs. In the mews, carriages and equipages of various kinds.

In the case of the Talbots, there was also a house in London, presumably with a caretaking staff.

*

At the bottom of Miss Leech's page, there was the second inventory – the one made in the parish of Gweedore, in Donegal, just before the decade of the Famine. I copied it into my notes, too. Slowly.

The teacher, Miss Leech wrote, lists the entire material wealth of four thousand people:

1 cart, no coach or any other vehicle, 1 plough, 20 shovels, 32 rakes, 7 table forks, 93 chairs, 243 stools, 2 feather beds, 8 chaff beds, 3 turkeys, 27 geese, no bonnet, no clock, 3 watches, no looking glass above 3d. in price, and no more than 10 square feet of glass.

Kathleen! Ella was shouting up from the bottom of the stairs. Kathleen! Daddy wants you!

Bertie was in the kitchen, his tongue sticking out like a child's as he concentrated on squirting blobs of choux pastry, in rows, onto a baking sheet. Ollie and Joe were standing on chairs looking on with interest.

That was a wet start, he murmured to me. I was afraid the rain was settled in for the day.

Your hair is all sticking up, Joe said to me.

I thought the rain was settled in for the year, I said.

Oh, Bertie said, putting down the icing bag and smiling at me – the forecast is excellent. Sunny for the weekend. Not that I believe it.

I'll be gone, I said morosely.

You'll only be gone to Mellary, Kathleen. It's much the same weather, you know. It's only an hour and a bit away. And you'll love the cottage – it's ideal for a writer.

I'm not a writer yet, I said. But I might be after today! The house might inspire me. Here – I passed him my list of the locations of the seven sightings – this is what we're after.

He started to take a pair of glasses mended with Elastoplast out of a pocket of his cardigan.

Bertie, I said. The animals they had up there. Did the people not get at the horses and cattle to eat during the Famine?

For God's sake! Bertie said, at the same time as Joe said, Eat horseys!

Nonsense, Kathleen! The people did bleed cattle and horses, and beasts of any kind had to be guarded for years. Nan Leech had a kind of drawing, from some English newspaper, of men with a razor and a bowl standing beside a horse, in her Famine exhibition –

Granda! Joe was pulling at him. Granda, I wouldn't eat a horse, he said piously.

No one's asking you to, Bertie said.

He took a battered waxed jacket down from behind the door and stuck a shapeless tweed hat on his head.

Ella, take those prawns up to the hotel kitchen, before we're evicted for breaking the food laws. And keep an eye on what the cleaners are doing up there. And generally hold the fort, like a good girl. I won't be long.

I heard him say that, and I was surprised. How could he not be long? But then, I'd been surprised when he'd said at breakfast that he'd take me up to the demesne before I had to leave today – given that the preparations for the wedding were getting quite hectic. But I didn't say anything, in case it looked as if I were criticizing.

The grand avenue to Mount Talbot started at a derelict but wonderfully ornate triple archway that made up one side of the square in Ballygall. It was a fairy-tale beginning, to follow Bertie in under the elaborate arch. But the avenue disappeared after a hundred yards, in a wilderness of deep, clay ruts full of water, where we had to climb the first of a series of metal gates swathed in barbed wire. This side of the estate had long ago become fields which the rain had reduced to tufts of grass in slicks of mud gouged by the hooves of cattle. We plodded along a slope above a stream that had flooded its banks, and made our way towards a high wall. My wet jeans scoured the skin of my knees and thighs. Already, this early in the year, ramparts of nettles guarded the breach in the wall, and twisted saplings bent from where earth had lodged between loosened stones. There was fallen masonry everywhere under the drenched grass. A branch whipped across one cheek. I stumbled, and my hands brushed a high patch of weeds, and were stung. My socks had wrinkled in under the heels of my boots. My face was scratchy with seeds and grasses.

I caught up with Bertie gazing at a convoluted tree.

Every time I see this, he said, I wonder if it would stand transplanting. It's an arbutus – a strawberry tree. I'd love it in my place. The Talbots made a lot of money – Nan explained it all to me – in the time of the war against Napoleon. So they made a sunken water garden, and started bringing in ornamental trees from all over the world. I remember an avenue of beautiful old trees between here and the town, but some professor from Dublin came asking about them once, and the oul fella that bought this place from the Land Commission cut them down out of pig-headedness. He said they might poison his cattle.

A water garden! I said. Just what you need in these parts.

We made a slow progress onward, pushing back high, wet weeds till we broke through to a wide stretch of cobbles, slimy with moss.

Bertie stopped.

Here you are, he said.

Where?

The house.

Where's the house? I said, looking around.

Here.

All there was ahead of us was a wide platform, stretching away. A broad, level, stone platform, covered in black moss and twigs and bird droppings.

There were twenty or thirty rooms, Bertie said.

This is all there is? I said, still incredulous. This?

His voice seemed to echo across the concrete. The heavy trees around were immobile and drenched.

This is it, he said. The oul fella took the roof off when they tried to charge him rates, when I was a boy of six or seven. There was a big room with bay windows that was the ballroom. It was all covered with broken glass when we were kids. There was a dining room, too, or at least, a room with a huge wooden table with thick carved legs. We used to play underneath the table when we went up to the house. But the whole thing went to rack and ruin without the roof. And someone bulldozed what was left of it in the sixties.

The house had been built on top of a rise. In front of the platform, a tussocky, weedy field stretched down between thick woods to a small lake. Beyond the lake, the inner demesne ended. Where trees had been felled you could see the high wall of the estate. It had fallen in parts, and been roughly breached here and there. Beyond the wall, the land became more marshy. Then it rose, on the horizon, to hills that barely made an impression on the low, mottled sky.

I brought my camera! I wailed. I brought the *Judgment* so as to go from place to place mentioned in it, making a map! I was going to read you out the relevant passage at each location.

You're too late, Bertie said. There's been nothing here since before you were born.

We turned away.

Some of the outbuildings are the same as they were, he said. The bell tower is there. And the walls of the orchard and the gardens. I've spuds of my own in the kitchen garden down the hill, just inside what was their back gate – the West gate. I go out there in the car. And there is this –

We had passed a great spill of daffodils at the foot of a flight of steps that led up to nothing, and made our way through a curved gateway almost hidden in thick foliage. All I could see where he was pointing to, ahead, was that cattle had been penned in the yard, and it was deep in pale, viscous mud.

Then I walked forward.

The stable yard!

Each stable had a wooden shutter over its opening into the yard, still.

One of those openings was what the two sawyers had peered through, when they saw William and Marianne abandoned to each other in the straw.

I'll be back in a minute, I said to Bertie.

He glanced at me. The rain had plastered his hair to his forehead, and the chill had reddened his nose, but his brown eyes were very alive. I could see from his face that my own was vivid, too. I beamed my excitement at him.

I jumped and slid along the edge of the yard to where the thick, roughly carpentered double doors into the first stable wing stood ajar, and I slipped in. The rows of empty stalls stretched away. The straw on the stone floor was as grey as dust. Nothing had disturbed it for many years.

I put out my hand and laid it against the bleached wood of the door. Their hands had touched this door. One of these stalls had been their couch. Under this roof, flesh had worshipped flesh . . .

I bowed my head. Thick silence inside. The sound of water dripping, outside.

When I came out, Bertie was pulling ivy off the archway.

I slumped down to sit on the dry earth underneath. Gradually, the inner curve of the arch revealed itself, and I saw that it had been made of finely chiselled small stone blocks, and that Bertie had uncovered a deep niche in its flat side, below the curve. Within the niche, he held the last strands away from – still perfect, though streaked green-black by damp – a small, classical statue of a hunter. A boy in a tunic and sandals, with laurel leaves in his hair, holding up a bow.

Oh, Bertie! I cried.

I'm the only one that knows that's there, he said. Oh! And now, you.

I rested, looking at the beautiful boy. Bertie squatted beside me, gazing at the statue, too.

This exact configuration had happened to me before, somewhere. I searched my memory. An arch, and a man looking down on me, and thick vegetation outside . . . Oh yes! And then the man sat down beside me, and the two of us were too exhausted to speak, and we shared a water bottle. And then there was a sudden sense of the other's nearness, and a parakeet high up in the canopy of trees squawked and I saw a flash of its scarlet wing, and the air was buzzing with heat and the endless chatter of cicadas, and the man turned his head and looked at me with longing. He looked at my lips, wet with the water . . .

Cambodia, it was. He was an archaeologist, working across the plain at Angkor Wat. Marcel something.

Bertie and I leaned against each other, gathering our strength to start off for home. Drops fell from the ivy on both sides of the archway, as heavily as if it had started to rain again. We were sealed in.

Nothing. I am almost fifty years old.

Would you like a mint? Bertie said, and he managed to get a roll of Polos out of his wet jacket, and we slouched there and sucked away.

Ella was peeling a huge pile of prawns when we got back.

They specified fresh prawns, she said. Never again. The hands are falling off me.

Let the girls above finish them! Bertie said. There's girls up there with nothing to do.

Ella, I said mournfully, there's no house there!

Sure what has you interested in that old place, anyway? Ella said. Have a cup of tea. Did I tell you the Coby bride is bringing her own wild flowers over from England? To strew in her hair, like.

Isn't that a laugh! I said. They come back to the ancestral spot in dear old Ireland because it's so picturesque, and then they have to bring their own bit of picturesque with them from Sloane Square.

She's going to wear flowing cream silk velvet, Ella said. Her secretary faxed the whole particulars to Dooney's that's doing the video. She's going to be barefoot –

Jesus! I said. How many barefoot Irish peasants starved –

Listen to you, Kathleen! Bertie said. Money's no object with this London crowd let me tell you. Thank God. The Ballygall people have no style – they'd rather go out to the Hawaii Beach at Tullabeg where they can have a disco after the meal and eat rubber chicken. Which way would you do a wedding reception yourself, miss, if you're so smart?

We're not a marrying family, the de Burcas, I said. Two out of the three of us aren't married. That's the majority.

Why did you never get married, Kath? Ella said.

I was saying to your father, I said, that I was always on the move. And, I suppose I just never met the right person –

But how do you know if it's the right person? Ella cut across me. I don't know, I said.

93

How do people know? Ella said again.

I sat at the table and took the pages of the *Judgment* out of my pouch, and turned them with the hand I had warmed on my mug of tea.

I don't know how other people know, I said. But this is how the lovers of Mount Talbot knew. This is what one of the nurses who guarded Marianne when she was locked up in Dublin told the court:

> *Mrs Talbot told me how it commenced and the way it commenced was this.*
>
> *She went into his room, and a part of his body came in contact with hers, which caused a thrill to run through her whole frame, and that was the commencement of her fall.*
>
> *Did she say that? – Yes.*
>
> *Did she say, 'commencement of my fall'? – Yes.*
>
> *Did she say what the room was she went into?*
>
> *I am not certain, but it must have been the tack room,' because she told me he was putting up articles in their proper place . . .*

What part of his body? Ella said.

Neither Bertie nor I answered.

It wasn't just physical! I said. It went on for three years! If he'd been nothing but a toyboy it couldn't have lasted that long.

How in God's name did they get away with it for three years? Bertie said. He had his glasses back on and he was leaning over the trays of profiteroles, inspecting them. That's news to me, that is. Everyone of my generation in Ballygall heard about the Talbot scandal. But I never knew the pair of them were at it that long. What was the husband doing, I'd like to know!

Give us a minute, I said. I turned the pages, looking for the passage I remembered.

As far as I can see, I said, Richard Talbot never suspected a thing, all the time, and the servants kept their mouths shut. But then two real desperadoes turned up and got jobs at Mount Talbot. They'd been fired from so many jobs in gentry houses that you'd nearly have to call them travelling servants. Halloran and Finnerty were their names. Did you ever see a cowboy movie where someone rides up to some isolated ranch house looking for work? They must have been like that.

Hud! Ella said. Wasn't *Hud* like that?

Anyway, I said, Halloran was taken on by Richard as a butler, and Finnerty as some kind of steward. And they went after Marianne.

Halloran and Finnerty had been watching the conduct of Mrs Talbot and they had traced her into Mullan's room, and then went and informed Mr Talbot; Halloran and Mr Talbot went to the room. They found the door locked; they called out, 'William, are you there?' There was no answer, and they broke the door open; and there they saw, according to that evidence, Mrs Talbot behind the curtain with her child, and this man, Mullan, standing by the fireplace . . .

A violent outbreak, the Lord Chancellor says, took place, and Mr Talbot separated himself from Mrs Talbot and took away his child. The husband rushed towards the wife, and took the innocent child from the hand he deemed no longer worthy to hold even her own child —

There's Finnertys out at the crossroads, Bertie said. Would they be the same Finnertys?

What could they have been doing in the room that was that bad, Ella said, if the child was with her?

Well, I don't know what they were doing that particular time, I began.

Joe had come into the room and was up on the chair again beside his mother, trying to eat the shell of a prawn.

Never mind what they were doing, Bertie said.

They paid for it, anyway, I said, dreadfully. She did, anyway.

On the 19ᵗʰ day of May, 1852, Mr Talbot discovered, or considered he had discovered, that his wife had been false to her marriage vows . . . A great excitement is described by witnesses as having occurred in the yard outside the house when Mr Talbot snatched the child, then about seven years old, from Mrs Talbot and quitted the place, and left her with the servants.

Mrs Talbot was in a state of very great excitement, and the following day the clergyman of the place, the Rev. McClelland, took her away to the railway station in the neighbourhood, and the mail train that night took her up to Dublin. He then took her to a hotel called Coffey's Hotel in Dominick Street.

In the course of two or three days Mrs Talbot was removed to a lodging in the Rathgar road, which is a suburb of Dublin. After having been about three weeks at this lodging the gentleman who had attended her, the Rev. McClelland, removed her across the Channel to this country and she was brought to a house in the neighbourhood of Windsor. In that house she was placed, under the suggestion, real or imaginary, that she was of unsound mind. The place where she was kept was or is alleged to have been, unknown. There she remained under the custody of a woman till about the month of December following, when her place of abode was discovered by connexions of Mrs Talbot, namely, by a Mr and Mrs Paget, Mr Paget being a gentleman at the Bar . . .

They took her child! Ella said, appalled.

He dumped her in a lunatic asylum, Richard did, I said. The bastard! He said she was mad, and he hid her away, and she could have been hidden away for her whole life if this Paget whoever he was hadn't found her.

That's our house! Bertie said. This house! He looked half shocked and half delighted. Where we are! he said. Mr McClelland's! This was the vicarage in those days and that man, Mr McClelland, was the vicar. I often heard that. This house where we're sitting now!

Richard just took off and left the child with the servants! Ella said. Which servants, I wonder? Where was the fella Mrs Talbot had been going with?

Joe didn't like the sudden excitement of the adults in the room. He slipped down off the chair and buried his face in his mother's side, like a much younger child.

It's okay, Joe, I said. It's only a story. Like your mammy tells you when you're in bed and you're nearly going asleep.

Ella sat down and hoisted him onto her lap.

Is there any more? she said to me. It's as good as the television.

That's enough, now! Bertie said. I can hear Ollie calling you, daughter. And you, Kathleen – I'm afraid I need you to pack up so we can do your room. I'm just going to put together a box of food for you, for Mellary, so you don't have to worry about shopping. Ella, I want you to do the hall and the stairs as soon as you've fed Ollie. Joe, go and get colouring books for yourself and your brother. Kathleen, I rang the Spar shop in Mellary for PJ to go down to the cottage and turn the heating on, and you've only to call there for anything you need and you can't miss it because it's the only shop in the place.

I ran up to the den, to phone Miss Leech.

I have to leave for Mellary this afternoon, I said. The Coby wedding party is coming in tonight. Is there any chance you could see me before I go?

I will see you, Miss de Burca, she said. But I am too tired to discuss the Talbot matter today. I do not share your apparently inexhaustible interest in adultery.

It wasn't just adultery! I protested. She got his shirts washed specially, and she gave him food and wine and she used to send for him to give him instructions about the carriage when she could easily have told one of the servants to tell him – that's all there in the evidence.

I wonder whether you have spent too long in England, Kathleen, she began. Because –

I braced myself when she used my first name.

– the Talbot story is just the kind of thing an English audience would be interested in. History without the economics, history without the politics, history without the mess. And the attraction of the Mount Talbot people to the ignorant English is that they think the people concerned were semi-aristocratic. Planter scum, most of them! And their values were rotten! This one sleeping with that one: that one sleeping with this one. While decent people starved –

Miss Leech, I interrupted. Miss Leech, those were people, too, you know, the people in the Talbot story. They had souls, too. Their lives mattered to them, too. And what if they loved each other –

Love! Miss Leech cried. I knew you'd bring love into it!

Well, I'm interested in love! I yelled down the phone. *People* are interested in love! Love is the best thing that ever happens to most people in their lives, rich or poor.

You are incorrigible, Miss de Burca, she said. But I shall put the kettle on as I always do, at half past three, and hope that you will join me in a cup of Earl Grey.

That's an English blend of tea, I said.

I have nothing against the English, she said, except (a) the Reformation and (b) their occupation of Ireland.

Bertie barely had time to say goodbye to me. The kitchen seemed to be swarming with girls who had come in to help. Spot's little black-and-white face was sticking out from under the table, quivering with excitement. The old dog, as usual, was asleep on his rug beside the Aga.

You'll be back to us in no time, he said. I've teachers booked in after the wedding but I can double them up. And if you want anything, just ring. I told PJ in Mellary to get the phone connected for you straight away because you're on your own.

Slán, a Sheosaimh, I said to Joe.

We haven't done that yet, Joe said.

Mind yourself now! Bertie said. He hugged me against his tweed front. Don't get into trouble, now!

He meant it as a little joke. I turned away before he could see my face, because it crumpled at hearing those innocuous words – the very words my mother said the last time she ever said anything to me, the day Sean was banging his high chair with a spoon. The day I left home to go to college. Don't get into trouble whatever you do! she said to me. But she said it leaning towards me from the corner of the room, not touching me. I need hardly say that my mother did not know how to hug.

Neither do I, I thought.

6

A sombre sky hung low over the bright shops on the square. I could easily imagine this hill before ever there was a town here, when wolves howled in oak thickets through the long winters. I drove past a stack of silvery buckets on a pavement. A video shop with a life-size cardboard Sharon Stone. Packets of marrowfat peas stacked in the window of an old-fashioned dairy. A big drapery store with chipped mannequins from the fifties and blankets hung around the deep doorway. The library, with its lovely flight of steps and tall Georgian windows, directly opposite the gates of Mount Talbot and made of the same whitish-grey stone. Next to the library the supermarket windows were covered with brilliant yellow posters advertising *This Weeks Bargain's*. One wall of its car park, behind, was a wall of the original workhouse, Miss Leech had told me. The supermarket owner wouldn't let the Famine Commemoration committee put up a plaque there. All that kind of stuff was best forgotten, he'd said to Miss Leech. I have to pay the schoolkids a man's wage now to do a bit of work around the place, Ireland's doing so well.

I drove down to a garage and filled up with petrol. I was getting ready to drive back up to the library, standing beside the car, taking the wrapper off a bar of chocolate, when I thought, This is ridiculous! and looked through my pockets for fifty-pence pieces. Then I waited behind two giggly little girls for the phone. When the coins dropped right through at first I thought, never mind, I'll leave it, there's no rush. Then I tried once more, and this time the coins registered and I tapped the numbers in.

Annie? Annie? Dan? But it was their answering machine.

Hello, darlings, I said, this is Kathleen. Wait'll I tell you – you'll never guess – I'm in Ireland! Just got here! I'm working, but I might have time at the end to nip over and see you all – see little Lilian especially. I'm on my way to Mellary now, to a cottage for a week or so – more work – and I don't have my mobile with me in Ireland but they're getting the phone connected there so I'll ring you when they do.

Then I said, I have to tell you something. Jimmy passed away. Heart. Two months and two weeks ago –

The beeps started.

I'm fine! I'll call again! I cried. I'll call again!

I walked back to the car with such a spring in my step that I laughed at myself. Why the hell hadn't I done that earlier? I was a woman who'd been caught in not one but two coups in her day, and the Fiji one wasn't a bit funny. And here I was working up my courage to ring one housewife and one small farmer, both of whom I'd known more or less all my life and neither of whom had ever said as much as one cross word to me! The vague difficulties between them and me were all in my head. And it couldn't have been telling them about Jimmy that had held me back. They only knew him slightly. The four of us went to an Ireland–England football match in Wembley once and we sang, 'There's only one Jackie Charlton' to the tune of 'Juantanamera' and afterwards we went for a Thai meal. The waiters did a folk dance around us, between each course, with silver bells on their fingers and Dan asked them did they have anything in the way of potatoes by any chance? Mind you, it was ideal that for the first phone call in quite a while they hadn't been at home . . .

I'd kept the message nice and simple. You can hardly say, after all, to a brother you hardly know – I loved Jimmy. I miss him dreadfully. He was like a brother to me.

I was light-stepped, still, going up the back stairs of the library. Miss Leech was wearing a little velvet beret, at a cocky angle, presumably to distract attention from her tired face.

Now! She glared at me, and began without a greeting, As to the 'Notes' you faxed me – the précis of Marianne Talbot's seven rendezvous with the young Mullan man –

Oh, never mind! I said. Forget the notes –

I am a professional librarian, she said. Just as you are a professional writer. My comments on your comments are as follows: yes, all the area outside the town was Irish-speaking until the 1870s, and William Mullan's first language would have been Irish. Second – the Catholic merchants of Ballygall had elaborate furniture, the same as the gentry had, and presumably the people of no property wondered at it, as they do the world over and have always done. Finally, I have no idea why Mrs Talbot wanted a drink of milk.

I could feel myself go red at how foolish she made my questions sound. She was sorry immediately.

I do think, however, she hurried to say, that the young pair are more worthy than a mere list of the meetings of theirs which were witnessed by servants would suggest. I must confess, as a matter of fact, that they are more worthy than I had always assumed. It may be that I never read quite to the end of the *Judgment* before – I was rather intolerant when I was younger – and I had not attended to the evidence that William Mullan may have cared deeply for Mrs Talbot, and she for him. Which is what I now conclude from the following.

She picked up the *Judgment*, and read out in her high, precise voice:

It appears that this man, Mullan, followed Mrs Talbot; he arrived in Dublin a day or two after Mrs Talbot arrived. She arrived and a day or two afterwards Mullan came and he wrote a note to Mrs Talbot when she was at Coffey's Hotel, and appears himself to have come to the hotel with that note. The note was put into the hand of Mr McClelland who was there as her protector, and he having read it destroyed the note, not allowing her to see it. It turns out that when Mrs Talbot desired to know what this note was, he mentioned that Mullan had called and wanted to see her. She was then extremely anxious to see Mullan. She expressed a great desire to see him, and said, 'Do let me see him; and not only let me see him, but I wish to go off with him to America,' or some expression of that sort. That took place at Coffey's Hotel.

I always thought that was the most important thing in the whole story, I said. I'd give anything to know what he said in the note.

It is altogether unlikely that we will ever know that, she said.

If I could find a record of the evidence as it was first given in full,

I began. Richard took a separation case in the Ecclesiastical Court here before he went to England to the Lords –

I thought of that, she said. But the records of the Ecclesiastical Court were kept in the Four Courts in Dublin and it was destroyed by fire in 1922, in the first act of the repression directed at true, Republican Irishmen –

There must be something somewhere I said. I came here with the *Judgment* and so far I haven't found one extra thing to put towards a book! Even the ruin of the house isn't there.

We were both silent.

I'd thought there would be other documents, I said, that I could start making a mosaic with. The daybooks of the Mount Talbot estate, perhaps, so that I could say, for instance, that on such-and-such a date – the day the lovers were seen going into the orchard, to take an example – a hundredweight of turnips was taken from the Long Field, or Richard Talbot ordered a new shotgun from Purdey's, or William Mullan was among the servants who stood in line at the office in the yard to be paid their wages. I'd thought there might be a Ballygall newspaper – maybe a monthly, or quarterly – so that I could interweave the private story with the public story . . .

We had a library here, Miss Leech said, from the 1890s. But the librarians didn't put much value on the relics of the landlord system, no more than anyone else did. My Local Studies collection is the first there's ever been – it took that long to accept our own past. But don't give up yet, Kathleen. There is one piece of help I could offer you. There's a very nice boy from the town who's studying librarianship in Dublin, but he's home at the moment. Declan is his name. His mother had hoped he might go for the priesthood but apparently, that is not to be, and she considers a librarian to be the next best thing to a priest. I shall ask him to search the national newspapers of the time for you. It will be good for him. Yours is typical of the kind of query he's going to have to cope with all his life.

You're very kind, I said. I don't know what I'd do without you.

You may have to find out, she said crisply.

I didn't dare ask her what she meant.

She came around the desk, all five foot of her. She'd pinned a vaguely Celtic brooch to the side of the beret. She was not moving with her usual briskness.

If you ring towards the end of next week, my young friend might have something to report. You'll be back in Bertie's then?

Thank you, Miss Leech, I said. Thank you for all your help. I am really very sorry –

I looked down at her wrinkled old face. A half-moon of skin under each eye was dark brown. My hand involuntarily moved towards her. She saw the movement and turned away.

I look back on my life – she said, and she was gazing out over the roofs of Ballygall – and I wonder whether something interesting would have happened to me if I had been born in America or Italy, or even China or Africa? Women of my time in Ireland, if they wanted to work in the public service – and I did want to be either a librarian or a teacher – had to resign if they got married. Maybe I should have attempted to be a wife, all the same? I wouldn't be playing bridge with ignoramuses now to pass the time.

I could not see her face.

Imagine that! she said, forlornly. Playing cards, to pass the time, when people of my age have so little time left!

Actually, she said, reviving and turning around to me, people of *any* age have very little time left, but they are too foolish to see that.

And whether she knew it or not, she smiled brilliantly at me.

It stayed with me as I began the drive to Mellary. Not the meaning of Mullan following Marianne. But the image of it – the powerful image of the man standing, waiting, in the Dublin street. There would have been flares in holders flanking the door of the hotel, and as he stood there, he must have been half visible out at the edge of their flickering illumination. In Oxford there's a brass cross in the asphalt in the middle of a street to mark the spot where early Protestant martyrs were burned to death. There should be a cross in Dominick Street, Dublin. Here Stood William Mullan, Faithful Lover.

As I drove along, that image began to merge with another that I had carried in my memory for many years, and that I retrieved now, perfectly intact. It was of an African pedlar I saw once, standing in a village square on a wintry night in Sicily – standing in the gathering night, snow beginning to dust his ragged woollen cap, his impassive face fitfully illuminated by the light thrown into the night sky when Mount Etna belched.

I made my choice to think about Sicily. Sicily was my own memory, from my own life. I wanted to retreat into myself. I was tired of all the effort I had to make in Ireland. I was exhausted by all the people, living and dead, I was coming to know. Too much feeling was being asked of me, when paying attention to even one person had been more than I wanted to do most of my life. It's not fair! I said to myself; I'm having to worry about people and there's nobody worrying about me! Alex not there when I rang! Imagine! It doesn't matter of course, I don't need him for anything in particular. But still.

It was the last day of a travel publishers' conference, when I saw the pedlar. I might easily never have seen him. We'd been in Sicily five days already, the three of us from *TravelWrite*, at the Grand Hotel et des Palmes in Taormina, in January, when there were still lemons on the leafless trees, and the sun was warm enough through the French windows in the morning for me to drink my coffee lolling on the sofa. I was very content. I'd made a home out of my luxurious room – supermarket wine cooling in the minibar, my corkscrew, my radio and my trashy novel neatly laid out, my make-up arranged in the marble bathroom under a spotlit tilted mirror. Alex was pleased with me because I'd chaired a workshop and given a highly praised report from it. He told Jimmy his only criticism was that I'd worn a thing like an old nightie when I was giving my report. When Jimmy told him my asymmetrical Yamamoto was the most distinguished piece of clothing in the town, Jimmy said he looked politely disbelieving. Jimmy himself was cross with me, because except when I was actually working, I was shy. I stood against the wall, at breaks, with a mineral water.

You frighten people, Jimmy said. You look as if you're saying, Let them come to me because I'm damned if I'm going to them.

It's not that, I said. It's half that I don't know how to chat and half that I don't feel confident anyone wants me to.

I'm going to tell Nora about you, Jimmy said. You need a therapist. Everyone here knows you're terrific except you. Anyone would be glad to talk to you.

The last afternoon we went up into the hills on a coach tour. I pressed my face past its own wan reflection and peered through the window. Broken walls, rough grass, an old man in a baseball cap keeping a herd of sheep back with a stick and a prancing dog. Just like every place on the planet where there are sheep. Yet that shepherd will speak a dialect different from the Sicilian spoken down below in the valley, never mind different from the language of other shepherds. As if there were some way in which place itself insisted on being creative . . .

The coach pulled over to the edge of the road. The driver switched off the engine.

Oh, wow! someone said, and then the aisle was full of video cameras being taken down and coats being put on for a dash out into the icy afternoon air. Across the valley, high above the horizon, a snowy peak had appeared, huge and remote, in a rift in the clouds. Etna! The sky around it was a deepening navy blue. Into the navy blue came – whoosh! – a great flash of light, and then smoke billowed and eddied away, and a red gash had been cut in the snow. Etna was erupting. The event was so simple and so big that it made children of the travel writers. When the cold drove us back into the coach, restraint had disappeared. Everyone piled into the front rows. The bus ground on up the mountain, night creeping into the great black amphitheatre of hills behind, where the primeval crimson light came and went.

It was almost too late to go on to the café the tour organizer had promised. But the coach drove up to a grey village in the hills, a place of blank, thick walls turned in on themselves. A few first flakes of snow fell as we hurried across a square to a dim bar, shouting for espressos and brandies. I turned at the door, to look back at Etna.

I saw an old man on the stone pavement outside the bar, with his back to it. He was an African – very tall and thin, standing behind a tray of what looked like small toys and packets of batteries and plastic tools. He stood there in an old greatcoat, a ragged woolly hat pulled down on his head. He was absolutely immobile, as if the cold and the dark had drained him of life. I saw that his eyes were staring into the dark.

This bar will close after we leave, I thought. The owner will turn the key and go home, and there'll be no more movement in this village on a cold night like this. There won't be any sound except the tinny laughter from television sets behind the walls. The snow will just come down on the dark alleyways.

Oh – where will he go?

Back in the hotel that night, I was haunted by the pedlar. I thought of the snowflakes on the shoulders of his thin coat. I sat at dinner with the Canadian delegation and I tried to be generous for once – to listen well and not to talk too much or too little. I had so much to be grateful for.

Let the others go to bed, one of the men said to me at midnight. You and I will drink and get to know each other.

And he flourished a new bottle of wine.

But I went into the Ladies Room and thought about it, and decided not to do it. I went straight across the foyer to the stairs to go up to my room.

Alex was walking slowly up the stairs.

Hello, he said. He stood and waited for me. He didn't know how unconsciously graceful he was, bent towards me, above me on the stairs.

Did you have a good night? he said.

We had come to a wide plate-glass window on the first floor. Grey flakes of snow eddied in slowly from the black night, and brushed the glass.

I did, I said. Better than if I was out there. I put my hand against the glass and shuddered at its coldness.

I saw you looking at the African chap, he said.

I stared at him, amazed. Imagine Alex looking at me and me not knowing! What had I looked like? If I was in profile did the bit of double chin show?

I could see you were worried. I was worried about him myself, Alex continued. I know some people in Palermo who I thought might be useful and I gave them a call.

You did? I was dumbfounded. You know people in Palermo?

They said they know the fellow, Alex said. He has family in Catania. They were going to arrange to get him back there tonight. And you, my dear, he said, smiling into my face. Are you all right?

We walked down the corridor together and he had his arm very lightly around my shoulder. You didn't catch a cold, did you, Kathleen? You're very quiet.

No. I'm fine, I said.

This is me, he said, and started putting his key into a door. He patted my head with one of the lovely hands I always watched at meetings in the office. Mad hair you have. He smiled at me. Nice.

The next morning, when we were all standing around outside the hotel waiting for the coaches to the airport, I said to Jimmy, I *really* like Alex. He has hidden depths, so he has. No, Jimmy – I *seriously* like him.

Jimmy took it in with one look.

Did fairy Puck by any chance sprinkle some potion into your ear during the night? he said, coldly. Alex is exactly the same extremely limited person today as he was yesterday.

I don't care, I said. I like him *very much*.

Bertie was right about the cottage in Mellary. I would be happy there. I went in through the porch and stood in the room. It was warm, and full of a powdery, golden, evening light, and I knew from my childhood that the distant slow sob – a disturbance of the air, more than a noise – was the sea on a stony shore. This was a white room with two small windows, a pot of pink geraniums in flower on one deep sill. A cooker and sink in one corner. A small fireplace. An armchair. Sisal matting and an old rug over it in front of the fire. A table and two chairs. A picture of the Sacred Heart and a little red lamp on the wall. A bathroom down a step broken through the thick rear wall, and electric space heaters, were signs of the modern world; otherwise, this was a house outside time.

I looked down at my feet on the matting. I could hardly believe that they had brought me to here.

This is the first Irish house I have been in since I was twenty years old, I thought. The last one I was ever in was the one I grew up in! I never realized that before . . . And I have hardly ever begun a stay alone in a house since then. I moved around between student shares when I was at college in Dublin, and when I was at the poly in London. Then there was the attic among the chestnut trees with Hugo, and then Caro and I lived in the mews her father gave her, and then I moved into the basement on my own. I walked across to the sink to fill a kettle for tea. I thought, I've hardly ever looked after myself, either. I hardly ever cooked. I kept wine in the fridge and long-life milk. I had tins of tuna for next door's cat, and sometimes a burger for it. But I never had a big bag of food, like the one I'd brought from Bertie's. I looked around. I'd never had a wooden draining board or a broom or a fireplace with a poker and tongs propped up beside it. Making tea was like repeating a ritual from childhood. Letting the tap run till the water was clear and cold. The little sigh of the flame of the butane gas under the kettle before it caught light from my match. Pulling open the milk, and finding a mug. And turning, to look again at the room. So thick-walled and crouched and low. Such a harbour of peace.

Exactly like Uncle Ned's place was, the only week of my life I was ever a housewife. With a man to approve of me, now that I came to think of it, in the unlikely form of my father . . .

While the kettle boiled I brought in the rest of my stuff and I went through into the little bedroom and made up the wide brass bed. It was so low and springy that I rolled on it for a minute, like a child, when I'd finished.

God! I'd love it if I had next door's cat with me here!

Then I pulled a sweater on and ran out in the early dusk to the stack of turf at the gable end of the house. I bundled the sods onto my arms. Rock-hard fragments of the bog. I hardly knew the feel of turf, because the coalman on his horse-drawn dray came out from Kilcrennan to where Shore Road straggled to an end and, when

Mammy had the money, left us a bag of gritty Polish coal. Near the porch of the cottage I saw dried-out gorse bushes on a rocky outcrop. I went back in and got the bread knife and cut a few knotted branches, and balancing small, broken bits of turf on them, I got the fire lit. I knelt on the rug and watched the flames and smelled the burning gorse. I could not remember how long it had been since I had lit a fire – a real fire, like this, not some ski-lodge log thing.

I sat back in the armchair with my tea and a plate of bread and butter and wedding poached salmon, and watched my blaze. I used to watch the little barred rectangle of the stove in Ned's with the same contentment.

Cait! *Cait!* Get into the car –

Oh, *no*! I had been lying on my bed reading *A Farewell to Arms* and praying to be left alone by all of them but particularly by him. He was home on his holidays and there was no peace.

Nora said at the dinner the day before that she'd love a miniskirt and Daddy started on a monologue about the native culture that was lost with the defeat of the Gaelic chieftains at Kinsale and how new forces were massing against Ireland to destroy it. He said it was a mystery to him why Nora wanted to look like a slut. Then when she recovered, she somehow mentioned she was good at maths and that she'd love to study accountancy. When they came up from the pub, Mammy went straight into the bedroom, but he got Nora out of bed and mocked her – making her take the coins out of the pocket of his overcoat and count them in front of him.

What's wrong with him? I whispered to her when she came back to bed. What's biting him?

Tell him nothing! she said. She was nearly crying at the humiliation. He hates us! What did we ever do to him? I have a miniskirt, anyway! Mrs Bates made it for me. White. I put it on under my uniform in the mornings and when I'm wearing it sometimes I pick flowers through the railings and I put them in my flip-flops . . .

Cait! *Go tapaidh!*

But Daddy –

Immediately!

I want you to come out to the old place, he said when we were out on the path. There are matters that need my attention.

That was the way he spoke.

As soon as we were on the road to Uncle Ned's he pulled in. He sat for a moment looking straight ahead as the car ticked in the silence.

Here, he said, and he took his black comb from an inside pocket of his jacket and passed it to me. Tidy yourself.

As you know, Caitlin, he began in his most fruity voice, as you know, I am a member of the civil service of the Republic of Ireland – a servant, you might say, enrolled in the defence of the state on the civil side, just as an army man is on the military side. I cannot be associated with anything that might bring my position into disrepute.

No, I said. Yes. That's right.

So I must ask you to refrain from discussing with others what I am about to reveal, he said. Even with your mother. Ned is in jail.

What? I shrieked, and I could hear the gratification in his voice when he said solemnly, Yes. Mountjoy Jail.

Ned is? *Uncle Ned?*

Yes, he said. The burden falls on me.

Then – with maximum emphasis on how much of a shock this had been to him, Daddy – he told me that Ned had gone up to Dublin the day before on a demonstration with the local Small Farmers Association about livestock prices. His crowd had joined in with a big crowd from around the country. Nobody realized it, but he'd brought a couple of hens in a suitcase that he'd made air holes in, and he deliberately opened the suitcase when the Minister came out on the steps of the Department of Agriculture and one hen flew up and roosted on the top of the microphone. That was a good laugh, for the farmers at least, but later that night things had got violent when the police rushed the building and the farmers occupying it wouldn't leave. Ned couldn't leave because he was trying to find his fowl.

A garda said Ned punched him –

Ned?

The officer may have been mistaken, I grant you that. But in any case, Ned got seven days. I want you to look after the place, Caitlin. Go out there every day, feed the beasts, leave a light on at night and lock up well and see that everything's all right.

But, Dad, I was going to say, why don't you ask Danny? Danny's always going out to Ned's place – but any mention of Danny was a red rag to a bull. So I said, But, Dad, what's secret about it? Sure, Ned'll be a hero.

I just want it kept quiet, my father said. In my position. And your mother isn't well . . .

How will I get in and out?

There's Ned's bike, isn't there?

But Daddy, Saturday –

What about Saturday? He whipped his head around to glower at me. You don't mean that you'd put a person of the type of Sharon Malone ahead of your only uncle, do you? Sure all you do is hang around the streets anyway. I have my sources in town, you know.

And he started the car.

We got out at the old place and walked up the lane and in through the high hedge together, and we got the key from where it was always hidden, under a jumble of old bridles, on the wall at the gable end of the shed. We pushed open the front door onto the tidy room. The tea towel was white and square on its rail. All the dishes were put away and Ned's two houseplants sat on the draining board in saucers with water in them. The clock tick-tocked busily. The iron door of the stove was open, and a twist of newspaper under twigs and sticks stuck out, ready for a match to be put to it. The most peaceful room in the most safe house in the world.

There was a tremendous commotion at the door. Ned's dog Elvis was prancing on the threshold, whimpering and pawing the ground with hunger and excitement.

I know how to do it, Dad!

Out in the scullery I got the sack of dried dog food and the scoop, and then I took a can of buttermilk down from a shelf and doused the stuff with it. I took the bowl to Elvis. The dog hoovered the food up, and then slurped up all the water I poured into his water bowl, and then he collapsed himself across the threshold with his head on his paws, looking up at us alertly.

Do you know how to do the cattle? my father said.

I do, I said. I often helped Uncle Ned with them.

Do you know how to mend a puncture if the bike gets one?

I do. He has a tin box, and you get a basin –

You're a great girl, he said. You're better than a boy. It'll be a lucky man that gets you . . .

That week I repainted the white stones along the edge of Ned's flower beds with paint I found in the shed. I weeded all around his canna lilies. On the Saturday I didn't even go into town. I was busy out in the house, putting flowers in a jug on the oilcloth table for Ned to come back to, and laying out the good delph for his tea under a clean cloth. I lavished feed on the cattle, and I left crusts I'd brought from home for the wild cats that lived in the shed, and I spent an hour outside the front door, trying to get Elvis to stand still while I washed him from a basin. Often, afterwards, I thought that that's what being in a happy partnership must be like. You love working, and you have endless energy for it, because you know you will be praised.

My father banged on the bedroom door for me, early on the Sunday morning of Ned's return. I climbed over Nora and was dressed in a minute.

Look at the sea! I said, when we went out to get into the car.

It was something that only happened a few times a year, on windless mornings like this. The water reflected the perfect sky like a mirror. Down at the end of the beach, where the land rose up before the bay with the German holiday camp, the low cliffs were reflected exactly in the shining water. Their every detail was duplicated as if, during the night, a magic trick had been prepared. Everything – the wide blue expanse of the water, the white road, the grass verge, the line of cottages, our faces and backs – was bathed in new, fresh sun. There was not a single sound except the distant, repetitive sigh that was the dry sand succumbing to the silent incoming tide.

There's a morning! Daddy said. A pet day! By God – this'd be a great morning for mushrooms!

We were up on the hill behind Uncle Ned's place for maybe an hour. The grass was short, up there, and like a living thing to walk on, so vigorous and green, so dense with rich dew. We moved slowly up the flank of the hill, above the beechwoods that followed the line of the road, up through Ned's little fields and then onto the turf above them. The air up there was new-made – playing around us, friendly, but with the chill of the dawn still in it. The larks clicked and whooped high above, and flocks of brown fieldfares wheeled just ahead of us as we moved along the brow of the hill, as if they were leading us through the glorious morning.

My father was singing. I could hear his rough voice, as he sang to himself. *Come, in the gondola, come. Komm in die Gondol* – and then something about Venice and gondolas and love and then a kind of call that must have been the gondolier's call or the lover's call in whatever operetta had come back to him. *Hi-ee!* I heard Daddy singing. *Hi-oh!*

And then he lumbered towards me across the grass.

Look! Look, Cait! His big palms cupped, full of small, white mushrooms with the most delicate, ecru undersides . . .

My Mellary fire was settling in on itself and beginning to glow – letting out the energy impacted in the turf just as memories release their power. Not one of the details of that morning with my father had ever faded. When I'd be somewhere beautiful in an English way in England – like the gallery at Petworth, with the great Turners on the walls and mist in the park outside, or in one of the creamy Georgian towns in Yorkshire, or looking across the curve of the Downs to the icing-sugar front at Brighton – I'd think, Ireland has nothing like this. But – the hill where we got the mushrooms! There was nowhere else I had ever been as crystal-clean and fresh.

Was there ever
A time of such quality, since or before . . .?

I went over to Bertie's bag of food. Yes, he'd put in wine, and he'd put in a corkscrew, too. What a nice man!

But for all the happy memories and the wine, I didn't sleep well that first night at Mellary. I had a bath, last thing, and the old bit of mirror on the wall beside the tub showed me, at some freak angle, when I stood up to get out, a grey hair in my pubic hair. Distress, like cramp, went through me. I had to sit down in the emptying water.

This will not get better, I said to myself. It will never not be grey from now on.

I woke to a car skidding to a halt at the bedroom window and a loud knock on the door.

One of our own, thank God, a man in brown overalls said, bobbing his head at me. It's usually oul Yanks and Germans that Bertie sends out to this place. I'm PJ from the shop, he said, scurrying past me with a toolbox. I'm going to get the phone going. And I read the meters, and I tidy graves, and my wife has the Spar shop above in the village so what I don't know, she knows. Bertie was saying you're a writer. Would you get much money, now, for writing articles?

It depends, I said. I'm not writing articles now. I'm doing some research about something that happened just after the Famine.

You don't look like someone that's writing about famine to me, PJ said.

What do I look like then?

More like a model, he said seriously. Or one of the girls on the television that reads the news. But – famine. The last time the Sudan was on the television I said to herself – that's the world for you now, the men out fighting and the women left trying to feed the children.

The potato famine I'm interested in, I said. Irishmen weren't fighting anybody at the time – the potatoes just failed.

Don't I know it? he said. How could I forget it, going around every day in the van? Look! he said, crouching to point along the window sill to the bit of field between the house and the gorse bushes.

And perhaps because the early light was picking out the texture of the land, I saw what he was pointing at. There were wide deep ridges, all across the field, under the topcoat of grass. Undulations.

Lazy beds, he said. For growing potatoes. Famine ridges is what they're called.

But there's far too many, I said, stupidly.

Sure there were hundreds living here, the postman said. Down this one lane. There were thousands in these parts one time. And that's what they all lived on. They all went to America, the ones that didn't die. And if I was a younger man I'd be off to America myself! Reading *Playboy* every day I'd be, and the hell with this dreary oul perch!

He started jiggling the phone.

Hello, *compadre*! he roared into it. Ring me back!

The phone rang.

No. No, I can't. Well, fix it when the van is back . . . They made a balls of it the last time, too. Sorry, missus – no phone till tomorrow.

And in an instant, he was gone.

I didn't care, except that I preferred to be in touch with Alex. I went out with my coat over my nightdress and followed the restlessness in the air to the sea, where it came in across a rocky shore to gnaw at the eroded edge of the field, not a hundred yards from the cottage. To be on grass beside the sea, again! But the sea at Shore Road was very quiet. A sheen on the horizon, for most of the day. Here, there was constant vitality. There was a shower so ethereal that I only realized it was passing from seeing the pockmarks of the raindrops on the silky surface of the water, swelling strong and calm, the raindrop marks forming and re-forming. Then a wind full of sun followed the shower. I saw the swell begin to break into waves. The wind blew stronger, and the waves began to lift and curl. My hair blew into my face, and I turned, and a gust blew me, laughing with joy, back to the house.

I jumped into the car as soon as I could, to explore. Up at the main road, I turned left for the road to Mellary village and the ferry to Mellary Harbour. And as I did, I saw for the first time a vista of the whole bay, and I pulled onto the grass, astonished.

I knew this Atlantic where it broke on western coasts, all the way down the curve of the earth. I could picture ten or twelve places I'd been where this same ocean met land, from a sturdy village among artichoke fields in Brittany, to the baking sand dunes of Namibia. I'd watched the fog roll in from it every day when I was writing a piece about golf courses in Portugal. I'd lived a few feet from it in a run-down tourist camp on a beach in Senegal, where the crabs clacked around the legs of my bed all night. But I had never before been on the west coast of an Atlantic island, at the turn of spring into earliest summer – never before seen such a wide slope of small fields, their grass patched with the brown of weeds and rushes, fields of a muted and glowing green that lulled the eye, that then was shocked by the huge vista of the turbulent, turquoise sea beyond. There was hardly a sign of life, except for the spire of a church in a village, over on the bay to which the green waves were racing. The land was as if abandoned. There were no barns. There were two or three small white farmhouses perched beside each other on a ridge, and a big strand far below and an open, empty swathe of emerald sheep pasture beyond. There was my cottage, out on its headland. But no boats, no harbours, no crops. There was just emptiness in the foreground, and behind, the fabulous sea, boiling with energy.

And weather danced across the wide vista like another dimension of place. In the short time I watched, a sharp squall of rain came racing in from the sea. The sky turned dark. Within a quarter-minute, the swirl of rain had passed. The steaming road ahead was framed in the dazzling drops on the windscreen. Then the mild blue sky and clear sunlight were restored and I was able to wind down the window again, and in the sudden peace, a robin, on a mountain ash that had taken root in the ditch, called so vigorously that I could see his plump chest rise and fall.

Very wet, the west of Ireland, I've always heard, Alex had said, the last time I'd been in the office. I laughed at the memory. The sky was darkening again, to spin down another rain shower. Won't you be sure, Kath, to take an umbrella? he'd said.

Mrs PJ was beady and unpleasant.

You're very welcome! she said. A famous writer! Don't be putting us all in your book, now! Did PJ fix up the telephone for you? It must be terrible lonely down there in the cottage without a friend.

Unless you have a friend with you? I'd say you have. I said to PJ, a famous writer – I'm sure she's not going out to the oul cottage all on her own.

I'm not a famous writer, I said.

Sure what would have you in the cottage only writing?

I looked at her and said flatly, I've been sick.

The woman looked me – the picture of health, no doubt – up and down.

Have you no one to look after you if you're sick? she said. Your mammy or your daddy?

No, I said. To answer with just one word was as rude, I knew, as a person could get in this country.

Do you have any soda bread? I said.

We have wrapped bread, she said. If you want fancy bread you'll have to go across to Mellary Harbour. Or drive around – it's fifteen minutes on a ferry one way or an hour in a car the other. But sure what's wrong with the wrapped bread?

Since when is soda bread fancy? I said.

Easy seen you've been away, she said.

I stood irresolute outside the shop. Now the sun had settled and become quite hot, for God's sake. I could do with a few T-shirts. The memory of my father smiling at me as he came towards me across the grass with the mushrooms would not leave me. I started doing sums in my head. Alex was about fifty that night in the hotel corridor when my attitude to him shifted and deepened. And wasn't fifty in or around the age my father was, the morning we went mushrooming? Could he have been a man you could suddenly *see*, like I'd seen Alex?

I got back into the car to go over on the ferry to Mellary Harbour.

Funny thing – Jimmy never condemned my father, even after I'd given example after example of his unkindness.

We used to go to Jim's parents in Scottsbluff, Nebraska, for Christmas. The four of us used to sit on the sofa in slippers decorated with fluorescent Santas and watch hour after hour of television in a mild and cosy haze.

Singing in the Rain was on once.

That's who Jimmy's like! I said. Gene Kelly!

Yes, his father said solemnly, but Jimmy has brains as well.

If an IRA bombing or shooting turned up when we were watching television, Mr Beck would say, as predictably as a clock, I worked with a few Irish boys. They explained the whole thing to me. There's right and wrong on both sides.

Banal as it was, that attitude made me relax, after England. I could blow off steam with Mr Beck because he didn't judge me in advance. I remember, for instance, telling him that Irish set-dancing began when the native people – barefoot, murmuring to each other in their language that no landlord knew, furtive and angry – watched from behind doors and through windows the Anglo-Irish gentry dance, and then brought the memory of the polkas and mazurkas to their earth-floored cabins, and struck up the fiddle, and made the ballroom dances into their dances.

They stole them, I cried to Mr Beck, from the oppressor.

Forget the English, he said. The English are just an old-style people from Europe. The only English person they ever have on TV here is Princess Di.

I used to sleep like a happy baby under the pink blankets each night, while the house's heating battled the snow outside.

But every year there was a variant on the first year.

After only a few days Jimmy had what was obviously a ritual row with his father about who would drop the hire car back to the airport. Jimmy insisted he would do it. And when we got to the airport and parked, Jimmy hurried ahead of me into the building – leaving me to carry the suitcases – and when I finally caught up with him in the bar he had almost finished a martini.

For heaven's sake! I said. What's wrong with you?

Parents! He was shaking, I could see it. Not just his hands – his shoulders.

But Jimmy, I said helplessly. They're such lovely people.

I know, he snapped. He called to the barman, Sir!

He's your father, I began.

They're fathers second, Jimmy said. They're men first.

7

A few cars and a truck were waiting for the little ferry across the estuary north of Mellary. I should have offered Alex a Great Ferry Crossings of the World piece, I thought. In Seattle I crossed and recrossed the harbour, and the water shimmered like a parachute settling. The Meuse, in the water meadows near Dordrecht. I sat under a huge oak tree in the summer heat, waiting for the wooden pontoon to swing back across the emerald water. The Tisza, when I ran the little Lada off the ramp to the ferry, and the men were shouting in Hungarian as they tried to lift it, and an old man sitting on the bank looking at them fell back on the grass, helpless with laughter. The high white boat on the aquamarine sea that brought me to Paros, and Hugo.

This gentle Irish place.

'A white road winds down between tangled woods to the wide estuary, and the smallest car ferry in the world comes huffing towards me, low hills of the blue-green so typical of Ireland behind it —'

Stop that! I said to myself. At least I hadn't reached for my notebook. The old habit of drafting *TravelWrite* descriptions in my head was not so easy to outgrow though it seemed trivial, now, to describe a place as if what it was was what I could see of it.

The radios of the cars lined up along the road were all playing the same station. A yearning woman's voice dipped and rose as people got in and out of their cars to stroll across to the sea wall.

Some day my happy arms will hold you,
And some day, I'll know that moment divine —

I stretched luxuriously in the sun, beside the car. I felt my freedom and my health. Free as a bird, and the summer not too far away. I picked up a flat stone from the road and bent over the sea wall and skimmed it carefully along the sleek water that was silently invading the shining black mud. We practised skimming stones when we were growing up on Shore Road. It was one of my skills.

When all the things you are —

The line of cars for the ferry began to move. A car door slammed exactly on cue.

Are mine.

Slam.

I could feel the bounce of the waves under the ferry. In the breeze and the sun, the water was so full of light that I turned away from the rail. Then, Ladies and gentlemen! an excited voice came over the Tannoy. If you look towards the ocean, you can see bottle-nose dolphins —

I turned back, and there came the first glistening shape, plump and supple, twisting up out of the green and white confusion of the water, and as it leaped, being joined by another dolphin, and then another, and another.

They're so cute! An American woman with a video camera was leaning out over my head.

Her child had squeezed in front of me at the crowded rail.

Can you eat them, Mom? she said.

Can you eat them? the woman said to me.

I don't think so, I said. I never heard of people eating dolphins, even when they were starving.

I think they'd be very oily, the man jammed in on my other side said. I think it would be like eating a rubber tyre soaked in fish oil.

Yuck, the kid said, so disgustedly that the mother and myself and the man laughed. We'd have laughed at anything, it was so exhilarating to be squashed in there together on the rail, in the sun and wind and sparkling spray as the ferry chugged across the estuary.

Within five minutes it was coming in to shore. The engines stopped, and the boat glided the last few yards. In the silence, the air was decorated by the tiny, continuous gurgling and squeaking of the larks high over the fields around.

I stopped for a second, charmed by the sound.

The man stood back to let me down the iron stairs to the car deck.

You know – larks? I said. They own as far as their song reaches. It's a kind of cone shape, spreading out from where they are. Where you can hear them, that's their territory.

Are you a teacher? he said, as we squeezed our way through the cars in the hold.

Ah no, I said. God! Am I that preachy?

The ferry bumped onto the concrete ramp.

Will you wait for me? he called over the clank of chains and the grinding noise of the boat's engine reversing. Will you wait for me in the car park?

I glanced back at him, surprised. Yes – close-cropped grey hair, a lined face, a stocky body. Nondescript. He looked like all the middle-aged men you hardly notice – hanging around outside department stores, maybe, waiting for their wives.

Buy you a coffee? he said, in the ferry car park, speaking from his driver's window to me at mine. I'm having a look around out here on my way from Shannon to the Sligo area. It's miles out of my way, but I decided when I got off the plane this morning and saw the lovely day just to take my time and follow my nose. I know no more about where I am now than the man in the moon. So – if you had half an hour?

I would have said yes anyway, for a hundred reasons. That I was in a holiday cottage with no work to do, that everywhere was so beautiful, that I hadn't had a coffee for days. Anyway, I always said yes.

I'm not from here, I said. I went to England years ago. I'm only in Mellary by accident.

Oh, right, he said. Now that I notice – you're driving a hirecar, too. I'm in England since I was fifteen. I often go down the Irish Club for a pint, but all they talk about is sport . . .

I liked him. I didn't like his voice much – he had a weird hybrid accent – rural Irish, but with the occasional word pronounced the way the Beatles would pronounce it. Loovely, he said. But he had small eyes that still had a kick of blue, and the rough skin around them crinkled up like Paul Newman's when he smiled. The collar of his shirt under his windcheater was crumpled. The points stuck up. His neck came out of the old shirt short and thick. He must work out of doors because under the shaved grey hair, and on the back of his big hands, the skin was a brownish-red.

Where near Sligo are you heading for? I said.

Ballisodare. Do you know it? he asked eagerly.

I don't, I said. I'm from over near Dundalk and I've been away since I was twenty. But there was a nun in our school from Ballisodare – I remember, because she told us about Cuchulainn trying to keep the tide back in Ballisodare Bay – like, she went out on the floor and did all the gestures –

What was her name?

Sister Immaculate.

No – her real name.

Gleeson?

One of the Gleesons from the garage?

How would I know?

We were both laughing.

Do you think do they do cappuccino in Mellary Harbour? I said. And an egg sandwich?

Let's go! he said, and started his car. Then he leaned out to me again. What's your name?

Kathleen.

I could have guessed that, he said.

How?

You look like a Kathleen, he said. You have curly hair.

Do I look like a *hungry* Kathleen? I said.

Oh, all right! He smiled at me. I can take a hint! And he pulled out of the car park with a flourish.

I drove behind him down roads sunk between green banks, and

around a rocky bay, and down the wide main street of Mellary Harbour to a grass-grown, cobbled quay.

The one thing I know about this place, I said, as we walked away from the cars, is that a reporter from a London paper came here during the Famine. The town was packed with people who'd been thrown off the land, and they were hungry, and he couldn't get over the noise. He just couldn't get over it – a whole town full of people shrieking.

What did they shriek? What words?

Save us! was one thing. And – Do something for us! The reports were so heartbreaking that people in England started to collect money.

They're very decent people, the English, he said.

The ordinary English are. Not the ones on top.

That's right, he said.

The first pub we saw did coffee, and it still had some soup, though lunch was officially over and the last customers were leaving. We sat side by side on a padded bench, at the short end of a big old table, and ate soup and bread.

His name was Shay.

Well, Kathleen, he said, and I waited.

You're pretty good at hopping stones, he said. I saw you, there at the sea wall, when we were waiting for the boat.

What happened was, that the pub emptied out. There was a fire near us, so we went on sitting in our dim corner. Perhaps if one of us had pushed in and sat where there was room to stretch out, on the long side of the table . . . But neither of us moved. We just sat there, quietly, close beside each other, in the peace of the afternoon pub, and the glass jug of water on the table in front of us changed appearance with the changing light from the high window above us. We talked a little bit. Muzak in pubs, coal versus turf – nothing subjects. We had coffee and then, after a while, we had more. It began to be that when his side brushed against mine, fine heat ran along the surface of my nerves. When we had to move our arms to stretch our hands for cups and milk, it disturbed the glow that had grown between the side of his body and the side of mine. The sky filled with clouds above the half-curtain on the window. We decided to have sandwiches. The barman went down to some room at the back to make them. Now there was no one at all in the pub except us. And the occasional small noise from the heaped-up coal fire, and the heavy tock of an old pendulum clock somewhere.

The shelves of bottles and glasses and mirrors gleamed like treasure. We sat side by side and watched the barman. He had his back to us, his head tilted up at a small television on a top shelf. Snooker. The red glow from the fire beside us was reflected in the varnished wood of the bar counter. Shay's thigh lay alongside mine. Where they lightly touched, the thinnest of shudders began.

The barman came around the bar and stood looking peacefully down at the fire.

There's a nip in the air, all the same, he said.

We'll have a drink, maybe? Shay said.

The barman ambled back behind the counter.

What'll ye have? he said.

What'll you have, Kathleen? Shay said to me. Wine?

How do you know I drink wine?

You look as if you drink wine. Good wine.

There's no good wine here, the barman said. You're in Ireland now.

All the pubs around where I live in England, Shay said, they serve a lot of wine.

Yeah, the barman said. I serve wine meself, but it's rotgut, I believe. So the tourists tell me. He laughed heartily.

Do you want to go somewhere else? Shay said to me.

Oh, no, I said. I'm happy here.

We had hot whiskies, and when the barman put them down on the table, we reached for them at the same time, and our fingers touched. Mine are wide enough, but his were wider. His nails were deep and worn.

He saw me looking.

I come over from the place where I live, between Liverpool and Chester, every so often, for a week or so, he said, to give my father a hand. He has a bit of a fuel and oil business in Ballisodare. I do the heavy deliveries and that, because he's on his own. And he's a kind of unofficial selector to the county football team, so we go to a few matches. I'm not going for the full week this time because I have a big job of my own waiting for me at home. I have a landscaping business, and I'm after winning the tender for the upkeep of all the council grounds in my area.

Then after a pause he said, Well, it's just me, really, my landscaping business. I'm more or less a gardener. I suppose I am a gardener, really. Plain gardening.

The smile he gave me at this admission was as sweet as a baby's.

You could be a gardener just as well here as in England, I said. I'm staying in a cottage in Mellary, and the man who connected the phone told me there's no one left in the place that can fix things around a house or a garden, so he's run off his feet. You could make a fortune if you came back.

I married an English girl thirty years ago, he said. I never thought of coming back after that.

People began to come into the pub. We sat on. The light was going, now, above the half-curtain.

I'd better be pushing on, he said.

There was the smallest hint of a question in the way he said it.

I said, I came over here for soda bread. I'd better go out and find a bread shop before they close.

Will they be worried at your place about where you've got to? he said.

I didn't look at him, and my tone of voice was casual.

No, I said, I'm on my own. There's no one to worry.

I thought I could feel the air changing.

What has you in a place like this, on your own? he asked frankly.

I'm a writer, I said. Well, a journalist. I was going to write something about a thing that happened long ago. Inland from here. But I'm finding it hard to get the facts of it straight.

Could you not make them up? he said.

No, I said. I couldn't make up facts.

He bent his big hand over mine, where it lay on the table, not holding it, but sheltering it, as if we were having two conversations now – the one with words, and this one. We sat there like that.

That's something I'm not one bit used to, I thought, dreamily. I seem to remember an awful lot of men who didn't hold my hand, much less protect it . . .

I was certain now that Shay felt the other half of what I felt.

A bunch of girls started to put their drinks and bags on the table.

I'll just settle up, he said, and he went up to the bar.

My hand felt exposed, because he had taken his warmth away.

I looked at him. Yes – he was an ordinary-looking man. He took his time moving, and he positioned himself solidly where he stood. His shoes were old, the leather soft, and someone had kept them polished. He'd taken off the windcheater and there was just the crumpled shirt, and a bit of a paunch and then the belt and shapeless trousers. Everyman's clothes. He leaned on his elbows on the bar, talking to the barman. I noticed the strong curve of his arse, and that he wasn't conscious of it. If that had been me leaning on the bar, I'd have been paralysed by the thought of his eyes on me. But he and the barman were entirely at ease. Middle-aged men who moved at their own pace. I could sense their pleasure in a properly conducted ritual conversation.

They were talking about dogs in pubs when I came back from the Ladies.

Where I live in England, they all bring their dogs into the pubs, Shay said. Cocker spaniels, they go in for.

Well, it isn't allowed here. The English visitors do give me hell. The Irish couldn't care less. The oul dogs you see around here are for working.

When I was a boy in Ireland, everyone loved their dogs, Shay said.

You're looking back through rose-coloured glasses, my friend, the barman said. I wouldn't want to be a dog in Ireland. They get a dog's life!

So we were laughing when we came out of the pub.

It was dusk; not dark. The street ended in a block of old warehouses and grain stores – half ruined, most of them. Between each building there was a narrow laneway with rough stone walls. We turned into one of them to walk down to the quay to the cars.

One moment we were side by side and apart; the next, we melted into one, and I felt the stones in my back as he pressed me against the wall. His eyes were closed. He pulled me against him. He put one thick-fingered hand up and began to feel my face, rapidly, tap-tapping the pads of his fingertips all over my face, as if he were trying to learn it in some primitive way, some way that came out of him without any self-consciousness.

Then he shoved two or three fingers into my mouth and I felt them on my tongue. I gasped. Heat whooshed up through me. I could feel that he was swollen and I was glad to make my belly taut for him to push against. We were the same height and I returned pressure for pressure, bracing myself against his thighs on thighs that felt strong and alive. My arms, my legs, tried to touch him everywhere. We stood with mouth plunged into mouth, eyes closed, blind hands searching, shaping, clutching. You couldn't get two people more candid about desire.

I actually reeled from the embrace to gasp for breath. There would have been nothing pretty about me. Kisses like that leave your mouth hanging open and your face slack.

I tried to get back to his mouth for more, but he held me away from him and to one side, so that the light from a street lamp shone full on me. My face must have had snail tracks of saliva across it.

You're a wonderful woman, he said, very seriously. Can I come back to where you're staying?

Is that what you want to do?

Yes.

You want to come with me?

Would that be all right?

Do you think you could follow me on the other side and not get lost?

I won't get lost.

Down on the quay, beside the dark water, before we parted to get into the cars, he held me to him.

He whispered into my ear. I'd forgotten, he said. I'd forgotten.

*

In the car, driving back to the ferry – his headlights coming and going behind but always reappearing in the end – every activity inside my head was suspended. I just drove at a medium pace, my senses tilted forward, as if it were a warm day and I was driving towards a swim. I thought there was a spicy smell in the car, but when I pulled the collar of my coat forward and ducked my head to sniff, all I could smell was heat. But there was a long wait for the ferry in the dark car park. And it was too cold, when it did come, to get out of the cars. I slipped in to sit beside him, but we were awkward, and the ferry was wallowing because the wind had come up, and he turned the radio on to a pop station and I didn't think I could ask him to turn it off. We've moved too fast, I thought, but we're stuck with it, now. By the time we got to the cottage, the spell that had come down in the pub had melted away. I had gone back into my normal self again, and he had, too.

We stood in the middle of the room.

You should get a dog, he remarked. Out here all on your own.

I'm only here for a week, I said.

Where is your home? he said.

It's in London. Or – it was. I'm thinking things over.

Then there was a stiff silence.

After a while I looked at the floor and said, Will we go to bed, do you think?

I suppose we will, he said.

We went into the bedroom. Strangers. We did, now, seem ridiculous to me. I didn't turn on the light in there. A bit of light spilled in from the main room.

I could feel that he'd left his T-shirt on, and his shorts, when he slid into the bed to face me. And socks – his feet in socks hooked themselves around my feet. The kissing was just wet and savourless now. Nothing that was happening got past my cold, defensive brain. As hard as I tried, I couldn't help him get erect. After a while he half crouched over me, and he did something to himself with his hand. But there was still nothing. I braced myself to endure being fondled until I failed, too.

I'm sorry, he whispered miserably into my ear.

It's okay, I said. Really it is. It was a lovely afternoon anyway. Never you mind.

I could feel him listening, tense, to the tone of my voice, to see whether I meant it. I did mean it.

He fell back on his pillow with a sigh of relief.

I'm really sorry, Kathleen, he said in an ordinary voice. I'm not making excuses, but I've been taking tablets for a bit of a blood-pressure problem and they mightn't be the best for this kind of thing.

It doesn't matter, Shay, I said. Honestly.

I knelt up in the bed beside him, suddenly full of energy. I liked him, sex or no sex. He was a very natural man.

Any chance of a cup of tea? he said cheerfully. Is there no bread in the house at all?

There's salmon, I said. There's profiteroles. I bent over to plant a little sign-off kiss on his forehead.

Tea! he said. Now! Are proff – what you said – are they little cakes? Roundy ones? I'll have some of them. He caught my face in his hands and landed a kiss on my nose.

What about equality? I said as I fumbled around in the half-dark trying to find my nightdress. Are you just going to lie there like a sultan while I toil in the kitchen?

I'll toil for *you*, he said. Just tell me what to do.

So he carefully raked out the ashes of the fire and started it going, while I laid out all the stuff I had left from Bertie's on the bockety table.

Hang on! he said. Have you a bit of paper? And he took a page from my notebook and folded it and tried it under the short leg of the table to even it up.

What are you smiling at? he said, looking up at me from the floor.

Nothing, I said. I'm just in a good humour.

I was remembering that Jimmy used to tell me that I idealized marriage, and that I used to say to him that I thought it was no less than a miracle that two separate persons sometimes work side by side, for shared goals, in mutual affection.

*

We had the picnic half at the table and half on the rug in front of the fire. He asked me about my home. I said that Irish people always asked Irish people about home, even when they were middle-aged, and Shay said that I wasn't middle-aged.

I'm middle-aged, he said. I'm fifty-seven.

Well, I'm forty-seven, I said. I was incapable of telling the truth about my age.

He was gratifyingly astonished.

I saw you leaning over the wall, pegging stones, he said. I thought, there's a great pair of legs! Though – I didn't mean to try to get off with you, he hurried on. Honestly! I thought you were a local. I never picked a woman up in my life. I wouldn't know how –

You wouldn't? I said, gesturing at him in his underwear and me in my nightdress.

He laughed, and leaned forward and tried to smooth down my hair.

Well, what about home, anyway? he said. What did your father do?

He was a civil servant, I said. A weights and measures inspector. He travelled up and down the east coast. He only came home at the weekend. He died a few years ago. I hadn't seen him since I was twenty. I blamed him for a lot of things.

Since you were twenty! Shay said, shocked. That's bad –

No! We had a hard time with him. My poor mother . . .

Shay wasn't that much older than me, and he was from a small place outside Dublin, too. So there were things that I wouldn't need to explain to him. It startled me to realize that he was the first Irishman I'd ever been with, unless you counted the boys Sharon and I walked home from the dances with, going into doorway after doorway for a quick feel. But he'd understand a thing like how it marked us kids out that Daddy was an Irish-language enthusiast and went for a walk around Shore Road every Saturday calling out, *Go mbeannaí Dia dhíbh!* to the neighbours, though no one else around ever said a word in Irish, and they just muttered, How're ya, Mister de Burca if they replied at all. Then Daddy would take Mammy to the lunchtime session in the pub. She'd go with him silently, in her good black jumper, with a lot of lipstick on and her hands trembling a bit on the strap of her big handbag. When they came home they would go into their room. Then he'd come out whistling and pad down the corridor into the kitchen and tell one of us to bring her in a cup of tea.

What I said to Shay was, it wasn't a happy house at all. My mother suffered from depression.

I didn't tell him that if we said, There's no tea, or milk, or whatever, Daddy would look vaguely surprised and give someone a fistful of money to go to the shop. And she would have the bedroom door open when the child was passing.

How much did he give you? she'd say, low, so he couldn't hear. Give me that! Or, tell Mrs Bates that's a pound off the bill.

We didn't understand them at all. I was always nervous when the two of them were together. Danny used to get sick, literally, from the tension.

I said to Shay, She never had a penny. I think he kept her short on purpose to dominate her. Do you know what I mean?

Oh I do, he nodded. I know the type.

She was lovely when she was well, I said. I remember being in a café in Dublin with her one time and the way she licked the cream and the raspberry sauce off a big ice-cream thing in a glass. It was called a Melancholy Baby –

I remember Melancholy Babies! he said. I was in the county Under-14s and we played in Croke Park, and we lost, but my father took me to Cafolla's and that's what I had.

Funny, I said.

My mother died when I was fourteen, he said. I left school then. I wanted to, but I'd have been made to, anyway. I'm as sorry as anything, now. I can see you got all the education that was going – your computer out there in the room, and the things you were saying, on the ferry.

Oh, I'd have got out of school if I could! I said. Me and my friend would have gone to dances every night of our lives if we were let. What did your mother die of? Were there many of you?

Car crash. No, I was the only one. It made it very hard. The good thing was when I went to England no one knew how young I was and I danced three nights a week. For years. I might as well have been at home. Irish bands. Irish girls. Though we did the twist as well as quicksteps and that.

Me and my friend were only let go about once a month.

He was leaning back from the flames of the fire, his face alive with interest at these fragments. He was much better-looking in his T-shirt than in his clothes. But you could see he never thought about what he looked like.

We would have been mad about you when you were a young fella, I said. Sharon and me.

Be mad about me now, he said. I'm here now. Or, I'll be here in a minute, when I have the dishes done.

I got a brush from the window sill in the bedroom and untangled my hair a bit and tied it back with a ribbon. Then I made the bed and got in.

It had been a good day, even if the sex had been a fiasco. But Shay wasn't the kind who hated me or hated himself about that. I could hear him humming contentedly to himself next door as he sloshed the dishes around over at the sink. A mystery, it was – who he thought he was with, or what he thought he was doing. But the hell with it. It was so nice to have another person in the warm house, with the wind and the sea outside. Someone easy. Someone that I could talk to if I wanted to. He was welcome to share the bed with me. There hadn't been any overnight guests in the basement for a long number of years. That oul morgue. I never even knew what the weather was like, down there.

I was getting sleepy.

Mammy *was* charming, when she surfaced. But I'd been pushing it a bit when I said to Shay that she was lovely. She had a lovely smile, fair enough – a girlish smile.

Anyway, that was enough about her. I needed to go asleep.

I just made it to the bathroom to pee and brush my teeth. The sisal matting hurt the soles of my feet, and Shay, who was pulling the bolt across the front door, laughed at me as I tried to hop across the floor. He turned the lights off and came into the bedroom and took his bits of clothes off. The big bed sagged and jangled as he snuggled down, naked, against my back. He started to say something, but he dropped down into sleep with one snort, right in the middle of the first word. His arm fell across me. My head was under his chin and his steady breath ruffled my hair. All the length of my body I could feel his warm, sleeping body behind me.

In the middle of the night, I came back up to wakefulness. I was lying on my side, turned away from Shay. He was half sitting up on his elbow behind me, like the husband on an Etruscan tomb. His hand was lightly, lightly, stroking the length of me. He took his time. His palm would begin, cupped around my shoulder, then slide down the side of my breast, then into the shallow indentation at my waist, then up over the roundness of my hip and down the flank of my thigh. Over and over. The hand was more like something breathing on the skin than touching it. I lay there, drowsily picking up the rhythm of it, half imagining myself the hand and half the body it was stroking. I began to melt. Deep down, under my pubic bone, it was as if black tar gave a first, thick, bubble.

Tell me about yourself, he whispered.

I don't want to talk, I whispered back.

Have you children?

No.

Are you married?

No.

Were you always a writer?

Yes. I don't want to talk –

Why did you go to England?

I sat up in the bed and snapped on the light.

Listen, I said crossly, why is it me that's being cross-questioned?

He smiled at me from the pillows. He really did look handsome, relaxed as he was, and amused.

Ah, come here, darling, he said slowly, and don't be running away from me.

He pulled me gently back into his warm arms. He opened my nightdress and stroked my breasts with one big hand.

With the other hand he cupped the back of my head lightly, and brought my face to his.

You're my little girl, he said to me confidently. Aren't you? Aren't you my little girl?

Without the slightest warning, I went open and wet at his tone. He rolled me on top of him. With one long, exquisite wince, he was deep in me. For an endless time, and also for only a few minutes, I was kneeling on him with my head thrown back and his big, solid hands pulling me down by the hips, strongly grinding me onto him. I crouched over him, and he chewed on one breast, and milked the other with his hand. Then his mouth slid away, and his head fell back, and from deep inside him, he began to moan.

After a long while he murmured that he'd better go and have a shower and I said there was no shower.

I think we both slept then, holding each other. He was definitely holding me in his arms when I woke again. Soft light was seeping into the room. Kathleen, he was saying. That's a real Irish name. *I'll take you home again, Kathleen*. I like it. I'm Shay in England, since I went over. But my father still calls me Seamus. I don't know who he's talking to, sometimes.

He went on talking to himself for a while, innocently. I didn't bother to wake up enough to answer. The boys Sharon and I used to court in the bus shelter – he could easily be one of those, grown-up. I fell back into sleep.

The morning was the best. He tidied me. He pulled my nightie down from my neck, and plumped the pillows, and fixed the bed so I could rest in coolness. I stirred when he came back into the bedroom carefully balancing the teapot and the milk on a breadboard.

I can't find a tray, he said. Sit up, chicken.

I didn't even have to hold the mug. He held it under my lips and I slurped the tea like an infant.

That's a good girl, he said, tenderly.

He wiped off my mouth with his fingers. Then he lay down on the outside of the bedclothes, looking at me.

I definitely think I must have a guardian angel, he said, smiling at me. What made me turn left to go out to Mellary Harbour? What kind of an accident was that?

Then he asked me was I a Catholic still, myself.

I felt like talking to him properly, now. Strange, what a bodily event could do. If we hadn't made love it wouldn't have mattered, but now that we had, now that we knew each other that way – everything was different.

I told him that my father was a good ol' Catholic boy, and he never stopped making my mother pregnant. I got out to England, I told him, when I saw that Ireland was run according to the rules of the Catholic Church and that the Catholic Church was based on pushing women around.

But England's not so great for Irish people, all the same, he said. Particularly when things were bad in Northern Ireland.

Yes, I said. I was often afraid. I was ashamed, too, sometimes.

His arms were around me. I was talking, lying across his chest, and his head was above me. Now he brought me up to him and laid his mouth lightly on mine.

You are a brave woman, he said. You have no one to look after you.

I was so happy. I began to sing 'Tea for Two' into his ear.

Day will break
and I will wake
and start to bake
a sugar cake –

And he joined in:
No one to see us, to hear us, to – oh, I forget the words! he said. Go to sleep now, and when you wake up we'll have breakfast. I'm just going up to that shop in the village we came through last night.

Fresh bread, I said.

Anything else?

Yes, I said. Come back soon.

I heard him fixing the fire. It was lovely to drift towards sleep and hear the house being started for the day.

He came back into the bedroom and kissed the top of my head.

Thank you, he whispered. I could never thank you enough.

And orange juice, I said. Get a carton of juice.

When I woke, I was cold. The bedclothes had slipped down. The cottage was completely quiet.

Shay! I scrambled from the bed. Shay!

I ran into the big room. Where was the clock? There. Midday! But it had been early morning when he went out! The village was only ten minutes away.

I looked to where he'd brought his bag in from the car last night and left it beside the door.

The bag was gone.

It hurt so badly that I had to repeat to myself over and over to keep the pain away – You only knew him for sixteen hours. It was just another one-night stand. The way he'd lied was the only unusual bit.

I tried to work. What else could I do? I wasn't a girl any more, to fall apart at these things. I pulled the table back to the window and sat at the laptop. I could do mechanical stuff.

I tried not to think about it. But every so often it would burst out of me – why did he do something so unkind? What had I done to deserve it? I did believe, from my experience of life and of looking at the world, that men hated women. But there were all kinds of exceptions, and I'd have bet everything that *this* man didn't hate me, *this* woman.

I turned the pages of the *Judgment* – I'd almost reached the last of them. I copied into my story file the little bit of narrative there was about what happened after William Mullan followed Marianne to Coffey's Hotel and sent in the note. The clergyman destroyed the note, though she begged for it.

He brought her from Mount Talbot to Dublin, to Coffey's Hotel in Dominick

Street and then, he says, to the Rathgar road. 'I made it my business to call, and was sometimes with her five hours a day, because I considered myself responsible for having her in my charge.' She was in a state of extreme excitement, and he tried to soothe her, and he says, 'I wanted her to join me in prayer. I never could get her to pray. But I drew up a form of prayer in which I put, in the way of confession, what I conceived to be the state of her case.'

'I never could get her to pray.'

The arrogance of them! Last night, when I was languid in the bed, do you think some old priest could have got me to repent? Repent for *what*? I did not regret last night one smallest bit, even though I was paying for it today and I'd go on paying for it. If I was going to pray I'd pray in *gratitude* for having opened up to someone again, at last. And for the miracle of people attracting each other.

I went into the bathroom and leaned across the bath to try to see my face in the speckled mirror. Today hadn't registered on it yet. I was still plump and pink from the night. If he had stayed, I would have trusted him – I would have let myself go. But could he have stayed? Maybe he was a widower. No. He didn't feel like a widower. He gave off well-being, as a matter of fact.

I walked from the room to the bedroom and back again.

What if I never have another lover? What if I have to go the whole way to the grave without ever making love again?

Don't say that! I said to myself.

I sat down and my head drooped forward onto the table.

I can't bear it, I said out loud. I stood up to ease the pain. My body was stiff. I could feel the path of him inside me. Did he not like me? I thought he liked me. His tenderness when he was feeding me the tea. The way he looked at my face. Maybe the car had overturned and nobody had seen it in the ditch –

He ran out on me. Simple as that.

I moved back to the table. I had to work. The time would never pass if I didn't work. But – what work? I'd copied out the story of Marianne and Mullan more or less as far as the *Judgment* knew it. There was nowhere to move to from there. I didn't have one piece of new material. All I had was the experience of going out to the bog and thinking about the people who used to live there, and going up to the demesne at Mount Talbot and thinking about the people who used to live there. And those were experiences that had happened to *me*, not to them, Marianne, or William, or Richard or the nameless Irish people, dead or flown. And they were feelings, not events . . .

I stretched, and felt the seams of my jeans press into me, between my legs, where the nerves still quivered. Suppose I had to go from now to my grave without knowing again the feel of another human being's arms around me?

Oh, Jimmy! I said to the air around.

After a while, I began to be more calm. It helped that I saw myself suddenly as if I were looking down from the sky – a tall woman moving agitatedly around a small house on a lonely headland, while outside, badgers and foxes slept under the grassy earthen banks covered in gorse. I went and stood outside the front door. There was a strong wind. The air was full of the sound of waves and the smell of salt. The wind was coming in off the bay, bending the grass flat from left to right. A west wind. Shelley's west wind.

> *Make me thy lyre, even as the forest is:*
> *What if my leaves are falling like its own . . .?*

What if I didn't think of it as the Talbot story but as Marianne's story? If I came at it from inside, not from outside?

PJ's post van was racing down the lane and skidded up to the porch.

He all but ran past me to the phone.

I was on to Pat, he said. Everything's game ball now. *Compadre!* Ring me back.

Pat rang back.

Great! I said to PJ.

Oh, I have your messages in the van, PJ said.

He ran out the door and in again, carrying a cardboard box. I could see milk and a baguette and the corner of a carton of orange juice.

Your friend said to bring them down to you as soon as the baker came with the fresh bread.

I could see there was an envelope on top of the groceries. Kathleen, in capital letters, in pencil.

I didn't touch the envelope. I didn't even look at it again, while he was there, though it glowed in the corner of my eye.

Wait! I said. PJ! Wait a few minutes for me, will you? I have something for the post.

I sat at the table and scribbled a note to Miss Leech. Well, it wasn't that scribbled – I found my notebook so as to get the quotation from Henry James impressively accurate.

Dear Miss Leech,

I very much hope you are feeling better, and thank you again for all your help. I look forward to seeing you again when I get back to Ballygall. I do agree with Henry James, that 'Historical fiction is condemned to be second-rate. You may multiply the little facts that can be got from pictures and documents, relics and prints, as much as you like, the historical novel is almost impossible to do . . . You have to think with your modern apparatus . . . you have to simplify back by an amazing tour de force – and even then it's all humbug.'

But if I gathered the bits and pieces of the Talbot story into a tale, just for my own satisfaction, I wouldn't be trying to humbug anyone, would I?

Mellary is marvellous.

Le gach dea-ghuí,

Caitlín de Búrca.

I gave the card to PJ, and as soon as the noise of his van had died away I took the envelope out of the box of groceries and went into the bedroom and sat on the bed. Shay had stuck it down with the edging from a sheet of stamps. Only one paragraph! Florid, loopy writing, on a lined page. He must have bought an exercise book. I remembered the furry feel of the paper from school.

If I did not go then I could never go at all. I could never leave you if I stayed. You are Everything a man could desire. Youre a Queen in any bodys world. You will Always be in my Memory. Shay xxx.

8

The Talbot Book

She hated the smell of the house. The very first day they came to Mount Talbot she knew that. They had stood in the flagged hallway, and Richard had been flushed with the stir of coming to the Irish house after so long a journey, and he had carried Mab over to the fireplace and put her on the bearskin rug there. There had been oil lamps on brass brackets on either side of the high mantelpiece, and down at the back of the hall, under the curve of the divided stairs, where the servants had gathered to see the new master and his family arrive, there were more lamps, though this time without glass: a twist of tow rope floated in each tin saucer of oil. Behind the smell of the lamps was the sour smell of old turf ash from the fires of many years.

She could hardly believe how plain and worn the place was, compared to her father's house in Harley Street. No monies could have been expended on the hangings and furniture for many years. She went and picked up Mab and buried her nose in Mab's clean skin, and listened to the servants talking among themselves in the Irish language.

The smell was worst in the mornings. By the time they had been at Mount Talbot for a year or so, they slept late into the morning, Richard and she. Sometimes, the two of them came reluctantly into wakefulness together, stretching and turning under the pile of blankets and quilts behind the musty hangings of the marital bed. Sometimes they woke in their separate rooms, if Benn had got someone to help him carry Richard up from his decanter of port the night before, and roll him onto the narrow bed in his dressing room.

Even then, the first thing she heard in the morning was his snoring, through the open doors between them. She would hear him snuffling and clearing his throat as he woke. She would hear him relieving himself in his pot. She would hear his bare feet make a slapping noise as he came towards her, moving as quickly as he could across the cold floorboards of the dressing room. She waited, down in the hollow of the old bed that her body had warmed during the night, her eyes clenched shut. If he pulled the bell cord beside the fireplace, then he wanted hot water for shaving now. If he did not pull the cord, he was going to have her.

But that was a year later.

It was different when they were new to Mount Talbot, even though the condition of the locality was much worse then, and she and Mab were not allowed to go outside the demesne. She and Richard always slept in the same bed, then. And he rose early. It might still be dark when he slipped out of bed; he'd throw a few sods of turf on the ashy fire as he passed it on his way to dress. On sunny mornings, he might whistle.

There had been much to rise early for. Barlow, the agent, and Tracy, the steward, waited for him in the office every morning. There were many plans afoot to do with reorganizing the estate. There was talk of Richard chartering his own ships to send the tenants away to Canada. Coby had done it. Sligo to the St Lawrence River: costs had been less by almost a third than paying for the people's food while they walked to Dublin and went across to Liverpool and were shipped from Liverpool to New York or Boston. If Richard had been sure he could trust Barlow, he murmured to Marianne one morning when he lay back on the pillow – she had woken to find him pulling her nightdress up to her neck – he would have done it.

'It is an investment, not a loss. There are two farmers in a substantial way from Scotland who think of taking the land we are clearing with the evictions. They have a plan for the intensive cultivation of turnips . . .'

She interested herself in matters like these, at that time. And anyway the Scotsmen might provide some company, for Richard if not for herself.

'Why do you not trust Barlow? Barlow is not Roman Catholic,' she said.

'His numbers change at each reckoning. On one day I am responsible for five hundred men and their wives and their old mothers and their score upon score of children. By the time he reckons it again it is eight hundred. Or else he is not quite certain how many. This when the whole upper field is gone on pits for the dead, and I may not dare to plough it! And still – when I ride further out – in the Mayo direction – I seem to have as many useless mouths on Talbot lands as before the potato failed . . .'

When Marianne came to Mount Talbot, the mansion seemed to her as artificial as the scenery in an opera. The bleak Irish landscape made it seem unreal. There were no cosy home farms to nestle against its walls. It wasn't even a household in the usual sense – the Talbot family had lived only half the year on their Irish estate. When the Talbot boys went back to England to school, the parents usually made their principal residence in England, and England was where wives were chosen. They were not farmers, and they had done little to the land. They had named the parts of it crudely: the Long Field, the Bog Field, the Lower Woods. When they called in the steward to discuss a shoot or a fishing expedition, they used those names. They did not know that every bend of the lanes, every rise and fall of the land, every clump of trees, every ditch and pond had a specific name. They could not have imagined how intimately the land was known to the local people. The real names were in Irish, and the only Irish words the Talbots knew were a few commands. The men and women working in the house or the grounds could mock the Talbots in their hearing, or plot against them, and the Talbots would never know. When Richard's aunt died in the house the first year of the potato failure, they stood respectfully along the avenue while her body was brought to the Church of Ireland graveyard. But in so far as they bothered saying anything about her at all, they said to each other that she was a black-hearted old bitch.

For all the talk of famine, Marianne had seen dead people only once. It was when the journey to Mount Talbot was almost over.

They had stayed the last few nights at Richard's cousin Letitia's place, in the next county, where there was a shoot. The ladies had driven themselves out in light carts at midday. They had brought, in white napkins in baskets, some fried mackerel and a roast chicken garnished with mushrooms and a leg of lamb with chopped onion and nutmeg, for the men. They pulled up somewhere in hilly country, where two tracks crossed. There was a well, and stepping stones had been placed in a ring around it. Letitia said the people said prayers there.

When Marianne was getting down from the dog cart she stepped onto a grassy bank. She cried out with surprise and might have fallen, but that the others came hurrying over, and one lady held her. Behind the bank, on the ground between it and the well, three bodies were laid side by side on their backs. There was a man whose face was yellow-grey. A boy of about sixteen. And a girl of five or six. Their faces were very pale and thin, but no worse than that. One cloak covered the lower part of the three. The stomachs were hugely distended and stuck up under the cloak.

'They died of the hunger,' Letitia said. 'I believe it is exceptionally bad in this area. They eat grass, apparently, and that is why their stomachs blow up in that manner.'

Marianne was shocked, but she was excited, too. Since she married she had often had those two feelings at the same time, but coming upon these dead Irish was the first time they had been prompted by something outside her personal life.

Her duties as the wife of Richard Talbot had shocked her terribly at first, and at the beginning of their wedding journey they had done only that. Then everything, including even those, became more tedious than anything else, though she never said as much, even to herself. Her husband was waiting for the uncle to die, at which time they would inherit Mount Talbot. Marianne would have been content to live with Richard's mother in Ardfert, in the south-west of Ireland, but Richard would have none but formal dealings with his mother. She had sent him to school in England, he said, no matter how he begged her, and the boys there called him 'Paddy Pig', and they tied him, once, to a bench in the schoolroom, overnight – on a winter's night! – and when the class filed in in the morning he was found snivelling and half frozen, and stinking of his own incontinence. He told his young wife that on one of the first nights they were together.

'Because I was small. That was why,' he said, shuddering in her strong white arms. 'And they said I was Irish.'

Richard and Marianne, with his manservant and her maid and Mab and the nurse moved from watering place to watering place while they waited to take possession of the Irish estate. They came down in the evenings to the ornate dining rooms spruce, and finely dressed, to sit opposite to each other. He began to complain at her quietness, and she said, 'But you said it was a delight to you that I am quiet!'

'Drink some of the wine, Missy,' he said. 'And smile at those other ladies. Attend to what I say – go on – smile! It is dull beyond anything in this place.'

The places were Carlsbad, Homburg, Baden. They were at Bagni di Lucca a year after the wedding, when to her delighted astonishment she became a full partner to her husband in their lovemaking. Now, she had an intimate life that soothed her. At that time, walking the soft paths among the chestnut woods around the little spa, she confided in him how long the years had seemed to her, growing up as the most solitary of children in the house in Harley Street. How her earliest memory was of waiting for her mother to come back, because nobody told her that, when Marianne was three, her mother had died of fever. And of how her first memory of her father was of his looking down at her small self with distaste when he found her exploring the immense hallway and then ringing the bell behind the ottoman and saying, 'Take this child, Horton, and see that it does not come down from the nursery floor except when I specifically so instruct.'

She told Richard, in bits and pieces, that she had become quite friendly with her papa when she was older and was learning a little Latin with her tutor, and when she ostentatiously purchased books instead of fripperies with her allowance.

'I asked to go to a course of lectures on the poetry of England,' she told him, 'when I was fifteen, and dear Papa gave his permission. My maid accompanied me and she said it was the worst thing ever

– the benches in the Athenaeum were so uncomfortable! But, you see, Richard, he did not like me to go to dancing class, and I had very little opportunity to talk to other girls, and I had no sister or brother. I loved my poetry so much because so few visitors ever came to my room. And my father liked to see me a bluestocking. If my aunt Paget had not taken me around for a month of every winter season, I would never have known anything but books and my father's conversation. I did not know the fashions! I knew nothing!'

Even at her most confiding she did not tell Richard that she had despaired of marrying until he asked for her. She knew she was a big, heavy young woman. Her father said so. Even Mrs Horton, who had always been her Nana, almost prayed over her as she dressed her, the three or four nights a year when she went with Aunt Paget to dances. Her father was the least sociable of men, and her dowry was no more than reasonable. If Richard Talbot had not asked for her, she might have had to spend her life with her father.

And Mab's birth! She was taken down to the *ospedale* in Lucca for that. Nobody had warned her. Again, the shock, and again, the excitement. She did not even need to sleep, the first year, so absorbed was she in the baby. The hands! The ear! The curve of the cheek! The folds between the tiny plump thighs, from which someday in turn a child would emerge . . . Marianne could hardly believe in the wonder of the child, and in herself, for having brought a child into the world. She became peaceful, and indifferent to her father, who had hurt her, at first, by hardly ever replying to her letters. Richard made generous use of her rich body.

And then there was the coming into Ireland. All the talk was of death and ruin and fever, and Letitia and the others clung together as if they were under siege. It would have been very exciting to live near Letitia, where the entertainments were so many. But Mount Talbot was quite cut off. At first Marianne thrilled to the isolation itself. Sometimes she would prop Mab among the braided velvet cushions on a window seat of the ballroom and stand across the room from her, and declaim the poems she could remember. The parquet had begun to buckle a little in the damp, and there were many cracks in the panes of the tall, clouded windows. But that made it more like a castle in a fairy tale.

'*So we'll go no more a-roving,*' she said in her most poetic voice, to the wide-eyed baby –

> '*So late into the night.*
> *Though the heart be still as loving,*
> *And the moon be still as bright . . .*'

The echoing room made the lines resound, and the infant laughed at the strangeness of it. Then Marianne couldn't stay apart from her one second longer and she ran over and scooped her up to hold her face to face and kiss her and murmur, 'Who's her Mama's little lambkin, then?' because she had learned the things mothers say to babies over the years from going down to the servants in Harley Street, when she did not dine with her father, and listening to their talk.

Husband and wife were friendly for a long time.

She learned that she could rely on certain reactions from him.

'The workmen are so wild-looking!' she might say, and that would make him smile. Or, 'There are a great many beggars still around our walls, Richard,' she might whimper, snuggling in to him, and he would tighten his arms protectively around her. Or, 'I dislike to go through the Great Gate to town, Richard. Mab will lean from the carriage and I am afraid they will touch her.'

'It would be better not to go outside the gates, my dear.'

'Oh, Richard, I must see the things that come in to Mr Hurley's. Mab grows as fast as anything! And I am lonely for Whiteley's. Papa allowed me to go to Whiteley's Emporium several times a week, with Mrs Horton . . .'

Richard talked to her, too.

'Hurley bought up the rough land beyond the big bog, during the bad years. Barlow says he offers clothing, and tickets for the car to Dublin, if the people going to the boat will sign. Old Mr Treadwell had to have a word with him when we went out with the guns. The

147

Treadwells have been in this wretched country since the time of Good Queen Bess. Fancy having to ask *Hurley* to allow us to shoot!'

And so they chatted, at first, of the things of their days.

The English midwife who had attended at Marianne's lying-in had said to her when she held the baby up and saw it was a girl, 'Lie still when your husband's seed comes into you. Don't move at all. That's the way to make the boys.'

Marianne told Richard, and they stayed immobile in each other's arms – sometimes seriously, sometimes laughing.

The hope of being with child again gave her something to look to the future for. Because time hung very heavy in Ireland.

'All the ladies say the same,' she told Richard. 'There is very little in this country for a lady to do, especially in the parts like this one. It is hardly possible to visit or be visited. Mrs Treadwell and Lady Coby did many good works – the Reverend McClelland is full of stories of their goodness and the soup they gave out during the potato blight and so forth. But they are older ladies, Richard. I am young, and I have the care of Mabbie. And Mount Talbot is in country so wild. If there were other ladies to join with me I could visit the sick, and so on . . .'

'You have me to care for besides our daughter,' he said, kneading her plump back with his small, hard hands. 'Let that be your occupation, my dear.'

Mab was small and delicately made, like her father. Her hair had been a silver colour which was much talked about in the locality when she first came. She was welcome everywhere. She was the only person in Mount Talbot who knew no boundaries. She played on the sweep of the grand staircase and she played on the back stairs. She loved and trusted her mother and father, but she also loved Mary Anne Benn and Hester Keogh and Maria Mooney and Mr Barlow the steward and Benn the butler and Margaret, her own maid, and the Boylan boys who did the fires and Mr Cooper who was the coachman in former years and Mullan who helped Mr Cooper and Mullan's dog Lolly. When Marianne heard the child's prayers she heard her include in her list for the angels' protection the names of men and women who must be working about the place but who she herself did not know. And the child used Irish names with as much ease as English, whereas Richard, who had spent half of every boyhood year in Ireland, had great difficulty with the native pronunciation.

She knows everybody in the household, Marianne wanted to boast. Girls from the bog, just brought in to help on laundry days – she knows their names. But Marianne had no one to boast to.

Mab even knew people in the town, because once or twice she had been allowed go there with Mrs Benn and her nursery maid and a couple of the men. She was shown off in there like royalty. She also knew her donkey and the house dogs and the stable dogs, and the horses in the stables, and Mrs Benn's tame jackdaw and the rabbits Mrs Tracy kept in a hutch outside her back door and old Mr Boylan's two lurchers and countless other animals and birds. They were in her prayers, too.

'Mama!' She would dart in under the heavy oriental curtain that was hung across the doorway of Marianne's small drawing room, rather than delay a moment to pull it aside. 'Mama! The hens came into the kitchen again! Mrs Benn had to run after them!'

'Not "hins", Mabbie. Hens.'

'Mama! May I go down to the house with Mr Tracy when he is going home for his tea? Because there is the doll there that Mrs Tracy had when she was small like me that her brother made from a piece of wood.'

She danced with impatience on the old Persian carpet. It had tints of blue and rose, and it warmed the dark room.

Behind the child the long, paned windows looked onto the rank grass of what had once been formal lawns. Richard's aunt had been a great gardener, in intense competition with cousin Letitia twenty miles east and Lady Coby twenty miles south. But Richard paid the two gardeners off the day he came to Mount Talbot, as an economy, together with three elderly house servants. One gardener was gone to Dublin, but the four others continued to be fed in the servants' kitchen, and two of them lived comfortably enough in a room behind the parapet of the ornamental archway that led to the deer park. Richard never knew.

The gardeners were of the generation that spoke nothing but Irish. The house servants had come from England, or spoke English. But in the yards and around the farm, even the ones who spoke English talked among themselves in Irish. Mab knew a smattering of the language.

'*A Dheaide!*' she would call in delight when she caught sight of her father. '*A Dheaide!*'

She did not even know that she was greeting her dada in Irish.

Richard would complain to Marianne.

'Ayadda, ayadda. What is this gibberish! Issue an order! They are not to speak in the native way in this house! I shall make it a condition of employment! Our people, when they come home from India, do not have children who sound like little Hindus. Mab is an English girl,' he said firmly. 'An English rosebud.'

Marianne wrote to her father almost weekly. Having a child was the first thing she had ever done that had interested him in her. Though he made it clear he wanted a grandson soon.

'Mab is the happiest, fastest child,' Marianne wrote. 'Everything she does she does speedily. She changes the whole house, even though she is only a little girl and it has twenty or thirty rooms. It was a dark and heavy place when Richard's old uncle was here, Lady Coby told me. Now Mabbie is everywhere – dancing and hopping and sliding, even though Richard and I implore her to be careful. She laughs all day!'

At night, Marianne sent everyone away while she said her prayers with the little girl, and tucked her into her bed among her toys. She often stayed with her for a long time, marvelling always that the child went from waking into sleeping in the course of just one long breath. Her mother studied her face. The delicate eye socket, and along the top of it, the fine eyebrow. The subtle shadow that hid in the cheek. The cut of her lips. Her fingers. The dab of hollow in the back of her neck, under the hair that was Marianne's pride and joy.

'It is hair so exceptional that we hardly know where it has come from,' she wrote to her father. 'Richard's head is sandy, and – dare I say it – is already somewhat thin. My own locks have never attracted any compliments. Yet there is our child, with hair so fair that every single visitor to the house says it is the most beautiful hair they have ever seen. It is like spun sugar, Lady Coby said on seeing it.'

But after Mab slept, Marianne had nothing to do. In summer, it might be full daylight still when the child went to bed. In winter there would be long hours in the chill drawing room before she might retire. Richard did not care for music, and in any case, the pianoforte had been badly affected by damp. The couple sat in close to the fire. Richard had his decanter, and Marianne held her embroidery tambourine, or one of the poetry books she had brought – there were no books of fiction or poetry in the house, only peerages, and pamphlets on animal husbandry, and the Bible. But she sat, dreaming, more often than she sewed or read. If Richard was away Marianne would go to her rooms early. Sometimes when she came out of Mab's nursery at the top of the house, she would hear rain on the roof, or wind, curling around the house. She would walk along the top corridor, shading the candle from the draughts, saying to herself without being conscious of it, What will I do now? What will I do?

At that time she was twenty-six years old.

She did not go around the house much. Mrs Benn sealed up two corridors of rooms, even, before she had looked at them. But Richard told her often enough that they might leave the place. He said that there was not and there never would be ratepayers enough in the district to finance feeding and shelter for the indigent populace. The situation, he said, though it was becoming better for the people, was ruining the gentry.

By the end of 1848 there were no longer bodies on the roads and in the ditches, though there were bones in the most unexpected places – sticking out of earthen banks; under a solitary thornbush in the middle of a field; behind the threshold of what had once been a shop. There were as many deaths as ever, but now the deaths were indoors, in the workhouse, and in the auxiliary fever houses. It was not possible to forget that, all the time. Coming down the outside stone stairs from the court above the Assembly Rooms, when he went to sit on the magistrates' bench alongside two or three of the merchants of the town, Richard was mobbed by living skeletons. They were silent, except for the hisses of *Your Honour! Your Honour!*

He said to Marianne, 'It sounds like cursing, when they say it. I would quite like to curse them myself, if truth be told!'

Inside the demesne walls, there was a comfortable life. Mab's laughter rang out. Her mother called to her. The smells of dinner being prepared for the Talbot dining room came from the kitchens. Mullan's little dog Lolly barked from the stable block. Mullan would not let her out of the yard without him. He had heard – it was part of the gossip of the time – that out in the countryside the wild dogs were fat. It was said that where there had been remote settlements of cabins the dogs had eaten the bodies inside, and the bones had been so tossed that no one could tell how many corpses there had been in the first place. He didn't want Lolly to run with those dogs.

Marianne wrote to her father.

I was in the town today to make some small purchases. It was like being in a dream. There are shops rather like the shops at home but with hardly any things in them. The street that goes up to the square has houses of some elegance that contain the offices of the professional men, but many of them have boards nailed across the doors, still. However, the Assizes are here. And there was a crowd on the Fair Green perfectly well shod and so on. The court is a handsome building of dressed sandstone something like what we see in our smaller towns in England. Richard is pleased that there is a force of the constabulary returned to Ballygall, because there is no regiment stationed nearer than the next county. He fears the people may become restless. He says that though the county is excessively quiet, now, your Paddy is ever an excitable fellow.

She wrote that, thinking the words most impressive.
Your Paddy is ever an excitable fellow.
At the same time, she knew that nothing about Ireland impressed people in London.

Mullan took Marianne's letters in the pouch from Mount Talbot all the way to the post office in Ballaghdereen each week and collected the mail for the estate. It was the first time the mail service had been in operation for more than a year. It was suspended, the postmaster told Mullan, not because in the wilder parts – out on the highway, far from anywhere – the poor people had lain out in the middle of the road crying for help, and not because it was difficult to keep the post horses secure, at night, against the people bleeding them, but because drivers could not be found in all the north-west strong enough to do the job. This might be true. The strong men took the emigrant boat first; the men who stayed – the men who thought they were lucky because they got work building the Relief Works road out near the lake – could barely raise a mallet.

The year turned. It was early February of 1849 – the dead of winter – the season of the year when Mount Talbot was most itself, because the harsh weather and the short days and the bad roads cut it off from the outside world. Her isolation was so complete that Marianne ceased to fret. In the mornings, at this time, she pulled back the curtain of her bed and looked at the pale woods down at the lake. On windy days, dry leaves lifted from the clearings swirled into the sky. Sometimes she had to wait for the thin sun to clear a dusting of frost from the panes of the windows before she could see the sweep of grass drenched and sparkling with the night's mist, and the grey trees.

This morning she rang for her tea. She would have liked to feel soft and poetic. She began to recite her beloved Shelley.

'I am the daughter of Earth and Water, and the nursling of the Sky –'

The words soothed her as if she were being rocked.

'I pass through the pores of the ocean and shores; I change, but I cannot die . . .'

Richard heard her through the open door, where he was shaving in the dressing room.

'What are those words, Marianne?'

'They are a poem, Richard, a famous one. By the poet Shelley, who died young.'

'I know of Shelley. He came to Dublin when my grandfather was there and incited the Irish people to rise up. The constabulary had something to say to the young pup, I can assure you!'

'You see the woods, Richard? He said the leaves were "pestilence-stricken multitudes." Is that not fine?'

'There is pestilence not a mile from this house. Your prayers would be more fitting than poetry.'

He came into the bedroom, his neat, booted feet clicking on the polished boards like a dancer's. He stood on his toes to see his face in the cloudy mirror that had half its gilded border missing. He smoothed his hair back with alternate strokes of his two brushes, and pushed his crisp shirt more neatly into the waistband of his breeches with his fingers. He came over to the bed and bent his smiling face into Marianne's face.

'Are you a naughty girlie! Are you? Naughty, naughty! Turn over!' Marianne moved patiently onto her stomach.

But then, abruptly, he lifted his head. He covered her buttocks with the blanket.

He had heard Mab's footsteps as she ran down the long corridor towards the bedroom – the tap of her shoes clear where the floorboards were bare, blurred where she was running across carpet. He smiled down as Marianne heard her too, and half sat up. Mab had games that she played with them that she loved to have repeated.

The girl peeped around the doorway.

'Do you know, Marianne,' Richard said, 'I thought I saw a little girl a moment ago?'

'A little girl, Richard? I don't think there are any little girls in this house. I certainly don't see any little girls.'

'Yes you do! Mama! You do! I'm a little girl!' And Mab burst into the room. Her father scooped her up. He kissed her tenderly.

'We shall dine at Coby's after the Board of Guardians meeting,' he said to Marianne. 'Do not wait up for me. I shall explain to the

Cobys that you are not going around at present due to the state of the country.'

He went.

She heard Hester Keogh talking to the scullery boy as they came towards the bedroom. He would light the fire in the room, and take away the chamber pot from under the bed. Hessy would put the tray of fresh soda bread and a boiled egg and tea on the table. She would go back down, and in an hour she would bring Marianne's jug of hot water.

There was nothing to do but supervise Mab's Bible lesson and write letters, and read her books, all day. And all evening: Richard was dining from home.

Mrs Benn tapped on Marianne's door and came in.

'We must prepare for my father's stay,' Marianne said to the housekeeper. 'There will be his man, too . . .'

Mrs Benn, on her way out of the room, barely paused. 'We are well prepared to receive any party of visitors,' she said. 'Mr Talbot has made all arrangements as regards the dinners and what he wants brought from the cellar, and the foddering of Mr McCausland's horses.'

Marianne stroked Mabbie's hair. She shrugged to herself. Her father must make the best he could of Mount Talbot. She had wanted him to come, only so as to show him Mabbie. The daughter of Marianne McCausland was as beautiful a little girl as any in the Empire, and she wanted to see his surprise at that. But then – he could go back to England for ever, for all she cared. It seemed to her a truly terrible thing now, that he had left her without any explanation of her mother's disappearance, and had not tried to relieve the loneliness of her motherlessness. When she thought of how Mab demanded endless love, and thrived on it! And in any case – he had married her to an Irishman, and if Ireland didn't suit him, it was not her fault. She could not play the hostess. She did not even know what the servants were saying when she heard them talking or singing. She could not bustle about. And there was no company to present to Mr McCausland. She had a reputation for being some kind of bluestocking because she did not garden, and did not ride out, and no one but cousin Letitia and the Cobys made the effort to visit, and the Cobys were trying to sell up . . .

It was Mr McCausland, when he came from London, who noticed that there was something wrong with Mab. They had told Mrs Benn they would take a sugar cube to the donkey. They had gone down the flight of steps outside the small drawing room and were walking under the archway that led to the first stable yard when the grandfather turned to tell Mab to come along. He saw that Mab was limping.

'Why is the child limping?' he said to Marianne.

At that moment Mab looked up at them, as she came towards them. Marianne saw that the small face, though pale, had somehow darkened. Mab's eyes were open but unseeing, as if she was looking into herself. It was as if she had become preoccupied. A frown had settled on her forehead. Her cheeks were shadowy. It was not a trick of the light – the child, hobbling as she came up to the other two, looked remote. She even looked old.

Marianne stood there. Black fear gave one great yawn through her whole being. She tried to speak.

Mab said, 'Mama! I hurt!'

'Well, then, we shall get the doctor,' Mr McCausland said brightly, 'and he shall take the pain away.'

His granddaughter and his daughter did not hear him. The child looked up searchingly into the mother's face, and the mother looked as greedily back. Then the mother fell on her knees in front of the child, and pulled her head in its cloud of silvery hair to her breast, and gathered her into a deep embrace.

She commanded her father, 'Get the child's dog cart brought here. Get Cooper to go for Dr Madden and not return without him. Tell Benn I want the laudanum unlocked and a draught brought here.'

They were alone, then, mother and daughter, wrapped in a solemn embrace.

And even when Mab was wrapped in a cloak, and Mullan lifted her gently and placed her in the dog cart and began to lead it with careful slowness towards the house, she twisted her head so that she could see her mother's face. Her mother stumbled behind her, looking only at her. Their eyes hardly left each other.

The child was very ill for nearly four months. When she came back down the outside flights of steps again – moving very slowly, and looking around at her mother almost every minute – she had changed. Her hair was brown and dull. She was much taller, and very thin and awkward, and her confident laughter had gone. And so was the place changed. The gravel was bare in places, and weed-grown. Almost all of the outdoor servants had gone when the weather turned clement, in the second draft of assisted passage to America. Everyone knew that the Talbots would be giving out no more tenancies. Most families were not even planting potatoes to lift later in the year. There had been too many years of blight. The estate had kept seed potatoes, stored in the attics of the house itself, where they could not be stolen and eaten. But none of the people around were planting.

Even the child felt the dereliction around.

'Mama! I am cold! I want to go in. I am too big now for my donkey cart . . .' She started to cry.

Later that day, Mrs Talbot came out and stood under the archway at the edge of the muddy stable yard and called for Mullan.

'William Mullan!'

He came down the outside stone stairs from his room above the near stables, his hair wet from the pump.

'Ma'am?' he said.

They were both young and full of health, but there their resemblance ended. His clothes were threadbare, and his second-hand boots were too small for him and painfully run down at the heel, and he was wire-thin. She was much fleshier now and more slow-moving than when she came to Mount Talbot, but her clothes were lavish – she had wrapped a cashmere shawl over a velvet jacket and a sweeping skirt of black silk embroidered with black.

'She knows the donkey is gone. It is gone, is it not?'

'Yes, ma'am. We could not get feed for it, and we could not let it out to graze because it would have been taken.'

He spoke slowly, because even though he had done his learning from the travelling schoolmaster in the English language, and the language of the servants' hall was English, his first language was Irish.

'Tell her you gave it to another child. A small child. And please to get her another donkey.'

'I think Mr Cooper said, ma'am, that the master said, ma'am, that Miss Mab should be riding a pony with a bit of life to him.'

She looked into his face. She was very capable, when it came to protecting Mab. Mullan looked away. He had noticed how the dry pink softness of the outside of her lip became darker where it was wet, on its inner side.

'Perhaps there is no suitable pony available at the moment,' she said. 'Perhaps it would be easiest for Miss Mab if another donkey were to arrive in the stable yard.'

He lifted his head and looked at her. He did not know the exact implications of the way she had placed the words. But he knew by her tone and the way she held her head that she was indicating something. After a moment, he understood.

'There are a couple of old donkeys straying out on the bog that would be grand quiet beasts to have around the place,' he said.

She smiled at him with a full, youthful smile.

'I will tell Mrs Benn to tell her that we gave the other fellow to a small girl like herself,' he said. 'And that a new fellow is coming very soon.'

She thought afterwards, he is quite a young man – I had not realized.

He marvelled at her skin. He had often been close to this lady and to other ladies, helping them in and out of the carriages and cars. But he had never taken note before of a skin not like silk only because it was finer than silk.

The mornings in Marianne's room were seldom happy, now. The winter had been long. Marianne did not turn her husband away during the time that Mab was sick, but he knew she was reluctant. It hardened him towards her: who was she to shrink from him, when he did not yet have a son? And that winter was very cold and wet, and there had been little or no turf cut the previous summer, and the woodmen had gone to America, and no place in the house could be made comfortable. Templeton's place and Castle Strange were in the Incumbered Estates Court, and Richard had to travel twenty miles to get a game of cards. Marianne was getting fat. Richard took a fold of the new flesh on her stomach in his hand one night and pinched it roughly, and asked himself out loud how he could get a son on a pig like this. But in the morning he said something about the wine the night before not being agreeable. There was no single reason for how they slept long into the day now, and woke without much of a greeting to each other.

She liked the smell of some of the trees in the arboretum, and she liked the smell of the pears on the heated wall of the inner orchard, and the smell of the carpentry shop, though there was hardly anything made there now. And the stables – she liked the smell of horses, though she was no horsewoman. She hated the smell of the curtains around their bed.

Richard said, 'I see no reason for you to buy new bed hangings. There is not a penny to waste. It will be many years before this estate recovers what the blight has cost us. Tracy had to make a tour up into Mayo to get men to work in the fields. They will not stay, he says, even for the best of wages. The first ones send them back the fare to America and they up and go . . .'

Even when the shops in the square reopened, half the town of Ballygall was empty. Not boarded up – deserted. Abandoned, simply. Whole laneways and streets, house after house – empty. Out along the roads, there were ghost villages. Sometimes they had been relinquished in anguish when the eviction crew went from house to house knocking the thatch down between the gables. But if the roofs were still on, then the people of that place had simply one morning begun walking along the lanes to the main road, and there had turned towards an embarkation port. With the very old and the infants on a cart pulled by a bony old horse, if they had kept a horse alive. With their possessions on their backs, or pulled along in the wicker creels on poles they brought turf out of the bog with. They walked slowly, and with much stumbling, because the people at that time did not move out when they were well. They believed, for as long as they possibly could, they might escape this fate. They did not start the walk until privation and sickness drove them.

Every human settlement was ravaged. But the landscape looked exactly the same.

If the Talbots had never known how many people lived on their land and had had to believe whatever they were told, it was because this was a landscape into which people could melt. The landlords and the landlords' men could not follow the Irish into the bog, where the settlements of low cabins covered over with sod barely disturbed the rhythm of causeway and hazel copse, grassy clearing and brown pond. Richard Talbot did not know how many people had died on land owned by him. He knew how many had died in the workhouse in Ballygall, because he signed the minutes of the Union. Since it opened in August 1847, until now, May 1849: 8,761 persons. He knew how many of those gave Mount Talbot as their place of dwelling: 3,080. But where the majority of that three thousand had lived before they were admitted to the workhouse – swearing that they were utter paupers – he could not have said.

She had planned to get Richard to allow her to buy the new bed hangings on account. At one time, Hurley's had almost ceased to trade, and most of the other shops around the square were closed. But then an ironmonger from somewhere up north opened a business with a cartful of buckets in an abandoned shed down at the outskirts of town, and his place was full all day not only with customers, but with men anxious to talk to each other and exchange news, as if they were coming out of hiding. Then the ironmonger up in the square reopened. Then Mr Hurley placed the first large order for two years, and soon he sent a dray down to the railway head at Athlone to collect the new merchandise. But by then, Marianne did not care. What was the use? The blankets smelled of turf ash, too. The threadbare velvet drapes at the window. Mab's mattress and bolster. The linen cloths Benn polished the glasses with. Benn's frock coat . . .

William Mullan saw what had gone, because he had seen it when it was there.

One wide lane circled the walls of Mount Talbot, and a path went out from that lane into the bog. It first passed a field with rough wooden railings, where Mullan used to keep the horses ready for saddling when he was waiting to prepare the carriage for old Mr Talbot's excursions. In the spring of 1847 a watchtower was built in the field, and at night the cattle and horses were driven in together, and armed watch was kept on the beasts all night. But within months, there were people so desperate that they were willing to risk being shot, and gangs attacked the field night after night. One morning, at dawn, two of the young O'Connors herded the cattle out and began to drive them east. They never came back, themselves: they took the price of their passages from what the cattle fetched in the mart at Moate, and sent the rest back to Barlow by hand of a Ballygall man. Mullan kept the horses in the stable at all times from then on, and slept beside their stalls, with his shotgun cocked. He kept half their rations of oats in the icehouse on the edge of the lake, where no one would think of scavenging. He cut grass for the stables, himself, with his scythe, to keep the horses in heart.

A half-mile further, there was a gap in the bank beside the path. That was where the shebeen had been. The thatch had fallen in and was rotted black at his feet with new grass growing from it, where a few years before there had been a floor of beaten earth and a wide wooden bench and two bowls for punch, kept in a niche of the hearth. But in 1847, as soon as the days began to get long, Pat had taken what he could carry into the town. His wife's Sunday dress and his own shoes. The battered pewter spirit measure. The very hook it had hung from. Hurley at the drapery shop gave him a guinea for his belongings.

William Mullan had been in the cold shebeen with a few men of the townland that night.

'*Beidh orainn imeacht*,' Pat said when he had every man served. 'Even if we leave the old people. *Beidh orainn éirí as an áit seo!*'

'*Cad é? Cad é?*' The deaf boy sat on the floor with his back against the earth wall and watched their faces.

Pat had pushed his face into the pale face of the boy, and made big, chomping gestures.

'Go! We have to get away from this place!' Pat roared at him. 'We will have nothing to eat! They are taking the houses! They are taking the fields!'

Now, William Mullan rode out there, and stood in the earth-floored room. The thatch had half fallen in, but there was no reason in the world why the shebeen should not be built up again. There was a whole colony of families living now on the common land up along the ridge of the hill, in shelters made of rocks and furze branches and earth. The men up there made poteen, and they drank poteen.

But the fellows that knew all the songs and the stories are gone, William thought to himself. We'd feel the want of them. The likes of the O'Connor boys. There'd be no fun to the drinking . . .

I should go out to America myself, he said to himself. Leave this place be. Get out, with the help of God!

Mullan had been an orphan since he was fifteen. His possessions were very distinct to him. Most of them were the clothes which had been passed to him when he became under-coachman. He kept them hanging from nails in the stall he had made his retreat, in an empty stable wing. He had a cloak and a tall hat, and a greatcoat, and a jacket for the light carriage, and a linen shirt for the times when he brought horses out onto the gravel to show to Mr Talbot. These hung from nails, driven into the wood of his box. He slept there on many nights, in a heap of old blankets. It was said that he had taken four horses from Ballinasloe out to some captain in an army on the Continent, when he was only a boy. He had the neatness of a soldier. When he came across the yard to the kitchen in the morning to get his tea and gruel, he would already have drenched his face and his cropped head. Even in the winter, when the other servants huddled in musty coats, he went about his work in a flannel shirt and breeches. He kept his boots cleaned, broken as they were. On Sunday mornings, Mary Anne Benn left a bowl of hot water for him out on the window sill, and he shaved with his cut-throat razor, lifting his chin high and checking his reflection in the kitchen window as he delicately pulled the blade across each jowl. Then he threw the dirty water across the grassy yard, scattering the hens.

He didn't talk much, but the other Irish took great note of anything he did say. The landlords around did not know, and even the Catholic merchants in the town did not fully grasp, that the Mullans had always been the leading family among the people who lived on the bits of land out in the bog and on the far side of the bog. The Mullan boys had been sent for schooling in every generation. They had been dispossessed – their land granted to the Talbots' predecessor sometime after the battle of Aughrim: William's grandfather had seen the first of the Talbots level it into a sheep run. William had kept a few cattle on a corner of it in recent times, but in the summer of 1847 he had sold them for a pittance. They had been thin, from being bled where they lay in the fields at night, by people too weak to steal them.

Now, he was riding through a landscape that had always looked, to the passer-by, empty of both animals and people. But he had grown up knowing the squatters who lived out there in cabins among the hazel scrub, a potato plot outside each low door. Those people had had little use for the town, and the town had none for them. The men talked all day in the shebeens, and the women talked among themselves in the clearings between cabins, their babies lain on the grass, or tied – for fear they'd fall into the ditches – by long halters of straw, when they began to totter. When William Mullan had ridden past those thin, half naked, smiling people they tipped their heads to him respectfully. They did not belong to anybody. But they looked on themselves as his, even though he had no wealth or power.

They had expected, in the long run, that he would protect them. But when the potatoes failed two years in a row, and the sheriff sent soldiers to guard the men pasting eviction notices on the boards of doors, he could offer them no protection.

All these people were gone. There was hardly a sign of them left.

He had a place out on the bog himself. His mother had lived there, and the cottage still had traces of the dead woman. There had been a garden in front and the eye could still make out where the big old sow she'd kept had worn a depression in the soft ground with her constant rolling on her back. Fruit bushes now gone wild had lined the outer edge of the potato patch. She had even grown beans – thick, round beans that she let grow hard and then podded, and ground into flour – and the plants had bolted and seeded themselves many times, and turned into bushes profuse with white flowers.

The house had not been lived in for years, and the warped door was easily pushed open into the room with its floor of beaten earth. There was no furniture but a bed in a press, with the mattress missing, and a small stool. On a ledge within the fireplace was a bit of mirror. This was famous in the locality, because it was the only such thing out in the bog. The mother's concertina, its sides perished, hung on the wall. The piece of mirror was worth money, but though terrible things had been done by hungry people, nothing had been stolen from the Mullan house.

William went out there to talk to his mother. He had valued her more than any other being. He believed she was in heaven, but also that she was near him, and never nearer than when he went back to the cottage which was still full of her presence.

'You know better than anyone, *A Mbama*,' he said to her in his head, 'that I am not a hasty fellow. Do you remember when Tadhg Colley wanted me to go to America? And I would not chance it? Well, is it not time now to be off? At the demesne, the big house is going to ruin. Since the child got sick, there is hardly a call for coach or car . . . Everything is still wrong! There is no one left, except far up on the hill where they live under the furze!'

He buried his head in his hands. Lolly crept behind him, where he sat on the bench, and pressed her body against his legs.

There was a band of near-savage children, who lived in houses that had been abandoned, in the lanes behind the main square. It was said they killed dogs and ate them. Certainly, they lived on what they could get. They pulled at cabbages, or they had berry-stained mouths. They sometimes had apples to gnaw on, too, in spite of the watch Tracy tried to keep on the Mount Talbot orchards. The Quakers' makeshift kitchen was gone, but three nuns had come from Belgium and were waiting for permission from the bishop to open a place where they might bring children in off the streets. They were learning English phrases and Irish phrases so as to talk to the children. These children did not remember, or would not remember, who their parents had been. Some of them had scars. When the Quakers were first in the town the children had gone into the fire itself and tried to reach over the iron rim of the pot to take a handful of scalding porridge.

The nuns tried to entice the children into their room with bread.

Hurley mentioned to the parish priest that since first the Quakers and then the Belgian nuns had come and were giving out free food, the Catholic shopkeepers were finding themselves left with unsold foodstuffs on their hands.

'They will bring ruin to the people who are the backbone of this town, Father.'

'Then ruin will be universal,' was all the priest said.

Two men from high on the hill came to see William Mullan. They were from families whose cabins in the valley had been tumbled by the men with the battering ram, on foot of eviction orders obtained in the name of Mr Talbot and Lord Coby. They had gone up the hill with their families, almost invisible as they climbed through the tall bracken, and they had made lairs deep in the furze bushes under the summit.

They waited at the end of the yard, sitting against the outside wall of the stable block near the well, where he must pass them when he went for water for the horses, but the house servants would not see them.

'*Bhfuil aon tabac agat?*' they murmured as he crouched to greet them.

'*Fan nóiméad.*'

Mullan went across the yard to the kitchen door.

'Mary Anne, give me down that tin of Tom Tracy's –'

'He'll have your guts.'

'He won't notice two pipefuls.'

The men from the hill sucked deep, with closed eyes.

'Is there food above?' Mullan asked them.

'There is more, now that so many are gone. William, is there e'er a chance of a bit of work? We could sow the seed potatoes that Barlow and Tracy kept for the master. There are houses everywhere we could go into and have them mended in a few days. We could work grand for the master. It is hard on us up on the hill. We have no teacher with us, and the priest that comes up to us has no Irish and the women do not know what he is saying. And there were two dead children after the winter that was in it.'

'We only need a bit of food to start,' one of them said. 'We are quiet people. We could live out there near the lake where the whole lot of them are gone to America.'

'No,' William Mullan said. 'The landlords do not want the likes of you. They are sowing no more potatoes. It is all going to be sheep. There are Scotsmen coming who will live in stone houses and do the work.'

'We would work grand, William.'

They began to whine at him as they did with outsiders.

'Do not think that there will be a better time,' he said, and he heard himself say it, and afterwards he thought that that was the moment when he gave up hope, and turned away from the world he had grown up in. 'Even if you keep your families alive for this year,' he said, 'next year, if you stay here, you will be sent to the different sides of the workhouse in Ballygall. Or you will die like poisoned foxes. *Beidh oraibh dul go Meiriceá!* You *must* go. *Beidh oraibh!*'

Mullan kept falling into an exhausted sleep as he rode home from his mother's place. It was dawn when he came up to the garden gate of Mount Talbot.

He rode past the encampment of the dispossessed that was now almost a settled village. The people had made lean-tos of branches against the walls of the demesne, and covered them with sods. There had been hundreds there at one time. Now, about twenty families were left. He knew most of them. He'd played with the men when they were boys together. He dismounted and picked his way quietly up to the gate. He didn't want anyone crawling out and beginning to pull at him, saying, Do something for us. Do something for us.

Lolly was waiting for him, sitting quietly at the door to the east stable wing. He jumped down to cup her face and smooth her silky ears. Her black eyes looked into his face, unwavering.

'*An raibh tú ag fanacht orm?*' he murmured to her. '*An raibh?*'

The horse clip-clopped ahead of him to its stall. It turned and stood for him, and lowered its head for the bridle to be taken off. The harness was unbuckled, the saddle lifted off. Mullan went into the next stall. He took off his jacket, but he left his boots on. He lay down on his blankets again and blessed himself. Lolly settled into the straw beside him, watching him over her long nose.

He asked God and Mary to watch over him in the night, as he had done every single night since his mother taught him his prayers. And he added the phrase he said often now, and that he and the other men had said when things were very bad, and the priest couldn't come out, and they had had to open the pit in the top field to push in more bodies.

And may perpetual light shine upon them. *Et requiescant in pace.* Amen.

Sometimes a clamour rose from the people camped against the walls so loud that it was audible inside the big house.

Marianne did not draw back the heavy brocade curtains over her drawing room windows. But even through them she could hear, when the low noise of pleading and begging swelled to shrieking.

Ocras! Ocras! she heard them shout, and she knew that meant they wanted food.

'It is a most curious fact,' she had heard Mr McClelland the vicar say to her husband once, 'that when their faces become altogether cadaverous, and they are near death, a fine down comes on the skin of their faces. Like the down on gooseberries.'

That was the summer of the worst evictions. The land was being cleared. There were young Protestant men in Scotland, it was said, who knew the most modern methods of farming, only waiting to come to the west of Ireland to start.

The evicted people would stay around the ruins of their houses for a while, trying to build up a corner for shelter, or to make a fire within, at least, the walls of the home. But eventually, they had to go. It was not just that the home made of mud or rough stones and sod would have been destroyed; whatever the family had managed to keep through the bad years of crops or animals would have been taken by the bailiffs for rent arrears.

They howled and screamed when the hired men rode out from the sheriff's office at the court and nailed a notice of eviction to their doors.

'This is the land of our nativity! We cannot go from it!' That was written in a letter to Richard Talbot by an elderly man who was camped with his old wife and their children and grandchildren on the square. Everyone around knew of the letter, and they waited for an answer to it, but none came.

Band after band of dispossessed people walked into the square, silently, before it was light, the women carrying whatever bowls or pots the family still owned. They walked down the hill through the sleeping town, without – as Hurley remarked to the ironmonger next door, when they were opening the shops and hanging their goods outside with long poles – a word of farewell.

William Mullan had grown up on the slopes behind the bog that were as busy and populous as a street. By the autumn of 1849 there was not one single family left in his townland.

Nothing moves, he said to himself one day, but the wind across the grass.

In his mind, he had already gone. The old world was finished. He would have to start anew.

But the way things were changing around them was not the start of it. Neither of the lovers knew what did start it.

They were in the tack room – the first room to the left of the main door into the stables, and she had just said something, and his

168

eyes had been cast down, as a servant's should be, but he was furtively looking at her mouth as it moved and at how it revealed a secret, juicy inside. She wanted a saddle mended – Mab's miniature red leather saddle, that Richard had had made for her by a craftsman in Galway, when Mab was only three. Marianne had thought of it as she lay in bed that morning – that if it was still about, it could be mended and cleaned, and it would be a lovely thing to keep from those happy days. She could have sent for anyone from the stables, of course, but she had the thought that Mullan would be the one to understand best what she wanted done. So, when Richard had been driven into town by Cooper she went across into the yard and in the door of the big stable and up to the threshold of the tack room. Her soft boots made no noise at all, and he did not know she was there until, sensing something, he turned around, and saw her standing not twelve inches from him, silently, the dim stalls stretching away behind her. She said something, and without the slightest premeditation his ungloved hand, almost of its own volition, lifted, and delicately touched her mouth. She gasped. But she did not recoil. And without fear or daring, but as in a trance, he, who had been little more to her than one of the human presences in the place, dropped his hand and delicately sketched the curve of her, in at her waist, out again at her hip. Barely touching her black coat. Transfixing them both. Under the thick cloth of the redingote her skin, where he delineated it, felt as if a magnet had been passed over it. She looked at him as if looking would save her from drowning. He was standing in front of her with his eyes half closed. She saw the bristles on his unshaven cheeks and the texture of his wind-roughened skin. Then his eyes opened and they looked, fully, at each other. She turned and walked slowly back to the big house.

She waited for him, after that, all day. She walked now, restlessly, where she had never cared to go before – along the back corridors of the house, across the half-empty farmyards, through the tangled trees in the overgrown arboretum, along the mossy paths of the orchard, and wherever she went, she watched for him.

She thought she could hear time passing.

But its passing did not soothe the ache that possessed her. She waited. There was nothing else to do but wait. She never doubted that what she was waiting for would happen, although she did not know what it would be.

9

I stood at the table and looked down at the keyboard.

I would leave my lovers there, before they hurt or were hurt.

Every present contains its past. I had given Marianne and Mullan fragments of a past, though the *Judgment* did not. My own past had sometimes pounced on me from nowhere and ripped me open. I heard the gondola song once, on the radio of a taxi, in Edinburgh. *Komm in die Gondol* . . . Fritz Wunderlich, the announcer said, from the operetta 'One Night in Venice'. And it was on another spring morning, too, like the morning my father and I went mushrooming, though not as perfectly high and blue as that long-ago one. He had been dead a year or two and I listened to the tenor sing the lilting song – the song of a man's fine expansiveness and exuberance – in a way. I could not go on. I got out of the taxi and climbed, half blind, up to the Gardens on top of Castle Hill, and I waited on a bench for the turbulence of pity and regret to die down. Such wilfully stunted lives, the lives of respectable Irishmen of my father's generation! I was terrified that I was as unloving as he, and that the only reason I hadn't done as much harm was because there was no one dependent on me, as we had been on him.

But even if I was unloving, I wasn't heartless. My heart was still sore from the loss of Jimmy. Would I have told Jimmy about Shay? I wondered. Hardly. Not in recent years, anyway. The bastard walked out on you! he'd have said. Jimmy would approve of me for writing a story about two people with a passion that burned its way through convention, but we'd probably argue about the Talbot affair, too. I could nearly bet that he'd brood about Richard Talbot and his ignorance, or silence. Maybe Richard Talbot was gay? he might have said, and I'd have said, For crying out loud, Jimbo, do you have to find gays everywhere? and he'd have said, They – we – are and were everywhere, and then we would have had our long-running debate about whether you can be called gay if you don't know you are gay. The only time we ever had a bitter falling-out was when Jimmy once speculated about Alex's possible homosexuality. That is what a vulgar, reductionist American, on the run from problems far worse than any Alex has, *would* think, I began. He never brought up that theory again.

I tried to track Alex down while I made the last bit of the wedding salmon from Bertie's into a sandwich. There was just an answering machine at his numbers, and there was no answer at all from our office. The bread was stale, I noticed. How long had I had it? What day was this? Friday I'd left Ballygall. Saturday I met Shay on the ferry. Sunday he disappeared, and I began writing the story. There had been a few times, since then, that I threw myself into the bed for a few hours' sleep. But I stayed at it, until I had written it out of me.

Alex should be in the office. It was unheard of for him not to be there.

The phone rang – maybe Shay – but it was Alex, sounding so exhausted that I forgot the leap of hope.

I got your number from the hotel I thought you were staying at, Kathleen, Alex said. It took for ever for someone to answer, and the background noise was terrible. I wanted to tell you that I'll be away from the office for a while. Just in case . . . But anyway, I won't keep you. I haven't been to bed yet. My mother is very, very poorly. The poor old lady is fading away because she says an angel told her not to eat, so the doctor is trying to get her into a geriatric ward. It might be quite a way out of London, so I'll take some kind of lodging nearby, and go in and look after her.

Are *you* eating? I said. What about looking after yourself?

I'm fine, he whispered.

I don't think you are, boss dear, I said.

Betty's going to look after things, and keep people informed, till I'm back. She's got a file of all the *TravelWrite* stuff that's ready to go.

Leave your new number with her, Alex, I said. And I'll leave mine if I move around. Don't get out of touch!

When have I ever been out of touch with you, Kathleen? he said. I wouldn't be happy myself if I was. I only hope you're doing better over there than I am here.

I said, I'm doing wonderfully well, Alex!

I heard my own words, which were meant to save him from wasting any of his energy on me. But – I *am* doing well in a strange way, aren't I? I thought. Nothing is happening as I meant it to happen, but still . . .

I must go, he said. Please, will you pray for my mother and me?

Me pray for *you*? I said lightly as I hung up. But I'd gone a bit pink. I liked him asking me.

I did pray for them. I walked around the room slowly and said an Our Father, a Hail Mary and a Glory Be. Then I didn't know what to do. I'd have to face Mrs PJ if I went up to the shop. Though – did I care? Compared to the shame that went through me every time I thought about Shay quietly putting his bag into his car while I lapsed back into sleep with bliss on my face? His letter didn't help much. It was like something an old-style patriarch would do – making up his mind by himself to creep out on me. Why not talk to me, like a modern person, and let me be an equal in making the decision? Though, I'd liked him for exactly that – for being old-fashioned. I would have said, *Stay!* if he'd asked my advice. No matter how it threatens whatever your life is – *stay!* He must have known that was how I would be.

I wandered restlessly down to the shore, and I would have started to tramp along the edge of the fields, but that I was stopped by the sight of the seals. Down below me, they were, on rocks the tide already lapped – a big thick-necked bull seal, and a sleek grey mother seal turning her head and her obsidian eyes from her mate, to the baby seal on its rock beside her, then back to her mate. The bull seal lay heavy and at ease on his side, like Shay had done. Solid male protecting presences, the two of them. And this big seal moved his supple torso slowly this way and that so that through his skin I felt what I had not felt for myself – the warmth of the morning sun of this day. Tears sprang to my eyes at the wonder of seeing the seals, and at the pathos of the three of them against the backdrop of the huge ocean. And it was as if the tears cleaned my eyes: after that I saw everything – the chain-mail sparkle of the small waves of the bay, and the flush of delicate new leaves on the thorn hedge of the lane. And the clear light that moulded the old fields like a loving hand stroking them – fields that were turquoise up at the top of the hill and deepened into jade green in their sweep down to the glittering bay.

I walked back up the field towards the cottage. The white walls had greyed, and spatters of mud had been flung across them in winter storms but it stood as if indestructible.

I halted, on the grass, near the ragged gorse bushes.

I knew why the seals made me want to cry.

Because they were a family group.

I practised a light tone for the call. Hi, Annie! That you, Annie? Guess who, Annie? Then I remembered that I'd left them the message about Jimmy. I couldn't be that perky, with my dearest friend dead. I sat for a minute in the armchair and closed my eyes and tried to calm down and find some truthfulness in myself. Then I made the call.

Hello? Hello, *Annie*? Hello, this is Kathleen.

Oh, Kathleen – we were hoping you'd ring. We got your message. We were so sorry – such a lovely man and such a good friend to you.

I know, I know. But will we talk about that again? I said. There's the rest of our lives, isn't there, to mourn? Listen, how are you fixed for receiving a visitor? I think I can get a day or two away from this bit of work.

Oh, that's *wonderful*! Annie cried. A bit of glamour in our lives at last! That's terrific news. When will you be here? Wait'll Lilian hears!

Have to go! I cut across her. Not my phone. See you tonight or tomorrow!

I'd left the arrangements open, by instinct. All the time I was tidying up the cottage I worried about it. The times I'd met the pair of them in London, over the last twenty-five years, I always had to brace myself for their scrutiny. Still no sign of a boyfriend for

Kathleen. Did you notice she wears reading glasses now? A gold Visa card, she used . . . They and Nora were the only people who could compare what I was now with what I had been. It wasn't at all hostile, the close way they looked at me. But it was judgemental. There was no way they could avoid judging me. And this time – I'd be on their territory. I wouldn't be able to look at my watch after an hour and say, sorry, but I'm going to have to fly. And who knows what they'd say about me afterwards? She's beginning to look her age, our Kathleen . . . Devoted couples like Danny and Annie – they never tell anyone but each other what they really think.

I stripped the bed and made it up quickly with fresh stuff from the cupboard. Then I put the tea and sugar into the empty fridge. I wrapped the plastic bag in another bag and put it in the bin outside the door and weighed the lid down with a stone. I brushed my teeth and collected my bathroom things and packed my weekend bag.

I left the laptop behind. I also turned the armchair beside the dead fireplace to face the door. For the first time in days, I'd thought about clothes. The suit and skirt and dress I'd brought from London were completely irrelevant to my Irish life, and I'd never worn my beautiful Manolo high heels. Now, I propped them on the armchair. If Shay came back, he'd know by them that I was still around. And there'd be no note for PJ to read . . .

Then I drove away, leaving the door unlocked. If that was found out, I'd say I forgot.

I slowed at the top of the hill and looked in the mirror at the great empty sweep of the bay. A corner, and it was gone.

I've hurt myself in my life, I thought, by leaving a thousand beautiful places.

I had never before made my way out of the west of Ireland towards the east – as if I were heading for the east-coast ports in the company of ghostly forebears. The people who had to emigrate from this place – they can never have found its like again. A west-facing hillside and an ocean coming in to rest below it, and fluent songs of robin and thrush and blackbird. The grass can never have been, anywhere else, as vivid a green as this. Perhaps, I thought, that was why the Irish who went to America stayed in the cities. It wasn't just that the land had betrayed them, and rotted their food before they could eat it. It was that there was to be no attempt at a second love.

I'm not a typical Irish emigrant, I said to Jimmy early in our relationship, but I was driven out of the country by pain.

Afterwards he used to say sometimes, You have to go back, Kath, before you can go on.

That's an obscure remark, I said to him once, and it's not made any less obscure by the soulful tone you say it in.

I'm an American, he said. We love these little spiritual sayings.

We went to *ET* together – starting to cry about one minute into the film because there was a rabbit lost in woods, and then crying at ET's wise little face, and then crying more because the blonde mother was all on her own, and then practically breaking down when the chrysanthemum plant revived, and the child had come back from the dead. The kids behind us were climbing all over the seats and shouting at their friends and paying no attention to the screen, while the two of us got more and more emotional. We meant it, too. Phoone hoome, Jimmy used to say to me from then on in his ET voice. And every six months or so I would phone Danny and Annie. There was no reason not to; nothing was wrong.

When I was fifty or so miles inland, I got a burger and a coffee and ate, hunkered down in the sun with my back against an old wall. Maybe this place was an inn, once. At this crossroads, straggling groups from all over the west would have merged. There would have been dancing and drink and music, as well as mourning and heartbreak. I left home headlong, cursing this rotten Ireland, dying to get out. How many of them were exactly the same?

I stood up. Another ninety miles to Kilcrennan. I went over to the garage shop and bought a cut-price Sinatra tape I'd seen, and got into the car. But it didn't get me through. I thought I'd be caught up by the authority of the dry voice, the precise diction, the divine phrasing – that I'd be made to forget myself. It usually worked. But these were amateur recordings of early radio concerts, and they made even Sinatra sound commonplace. As if Sinatra were in the conspiracy to make me remember . . .

I had to face it. I was going home. Well, I was going to the locality of home. For all I knew, my actual home – the cottage on Shore Road – wasn't there any more. How would I prepare myself? I picked over my memories . . . Yes! I had one very good one . . . Well, it wasn't as good as the mushroom morning, or as good as going to Dublin with Mammy when I won the essay competition. But it had more people in it. Nora was gone to the States, but everyone else was there. Both Ma and Da were at the table, which was unusual in itself. Annie was there in her capacity as Danny's steady girlfriend though she was only thirteen or fourteen – not that anyone had invited her, but she had nerves of steel where Danny was concerned, and she'd made herself a part of the household. My father was much more pleasant to her than to Danny.

And Ned was there – specially for me, because this was the Sunday I was leaving home to go up to Dublin to Trinity College. Nobody had ever formally left home before, because Nora disappeared with only what she had hidden in her schoolbag.

Maybe that's why they made an effort for me.

Mammy didn't try to light the range on Sundays – she cooked the meal on the bottled-gas stove. The day I left home she left the bacon bubbling when they went down to the pub, and myself and Annie washed the potatoes and put them on when the football match started on the radio. My mother came home by herself a bit early. She'd bought a tin of peas and a tin of carrots in the shop for the special occasion.

And I don't think my father meant to start getting at her. I mentioned myself that I was getting a room in Templeogue.

Teampall Mealóig! my father intoned. *Mealóig* – belonging to St Mallock. And it was where his church – his temple – was situated, hence, *teampall*!

He pushed his big lips out and rolled the ll's as if his tongue were stuck to something gorgeous. This was one of the most boring things about him, I thought, not for the first time. If the name of any place gets mentioned he puts it back from English into Irish, and then starts telling all and sundry what the Irish words mean.

The number 49 bus from O'Connell Street. Am I right or am I wrong, Eileen?

That's right, she murmured.

Sean was sitting in the high chair behind her, making an awful noise. Mammy had given him a boiled potato in milk on a saucer, and he was trying to make it jump in the air. I remembered that now. He was such a funny little kid. Some blood thing, Danny said, when he phoned me at *The English Traveller*. He just faded away. But did the child let himself die?

Templeogue was where your mother lived, Daddy picked up again. You might ask around, Cait, and see whether any of your relations on your mother's side are interested in knowing anyone by the name of de Búrca.

We didn't know what he was getting at when he mentioned her family.

He must have had to marry her, Nora said to me once. The wedding certificate in the cardboard box under their bed said January, and Nora's birthday was in July. The certificate said 'clerical assistant' for Daddy's occupation, and 'shop worker' for Mammy's.

I don't know how she ever kept a job in a shop, Nora had said. She doesn't know what day it is as long as I've known her.

She had to marry him, too, I said. Don't forget that.

If this had been an ordinary Sunday Ma would have gone into her room at him jibing at her, and he'd have been satisfied with himself, and poured a drop of whisky into the mug of tea he had with his meal and given us whatever lecture on politics came into his head. But Mammy wouldn't be hunted out on this day. Actually, he was only trying to annoy her from habit. He was in a nice mood.

She said, Will you write to us, Kathleen?

I will, I said. And then, because I might as well say it, anyway, And you could come to Dublin and see me.

Don't wear Mrs Bates's suit on the bus, she said. You'll get it all creased.

The suit had been a present for winning the scholarship. It had been Mrs Bates's sister's in Boston. Mammy said the buttons on the jacket alone were worth a fortune.

It'll get creased in the bag, too, I said.

Daddy said, I'll go down to Mr Bates and get a few sheets of brown paper to wrap it in. When I was in the FCA I kept the spare shirt in brown paper and it was often remarked that my shirts were pristine. Danny! What does FCA stand for? Quick!

Fórsa Cosanta Áitiúil, I said, ruining his little game. Do you know, Daddy, if I was a man, I'd love to be in that, too. Go on courses and learn drill and how to fire guns . . .

He looked at me suspiciously, but he went off down to Bates's. He never did things like go to the shop. It made me take the whole going away more seriously.

My mother came after me into the bedroom and watched me put the parcel of the suit, my school jumpers, my pyjamas and my signed photo of the Beatles into the bag.

I have a little present for you, she said. For being such a great girl, Kath. And for getting yourself into Trinity College.

It was in a shiny black cardboard box with the name of the jeweller's in Kilcrennan town stamped on it in gold. The box was lined with white satin. On a little puff of cotton wool lay a thin necklace of crystals. I looked up at her, and she was looking at me, her mouth just straightening at the corners – ready to smile at my smile. But it was like a knife in my heart to picture her pushing open the door of the jeweller's shop and going in carrying her big handbag, that was almost always empty because she had no money of her own.

Oh, Ma . . . I could have cried.

Don't get into trouble! my mother cut across me. She was standing in the bedroom and the light from the window was full on her face. Kathleen, whatever you do, mind yourself! Don't get into trouble whatever you do!

Which might have meant, Don't get pregnant, in which case it was about herself. Or it might have meant, You are a reckless person and you could ruin your life by being too casual about danger. In which case it was about me.

The parents didn't come down the road to where the bus turned around above the shore. Danny and Annie saw me off, and Sean, staggering around like a little drunk, until Uncle Ned gave him a piggyback. Bye, Attly! Bye, Attly! My mother and father watched from the window of their bedroom. The chain that crossed his waistcoat gleamed, and her face was a pale patch behind his shoulder.

Of course, suits were gone out: I knew when I took the parcel. I always wore my old jumpers and a miniskirt in Dublin.

I lost the necklace, within a week of getting it. I'd never had anything like it and I wore it all the time and I never even noticed when the chain must have parted.

I did hang on to Mrs Bates's suit. While I was at Trinity, my friends had a landlady who let them keep their things in the basement in the holidays. I used to bring my cardboard box to store it there, and every time, on top of the books and LPs, I'd see the brown parcel with the suit in it. My mother died. When I ran off to London I didn't stop to bring anything, so I didn't bring the suit. If I had brought it, it would have gone into the bin when I heard she was dead. When I was certain she was dead.

I told Jimmy all that about that last meal, once. He looked at me very seriously and said, Did I hear you say that that was one of your *best* memories?

Well, I said after a minute, I see what you mean. But in reality it was a lovely occasion. Maybe I haven't explained it right. But everyone was there – that was one of the good things. And there was no fighting at all. And Mammy gave me a present. And, you see, I took to being a student like a duck to water and I had a great time and I had two or three jobs and I didn't bother going back home – not even at Christmas. I never went back in the nearly two years before she got sick. So her words that day were the last she ever said to me.

Now I wished I'd had a chance to tell Shay about that day. He would understand a few little nuances that Jimmy didn't. The treat that tinned vegetables were. How unusual a thing it was for a father to go to the shop for brown paper for a daughter. And I bet Shay never got a special meal in his house for himself, unless his mother and father gave him birthday parties. And there was no badness at all – Daddy didn't even want the crack about Mammy's family to start anything. And Annie held Danny's hand defiantly when we were going down to the bus stop, though Daddy could see them. And Sean chuckled like a little elf, up there on Uncle Ned's shoulders, and clutched that patient man's eyes with his plump, grubby hands when the breeze off the shore made him sway.

My stomach began to hurt as I got nearer Kilcrennan. It really might have been a better idea to stay away – maybe come home another time. Not that this was at all like the place I remembered. There were suburbs on the western side of town that I'd certainly never seen before and yet the trees in front of the semi-detached houses were mature. I drove towards the centre as slowly as possible. I wasn't feeling well at all. I could easily go on to the bridge beside the hospital and turn right for Dublin. Ah – a hotel. New. The Shamrock Manor. I drove in and checked that they had a night porter in case I came in late, and I paid in advance for a room for the night. I washed my face and combed my hair as well as I could and pinned it back very, very carefully and put on a dab of pink lipstick and a hint of mascara. Annie thought I was glamorous, after all. I put on earrings. I had a suede blouson to slip on over my jeans and sweater. I hoisted up my bra straps to give myself a better line.

An only life, I muttered to myself, *can take so long to climb*
Clear of its wrong beginnings, and may never . . .
I often used poetry to keep harm away.

All the time, I kept glancing at the phone. I could cancel without the slightest problem. It would never occur to Annie that I'd be lying to her. Then I put all my things back in my bag. I wouldn't necessarily mention the room to anyone, but I'd have it in reserve in case anything went wrong.

I drove down the hill past the station – the hill where I'd stayed in the B&B when I came back from college to see Mammy when she was in hospital. And then, with everything inside me trembling from shocks of remembrance, I parked the car on a bit of waste ground, and I went down an alley that I knew well from my teenage prowls with Sharon, out onto High Street, and turned right. There was no one behind the counter of the dry-cleaning shop, but through a rack of garments I could see my sister-in-law sitting at a table, mending something.

Annie! I called softly.

Without saying my name or any other word she hurried towards me, and we held each other for much longer than we ever had before. We were like survivors, finding each other after a disaster. Partly, she was telling me how much she sympathized about losing Jimmy. But she was also saying that this was not just a greeting, but a welcome home after half a lifetime. I didn't really know how to touch people, except as part of sex. With Nora, my greetings were bony, wary. But this once I was able to be natural. I held Annie as tightly as she held me. I know goodness. Annie is good.

Hi, sweetheart! I said nonchalantly.

Hi globe-trotter! she said. You look great in jeans. It's twenty years since I got into a pair of jeans.

See your ears, Annie? I said. Models have operations to get ears that sit into their head like yours.

Then I saw that little Lilian in her convent uniform had slipped into the shop and was standing with her school bag in her hands, gazing up, rapt, at the two of us. She put down the bag and absently felt her own ears.

Don't forget to tell your daddy, Annie said to her, that your mammy has beautiful ears. Auntie Kathleen says so. Now – a cup of tea? Are you going out to the house to see Dan? He knows you might come today. Lilian does her homework here, and then we'll be out after you around six.

Lilian was too shy to speak at first. She stood half hidden behind Annie – a plumper Annie than when last I'd seen her, and an Annie with grey hair instead of hair with a touch of grey. I did not want to speak myself. The little girl's hair sprang back from the perfect oval of her forehead in a certain way, which was exactly her father's way, which in turn was exactly the same as on our mother. I don't know how often in childhood I had looked at the way that curve of hair went back from Mammy's face and thought it was like what you'd see on a film star.

I'm your god-daughter, Lilian suddenly darted her head forward and said. I'm nearly nine.

Then she blushed and went back in behind her mother.

A couple of customers came into the shop.

Miss Lilian and I will go and get something nice to have with the cup of tea. Then I'll go out to your place to see Danny. Is that an okay plan? And will you show me what shop to go to? I said to the child.

She looked back at her mother, but she took my hand and led me out to the street. I stood there delighted at how little it had changed from when I was at school in the convent. It was a narrow street lined with small old shops that were the front rooms of houses, that you went into through street doors with knockers. They had curtained-off kitchens behind, and women ran out to serve the customers between feeding meals to their families. Traffic barely crawled along, and people strolled in and out between the cars.

Do you want to hear a joke? I said to Lil, because I could feel her tension. What did the bra say to the hat? Do you give up?

No answer. But she held my hand more firmly. I guided her across the street. The palm of my hand tingled with the detail of her – the satin of her hair, the knob of her shoulder, the shoulder blades like the beginnings of wings.

What did it say? she breathed.

What?

The bra to the hat?

Oh. You go on ahead and I'll give these two a lift.

The old woman in the shop shuffled down behind the counter.

This is my auntie home from England! Lil announced. Her voice was suddenly strong and her tone proprietary.

The woman peered at us from between the sweet jars.

Sure I know that, she said to the child. I was having a good look at her, standing over there. I thought she was a stranger first but then I caught on.

She turned to me. Your mother was a handsome woman, too, of course, Lord have mercy on her . . . She used to come in here for a few sweets when she came into town to the library. I never saw the like of her smile.

Where is she now? Lilian interrupted.

She's flying around with the angels, the old woman said. You can't see her but she can see you. She's watching you to see are you a good girl.

She's a very good girl, Missus, I said. So could you let her pick out a few nice cakes there?

After our expedition, Lilian never stopped chattering, even when no one was listening to her.

I grew up four miles from Kilcrennan, where Shore Road ended at the sea. Halfway there, the road from the town went through a stand of beech trees. That's where the old place was, the family farm, where Uncle Ned had lived, and Danny and Annie and Lil lived now.

I tucked the car onto the grass verge, and got out under the beautiful, still near-naked trees. I envied Danny and Annie that they had finally got to live here. I had envied Uncle Ned in his day. When I was growing up in Shore Road our house was ordinary and this place was its magical opposite. The massive, smooth-trunked trees, elephant grey, flanked the road, and the ditch was lined with mossy boulders. Tissuey beech leaves were still folded close and scaly along the filigree of branches, but today's sun would open them. The day I bumped into Uncle Ned in the car park, after the school history pageant, when I was still barefoot and carrying a bucket of potatoes from being in the Year of the Big Hunger tableau, it was these beeches he was worrying about. Katey, he'd said, you know that stand of beech trees at the bottom of the three-acre field? Well, those are fine trees and many a one stops to admire them. But those are the old landlord's trees. The old Cooper-Bellews. The Cooper-Bellews weren't the worst, and they paid the fare to America for a good few they evicted off their land. But still . . .

My feet in trainers made no noise on the soft earth of the lane. I walked up the hill between high thorn hedges, barely dabbed with colour where young leaves had begun to open out on the old briars. Celandine glowed dark yellow and glossy green in the ditch. The blackthorn was almost at the end of its foaming blossoming, but I could smell its sweetness still. At the bottom of the next field there was a stretch of the silver of a spring flood, and there were two swans on the water. The air was lively with the baa-ing of lambs, but Danny must have heard the car stopping a hundred yards away. He was leaning on the gate between the ramparts of evergreen hedge that hid the cottage, exactly as Uncle Ned used to lean. He had on a crumpled white shirt, and he'd combed back the hair that sprang from his high forehead. He had a round face dominated by my mother's eyes, limpid in him where they had been clouded in her. I wasn't shocked; I had become accustomed to the ghost of her that walked into the pub in London, when he met me for a drink the times he came over to soccer matches. His mouth had a downward curve but smiling completely transformed it.

I seemed to have seen his smile before. Would it have been in my own mirror?

You've a lot more hair than I thought you'd have, I said.

So have you, he said. You have more hair than most people. Annie says she and Lil will be home round six.

No problem! I have the spuds peeled. My time's my own . . .

The place looks just the same!

It is the same. Annie is slave labour in that cleaner's and we've never had the money to change it.

But do you not have a job? I said.

He'd had a job in maintenance in the computer factory but he'd given it up, he told me when we went inside. I looked closely into his face while he talked. His nose was bigger than I remembered. Bulbous, even. But his eyes were as clear as ever. I could remember them looking out of his fat baby face.

A few of the lads are musicians like myself, he was saying, and if we were playing at a wedding or that, we wouldn't be able to go into work. So I jacked the job in. It didn't pay much after tax, anyway. And I wanted to try selective breeding.

What's that?

You buy pedigree stock in. Then you sell on the young.

Sounds great.

Oh, it is! he said. There's great money in it. I'm raising the capital at the moment. Annie's getting tired of being on her feet all day in that oul shop, and sure her car nearly takes what she earns. But we're a bit stuck at the moment till I get my scheme up and running.

He made tea.

At last, I felt able to look around. I was sitting beside the little square table, under the shelf that held the radio, the Sacred Heart and its red lamp, and the big tin clock. There were biscuits ready on a tray, and the good cups. Flowered ones. That's what my uncle would have done for a guest, too.

The feel of the oilskin on the table under my fingers brought happiness back in a flood.

Are these Uncle Ned's things? I asked. How could they be?

Daddy used to come out here and just mess around the house, Danny said, because the land was let in his day. He never changed anything. And we've left the place much the same. Anyway, the shops in town that farmers like me go to, they're the same as they always were. The design of things is the same as in Ned's time. Sure, they were all made in China anyway.

I realized with a start that a thing I thought was a cushion on the chair beside the range was an enormous cat.

Annie's, said Danny, following my look. Furriskey by name. The laziest, greediest cat in Ireland. Cat – *amach leat*! Lil says he understands Irish. The stepmother wouldn't let the old man say anything in Irish, did you know that? She said it put people off her nursing home. He used to speak Irish to me when her back was turned but I could hardly understand him.

I didn't understand him anyway, I said.

Fair enough, he said, vaguely. But he was glad I was playing the old music, the da was. I played at his funeral. It was packed.

I'm out of date, I thought to myself, almost panicking. I thought Danny and he were enemies . . .

We sat and drank our tea. The range was a new, oil-fired one, but it squatted where the old one had been, with the dishcloth airing on it in the same place. The lino on the floor was the same kind of lino. The home-made wooden bench I was sitting on I'd sat on as a little girl. It had seemed to me when I was a child that there was an invisible point of peace in the middle of this room, and that everything in the room bent in towards that peace. The new things made no difference to that sense of being in a benign space.

Danny got a dusty pair of rubber boots from under the stairs for me and we went out to look at the fields. He held the first gate open for me.

You look like you're showing off the country fashions, he said. I never thought that anyone belonging to the Burkes would look like that.

Well, there you are, I said – limply, because I was still feeling the impact of the word he'd used. Belonging.

A few cattle came towards us, ponderous and swaying.

What long eyelashes they have! I said.

We don't talk much about their eyelashes around here, he said, laughing at me.

He took a long time to untwist the bits of wire, or unknot the lengths of baler twine that held his gates together. It wasn't picturesque, the farm. The fields were rutted and thistled. But still, the new foliage on the untidy hawthorn hedges shone emerald green and the air was wonderfully fresh and light.

You must be very grateful to the old man for leaving the place to you.

He didn't leave it to me, Danny said. He left it to the stepmother. She put it up for auction.

I thought it was the family place! I said. I thought it kind of had to go from man to man. Isn't that why Ned left it to Da? And how did you buy it, anyway? Is it not worth a lot of money to a builder?

We were picking our way back across the trampled muddy laneway where his cattle came for feed.

I got it at a very fair price, Danny said. There were no other bidders at the auction. They all know around here that this is the Burkes' place. It was always the Burkes' place. Before the Famine, even, it was in our family.

A lady – a librarian – who knows a lot about the Famine pointed out to me recently that if we're here at all, we survived the Famine.

It's obvious, when you come to think about it but who ever thinks about it? Have you any idea what the Burkes did, to survive?

I haven't a clue, Danny said. Maybe Lil'll do the Famine in school, but until then I know as much about it as that gatepost there.

I'll take you out to Shore Road, he said.

We drove towards the sea. We rattled and whined down the hill in his ancient mud-spattered Ford, past Bates's shop and the pub, and along the row of cottages facing the shingle bank where the river spread out into the incoming waves. I got myself ready, and then gathered my courage and glanced at the end cottage. There was nothing to see. Whoever lived there now wasn't like us. There were flowering plants in both the windows, and white blinds, and a glass porch had been built on to the front door.

Half the hill behind the cottages was striped with new houses in geometric ranks. The other half looked for a moment as if it were covered in litter. Then I realized that those were graves – that the old enclosure there had been behind the church had spread up the hill.

She's up there, Danny said. Somewhere in the first row, I believe. Sean's in Kilcrennan – they've a special children's bit in the big graveyard. And the oul fella is buried up there, too.

You're not serious! In the same grave as Mammy?

Oh, yes. In Ireland you'd never be buried with the second wife.

And where's Ned?

Ned is out near our place. They opened the old graveyard specially for him because he was a hero in the Small Farmers.

We'll leave it, I said. We won't bother going up there.

I walked a few steps to the end of the road. I closed my eyes and listened to the sound I knew like my own breathing – the river's near, shallow rippling, and the distant chop of the small waves further down the beach. There was an asphalt car park where the thick, green turf and the bunker-like holes of cold sand used to be.

We'll go back, I said to Danny when I walked back to the car. I'll look for her grave some other time.

So he turned the car around. There was a jumble of cassettes on the floor of the car, and his face smiled up at me from one of them.

Danny Burke! I read out. *Tin Whistle Treasures*. Well, well, well!

Did I not send it to you? he said modestly.

I slipped it into the tape deck and turned the volume to high and we climbed up Shore Road with the broken exhaust puttering and a jig tune pouring out behind us, and the two of us laughed with a slight hysterical edge like kids who have just got away with something.

That evening I sat at the table in the little kitchen in the familiar smell of boiling bacon, and helped Annie with the Brussels sprouts.

We had got as far as Sharon in our round-up of Kilcrennan gossip.

She's as rich as Croesus, Annie said. Her and the husband. They go round to the chain of discos they own in their matching BMWs and collect the box-office money personally. They have a place in Florida. Two swimming pools. You should see the tan on her. And she's enormous! Annie threw her head back and laughed. I'm not exactly petite myself!

I looked at my sister-in-law. Her face was a girl's, except for a few deep nicks between the brows.

You look so young, Annie! I said.

Why wouldn't I? Annie said. Haven't I had a great life, thanks be to God? Like – for Him to send us Lilian, after we'd waited so long! I've been blessed so I have, in every way. But I put a fierce lot of weight on with the HRT. Did you have any trouble with the change of life, Kathleen?

I don't think I'm having it yet, I said. I haven't dried up, anyway. But things are happening. My ankles swelled up on a bad flight, and they never really went down. And I'm getting big brown spots on the skin of my body. I don't think they're any harm. I think they're just age.

How are you getting over poor Jimmy?

The shock of hearing someone say his name! For it actually to hang on the air . . . She went out to the scullery to give me a minute to myself.

You didn't bump into your stepmother down the town, did you?

she said brightly, coming back in with cooking apples to peel. You wouldn't know her, but she'd know you – she's not that much older than you and you always stood out, with the hair and all, and being so wild. Kathy Bates they call her around here. You know? That Stephen King one where she won't let the fella get out of the bed? There's a rumour going around that she was cruel to your da – that she made him go to bed after his tea.

At least she didn't have seven or eight children for him, if you count the ones that died, I said. Like my poor mother.

Sure she was a trained nurse, Annie said. If she didn't know how to mind herself, who would? Your da got very popular – did you know that? He used to run an Irish class and it was mobbed. He used to call in to me in the shop on the way back from it. Half of Sinn Féin was in it but so were lots of different people from the town. I was sorry for him, going home to that one. He was well punished for marrying again.

She paused and then she said, And how about yourself? A catch like you? And such lovely clothes! I wouldn't like to think you have nobody, especially now that poor Jimmy has passed on . . .

Well, I don't really know, I said awkwardly. I don't really know what happened, to tell you the truth. If I'd stayed in Ireland I suppose I would have married . . . I've been looking around since I came back this time and there's a kind of Irish couple where he trains the GAA team and she's big and good-looking and shy and they have three red-haired little boys all wriggling away in the back of the Toyota. I wish I'd been that woman –

She put down her knife.

Is it joking me you are? Sure – you could never have been like that, Kathleen! It wasn't in you! Taking the mother-in-law out to tea in a hotel every Sunday. Washing the boys' gear. Your husband out every night and talking about football games non-stop as if they were life and death – you'd have gone crazy! I might have settled for that if I hadn't met Danny. But you, Kathleen! You were always going to get out of Kilcrennan. The very first thing you ever said to me, when I was thirteen years old and I'd never met anyone like you, was that you were saving up to run away.

*

At the dinner, Lilian sat on my lap, and the cat glowered at all of us from the shelter of a cardboard box.

We told stories about the family. Everyone lavished charm on their little anecdote, and we laughed a lot. Danny told about the first time he brought Annie out to our house and how Mammy didn't say anything to her for an hour and then she asked her who her favourite writer was and Annie had to say she didn't have one. And Annie talked about Danny coming home to her house after a famous soccer match when they'd just got off with each other, and her father refusing to believe that he was any relation of what he called that oul gobshite crank Inspector de Burca. And I told about how Nora and I fought to take the infant Danny out in the pram, and how I'd lost control of the handlebar of the high, bouncy pram because I was too small, and Danny had been tipped out onto the road on his head.

Lilian ran over to her father and grabbed his head and started feeling it. Then she triumphantly announced that she could feel a bump.

I did not say that the floor of the pram was made of three yellow Rexine panels, the middle one detachable, and that under it, old bits of bread tainted with baby's pee rolled around in the hollow undercarriage. I did not say that Nora and I fought to take Danny out just to get Mam's attention.

I did not betray that when Lilian perched for a minute in my arms and leaned her head against me, I had a flash of Shay saying, looking up at me from where he lay, A man could stay at this for ever, and that longing for him went through me like a bolt of lightning.

Who knows what the others did not say?

I told them about the Talbot story.

You never think of them having sex during the Famine, Annie said.

That's what everyone says, I said. But they did. Or – these two did. And everyone spied on them all the time.

Oh, that kind of thing'll sell for sure! Danny said cheerfully. Sex always sells. Are you putting in the details? Sure we might get a few tips from it ourselves, Annie!

Were there children? Annie said.

There was the Talbots' daughter, Mab. She's described in the evidence as 'remarkably shrewd and intelligent'.

Like our little Lil! Danny said delightedly, swinging the child up onto the table and giving her a smacking kiss. And Lil will read her auntie Kathleen's story when she grows up. Won't you, darling? But it's bedtime now.

She's going to be a traveller, Lil is, Annie said. Like her auntie.

The child ran to the cupboard and took out a shoe box full of the postcards I'd sent from all over the world. She riffled through the cards and held them up to me. She had so much self-confidence in the presence of her parents that she even had a go at reading out the words. The Eiffel Tower. The Great Wall at Xi'an. Spring Flowers near Heraklion.

It had been a small ritual with me to choose a card for Danny's family, the first time I was in a new place, and track down a stamp, and then sit at a café table or on the steps of a monument to write to tell them where I was. I did it without fail. But I did it for myself. I had never imagined the cards being kept. I was astonished at the family caring that much about hearing from me. And I was struck by the tens and tens of cards I'd sent. I must never have stopped moving around. Permanence, I once copied down from a magazine, is what we all want when we can love and can be loved; change is what we want when we cannot.

Now that Jimmy was gone, I didn't know a single person that I could talk about that kind of thing with. Not that he'd much liked me in philosophic mode.

You make me lonely, I complained to him once. Always wanting a laugh. Never taking me seriously.

Oh, lay off, Kath, he'd said. You're *such* a gloombug.

I carried Lilian into her little room off the kitchen when she got sleepy, and after I'd tucked her under her quilt, I stayed there. I could hear the murmur of the other two outside. She slept as lightly as a feather. I liked the darkening evening, and her breath coming and going. I lay there, content, looking at the ceiling. I could just make out that someone had painted it with a brush that was losing its bristles. Lilian sniffed loudly and then went quiet again. She slept more deeply, and kicked out her legs, and then she threw herself against my side, as if she were asking to be held, and I put my arm lightly around her.

On the bus back to Shore Road, the day I went to Dublin with Mammy when I won the essay competition, that's how I must have felt to her. We sat huddled down at the back and I was in under her arm close to her. Same arm, even – the right arm. It was because the day had been such a success and we were so tired. We'd been around the clothes departments in Clery's and Arnott's not once but twice. Mammy said on the way to town that that was the way to do it – get our eye in first, see what was value, *then* buy.

I'd love a coat, I said. Poodle wool – do you know that stuff, Ma? I only have my Confirmation coat. We both need coats. Your coat is too big for you, and mine's too small.

We haven't enough for coats, she said. Coats are very dear. Forget coats.

I'm going to get a miniskirt, I said.

You are not! she said. Your father will murder you.

I'm getting everyone a present. I'm getting Nora tights. I'm getting Danny green stockings for football. I'll still have a lot left.

She didn't want to come into the newspaper office, and I had to be bossy with her and say that she couldn't stand outside like a beggar. But she melted away against a wall when I went up to a girl at the counter inside to inquire what to do. The three or four women on high stools along the inside of the counter all heard the girl talking to me and they smiled at me and said I was a great kid and congratulations.

That's my mother, I said, pointing to her.

She's a credit to you, Missus! one of the women called across to my mother. She just nodded shyly, and clutched her big handbag. But her eyes were glittering. I don't know what the woman saw, but she came out from behind the counter with a wooden chair and brought it over for Mammy to sit on. I was taken up the stairs to the photography department, and then a man in an office gave me ten one-pound notes in a beautiful thick white envelope. Even the envelope was precious to me.

We counted out the notes again, when we were outside, leaning into each other for fear a thief would see us, on the low stone wall above the salt-smelling Liffey river, with seagulls squabbling above our heads.

That's for you, I said, giving her five of the notes. That's your present.

Five! she whispered. Five! Oh, what'll I get? she said distractedly, as we turned, our money stowed away, to go back across O'Connell Bridge to Clery's.

We went for our meal to an ice-cream parlour. The waitress put Ma's order down in front of me and mine in front of her, because I had egg and chips, but she had a sundae in a tall glass with streaks of raspberry cordial through it and ivory-coloured cream on top – so much cream that it ran down the side of the glass, and she leaned forward and licked it.

Then – What did you say, anyway, she said, that they gave you the prize?

Huh? I said. I was completely taken aback at her asking me anything about myself.

What was it about – the competition that you won?

'The Beauty of this World hath Made Me Sad, this Beauty that will Pass,' I said. Padraig Pearse. You wouldn't think he'd end up in the Rising shooting people, would you, and him that poetic?

And what did you say?

Oh . . . I was embarrassed to tell her. Oh, I put in stuff about the beach, you know, on winter evenings, and the birds down there in the dark, the way they call out. And music. When I pass that piano teacher's house on the way to the bus and I stand outside . . .

You have your father's brains, she said admiringly.

I get the most of my ideas out of books. I frowned at her – I didn't want anything to do with him.

She leaned back in the chrome chair, smiling at me, as if we were two girls out together. Our table was in the window, and behind her I could see the people hurrying past and the traffic in the street.

You're like him, all the same, she said. You're a great girl, Kathleen. One of the best. But you're a chip off the old block, all the same.

Block is right, I said – meaning, that he was a big, solid man. We both started to giggle, then.

She bought a cotton frock in Clery's, after trying on a whole lot of frocks. I bought a black polo-neck jumper, because that's what they wore in Paris. And in the bus on the last lap back to Shore Road, as we drowsed in our seat, swaying along in the dim light, she said, That was a great day! I'm proud to be your mother.

Was your mother proud of you? I was chancing it.

No, was all she said.

Do they know about us?

About who? she asked, vaguely.

For God's sake, Ma! *Us.* Your children.

They know I'm a married woman, she said. After a while she added, Or – they knew. They could be dead now, for all I know.

And then there was quite a long pause before she added, Or care.

I couldn't see the ceiling any more. I took off my clothes except for my bra and pants, and lifted the quilt and slipped in beside Lil. The miracle child. They'd been married for years and years before Annie got pregnant. They must still have been making love. Though, would you call it that, when you've been married to the other person for ages and you wouldn't dream of going with anyone else and you're so sure you love each other that you never even think about it? What's it for, lovemaking, if you love each other already? If you know the other person? I couldn't imagine sex that wasn't trying to find something out – that wasn't a venture, an exploration.

I couldn't imagine sex that wasn't a looking for love, I thought, as I deliberately matched my breath to the child's breath – in, out, in, out.

I must ask Nora to ask her shrink – if a person's mother does not love him or her, then, so everyone says, they spend their lives looking for love. But, do they mean it? Do they really want to be loved? Or are they forced to do almost anything to manipulate those who love them into *not* loving them? So that they can return to the first state – the state of *not* being loved?

I heard Danny out the back calling the cat.

Furriskey! Furriskey!

Then I heard him laughing as he came back into the scullery.

That cat of yours is so thick he can't remember his own name . . .

Then there was a gale of laughter from the television set.

Turn it down, love! Annie called. They're asleep!

And the sound track dropped abruptly to a distant, cheerful hum.

10

I couldn't take any more of it in the morning. The bathroom was freezing cold and not very clean. I'd noticed the same thing when I carried the plates over to the sink after the dinner – there was dirt around the taps, and grease spots on the wall. In Uncle Ned's time, the place was spotless. Annie said she'd get into trouble for being late opening the dry cleaner's, and Lilian was whining that she'd be late for school, too. And if I was left with Danny, what would we do all day? We'd done the important things yesterday. What would we talk about? Danny must have felt the same, because he said something about getting the Ford fixed and gave me an awkward kiss and disappeared before he even had a cup of tea.

He's gone off now as happy as Larry because your visit went so nicely, Annie said. So. Leave it so.

She went out to the scullery to make the tea. I got my bag while she was out of the room.

One last thing, I said when she came back – as if it had always been understood that I was only staying till now. Would you have an envelope, Annie?

You're not going, are you? she said, standing there blankly. You're not going so soon? I have a bed made up for tonight . . .

I couldn't look at her. I could hear how hurt she was.

I wrote a cheque for a thousand pounds made out to Danny, and I put it into the envelope she got for me. I scrawled on it – 'For your farm developments. Gift not loan.' She watched me doing it, impassively. She couldn't have seen how much the sum was and I didn't tell her – it was a big sum by Kilcrennan standards. But I might as well do it handsomely if I was doing it at all. Give poor Danny a chance while he still had a bit of life ahead.

Give that to him? I said, and she nodded. She didn't smile.

C'mon, I said then. You and Lil – lead me to the car.

And they did, and the last I saw was the two of them standing in the road waving at me and blowing kisses. All along that stretch of the road flickering polka-dot light danced down through the lacy young branches of the beech trees, and it danced on them.

I considered for a minute turning the car around, when they'd have gone, and going out to Shore Road one last time, and visiting Ma's grave by myself.

No.

Enough.

Would there be anywhere in Kilcrennan with good Italian coffee in a minimalist room with linen cloths and a brushed steel and pale wood decor and maybe crimson cranberry juice on a lacquer table and something like a brioche with fig jam to eat? The lounge, maybe, of a gym where tanned, young people in pale grey sportswear exercised before going off to beds with Frette sheets to bring each other to simultaneous orgasm?

The notion of finding such a place between Kilcrennan and Mellary . . .

Well, what about going to Dublin? I didn't have to be back at Bertie's till Saturday. Everyone said Dublin was stylish now, though I remembered a derelict, smoky city, full of decayed, handsome things, where tired children waited in the dark doorways of pubs and the queues for the buses shuffled forward in the rain, umbrella behind umbrella.

I could go to the National Library. But I didn't need to. I had Miss Leech looking after me – my own salty little Virgil.

I could go up Merrion Square, to the steps of the Department of Agriculture, and pay my respects to Uncle Ned . . .

I saw him for the last time on a night when I believed I was beautiful. It was when I was at Trinity – my second year, when I was earning enough at my waitressing jobs to have a great time. I went with a gang of the others to the Trinity Ball in a wonderful hired gown and at dawn, after the night's dancing, we were drifting, tired, down the wide pavement of the square. There was a huddle of blankets and heavy coats on the steps of the Department of Agriculture – a delegation of protesters from the Small Farmers Association, asleep now. One man was sitting up in a sleeping bag, his back against a pillar, and as we passed, I saw that it was Ned. I stopped dead in front of him and he looked at me without moving. The ballgown was moss-green velvet, and my friends had threaded silver beads through my hair, which was wilder then than now. He looked at me for a long moment with a sorrowful, longing look that I had never seen before and – I realized at once – that had nothing to do with me.

I had suspected that Ned cared for my mother. It crossed my mind, that time I looked after his place. Because it was supposed to be a big secret that Ned was in jail, but he let it out at the first opportunity. He brought Mammy in her tea the Thursday after he got out, as usual, and he asked her how she was and she said she couldn't sleep. He said she should try the Dublin air, that he never slept better than in Mountjoy jail, and she said than in *what*? Then it all came out. I thought at the time that he let the secret out innocently. But when his eyes met mine in Dublin that morning, I knew that he had wanted her to know about his adventure – he had wanted her to admire him. I knew, from the way he looked through me, that Ned Burke had loved my mother. My face, responding to his, curved into a loving, womanly smile.

No. I would not go to Dublin.

I'd go back to the cottage.

The thing was, that if Shay wanted to find me, that was where he'd try.

I headed for the west, but after a couple of hours I went off my route, and drove down to Athlone. I asked the women in a dress shop about a good hairdresser and spent a couple of hours in a surprisingly chic salon getting my highlights done. The coffee was very good, and they had all the latest glossies, so I was renewed when I came out. I felt more in charge of things. I passed a delicatessen on the way back to the car and it was lovely to buy French cheese and country bread and organic tomatoes and expensive wine for the last few nights in Mellary. To be my cosmopolitan self, but have a little Irish house to provide for as well – sure, that was ideal!

I stood outside the deli, absent-minded. It was a lovely day. The freshest and newest of summers seemed to have settled on Ireland, but tentatively – so tentatively that the fine weather might have been on loan. I wondered if there was the remotest chance that I could get Alex to come on a very short holiday with me. If his mother was safe in the hospital, would there be any way I could get him to come somewhere warm, even for a week? Before he had to face the worst? Maybe somewhere with a beach, but a spiritual side as well. Say the Halkidhiki peninsula. The hotels were luxurious, by Greek standards anyway, and there were day trips to the monasteries of Mount Athos. Men only, of course. Blatant misogyny dolled up as religion. Though, Alex didn't know how to do beaches. He couldn't swim in the sea, he'd told me once – only in a pool. Jimmy could have lived on a beach. Jimmy said once that he and I would buy a house on a Greek island when we were old, to which I said, Okay but *not* Mykonos – I never want to see another beautiful German boy in a thong. Now, I was sorry that that was what I said, even jokingly. Jimmy wouldn't have wanted to be on Mykonos when he was old, would he? Did old gay men stay around where the young men were? What view of his life in his old age – if no partner came along – had he had? I was his friend: I should have had a feel for the things he didn't say! Oh – how was I going to get through without him? Summer holidays, Christmas, anything that needed a plan – he was my comrade! I would never buy a house on a Greek island by myself. Sitting on some patio in my seventies, watching the blue sea, a trembly old expatriate with the alarm system always switched on.

I found the car and started off again for Mellary. I still had only the bad Sinatra tape so I tried to listen to a discussion about Irish party politics, but it was impenetrable. I turned the radio off.

Anyway – I didn't want to be old in Greece! Not there! Not when it was the scene of my greatest happiness, when I was young. Not when I saw it first when I was unspoiled. Or – unwary, might be a better word; I certainly might have been already spoiled inside.

*

I often looked at my first love, Hugo, around the halls and in the canteen of the London City Poly. He was my idea of a hero out of a book. He looked like someone who should be at Oxford or Cambridge – not now, but in the 1920s. Rowing, or picnicking, or lying in the long grass beside a cricket pitch.

We opted for the same module in the second year of the journalism diploma. He sat at the back of the room during tutorials, and so did I. We exchanged basic information. He was interested in politics and he was getting a legal qualification at the same time as the journalism, with a view to starting in newspaper management. I just hoped to get a job on a newspaper in London. What did I think of the Northern Ireland situation? Gosh, I said, I haven't really kept up with it. Perhaps a job on a magazine would suit you better, he said.

I admired his ways. I noticed, watching him reading when we were waiting for the tutor to come into the room, that he read only one book at a time, and read it slowly. He had the same Penguin Classic of some medieval German fable for a few weeks. I was trying to read everything on earth immediately. I'd have four or five books on the go – Dostoevsky, *Love Story*, Françoise Sagan, Angus Wilson, Hart Crane, Catherine Cookson; I'd read anything. But I learned from him, I learned to be more selective. I admired his clothes – he wore men's clothes instead of jeans – old clothes. He asked me once whether I liked Schubert. Oh, yes! I said, needless to say, and I listened to a couple of LPs in the big record shop at Oxford Circus as soon as I could. Funnily enough, I did like Schubert. I listened to some wonderfully emotional songs sung by a man, the piano accompaniment weaving in and out of his voice like another song; then I listened to the 'Death and the Maiden' quartet. This was the first piece of chamber music I ever listened to. The next week, when we were waiting for the lecturer, I remarked to Hugo that the tune – the slow tune in the middle – reminded me of cats, the way they flick their tails into a perfectly elegant coil when they choose to sit.

He looked at me.

Don't you go around with the long-haired crowd? he said.

Oh, I don't think so, I lied. I'm usually more on my own, I'd say, than with a gang.

Mammy would have loved his voice, I thought. He's a bit like Leslie Howard in *Gone With the Wind*.

The media students were sent out in pairs with a tape-recorder, to come back with either a news item or a feature. The lecturer quite casually paired me with Hugo. I could hardly breathe with delight.

My uncle is an utterly unimportant baronet, he said. We could go down to the House and see if he knows any news.

That's a bit obvious, I said.

There was a pause.

The landlord of the pub I work in and his wife never stop fighting, I said. We could go and record what he thinks of her and then what she thinks of him, and then we could cut them together . . .

I'm not sure that that's journalism, he said.

We were sitting in the empty lecture room.

There's an old man who drinks in the pub I work in who fought in the Spanish Civil War, I began.

My cousin was in Albania last year, he began.

Don't you know anyone besides your family? I said, smiling at him, willing him to keep me with him.

Do you have any family? he said. Or is this pub you keep mentioning your family?

His smile was a signal to me, too.

When we broke up for the holidays the following June he told me he was going to Greece – to Naxos, with his parents, to a villa.

I'll miss you terribly, Kathleen.

What's the next island? I asked.

Paros, I think.

I pretended to take no notice. We went to the pictures a few times in the last few weeks and held electric hands. And when he came around to the pub where I was washing the floor, the morning of the day he went away, I said, I'll be on the quay of Paros. On my birthday. The twenty-eighth of July. The Feast of Saints Nazarius and Celsus.

He just stared at me.

Early Christian martyrs, I said, as if that explained it.

He still just stared at me. It was a very gratifying response, but it kept me awake at night worrying, too.

I paid in sweat and blood for the flourish. I worked two shifts in the hotel, and cleaned the pub every morning. I wrote to Uncle Ned to get me my birth certificate. Then I wrote to him, with shame, for the last bit of the money I needed for the trip. He sent a little wad of Irish pound notes in an envelope with the address in capitals on both sides and every seam covered in Sellotape.

> . . . All here are well thank God and Danny is a great help to me. I
> hope your boyfriend knows what a great girl you are Kathleen. It is
> very dry here and there is not the grass of former years. Yrs. Uncle Ned.

Often, over the years I was a travel writer, I'd be standing in a new hotel room, gazing inconsequentially at the corner of the lawn below, or at the bland, fake watercolour on the wall, and I'd feel gathered around my own core, as if, with anonymous space all around me, the boundaries of my self were secure. And I felt that ease for the first time when I was moving down through Europe and then off the edge of it, at Piraeus, and then on across the sapphire Mediterranean past the white islands, to the quay at Paros, to be united with Hugo. The journey stayed with me like a passage in music – the idea of journeying . . .

I wore a pair of sandals that had seemed good enough in England. I had bought a small bottle of red nail varnish from a 'Reduced' basket in a shop. I told the girl in the shop my theory – that painted toes signalled how feminine a girl was, deep down, even if she didn't make any other show of it. I was going to keep my bra on till I got to Paros. I had the notes tucked into my passport and the passport held firmly on the slope of my breast under the fabric. The other precious thing was tucked into the other cup – a plastic envelope of contraceptive pills. I had started taking them a month before. Just in case, was all I said to myself every morning. Just in case. Like a mantra. I had two panties and a clean bra in my bag and another T-shirt and a frock and my bathing suit and a plastic bag from the supermarket with my washing things. I had my nail varnish. I had *The Sun Also Rises* and a book about Greece in the 1930s by some sensitive Englishman and *War and Peace* and a notebook to write observations in and a pack of cards to play patience. I was as compact and efficient as a snail.

Right at the end of my mind there was a golden blur. This blur was love, or Hugo, or passion. No matter what I was thinking or doing – talking to a boy in the queue and letting him buy me a cup of coffee, reading the wonderfully glamorous place names on the sides of the Wagons-Lit carriages on the platform at Calais – all the time, the centre of me was immobile, rapt, in front of that golden light.

In the heat of Paris that evening, while I waited for the night train, I walked the streets around the Gare du Nord, half frightened, but drawn on by surprise after surprise: the displays of glistening seafood outside the restaurants; the way the women – ordinary office workers – wore little scarves flicked around their necks, and click-clacked sexily in and out of the grocery shops; a six-foot-tall woman in tribal dress and a great scarlet turban, screaming at a black child in a spotless white tuxedo, *Venez! Venez!* The streets were hot. My feet swelled up. When I took off my sandals in the compartment of the train that night, the straps had sunk into the flesh. I had weals, part of them cuts, in an X pattern on the front of both feet.

I was so hungry. Then the massive mother of the family with me in the compartment started to open packet after packet of things tied in brown paper and rolled up in newspaper, from the shopping bags at her feet. Her wide legs parted and showed the white skin above her black stockings, as she cut slices off a crusty loaf of bread, the loaf digging into the skirt tightly stretched across her lap. Her gold earrings dangled almost to the massive shelf of her chest. Her son and daughter were about ten years old and they had wide white smiles; they were both so plump that they had bosoms, too. The father had a nut-brown face and a crew cut, and he took all the food his wife handed to him without expression. But she kept up a monologue that demanded response. *Mais oui*, he'd say, with rhythmic regularity. *Mais non.* The children chomped away. And I chomped, too. I'd tried to be polite and refuse, but both husband and wife burst into torrents of persuasion. I had skimped all that long day, worried about my money. Now, I sat in the warm compartment and ate bread and a wedge of ham. I had a pear and a big mother-of-pearl plum. I had a cold lamb chop. I had chalk-white cheese and a twist of olives. I had a slice of gooseberry tart. I had two glasses of ruby-red home-made wine from the father's plastic bottle. I had a can of Coke that the little boy pressed on me with all his parents' courtesy.

C'est bon – les voyages! I said. I didn't know the exact French for what I wanted to say. I wanted to say – travel is lovely. I wanted to say – if this is travel, I want to do it for ever. I meant the train cleaving the night, and our temporary human settlement in the compartment, and the pleasure of meeting such generous people as themselves, and the unknown places outside the ink-black windows – the ponds, the deep lanes, the shuttered villages, the streets with traffic lights winking at empty intersections – all tethered out there to the ordinary world, while we flew past, safe and well.

Les voyages – ils sont beaux! I wanted to say that everything that would have been claustrophobic in an ordinary room was made magic by the drama of the train. A station whipped past – a gaping face, sodium lights, the *wuhoooo* of our train's whistle. The wheels pounded on. We slowed. A border. Every thriller I had ever read came back to me. Richard Burton movies. The bodies of the failed escapers hanging on the wire. I went out into the corridor and slid back the window. A ditch of weeds that were black in the light from the train. Behind us down the track, the edge of a building, and lights, as tall as if they were on watchtowers, refracting into rings of coloured light in the night sky. Someone called out in a foreign language.

A boy stopped beside me and clutched the handrail and peered out the window. He showed me an unlit cigarette, a watchful smile on his gypsy face.

I do not have a light, monsieur, I said, and slipped back into the safety of the family.

The mother had tidied everything away. When I had settled myself, her husband turned the lights to dim. The little girl was asleep wrapped in his coat, on the seat beside him. The boy was asleep on one side of the mother. And I fell asleep on her other side, my head pressed into the springy pillow of her hip, only waking once to protest with a cry when she gently moved me off, and laid my head on the seat, when the family left the train at some stop during the night.

There was a bad incident in Switzerland, when I turned out to be on the wrong class of train and I was put off in a station to wait for the right one. I trusted a North African cleaner who said he'd buy me a coffee, but he had misunderstood me, and when I wouldn't go up to his room, he took out his anger on me, in a hallway of a lodging-house near the station. But on the ferry from Italy I met another man, a Greek man, and he said I could have the other bunk in his cabin, not to worry, he had a daughter at home just like me. He was a lovely man. He did look at me – he stood in the doorway of the tiny little cabin in the smell of diesel and he looked at me. I looked back, mutely telling him that my feet hurt and my shoulders were sore. A tired-looking man, in a Marlon Brando white vest. He was driving a tanker of vegetable oil for Bulgaria. He looked at me for a moment too long. I just started to cry. He turned away, and he didn't come back to the cabin the whole night. He must have sat up. He knocked on the door in the morning, and brought me up to the café and bought me bread and slices of cucumber and a tin cup of black coffee. And when I looked out the window, we were going past a long headland covered in scrub. And that was Greece. Just coming into Igoumenítsa.

Years later I read *Eleni* and there was the name again; the family got out to America through Igoumenítsa. It's supposed to be a dump. But I adored everything about that hot, dusty concrete town with its flyblown cafés and swarthy lorry drivers squatting in the shade reading sports comics.

I got the long-distance bus from Igoumenítsa to Athens. Ten hours, it took. I didn't mind. I could hardly walk on my infected feet in any case. There was a boy halfway down the bus who was in charge of us. He sold ice-cold water from a wooden box. And every so often he came around with a towel dipped in rosewater. Just one between all of us – this wasn't Japan Air Business Class. You wiped your hands and sent it on. The driver had a radio tuned to bouzouki music and Middle Eastern rock and women with deep voices howling about – I supposed – love. The road was terrible the bit I saw of it, because the old ladies around me wouldn't let me pull back the threadbare curtains. They made clucking noises and pointed at the sun. And they were wearing black jumpers with long sleeves and woollen scarves, in ninety degrees of heat. But once I peeped out and saw a road sign for Thebes. This was where Oedipus himself really lived – just there, where there was a petrol station at the crossroads! In Athens I went up on the top deck of the bus to Piraeus and sat on the front seat as it ground across the city that was swarming and busy in the dusk of the evening. From my perch I saw it all – dazzling lighting showrooms, surly prostitutes in hot pants, sweating waiters gasping at cigarettes at the back doors of restaurants, groups of statuary, policemen whistling at traffic jams, fountains in dark gardens.

Then the bus emptied, and we began to rattle down a wide boulevard. The hot air that blew across my face from window to window took on a new tang. I lifted my head and sniffed. The sea! Oh – the sea!

The wind came up that night. Some English girls showed me where the hostel was, but I was too excited to go in. The hot gale slapped the water against the quays and banged the yachts and the fishing boats against each other and their masts and metal guy ropes rang like bells and cymbals. The big car ferries to the islands strained at their ropes, and the wind got hotter and small waves slurped over the edge of the quay and water trickled across dark parking lots and spray broke on the quayside huts where men sold ferry tickets. All the time, people called and cried out in the dark, and the men sat in the drab cafés and shouted with laughter, sitting side by side in rows, in a way I'd never seen before, and they threw their playing cards down on the plastic tables and moved the big brown worry beads along between their thick fingers. That night, as I lay under the thin sheet, breathless with the heat, I felt how near I was coming to Hugo. Nothing could stop me now.

We were held up in Piraeus by high winds, and by the time the Paros boat got away, the seagulls up in the pure air and our prow cutting a foamy wedge through the lively water were things of heavenly cleanness. I made a nest in the corner of the upper deck, behind a lifeboat. The long day caught me into its peace. My feet healed in the sun. My tired body rested on the warm wooden slats. I'd pick up my book and then I'd let it fall again, because I couldn't think any more – my mind, stuck in neutral, could only say, Hugo, Hugo.

Then, at the beginning of the evening, I got cold, and I gathered my things to go down to the lounge. I stopped to look in at the kitchen behind the café on the top deck. An old man toiled in there, flinging coffee grounds into a row of plastic sacks and walloping plates and mugs through a sink. All the time he sang at the top of his cracked voice. His galley was open to the glorious air on both sides, and behind him I could see a vista of the darkening sea on the other side of the boat. I could see, behind his bowed head, that we were passing a small island. He slammed his dishes around, and, suddenly, beyond him, on the high point of the island, the perfect columns of a classical temple slid into view. Illuminated. Gold, against the navy blue of the sky. A high frieze of fluted golden columns, thousands of years old – the first my eyes had ever seen. Me and my bag, the kitchen porter, the ancient temple – all one. All mixed together, while the big boat throbbed and swished through the dark Mediterranean, moving on towards what would be love.

When I got to the island I hardly ate, so as to save funds, and I paid the minimum for a garage with a cot and a sink in it, and the use of a bathroom across the garden. I swam and lay on the beach, getting brown for Hugo. I was frightened by the heat that made me gasp, by the notices in writing I couldn't understand, by people who approached my little heap of belongings on the beach who might steal my money and my passport, by the man who owned the garage who stood among the lemon trees pretending to water them. But I would be where I'd said I'd be, when the boat from Naxos came in.

The width of flawless blue sky. The big white ferry coming around the headland and cutting its engines as it slid heavily along the quayside. Cars, trucks with crates and sacks, a crowd of people. The old women calling and jostling and holding up colour photos of the rooms they had to let. Vans. Motorbikes. Bicycles – more people . . . No sign of Hugo. I could hardly move for disappointment as I turned away.

A motorbike had wheeled around and come back. Hugo pulled back his helmet.

I didn't recognize you, he said. You look like a movie star.

It was worth it a hundred times over. He looked at me all through our lovemaking, as if we must not lose a second of seeing each other. Sweetness saturated me, spreading from the well of sweetness he was drawing on, down where our bodies were joined. I hadn't even guessed there was such a reservoir within my body. I'd lost my virginity soon after I went to college in Dublin, in a hotel where I worked in the bar, the night of a rugby international, to a man from Scotland. It was horrible. I was terrified of getting pregnant too, and after that, though I knew lots of boys, I did not have sex with them. But now! The whole of my inner self lifted towards Hugo. Our eyes closed at the end, as each of us turned in towards ourselves. My being was caught up in a river of sensation that ran faster and faster towards a silken weir. I was held on the edge for a moment and then I overflowed, and slid over and was carried down into the thunder of a waterfall. The explosion went everywhere, spray after spray after diamond spray of it.

I wept with happiness and relief, and he held me passionately close.

I whispered to him, Thank you. Thank you.

We didn't sleep at all that night. The metal cot in my garage room was unsteady, and the sheets and the foam mattress kept sliding off and eventually we lay on the floor. Towards dawn, we walked down the rough lane to the little town. A flock of pure white birds stood on the beach, all facing towards the brightening horizon, beside the motionless sea. We walked along to the harbour. A café was open, and there were two or three fishermen in there, each at his own table, sitting quietly in front of a coffee cup and a glass. We sat as quietly.

All day we never got tired. He took me on his motorbike up into the hills. We sat under great plane trees outside village cafés. We held our heads that were hot from the helmets under the drainage gullies that trickled onto the road. We slept for a while, like Hansel and Gretel, on the soft floor of a stand of pines. Over on the remote side of the island, as dusk came down, Hugo got us a room with a big lumpy bed in an old woman's cottage. The shower was a hose draped over the thick vines outside the window. The water made my skin soft. I washed my panties for the morning with the bit of soap and hung them on a branch, and walked down to the taverna with Hugo's hand splayed across the small of my back. I felt he was claiming my body, and that it had never been alive before as it was now, naked and humming under the thin cotton frock.

I was beautiful that night. I know, because I saw it in his eyes.

There have only been four times, ever, that I felt beautiful. Merrion Square, when Uncle Ned saw my mother's face on me, was the first time. And in that taverna on Paros, sitting under a tree full of restless little birds, in the hot evening, across from Hugo, I was beautiful for the second time.

Stop there! my present self said. Leave it there!

I pulled into a petrol station, just before the turn-off to the Mellary Road, and I stood and ate two microwaved hot dogs and drank a bottle of mineral water.

But I couldn't stop.

We moved in together when we were back in London. I grew very confident, sexually. A year and a half passed. We'd got our journalism diplomas and I was working in a travel agency and hoping to get a job in travel writing. Hugo was finishing off his law studies. He gave me the xerox of the Talbot *Judgment* but there was nothing significant about that, then. Our future as a couple was never mentioned.

One Sunday morning, wood pigeons called from the dusty chestnut trees in the park. The sunlight streamed around the makeshift Indian curtain on the window near us, and fragments of warm colour fell across the whiteness of our bed on the floor.

Let's get up and go to Mass, Hugo said.

Oh, you're not serious, I groaned from under the duvet. I wriggled across and fitted myself against his back. Mass! Why don't we brush our teeth and do some really serious kissing instead?

I like Mass, he said. The Jesuit church up the road has the Latin Mass with a choir at eleven. It's beautiful.

I know the words, I said. Well, I know the *Gloria* and the *Credo*, anyway.

That's my girl, Hugo said. I caught the note of satisfaction in his voice.

Hugo was a convert. He'd been baptized a Catholic when he was fourteen by the Bishop of Somewhere or other in the private chapel of Lord Something's castle. We weren't the same kind of Catholics at all, to put it mildly.

Give us one last hug, then, I murmured into the skin of his back. My limbs felt half liquid with the night's sex and too little sleep.

No! Hugo rolled off the bed and stood up in one movement. You have exactly one hour, he said. I'm going for the papers and milk. I'll bring you a cup of tea when I get the milk. And then it's Mass.

When he was gone I kicked the cover back and sprawled naked in the sun.

I could feel a steady and deep throbbing, as if life itself were coursing through me underneath the top layer of tiredness. I cupped my hand over the lips between my legs. I could feel the heat coming off them. I stretched my legs, relishing the slight friction between the skin on the back of my calves and the texture of the sheet. I moved to bathe my breasts in the warmth of a lozenge of sun. They felt springy.

Even my head feels perfect, I thought. Even my face. I turned my head to one side and caught a strand of my hair in my mouth and licked it.

Oh, oh, oh! I said aloud. I could burst! I twisted up and onto my knees and buried my face in the pillow and knelt for a minute.

Thank you God! I said. If I never thank you for anything again, God, thank you for all this!

Then I began to laugh at myself.

I was in the shower, my eyes tight shut against the suds streaming down from my hair, when I heard the bathroom door open.

Hello sweetheart! I sang out.

There was no reply. I opened one eye. Sasha, the French guy from upstairs had come in and closed the door and was leaning against it.

Hey! I said. Out! I said it smiling. I didn't feel naked because the water was sluicing down my body, and because he was looking into my face, searching it for something.

I think about you all the time, he said. I don't know what to do.

He had soft hair cut close to his skull. His brown eyes looked into mine.

I saw you, he said. I didn't mean to, but the door was open. You and Hugo were on the mattress and he was fucking you.

I turned off the water and stood there. My mind was completely empty.

Kathleen! he said. He stepped out of his shorts. When he clasped me his T-shirt spread with damp from my wet body.

He just came into me, with ease. I was full of him. When his movement stopped because he was all the way in, that was what I was: I was a receptacle that was completely and deeply full. I wanted to groan with disappointment when he began to move faster and took the feeling of fullness away, but I made no sound at all, as if I were not present. He dropped his head onto my shoulder while the last shudders went through him. His hair was like fur.

After a minute, he leaned past me and turned the shower on again. He took the soap, and gently and quickly washed me as I stood there, beginning with my shoulders and arms, and ending, crouched, at my toes.

We both heard the thump of the front door through the floor when Hugo came back in from the shop. Sasha slipped out of the bathroom. I went over to the basin and started brushing my teeth.

When I walked into the kitchen, Hugo looked around from the counter where he was making toast and reading a newspaper.

Well, Kathy, he said, you look good enough to eat!

It was warm in the church. The sun striking through the stained-glass windows threw a hazy rainbow of dust particles across the shining pews. My legs were so weak that I had to haul myself up to stand. I used to go to sung Mass in school on big feast days. I had a shape in my head, like a beloved landscape, that was the shape of the Mass. When the priest began the move towards the moment of transforming the bread and wine, I felt it like the beginning of the ascent of a sacred hill.

Sursum corda. Lift up your hearts.

We have lifted them up to the Lord.

Then the priest intoned the Preface and the pace of the recitation quickened. I waited, happy, for the moment I loved, when the words of the prayer – no matter what form they might take on any particular day, issued – burst – into the affirmation, Holy! Holy! Holy! I folded gratefully onto my knees and buried my face in my hands. The exhaustion in my body opened my mind. I saw, as if it were in front of me, the rough stone wall of an upper room in Palestine, and the baffled faces of the men at the table when Christ took a crust, and said the impossible words. This is my body. A crust of bread! This – lifting the ordinary wine – is my blood.

The priest reached the Our Father, and the moment when I would turn to Hugo to offer him the sign of peace flowed towards us.

Let us offer each other the sign of peace, the priest said.

I looked up at Hugo and tried to put all my joy and gratitude into my expression.

Peace be with you, I said to him.

Peace, he said, taking both my hands in his.

When I was caught, and Hugo threw me out, I had to tell Nora, because at that time she rang me from New York once a week, and I had to head her off. She'd never met Hugo, but his good manners when he picked up the phone practically made her grovel.

I only did it a few times, I said.

Oh! she said. How could you? How *could* you, Kathleen? She was nearly crying. Could you not respect yourself, even if you couldn't respect Hugo?

The short answer to that was no. I didn't know what this self-respect was, or what it felt like or what its rewards were. I wanted to try things! I wanted to try everything! I hardly spoke to Sasha, but I went with him almost as often as he was waiting on the stairs when I came in from work. I got no pleasure out of the sex except the athleticism of it, and what it did to him. I got no sexual pleasure out of my other infidelity, either. That was at work, where I would sometimes go with the porter the girls called Sexy Al into his office under the staircase. He was the first coloured person I ever touched. Nora would have choked if I'd been insane enough to tell her about Al. A *janitor*! On the *floor*!

I was on top of the world for the few months I had the three of them – I looked terrific and full of confidence and energy and I was *nice* – nicer and kinder to other people than I'd ever been in my life. And I got on very well with Hugo. I always wanted him more after I'd been with one of the others. But still, it wasn't about sex, what I was doing. I didn't need anyone besides Hugo for sex. It wasn't about men, necessarily. I think that if a woman had shown that she wanted me I would have gone with her, eagerly, so as to learn another part of the great world. The satisfactions I got were in my head. If there had been some other way of doing what I was doing . . . But I had nothing else to barter my way forward with except the body I stood up in.

I was lying on my side on Sasha's bed. His head was buried in my breasts. Hugo came in smiling, and then I saw his face change into a gargoyle, and then hell came tumbling down on me. He physically threw me out of the house. He pushed me down the stairs, sweaty hands on my back, his knee jabbing into my buttocks, jabbing me hatefully – get out! get out! – exactly where he had loved to lick me and smack me and kiss me. He was shrieking. He ran back upstairs to hurl my clothes and my books into boxes to empty them out on the front step behind me.

But then Caroline intervened.

She was standing at the back of the hallway. I hardly knew her, but I knew we liked each other from the way we smiled when we noticed each other, even though she looked at first glance like an ice queen – tall and calm, with straight, butter-coloured hair. She visited the house from time to time, and she'd come that day to make hash cakes with some of the other kids. I'd been laughing with her earlier, before I sneaked upstairs with Sasha. He stood behind her, and he made a sucking shape with his mouth. I pretended to ignore the signal; I liked keeping him unsure. I turned away and said to her, For God's sake, why don't you just smoke the dope? and she said she didn't approve of smoking.

Now, she crossed the hallway and began picking up my clothes. She was going to help me! Even though she was a rich English person, like Hugo. The clothes were strewn on the doorstep. A blue minidress. My old jumpers. My black panties that Al the porter told me turned him on.

Hugo was bloodless around the eyes with rage.

Oh come off it, Hugo, Caroline said.

She had the same accent as him.

You hop in the car, she said to me.

Hugo . . . She turned to him, and tried to take his hand.

I got out of there.

*

What on earth did you do to make him so furious? she said as we drove away.

I was having a little scene with Sasha. Hugo came into Sasha's room. But it was nothing, Caroline. I don't care if I never see Sasha again.

Oh.

After a minute or two she said, If you didn't like him, why did you do it?

I don't know! I said. I didn't think I'd be caught. I didn't think about what might happen at all.

She drove towards the city.

Where can I drop you? she said.

I don't actually have anywhere to go. I lived there, you know . . . I started to cry.

Oh, don't cry! she said. You come with me, Kathleen. I haven't much furniture yet and you'll have to sleep on cushions and there's no cutlery or glasses or anything like that. But we'll manage perfectly.

Not many people would have been as kind. I used to think secretly that she looked like a fairy godmother. You could imagine her with her golden hair, in a white robe, holding a sparkling wand.

After a while she said, I always heard that you and Hugo were crazy about each other.

Oh, we were. I am. I don't know why I did it.

Oh, for heaven's sake, Kathleen! You can't keep saying you don't know, like a baby!

But I don't know, Caroline, I said sullenly.

Then I made the best effort I could, at that time, to explain myself.

I never can see any reason for saying no, I said. I know you're supposed to be faithful and all that but I don't know *why*. Like – if Hugo hadn't found out, he'd have gone on being happy. So Caroline – what does that mean? I was only trying to live life to the full . . .

I started crying again.

And did this apply to him, too? she said. Could Hugo live life to the full, too?

Oh, I don't think so, I said, surprised into stopping crying. It never happened, so I don't know what I would have felt. But I think I'd have been devastated –

216

How do you know it never happened?

Caroline!

No! I only mean – if you were getting away with it, he could have been, too.

But he wouldn't, I began, at a loss when it came to thinking about Hugo.

He'll come looking for you, soon, she said, comfortingly. When he gets over the shock.

He won't, I said. I bet you. He was mad about me, all right. But he didn't love me.

This complete recall of the Hugo time from beginning to end, as I drove across Ireland to Mellary, was something I'd never allowed myself before. I had often thought of bits and pieces of it, of course. When I saw a particular dazed smile on a girl's face. When Jimmy talked about Greece. When I'd hear a man shrieking in anger.

I explained what happened in different ways to myself at different times in my life. My *availability*, I'd call it, rather than promiscuity, was Daddy's fault for not loving me, or Mammy's fault for having sex with Daddy when they never even talked to each other, or both their faults for showing me no other version of closeness between a man and a woman except sexual closeness. It was Catholic Ireland's fault, for sending me out into the world without a shred of inner moral sense, and it was England's fault, for making me feel inferior and unwelcome except when someone wanted to fuck me. It was the fault of the 1960s, for inventing the pill and the miniskirt; and it was also the fault of history, for making a world in which everyone had to pretend to bow to the bourgeois ideal of fidelity.

Now, I think that I always shied away from happiness. I steered as near as I could to arranging for fate to destroy my happiness, always, because that was what I *knew*. I *knew* disappointment. I was familiar from infancy with the sad air of the house in Shore Road. And not knowing what ordinary happiness looked like, I picked Hugo to adore, then, apart from the bliss of sex, I treated him as if he had no reality, as if he were out of a book.

I did my best to blame him for what happened. That way I was able to believe for a long time that there was still a relationship waiting for me where there would be *real* love. Disloyalty wouldn't be an issue. I wouldn't need to be good because I wouldn't ever want anyone except my partner.

In the meantime, while I was waiting, all through my life, for as long as I was asked and no matter how often I was humiliated, I always said yes. But it was such an empty yes! By the time I was twenty-five I'd closed down. I crawled into the basement off the Euston Road, and the only man I ever revealed myself to was Jimmy. I forgot the ardent girl I had been. I forgot the sweetness of desire, until I woke up the other night and found Shay stroking me so delightedly that my soul told my senses that it was safe to respond, That this was the real thing . . .

I turned off the main road, and I began to follow the winding lanes up to Mellary. I'd see the sea soon. Five minutes beyond the village I'd come to the vantage point and the whole sweep of the bay would be beneath me, and my little cottage, in its field out on the headland. Oh – such a promise of loving there'd been with Shay, and what memories of loss his disappearance had woken!

What hurt me now was that back then, I wasn't a bad girl at all, though I thought I was. Hugo saw a whole bad person when he looked at me but I wasn't whole – I was pure chaos, behind my façade. I was reckless out of confusion. And I blew my pride in myself terribly early. I started out as a woman so vigorously and in such a wrong direction, and I got such a shock from what happened with Hugo, that my life eventually turned into a vigil outside the shrine of Eros – believing in sexual love more than anybody, and further from being able to know it than anybody.

But I didn't foresee that that's what would happen – that my life would be marked by my misunderstanding of passion.

What I saw – the explanation I gave to Nora when I had to phone her to tell her I wasn't with Hugo any more, was what a twenty-four-year-old immigrant to England would see.

He wasn't that keen on me, Nora, you know. He'd never have married me.

How do you know? Nora said.

He never brought me home to his people.

Count your blessings, she said. If he had, you might have had to bring him home to yours.

No, Nora. We were in a pub one night with all the others and I was having a great time and talking away and I overheard him saying when I was coming back from the Ladies that he agreed with John Betjeman that there was nothing more tedious than all that Irish guff.

Did you say anything about that to him? Nora asked.

No.

You cheated him, instead?

No I didn't! It was a separate thing!

Silence.

Hugo looked down on Irish people, I said. It's a real put-down to say we talk too much.

But we do, Nora said.

He was too much an Englishman to ignore the outside of a person, Nora. He would never have respected me. He didn't take me seriously.

That's the greatest load of rubbish! Nora said. You *screwed* his *room-mate*!

He could never just *forget* that I was Irish, I said stubbornly.

Hugo didn't come after me. I wrote and told him that I didn't know why I did it and that if he'd take me back I'd never do it again. Or, could we at least meet to discuss it, like friends? A young person's letter.

My letter came back, unopened, but torn in quarters, inside an otherwise empty envelope. That was another thing. If he'd been just a friend he'd have been kinder to me than that. But lovers – lovers are allowed to be as cruel as anything to the one who disappoints them. And that was how I got over it, in the end – by saying to myself, well, if that's love, you can have it.

I'd arrived at Mellary without even noticing the end of the journey. A straggle of cars was trying to get into the square, so something was happening. I had to go down a back lane to get to the car park behind the High Chapparal pub. Milk, I needed. Butter. Firelighters. The air felt marvellous, over here near the Atlantic. I breathed deeply, walking through the alley to the Spar shop, and I said to myself, This is Ireland; *be here now.* But I couldn't shake off the net of reminiscence I was caught in.

PJ was getting down from the chair where Mrs PJ usually sat.

Service is suspended! he said cheerfully. We're closed. We haven't all sold out, thanks be to God!

What are you talking about? I said.

There's a great man here this afternoon that has spent fifteen years in jail in the north on the word of a thug of an RUC man –

Here where?

Here. In the square. We're putting up a plaque to the centenary of the 1798 Rising. There was two fellows from this locality hanged, and four transported to Australia.

It can't be the centenary, I said.

Why not? he said belligerently.

1798, I said. This is 1999.

Oh, he said. Right. We were waiting for your man to get out of Long Kesh –

But was 1798 not, like, about equality? I said. We did a pageant at school and they had the French flag and the American flag in the 1798 tableau, and the idea was that the poor people – the lower classes – were rising up against the upper classes everywhere around that time – it wasn't just about Ireland wanting to get the English out –

He looked at me blankly.

Were there not all kinds of people involved in 1798? I said desperately.

So what if there were? he said.

Protestants as well as Catholics, PJ.

So what?

But your speaker that was in Long Kesh – was he not in the IRA? And, well, is the IRA not sectarian?

Certainly not! PJ said. The Irish wanted the English out of this country before there even were any Protestants.

Oh, forget I spoke! I said crossly.

That's exactly what I'm going to do! he said, just as cross.

The stage was a flatbed truck pulled across the top of the square. Three unmatched kitchen chairs had been placed in a line behind a microphone, but there was no one up there. Someone had put a tape-recorder on a bar stool near the microphone, and the fiddle music was coming from there. A large and grubby tricolour had been pinned to the back wall of the stage and along the front, weighed down by bricks, was a frieze of computer-lettered sheets of typing paper. MELLARY REMEMBERS 1798. MELLARY REMEM-BERS 1798.

They were handing out plastic chairs from the hall beside the church. An old man handed me one.

The press is very welcome! he said. We have nothing to hide in Mellary!

I'm not the – I began, but he was gone.

I tucked my chair in under a budding sycamore tree. The fiddle music ended.

Testing one two three! Testing one two three!

People began to gather. The man from jail spoke into the micro-phone, softly, in Irish that he'd obviously learned from a book –

Fáilte romhaibh a dhaoine uaisle go léir . . .

Our prisoners should never have been in jail! he was saying.

There were not more than twenty people on the rows of chairs, this being a weekday afternoon. A couple of boys going along the pavement shouted up, Fair play! Good man yourself!

I looked at my hands as the man spoke. I had never done anything with them but type out words. And caress, if you counted caressing as an activity. I looked at the ex-prisoner closely to see whether the fact that he read the world so differently from me somehow showed itself. Nothing. This man had a narrow face with cheekbones gouged in it, and nervous eyes, and his fingers were very white except that two of them and his right palm were stained dark brown from nicotine. The world said he was noble and that he'd responded to injustice, though he'd probably killed people – assisted in killing

221

them, anyway. Misguided, but an idealist, would be the consensus about him. But had I not been an idealist, too? How could I have been so sure, when I was a young woman, that I had got life wrong, if I hadn't had an ideal of what the right would be like?

I had the freedoms of a man all my life, I thought. But their satisfactions are a mystery to me.

An elderly gentleman with medals in his lapel was approaching the microphone now.

A Athair, a Chathaoirligh, agus a dhaoine uaisle go léir –

And then – to murmurs of approbation – he said it again, but this time in French: *Monsieur le Curé, Mesdames, Messieurs, vous êtes la bienvenue,* and we have among our number here today, and thanks be to God we have them, the descendants of two of the gallant men of Mellary sentenced to transportation to New Geneva, Australia, for the alleged crime of administering and taking an illegal oath to be members of an illegal organization – the United Irishmen . . .

Suppose I jumped up on the lorry and grabbed the microphone and said, I have hurt other people very deeply and they have hurt me. I want you to help me to see how to bring this evil to an end. Suppose I said, I have had my own English wars? I have been defeated, in my time.

Caroline's father was part of it, and he helped fix my direction towards the half-lit basement. Sir David mattered greatly in my life, I was beginning to realize, even though he only figured in it for about a month. Maybe I was right to explain what he did to me – and what I did in response – in terms of our nationality. But it had a lot to do with the times. In England in the mid-1970s, after all, there was an IRA bombing campaign going on that involved Irish people killing domestic workers and teenagers out for a beer and housewives doing their shopping, and children playing. It would have been difficult at any time to be unselfconsciously Irish in the company of English people like Sir David, who wouldn't have known any Irish people except in the form of chauffeurs, jockeys, gardeners. In the atmosphere of those years, it was more than difficult.

I moved in with Caro, the night Hugo threw me out, to the mews her father had bought her as a reward for getting an arts degree. He lived in Hong Kong but he'd come to London for a few weeks, and he was enjoying helping her set up house. When I materialized as the person who'd be taking the other room, he bought each of us a beanbag and a futon.

No favourites! he announced, with his usual jovial laugh, when he rang to say the shop would be delivering them. I intend to treat both you young ladies exactly the same!

But Caroline flirted with him like the cherished daughter she was, and rang him up to complain about her boyfriends, and he rang her back in the early mornings to give her advice. I envied her, sitting in her expensive kimono at the kitchen table in the sun, murmuring away to him. She would gesture – smiling at me to pour myself coffee from the pot – and curl herself into the phone like a baby.

He watched me, at first. Perhaps he'd heard a version of why Hugo had thrown me out. Or else he made a judgement about how poor I was and how insecure and how much I needed Caroline's patronage. Or maybe he sensed some corruption in me. Or fatalism. It doesn't really matter why he eventually waited for me in the corridor of the flat and followed me into the bathroom and pushed his meaty tongue into my mouth, or why, when he offered to drop me at the Underground he locked the doors of the car with a flick and, without a word, lunged and would not let me out till I rubbed him through his trousers. What matters is that I put up with it. I just bore with it, as if this were some past century and that was what always happened. The squire and the serving wench. Though, I lit a cigarette when I got out of the car that first time and smoked it standing outside Hampstead station, and I only smoked in the street in an emergency.

He got the two of us our first proper jobs – Caro on an education magazine, and me on the genteel monthly called *The English Traveller*. Just a few phone calls was all it took. He sat at our kitchen table and did it while the two of us looked at him, and afterwards we cooed at him and gave him pecking kisses, like little girls.

The groping went on for the month he was around. I knew that a lot of people would have expected me to walk out, or to complain to Caro, or at least to threaten him with telling Caro. But I couldn't.

I was on my own. It didn't seem to me that there was anything I could do. They were very close, the two of them, because Caro's mother had retired to Cornwall after the divorce and barely kept in touch with her daughter. Caro had chosen me over Hugo because she always helped the underdog, but she wouldn't choose me over her father. I'd lose my precious home. Above all, I'd lose her, and being her girlfriend, and she mine. I'd lose going out for a coffee with her late on Saturday mornings, and laughing our way around the supermarket together – me secretly so proud to be with such a beautiful, blonde, privileged woman. I'd lose our nights in our pyjamas lolling on the beanbags in front of the television that sat on the polished wood floor of the empty living room. Just because of a few gropes! And I liked her so much. I didn't want to tell her anything unpleasant about her beloved Poppa. For that reason I was even more careful than he that she would never suspect. I was not unconscious. I'd read *The Golden Notebook* and I'd been – by myself, but chanting along with the rest of them – on women's marches: I read *Spare Rib* every month and I was always telling Caro, who was no more than vaguely interested, about the women's movement. But I didn't stand up to Sir David. I didn't even stay out of the flat to avoid him. I behaved as if nothing at all was happening. Sure – what harm is being felt up, anyway? I thought. Though after a while I said to myself with a certain bitterness, He's not feeling me up, actually. He's not interested in me. He's using me to feel himself.

A priest had arrived on the platform now.

Before we ask Mr Molloy, County Councillor and former member of Dáil Éireann, to pull the curtain on the plaque, let us commend this event to God, through His Blessed Mother, with her holy Rosary. The First Glorious Mystery, the Resurrection . . . Our Father . . .

You could hear the Sinn Féin man praying along in Irish in a Belfast accent. *Ár nAthair*. Or Nohir.

We'd all moved onto our knees. They were kneeling on the flaps of handbags, on folded newspapers. I took off my jacket and knelt on it. I hadn't said a Rosary since I left school. A nice, easy prayer. Rocking along repetitively, like the chants in any religion.

Caroline entranced me. She was the first rich girl I ever knew. Her wealth seemed to me to show in things like the delicate little ankles, made of fine bones like a bird's, which sat so easily in the strappy high heels she tapped around in. She was slender and light, and she had tiny breasts, almost covered by areolae like the velvet petals of brown pansies. She wore no bra, and her panties were as small as handkerchiefs under the simple, expensive clothes she pulled from the jumble in her wardrobe and threw on in the mornings. Her hair dried into a sheet of gold: she brushed it back with the brush she'd had at boarding school, and clipped little earrings on while she talked on the phone, and pushed expensive things into her shoulder bag. A miniature tape-recorder; a bottle of Joy, her big black diary, tampons. I've got the curse, I might hear her saying on the phone as a normal part of gossip with her girlfriends or boyfriends, and I, who would not have said such a thing under any circumstances, was impressed and repelled.

I wouldn't give her father blow jobs. Those were the only times I was his equal – when he was panting, and I was dumbly refusing.

He went away. I used to ask myself whether he behaved to the Chinese girls the way he did to me – Hong Kong had been part of the British Empire, too. Or whether it was only with me he took the risk. I was afraid that there was something about me that said that I would collude. Caroline had the occasional boyfriend who stayed the night and she worried about me because, though I went out with blokes, I never slept with any of them. She'd say, Kathleen, if you want to bring someone home you're very welcome – it's your room to do what you like in, you know. She didn't know that I was frozen deep. That I could still feel Hugo's knee kicking me in the small of the back down the stairs. That I still asked myself – long after he had gone away – how did Sir David know I'd cause no trouble? I felt as far from the girl who went to Paros as the cold moon is from the hot sun.

The Second Glorious Mystery, the Ascension of Our Lord.

Hail Mary, full of grace . . .

At least I had my wonderful new job. I hero-worshipped the elderly lady who was the editor and sole other writer for *The English*

Traveller – a surprisingly lucrative, badly printed little magazine which had been going since the 1920s. She behaved as if she were a head girl and I was her trusted prefect and everyone else was a silly first-former we were entitled to bully. I worked as hard as I could for her.

But my own, personal Anglo-Irish war went on. Once while I was doing a piece on 'Hidden Beauties of the Peak District', I came back to the hotel and found the police waiting. I was a learner driver and I thought I'd done something wrong on the road. But they took me around the back, across a yard, to where my bag was sitting on a packing case in the doorway of a garage.

The manager and the chef in his white hat were watching from the kitchen door.

Will you open the bag for us, please?

I will of course.

Take the back off, they said when I took out my travelling clock. Take the battery out.

I pulled the contents of the bag out in front of them. Black underwear – old and worn, from my time with Hugo when I thought I was sexy and I loved myself and I bought underwear so that he – no! I said to myself, don't think about it. And now the underwear meant that my things didn't look like a terrorist's things. The cop picked up the book I had in the bag and shook it out. Then he looked at the title. I was going on to Sheffield so I was reading Arnold Bennett, *Anna of the Five Towns*.

Sorry about that, the senior policeman said. They don't get many Irish here . . .

It was nothing, the little episode. It didn't take five minutes. They had every right to do it. But for a long time afterwards I thought, They could have set me up! God knows, it happened to other Irish people . . .

I learned to ask for things – a meal, a drink, directions to a place – in a low voice and as neutral an accent as I could manage. I learned to look up at the television – at the pictures of tape across driveways, shoppers staggering forward with blood on their faces, white ambulances screaming around the curves of quiet housing estates – with no expression on my face. And to read my newspaper, and smile at everyone, and say nothing noticeable. It was like my life in Caroline's flat: I appeared to be as blithe as everyone else, but I concealed a watchful underlife.

The Rosary was droning on. No point in sneaking away. Both the PJs were very much in view and praying con brio, so I couldn't get my groceries anyway. I eased myself up onto a chair. I could see from a few expressions around me that not everyone had expected the priest to go through the whole five decades and they were none too happy about it. And it was getting chilly, too. Spring hadn't quite softened into early summer. I looked at my watch. Quarter to six. I felt my hair. Lots of conditioner the hairdresser had put in in Athlone, when he was doing the highlights, and it felt glossy. The Sinn Féin man was still saying the prayers in Irish though no one else was.

The Fourth Glorious Mystery, the Assumption . . .

The anti-Irish thing in Alex came as a complete shock. Especially since it was well into the 1980s when I stumbled on it, when things were quite good between the Irish and the English, most of the time, in England.

We were on a train going to a general NewsWrite meeting in a country house hotel in the Midlands, Alex, Jimmy, and I. Alex snapped his laptop open on the table top. PCs were still a new thing then, and I could see how much satisfaction he got from playing with his. I saw an ad once – a man lying on a hotel bed, his tie loosened but his cuffs buttoned, as he played on his PC. With Our New Global Modem You Won't Get Stuck in a Foreign Country. Stern and capable the man in the ad looked, the way Alex was arranging himself to look. When Alex became absorbed like that it made me behave like a brat. I heard myself, helplessly, becoming loud and looking for attention.

Toss me! I said to Jimmy, taking out a coin. For the next 'Twenty-four Hours in Hellholes You Hate'.

This was our name for a series on European cities TravelWrite was offering around.

Please, please swop me Düsseldorf, I said. I'll happily take Nicosia instead. Though – I could go on to Vienna to see the Vermeer –

No, Jimmy said. I want Düsseldorf. The gay scene in Germany is a lot more evolved than the scene in Cyprus.

Alex cut across us. I tried to persuade myself, afterwards, that he was unconsciously jealous of my larking about with Jimmy. But probably we'd insulted him by not even consulting him, as the editor.

I thought you Irish people were very keen on the Germans? he snapped at me. Seeing as how you were on their side in the war? Stuffing yourselves with steak, your lot were, when we were willing to fight to the last man. Got your reward, too, didn't you, in the so-called Common Market? Your old pals just shower money on the Emerald Isle, don't they?

At that point Jimmy ostentatiously opened the morning paper and disappeared behind it.

I wish you English would stop talking about 'you Irish', I began slowly. There's Irish and Irish, including the tens of thousands who joined the British forces, many of whom were killed. It just so happens that I've looked into this, and I know that at the time Irish labour was so badly needed, especially to build aerodromes, that Westminster did not want Ireland to introduce conscription. Your leading spies in MI5 were able to assure Churchill that the Irish were neutral but neutral on the side of the Allies. So there!

Actually, Kathleen, Alex said awkwardly, that was an uncalled-for remark about eating steak. I'm sorry.

We had to go to a management strategy seminar that afternoon in a wonderful Jacobean room in the country house, with peacocks on the grassy terrace outside and great oak trees shading the lawn. I sat there thinking about what Henry James would have made of the setting, while I had to endure a tense young woman in Armani babbling on about the three steps to customer satisfaction while the big boss sat beside her, assessing us for enthusiasm. Alex fell asleep. I moved my chair to hide him from the boss. He began to sag towards the floor. I moved again, and physically propped him up by leaning into him. He breathed deep and slow like an innocent little boy.

The truth was that I did feel shame about the war. I'd see something in London – an old tube station entrance, maybe, uncovered in building work, that would have sheltered Londoners at night during the Blitz. Or someone's father would die and I'd hear, He was at Dunkirk, or, He was on the Burma railway . . . I was always alert to bits of information about Ireland's role in the Second World War – that was how I was able to blow poor Alex out of the water with my quotations. And I often felt bitterly ashamed in central Europe. Standing at places like the deep quarry where thousands were flung to death in the extermination camp at Mauthausen on an autumn morning, when the mist rose from its floor like evil visible. And Anne Frank's house in Amsterdam – the heartbreak of her heights as a girl, getting taller for nothing, marked on the wall. And the recital of the names of the dead, going on for ever in the Holocaust museum in Jerusalem. And the candles for dead children. And the marshalling yards in Thessaloniki where they put the Greek Jews into wagons for Auschwitz. And the stadium near the Père Lachaise cemetery where they held the Jewish children of Paris before sending them off.

I once got drunk in Munich and I spent an hour trying to get the telephone number of the convent in Kilcrennan. Then I insisted that it was urgent I speak to the nun who taught us history.

I'd been sitting unsteadily on the edge of the bed, weeping.

You're old enough to remember, Sister! Why didn't we fight the Nazis? Why? Why?

Where are you, Kathleen?

I was in Dachau today.

We didn't know, dear girl –

We *should* have known! I said. The English were so brave! And the privations they endured! I saw a recipe for wartime apple tart, Sister – a layer of stewed apple, a layer of wood ash, a layer of stewed apple, a layer of ash –

The Civil War would have started here again! the nun said. We hadn't been independent of Britain for even twenty years, in 1939!

Two wrongs don't make a right! I cried down the phone.

Don't be such a baby! the nun shouted back.

We had to stand around drinking sherry that evening at the management conference before going in to dinner. Even Jimmy agreed that Alex looked terrific in evening dress.

I must apologize, Kathy, he said. I was way out of order this morning. And as you said, I really don't know a thing about history.

Don't worry, Alex, I said. I hope I wasn't rude to you.

Oh, no! Alex said. I'm afraid I started it.

It doesn't matter, Alex, I was beginning, when Jimmy started to groan.

What sins could I possibly have committed in a previous life, he implored the ceiling, to have to hang around with the two of you?

The murmur of the Rosary suddenly ended in a heartfelt Glory be to the Father. We asked God in a hurried PS to lead all souls to heaven, especially those who had most need of His mercy.

And now, the priest said, Mr Hughie Shannon, whose great-great-great-grandfather was sentenced to one thousand lashes and imprisonment in 1798, will now play 'Boolavogue' on the accordion!

Sustained applause from the small number of people who hadn't hurried away in the last few minutes.

A very old and small gentleman, all but hidden behind a massive accordion, was helped up the steps onto the stage.

At Boolavogue as the sun was setting
O'er the bright May meadows of Shelmalier
A rebel band set the heather blazing . . .

The priest sang it loudly into the microphone.

It's great, isn't it? the woman beside me said to me. Mighty stuff!

I walked down the street towards the grocery shop. Behind me Mrs PJ in a lettuce-green coat was up at the microphone reading a list of thank-yous to everyone who had helped to make the day such a success, but there was no one left to listen to her, and dusk was beginning to set in.

I walked past the High Chapparal pub, and saw through the open door that there was already a gang of young people in the dark lounge, their faces intermittently orange and purple in the disco lighting. They were singing, too. A fabulous-looking boy in a stetson was belting out Garth Brooks, standing on a table, leaning back and bumping his pelvis up and out. A barman toiling behind the pumps at the bar lifted his face. He saw me at the door and smiled and beckoned me in.

Oh I've got friends in low places –

A line of girls were swaying with their arms around each other, waving their big backsides in jeans to the room –

'Cause I've got friends in low places,
Where the whiskey drowns and the beer chases
My blues away
And I'll be okay –

On an impulse, I did go in, and sat in a dim corner near the door. The barman dropped everything he was doing and came over and wiped the table in front of me.

He said, I've seen you around the place. I was wondering do you take a drink at all.

He was too bashful to look at me, and kept wiping the table. A man of about forty with a homely face and a strong, footballer's body.

I'll just have a Coke, I said.

On the house, he said when he brought it back.

I laughed to myself – it must be the highlights. I was honoured, really.

Caroline and I used to go to a pub on Friday nights. We were part of a young crowd that socialized there. I began to imitate her. I sometimes called someone a poppet. I felt thinner. I ran for the bus with a high step, as if I had her grace. I bought a shoulder bag and threw it over my arm like she did hers. But I was never like her. Her duvet and pillows, always strewn half off the mattress onto the floor, were white and luxurious, and smelled of perfume. Her forearm was so faultless that I decided that rich people are actually less hairy than poor people — that they've bred out the hair and the smells and the pimples and the rolls of fat over centuries of mating with their own kind.

Then she fell madly in love with Ian, and that was the end of that.

But just before that happened we went on a trip — a trip that we remembered afterwards as if it had been a hallucination.

The silver-haired lady editor of *The English Traveller* offered me the freebie to Belfast as a treat.

But, I said. The Troubles —

This was 1975, when things were very bad in Northern Ireland.

I think you'll find, she said, that they'll be awfully glad to see you. I expect they're like us during the Blitz — best foot forward, you know. The woman from the tourist office is absolutely delighted you're coming. You might like to bring a friend — a suite was mentioned, and a car to meet you at the airport.

Did you tell them that I'm Irish myself? I was brave enough to ask.

I told the tourist woman, the editor said firmly, that *The English Traveller* is completely non-political. You will be visiting museums and parks and so forth.

I invited Caroline to come with me.

It's only one night, I said.

Belfast! she said, wonderingly. *Belfast*? Gosh! I can't say I ever thought of going to *Belfast*. But it certainly would be interesting to see your country.

It's not my country. That's what the fighting is about, Caroline. It's yours.

Well, I don't want it, she said politely.

Well, it wants you, I said. The unionists want you. The republicans don't.

Will we leave politics out of it? she said hopefully.

Listen, Caroline, I said. Politics are the only interesting thing about Belfast. Take the armoured cars and the graffiti and the hatred and the murders away, and what is Belfast but a British mercantile city? The kind of place that if it had a wool trade J. B. Priestley would have written novels about.

Who's J. B. Priestley? Caroline said.

We went out to Heathrow early, to get started. Caroline bought me a satin slip in the underwear shop, in the hope that I'd get a lover someday. I bought her a tape of Kathleen Ferrier singing Bach, in the hope she'd get good taste. Then we had vodka martinis with onions in them. Then on the plane we had two mini bottles of champagne each and then we asked the snooty hostess for two more to put in our bags.

Note well, Caroline, I said, trying to raise Caroline's consciousness, that that hostess only smiles at the men. She doesn't bother when it's us.

We're the only women in first class, Caroline said.

Yeah. I'd say our kind of woman hasn't happened in Belfast yet.

Sammy the driver was a middle-aged man with a tiny pony-tail behind a big round head, and a pouty chest in a bomber jacket, on top of neat hips in jeans. He moved with real loyalist bounce on his thick suede shoes. He seemed unfazed by meeting one ordinary-looking woman with an Irish accent and one rich-looking one with a Hampstead accent, both wild-eyed from quick drinking.

He dropped the bags at the Europa Hotel. We wouldn't get out.

Register for us, Sammy darling, we said from the back of the limo. And then let's go and have a little drink somewhere very, very Belfast.

He took us up the Shankill Road to a drinking club on waste ground deep within a maze of tight little redbrick houses. We had a hard time crossing the rubble in our high heels. Sammy had to get Caro across and then come back for me. Then – as far as I could remember next day – silent women with baroque blonde hairstyles watched us malevolently across Bacardi and Cokes all night, while Sammy brought a stream of small, witty men to our table.

They certainly seemed very witty at the time, Caro agreed, after-wards. Oh God, she winced. I think I went up on the stage and sang Neil Diamond. 'Sweet Caroline!' Oh, tell me I didn't!

You didn't. It was a Tom Jones medley, I said. You did a kind of pelvic dance to 'It's Not Unusual'.

Oh *no*!

Then Sammy had brought us back to the hotel. He steered us in through the revolving door and abandoned us.

A doorman came over and said, Ladies! Can I send anything up to your suite?

Caroline, they're trying to make us go to bed, I said.

Caroline said, No! No! I won't!

And we wobbled up to the first-floor lounge and ordered – I remember the duet with the waiter – a glass of, no, do you do half-bottles – no – make that a bottle of – oh all right, champagne.

Because we began with champagne, Caroline said. I think we did, anyway.

The last I remembered I had decided to hand Northern Ireland over to Caroline so as to stop the war.

I swayed upright on the sofa, spraying champagne all over myself.

Men and women have died over the centuries for these fair six counties, I said. Well, not so much over the centuries maybe but quite recently they did. But they definitely have died, Caroline. It wasn't fair what was done to the Catholics, Caroline. The land of Ireland for the people of Ireland. Well, now this land is yours to bring forward in peace into centuries to come.

Caroline in turn swayed into a sitting position.

All right, Kathleen. I promise you I'll do my best.

Promise, Caroline! I said, nearly crying. Promise?

I promise, Kathy. Really I do.

We somehow got ourselves up to the suite with its two huge beds. We were going to watch the late-night movie but we couldn't find any television sets.

I was woken an hour or two later by a noise and sat up abruptly, dry-mouthed and sick. I was on top of my bed, wearing my new satin slip and one shoe.

Oh, *fuck off*, I shouted at the army helicopter hovering like a huge lawn mower on the level of the penthouse windows. Then I took four Anadin and got into the bed and fell asleep.

I'd finished my Coke in the High Chapparal, smiling to myself at the thought of the two of us girls.

Thank you! See you again! I called across to the barman.

Don't forget! he called back. Come in any time. I'll look after you!

I walked out, still smiling, and bumped into a stocky man who was walking up the street.

I was afraid you'd be gone, the man said.

It was Shay.

I looked at the man. Commonplace clothes, worn-looking blue eyes, a tense frown on his face.

You said you were going for the paper –

I'm here now, he snapped. I'm supposed to be on the plane to Liverpool . . .

There's nothing to eat, I said.

I couldn't think of anything else to say. But it was enough.

That's a pity, he said, and his whole face eased out into a smile. Because I've been on the go since seven o'clock this morning and I'm hungry.

There's a hotel – I began.

Could we not go home? he said.

I opened up inside at that word – home.

He stood patiently beside me while I tackled Mrs PJ, still in her good green coat.

Fresh fish? she said. Don't make me laugh. This is the west of Ireland – you can only buy fish here by accident. The fish from that bay out there go past this village in a refrigerated lorry every morning, and they come back in a different lorry from Dublin to the supermarket in town. Is this another de Burca, Kathleen? She beamed insincerely at Shay.

No, I said.

We chose two big purple steaks from the meat counter, and a bag of potatoes covered in soil.

They're best like that, Mrs PJ said. Wait'll you see – balls of flour, those spuds are. I'd say now, mister, that you don't often see potatoes like that where you come from?

Shay didn't take the hint. He just paid, and he took the two plastic bags, and he carried them to my car. Not many men had carried

plastic bags full of groceries for me in my life. That's what saved us
– the shopping, and then the peeling the potatoes standing together
at the draining board cursing the blunt knives, and him telling me
about the new generation of lawnmowers, and me telling him how I
used to bring Big Macs back to the flat for next door's cat but that
when I gave up smoking I didn't dare go into a McDonald's, I was
so hungry all the time.

We'll leave this stuff, I said, after we had eaten with pleasure –
steak fried black, on top of white, boiled potatoes, beside bright red
tomatoes. It was eating of a completely different kind from the
picking at food I'd done in restaurants all over the world, in company
so meaningless that I prayed for time to pass.

Ah, no, he said. I'm a dab hand at dishes. But don't rush me.
Finish your wine.

I sat beside the fire. The radio was playing ballroom music.

I love that kind of music, he said. It's for fellas my age.

He hummed 'Cherry Pink And Apple-Blossom White'.

We were as relaxed as an old couple.

Which do you prefer, I said to him, England or Ireland? I'm
thinking all day about all the trouble I had when I was starting off in
England.

That's the sixty-four-thousand-dollar question, he said, seriously.
I never had a choice, when I was a boy, and then when I made my
bed in England I had to lie on it. I think America would have suited
me much better, but no one had the money for the fare to America.
But I definitely think English people are straighter than Irish people.
I notice it doing my father's books in Sligo – they're as slippery as
fish when it comes to paying their bills, his customers.

I believe you, I agreed. English people are straighter. My boss
wouldn't take as much as a sheet of paper from the office to use at
home, he's that honest.

Shay was putting my laptop back on the table he'd cleared.

You know you told me you were writing about something that
happened long ago? he said. That you couldn't get all the facts of?
Well, what? What kind of thing?

It's about mad, passionate love, Shay, I said, batting my eyelashes at him.

Oh, he said. Well, I'm sure there's not much anyone can teach *you* about that.

He knelt beside me and bent his head and leaned it very lightly against my chest. I lowered my own head, and my chin rested on the soft grey stubble on his head.

I'm surprised at you remembering what I said, I murmured.

Everything, he said. Every word you say. Always, I'll remember . . .

We were there together – barely touching, immobile – and after a while a throbbing started deep inside me, and gradually it began to beat a heavy rhythm through both of us. I heard him swallow, to try to speak. But he couldn't. And I couldn't. Then I stood up to lead the way into the bedroom.

It took just one moment to succumb to the seriousness of his closed lips as he delicately laid them on mine. My fingers felt the skin on his face. It was rough along the line of his jaws and then smooth, under the closed eyes. He suddenly pushed his tongue into my hot mouth and began to suck fervently, as if he wanted to drink everything in me. His hand had pushed my thighs apart, and he was stroking me between the legs. Down. Down. The cloth stuck in the folds of my skin as I began to get wet.

He moved his mouth away from mine.

I thought about you morning and night, he said.

I might not have been here, I said.

I said to myself all the way from Sligo, she will be there, she will. She has to be –

You said you were going for orange juice, I whispered into his face.

But I explained! he said. He started back, and his face was alive with the effort of convincing me. Did you not get my letter? I told you I had to go or I'd never be able to go!

The impassioned words. The ordinary face. I had never heard a man talk in this tone.

His fingers were stroking me urgently, as if they could convince me, too. His fingers pleaded. They felt as if they would never tire, as if they must stroke me until I dissolved under them.

Afterwards, I watched a bar of moonlight establish itself across the deep sill, as our exhausted bodies lay apart from each other on the bed.

Will we go down to the shore for a walk? I said.

We put some clothes on in silence.

The mild night soothed us both.

Oh! he said, throwing his head back. A thick bank of charcoal lay along the horizon. Behind it, a remote cloud was still suffused with candy colours.

Oh, I'd forgotten what clean air is like! he said. You could cut the air where I live.

I don't know what that sky means, I said. It's weird-looking –

But it's red, he said. Look! Over there, far out. Red sky at night, shepherd's delight.

Yes, but look at the pattern. Like the markings on a fish, I said. Mackerel sky, mackerel sky, never long wet, never long dry. If only that cloud would clear we might see seals. I saw three the other morning. Mammy, Daddy, Junior.

Believe it or not, he said, I rescued a seal pup once, in Ballisodare. It was lost. In the morning, very early, when I was fishing. I took it back to the house and I made a kind of pool out the back from rocks and a black plastic sheet. I came home from school, and the seal had got indoors, and he was sitting in an old armchair, with his flipper resting on the arm, listening to the music on the radio. My father made me take it back to the sea . . .

I put my arm around his waist, and slipped my hand under his waistband and laid it on the soft skin of his belly, lovingly.

The sea, underneath the lip of the last field, was almost unmoving. But it was very full. It swelled, in great sliding curves and hollows, its surface like black oil.

Shay said, I'll be able to see what you look like in the moonlight.

I was confused – relieved that he was staying; but shy at the thought of him scrutinizing my body and wary, in case he was going to become sentimental and false.

Are you staying, then? I asked.

Will you have me? he said.

Do I have any choice? I said.

Oh, yes, he said. He swung around, with the sea and the darkening sky behind him, and he took me in his arms. He was a hundred times more confident since we had been to bed.

Oh, indeed you have, he said. You can choose.

How long can you stay? I said.

Tomorrow afternoon.

Yes.

Okay, I said later. Tell me.

I'm from Ballisodare originally, he said. I went to England to find work, when I was young. I married a local girl I met at a dance when I was on the buildings. We live near Chester, and we have two daughters and they're both married near us. I called my gardening business 'and Daughters' for a bit of a joke and because we're very close.

What and daughters?

What?

What's your second name?

Oh, he said. After a moment he said, Does it matter?

Mine's de Burca, I said pointedly.

Is that Burke? he said. Kathleen Burke, he said slowly. *And when the fields are fresh and green, I will take you home again, Kathleen . . .*

De Burca, I said. My father changed it to the Irish version in a fit of patriotism.

My wife minds the grandchildren when the girls are at work – a little boy and a little girl. I have my bit of a landscaping business and I used to go to the pub. But a few years ago I started coming back here every so often to give my father a hand, and I've got back into the Irish way. My wife isn't that interested in the Irish side of things, naturally enough – she hasn't even been here since the girls were small. So I go to the Irish Club now when I go out for a drink but she usually stays at home and watches the telly. Or, the girls come over to her, most evenings.

His voice was warm and fond.

There's nothing in this for me, I said. You being happily married.

I know that, he said.

Murphy's my name, he said after a pause. I'm a bit self-conscious about it. Every second Paddy in England is called Murphy.

Some time that night he said, Do you like me?

Ah, well, liking . . .

We don't know each other long enough? he murmured. He was lying back in the broken old armchair in front of the fire he'd managed to make burst into flame. He was wearing just the trousers he'd pulled on, with me in my nightdress held on his lap. I shivered, and he put a heavy arm around me and tucked me into his chest, like a father would.

We hadn't turned on the lights, when we came out of the bedroom. He'd thrown a heap of briquettes on, while I was making tea.

I think we know each other, he said. It's as if I knew you before. I never did anything like this. I never even told lies. Well, hardly at all. But something happened, with you. I saw you leaning over the wall pegging a stone along the water, the day I went out to the ferry. I saw the wind lifting your skirt and something happened in me. I can't find the words, Kathleen. It was that I had to try to talk to you, no matter what.

His hand had been resting comfortably on my belly. He gently pinched the fold of plumpness there. I usually pulled the muscles in, automatically, to disguise the fat. But with him, I let everything about myself be.

My little girl's little secret, he said.

We were half asleep, the two of us. He was humming something tunelessly under his breath.

The llama hums to its young, I said. Not many people know that.

The world around us was absolutely quiet. I could feel the heavy, slow rhythm of his heart. I tried to remember when I had felt such peace before.

241

Only when I was alone, I thought to myself, and this seemed to me a great revelation. I turned my head lazily into his arm and kissed its smooth underside. If being with him was like being by myself, maybe he was my other half?

Maybe you're my other half, I said, into the warm skin of his arm.

Ah no, he said. I'm not a bit like you.

I was lying in a bed, once, on a summer night, in a hotel on the waterfront of a village on Lake Constance. It must have been midsummer: the pale and silvery light of the night never quite faded, and I never fell out of its hold on me, into full sleep. I'd cycled there from Konstanz, I remember that. I'd been at some kind of tourism thing in Strasbourg and I'd come across the Black Forest on the train, and hired a bike. The exquisite night was my reward for a day of cycling. The bedroom was over the front door of the hotel: the bottom of the tall window was on a level with the tops of the linden trees that lined the little promenade. Decorous couples had strolled up and down under the lights threaded through their branches, all evening. I'd eaten out there, my book propped on the salt cellar. A brown trout with firm, pale flesh. Now it was the middle of the night, and the window was open wide to the lake that shimmered, as I lay on the high bed, on the level of my face. It was as if I had only to be carried forward, and I and the lake would be one. I remember the feel of the linen on the pillows behind my head. Occasionally, a bird's distant wail or the sudden soft chirp of a waterfowl would emphasize the great bowl of silence in which room and bed and lake were suspended. A pearly mist rose from the lake.

That was what I felt, in the middle of the night, in Shay's arms.

The fire died down.

My Kathleen, he whispered. You'll get cold.

I'm not cold . . .

But I did fall asleep for a little while in his arms. When I woke, he was watching my face.

Did you sleep, too? I murmured.

I haven't got time to sleep, he said.

Don't say that yet! I sat up, agitated. We have time left!

He was looking down at me.

I don't want everything I built up to go to rack and ruin! he cried out, as if I had been threatening him.

He left halfway through the next day. I didn't even go to the door. I couldn't. I asked him when he might be back. He said he didn't know. I said I wouldn't be here; if I was in Ireland at all I'd be at The Talbot Arms in Ballygall.

You are Ireland to me, he said, looking at me sadly from across the room, his bag in his hand. Your curly hair and all. And that it breaks my heart to leave you.

So I just wait around, do I? I asked. I was crying bitterly. Is that all I can do?

That's all, he said.

I lay in the armchair, after he went. The top of my nightdress was open. I could see one breast. There was a wide band of rash – raw speckles of pink on the white skin – stretching from the nipple halfway up the breast. At one point in the night he had been sucking me, and then his mouth went away, and then it came back and the sucking began again more strong and deep than I ever dreamed it could be. I had looked down, voluptuously – revelling in the sight of the fat curve of the breast and his head buried in it – when I saw out of the corner of my eye a thing on the bed. His false teeth! His denture! He had taken his denture out, to give me pleasure without hurting me!

I'd felt disgust and shock, at first. But those reactions happened somewhere distant, in my head. The strong gums chewing on me were thrilling me from the inside out. I never thought about the false teeth again, or noticed when he slipped them back into his mouth.

Now, I pinched my sore nipples to make them more sore. To make the memory of him last longer.

I'm getting old. If I am never with him again I will die before I die.

But when I washed, an unlined, bright-eyed Kathleen looked back at me from the speckled mirror across the bath. I made the bed, tenderly smoothing the sheets and pillows we had used. I thought of getting in and going to sleep. But I was too restless. Four-thirty. Thursday? Yes – Thursday. I'd better make a few calls. Nora. Caroline. It was ages since I spoke to Alex. But I didn't go to the phone. I could make the calls tomorrow, when I got back to Ballygall. I didn't want to come back into the daily world, yet.

The bedroom seemed full of a light that came and went. I opened the front door and peered out from the porch. Yes! A windy, rolling, white-clouds-bowling-across-blue-sky day. I put an egg in a saucepan of cold water and turned the flame to low. Then I went out again, and around the back of the house, fighting the breeze, and across the grass the wind kept shaved and dense, to where the ridges of an old potato bed began. I squatted down, and with my eyes closed, the better to feel, I ran my hands along the rough edge of the furrow. As if there might be consolation for me in the sweep of time. As if, if I could see myself small enough in the scheme of things, I might not care about losing the sweet lover I had found so late. But I heard the wind break in the hawthorn hedge and I heard the scrappy, splashy waves coming in fast along the shore, and the pain was as energetic as they.

I rescued my boiled egg and made an eggcup out of a wineglass stuffed with twists of newspaper. Then I sat in the racing sun and shade beside the deep window and ate. Someone on the radio sang 'If I Loved You'.

> . . . *Off you would go in the mist of day,*
> *Never, never to know,*
> *How I loved you . . .*

I turned the pages of my anthology of poems in translation, looking for a particular poem in German that was the poem I needed now. Rilke. Its tone said: resign yourself. It said: this is how things are.

Immer wieder . . . was how it began. *Immer wieder ob* – something –

Und den kleinen – was it *die*? No. *Den kleinen Kirchhof, mit seinen Klagenden Namen* –

I found it. Yes.

Again and again, though we know the lie of love's land,
And the poignant names in its little churchyard,
And though we know that the others ended in a terrible, silent
    ravine.
Again and again we go out together under the ancient trees,
We lie down together, again and again, two by two –
Zwischen die Blumen, gegenüber dem Himmel –
Among the flowers. Faces up to the sky.

Then I turned to the Italian section, and, holding the book open at
the lines I wanted to begin with, I went over to the table, and
continued the Talbot book.

I 3

The Talbot Book (Continued)

L'attesa lunga,
Il mio sogno di te non finito.
The wait is long,
My dream of you does not end.

After Mullan touched her waist, Marianne was in a state of waiting, without any certainty that waiting would ever end. She plotted and planned.

She took Mab's hand and brought her down to the kitchen.

'I hear, Mrs Benn,' she said brightly, 'that there is a sweet little orphan lamb in a box –'

'The lamb is gone out to the yard, ma'am.'

She had gone down at midday. She could not help herself, when she heard the servants' bell. It still hung outside the kitchen door to call them to the meal, though there were only a handful of them left. Four or five girls and three or four men, were all the company at one end of the massive wooden table. Barlow the agent had gone south to an estate of his own. The steward had gone to America, to farm in the Susquehanna valley. Both dairymaids had gone to a hotel in Boston.

What if William Mullan went, and never touched her face again?

Marianne advanced a few feet across the flagstone floor. She looked at the wall of whitewashed brick, not at any of the servants.

'If she had a little bridle for it, Mab could lead the lamb about,' Marianne said.

'William Mullan!' Mrs Benn said. 'Did you hear what the mistress said?'

Marianne felt the heat flush through her as soon as she knew he was there, bent forward at the table, his back to her. She advanced from the door towards his back: six feet, five feet, four feet . . . She could feel their resentment at her visiting the kitchen. She dare not look at him. Then she retreated to the doorway. That was a thing that had never happened to her with her husband – that gush of heat. She had not known it could happen. There was no one she could tell it to. No one would ever know.

Except – he would know. If she could but be with him!

As it was, she had to lean against the wall as she went up the stairs. She ached between her legs from being in the same room as this under-coachman.

So, she paced and paced the house. Waiting.

There had been no visitors to stay for nearly a year, such was the risk of fever. And the town was quiet even on fair days. It used to be that commercial travellers and factors and pedlars drank beer and ate their bread with the local farmers in the licensed houses on fair days. But the constabulary patrolled the place now. The public houses did not open their front doors. Still, the back doors were more and more busy with comings and goings. Life was creeping back, at least into the town. But at Mount Talbot itself, exhaustion now reigned.

'Coby talks of selling up,' Richard said one night. 'And old Mr Treadwell is ill in London, I am informed, and may not return to Ireland. I am the only gentleman of any substance in half the county. This cannot endure.'

But Marianne walked the corridors and climbed the flights of stairs with new energy. For the first time, she began to learn the house. If she had dared, she would have asked Benn for the great ring of keys to the household, that she had never taken into her charge. The drawing room and the big dining room and all the reception rooms were more and more dusty. But down where she prowled, at the level of storerooms and cellars, it seemed to Marianne that life was pulsing through the house.

*

A week later, William Mullan rode out to the cottage behind the bog that had been his mother's.

One of the reasons he had never married was that he had held the memory of his mother very close. She had been soft with him far beyond what was usual in that place. Most of the women around had many children, but she had been widowed when she had only the one child, and William was her pride and joy. He learned tenderness from her. For example – the men around rarely showed affection to their dogs, though they were often proud of them, and competitive with the other men about them. No one rebuked the children for roughness or even calculated cruelty to pups or old dogs. But William and his mother, when they were alone, doted on their dogs. They had once had a greyhound so candidly emotional, and so gently insistent on showing its love for them – laying its fine head in the lap of one or the other as they talked – that William would not let the men race it with the other men's dogs, though he was only a boy himself when he stood up to them. He never told lies about himself; he had no need to tell lies. But he put it around that the dog had a hamstring defect. He didn't care if they mocked him for girlishness, but he didn't want them to mock the dog.

There were people from far back in the bog waiting under a stand of birch trees at the beginning of the causeway. They did not grudge it that Mullan still had a horse and a dog. Everyone who worked at the big house got plenty. Besides, it was in their memory that the men of the old chieftains' families always had fine animals.

The women fell on their knees on the causeway, blocking his path.

'Do something for us, *a Liam*! Do something for us!'

He could only pick his way past.

Out at the cottage, he looped the bridle around the branch of an alder tree. The grove of alder trees stood in water – the cottage on its knoll was only a few feet higher than the watery marsh. Lolly loved this place. She turned giddy, skidding past William and across the short grass and into the water, throwing arcs of bubbles into the still air, racing out again and up to William, circling his legs, panting, and then flashing back into the water as if she were fleeing from hot pursuit. When she had exhausted herself she would collapse onto

248

his feet, her flank across the front of his boots, and throw herself into instant sleep. At his stall in the stable, he sometimes came across her awake in the night, sitting watchfully in the dark. But out at his mother's place, she slept deep after her ecstasy, and her sighs and small whimpers kept him company in the silence.

A Mhama, he said to his mother's shade, *tá fíoreagla orm*.

He tried to describe the kind of fear that was gripping him, and also the humiliation it was to him to be afraid – he who had never been afraid, not even when the potato crop failed for the second year running, and the people started to get sick. Children's faces, turning black. But he hardly got beyond saying, over and over, that he was afraid.

Nior chuimhnigh mé uirthí! he said. I never thought of her!

Silent as he was, sitting on the stool with his back to the wall, looking across the room at the empty hearth where his mother would be sitting if she were alive, the dog felt his agitation, and growled.

He did not directly say that what frightened him was how ravenous he was to touch and be touched by Marianne Talbot. Such words could never be used between his mother and himself. He had never spoken intimacies to a woman. When he delivered horses from Ballinasloe, once, to a troop camped above Turin, he had spent some of his pay on the women who followed the regiment. A huge orange moon such as he had never seen in Ireland shone on the backs of the tethered horses he had stayed near, even as he rolled with the women. He hadn't been able to talk their language, no more than he could talk the same kind of English as Mrs Talbot. He might have been able to talk to a woman of his own people. But he hadn't thought of marrying. In these times? And what would he have to leave to a son? These two rooms? One field, and these few acres of water and reeds?

'I am lost,' William Mullan whispered to himself. 'I am gone astray.'

The dog slept pressed to his legs. The room filled with shadows.

That first time Marianne went to the tack room to inspect the bridle for Mab's pet lamb, she and William were delicate and shy, and did not even look at each other. But the next day, when she crossed the yard again, to ask for some decoration – a pattern of Mab's initials, perhaps – to be embossed on the leather straps, they moved towards each other. Everyone around the yard saw Mrs Talbot go to the stables, but it was merely a detail of the daily life of the place.

He put his hands on her waist, at the back of the room, behind the screen of hanging harnesses. Both of them were shuddering. He bent his head and rested his mouth, half open, against hers. There was no kiss. But what was within them broke its banks.

They used the fewest possible words from then on. He might murmur, as he led a horse past at the moment when she was coming down the side steps from the morning room, The old buttery, after the meal. Or she might whisper, if he brought a basket of turf up to the grate in the hallway, I will be in the orchard this evening. But they said nothing about what they were doing. Neither of them knew many words for the parts of their bodies. And they had never talked to each other, though they had often been alone since Marianne came to Mount Talbot.

The habitat of their passion, where they roamed like two animals on a great plain, was silence. Not perfect silence – there were always the sounds of the household and sounds coming in from the estate. Sheep, penned in a far yard. The creak of turf carts coming in from the bog. But the couple were habitually mute. Except that they panted and grunted when they forgot themselves in each other. Then afterwards there was peace, and silence again. And after that, she lived in a hot dream of him.

She had a marquetry box on her dressing table. She kept trinkets in it. The jewellery she had worn as a child; loose pearls; a few grimy medals. Someone had given her a pouch of diamond buttons from an old costume. She used them now to play the serious game of counting over her times with him. She sat in the window embrasure of her dressing room above the flight of steps at the side of the house. She had seen the sandy crown of her husband's head as he stood on the steps below her window, waiting for Mullan to bring the carriage around. She saw down onto Mullan's dark head, as he led the jangling horses to the steps. Fair head disappeared under the black roof of the carriage. Cropped dark head suddenly came near, as Mullan jumped up into the driving seat. She glimpsed his closed face as it lifted for a moment, as he twisted himself into position.

That was the look that set her on fire. That closed-away look. She crossed her legs under her skirt and pressed her fists down between the clenched legs, pressing through the aching flesh onto the bone. His unseeing face was what she craved – to make his face turn in on himself. She wanted to see it again above her, when he trapped her between his thighs and reared back and slid into her. She wanted to see it beneath her, when his slack lips fell away from her breast. She remembered his rapt face lying brown and russet on her white thigh, the day he first licked her between her legs. His mouth like a muscle had fastened on the tender jumpy thing at her core that she knew no name for.

She had been lying in the pantry off the lower buttery, among sacks full of grain. There were still so many thefts of grain that the sacks had been moved there – into the house. He had led her there that afternoon, pushing her ahead of him, lifting her skirts. She could smell grain and dust and her own smell, rising from her.

'I'll eat you up,' he had half groaned into her ear. He pronounced it ate. I'll ate you up. That had been on their fourth time. So far there had been six times. She put six diamond buttons in an exact row on the window sill.

She spent much of the day in her morning room. The sounds of the world outside would come into the silence around her. Rain splashing from a gutter. A cart with squealing wheels, going out to the bog. She could not sit at the piano, because of the tension in her, swirling, and because she was too sensitive to sit comfortably. At night, sometimes he was waiting quietly in the corridor when she went up, after Hessy and the indoor servants had finished household prayers and were locking up. She could not tell him to be there – she could only pray that he would be. She would see him in the flickering shadow at the edge of the light of her candle. He would step forward, and take the candlestick, and put it down, and begin to touch her. There was always some secret in her clothes that would tell him that her passion for him was always with her, like a flagellant's chains. She prepared these secrets, passing the days in a dream of him. She would have half unhooked her skirt from its bodice, or her stays would be already unlaced, or she would have taken off the horsehair petticoat and the stiffened one beneath it so that he could feel her limbs through the muslin underskirt. Sometimes she left off her pantalettes, and was naked for him under her crinoline, when he ran his hands over her in the first, mute minutes of being together. Sometimes, after a while, he had forgotten everything except his excitement, and she would hear him saying something over and over, under his breath, in the native language.

He had occasionally seen her smooth Mab's hair when it was the exquisite cloud of silver, when mother and child were sitting in the carriage, waiting for Richard. He had seen her perch the little girl, when she was crying about something, on her knees, and jump her gently up and down:

Who's the flower of the flock?
Who's the rose of the garden?
Who's her mama's pet?
Who's her little darling?
Toss her up! Up!

He remembered watching her carry the child towards where he stood readying one of the light phaetons for the mistress to drive out herself. It had been a brilliant summer morning, not long after she came to the house. She had come towards him across the white gravel and everything had dazzled. The infant was asleep, one small arm around her mother's neck, her body tucked into the shoulder by the mother's white hand.

He wanted to protect Marianne like that. To treat her finely, to show her he cherished every hair on her head, to make her his child, to lavish on her the protectiveness he had seen her show to Mab. These emotions were entirely new to him. Since boyhood, when his mother used to fine-comb his hair looking for lice, he had had little cause to touch or be touched by other human beings. There had been the greasy camp-following women near Turin. There had been his mother's hands, going from warm to cold when he held them for a day and a night, as she died. Horses. Dogs. But dogs were not persons; he drowned Lolly's pups without a thought, though she looked around for them in pitiable distress.

Mullan drank a little whisky when he was with men: that was all. Marianne brought a bottle of wine to him one time, and she drank it when she was with him, and she became languid, and lay beside him on the straw in her evening dress, holding him in her arms. Once she lifted herself half up and pushed the velvet of her dress down, and freed her breasts. She poured wine over her breasts. She said, Taste that! to him, and stuffed her breast into his mouth. He sucked at her for so long that a muscle rose in her breast behind her nipple and became a hard snout.

'Oh, look!' she said, amazed.

In the drawing room, a half hour later, she sat on a sofa across the fireplace from Richard, and seemed to look at an album. When Richard dropped off into a snoring sleep she plucked at her breast through the fabric of her dress. But it would not harden again for her fingers.

In the sod shelter under the furze bushes, someone said, 'William Mullan brought a bag of the landlord's food to the places around the crossroads. They're all sick there. They're on the ground. I went to get Paudie and he was lying on the ground in his place and the wife was beside him under his cloak and the children were under the cloak, too, and they were all whimpering like calves. Mullan is giving that food around there. But they don't want it. They want the doctor's medicine.'

Marianne would remember a touch or a sound and a cramp of ecstasy recalled would stop her dead – walking on the avenue, or crossing the hallway, or lifting her arms when her maid was dressing her for dinner. Sometimes she had to close her eyes for a moment. She didn't see exact pictures, or talk to herself in words. She was held in an atmosphere as thick as smoke.

She did not care to go through the town. The wraith-like people in the streets, that Mullan shoved and prodded away from the carriage with the stock of his whip, were the strong ones. The doctor had told her that. Weak people, especially old people, had stayed in their cabins, and died there if they were going to die at all.

'But it is over now, Dr Madden says. The worst of it is well over,' Marianne said to her husband one evening.

When they took their places at the table that night they had been disturbed by grotesque figures who had come up the lawn, and tapped on the long windows of the dining room, not twelve feet from where Richard Talbot sat.

'How did they get over the wall?' he asked, and rang the bell. 'Get Benn.'

Richard was looking across the table, through the candelabra already lit against the dusk of the evening, and past his wife's bare neck, at the faces and hands pressed against the glass.

They stopped eating, though Richard slowly drank his wine.

Mullan and Benn arrived outside. The intruders were pulled away from the windows.

After a while, Benn came in and stood just inside the door.

'They are from outside the walls, master,' he said. 'They used to live in that village at the top of the lane behind the West Gate. Cousins of Michael O'Connor. They are not begging for food. They are looking for work, or to be let back into their houses to work for themselves.'

'Get the constables,' Richard said.

'It is over, the doctor told me,' Marianne said. 'The bad time. Any of those we see moving around are strong, even when they are so thin. All the ones who are not strong, died.'

When Benn came back into the dining room, Richard said to him, 'Instruct all who answer the front door that Dr Madden is not to be admitted to this house, except by my specific invitation, until all fear of fever in the Mount Talbot district has passed.'

*

The lovers had the luxury of time only once in the first year or so of their affair. That was when Richard instructed Mullan to drive Mrs Talbot over to bid cousin Letitia farewell, in the next county, twenty miles away. The track lay over low hills where all the people had either died or taken the ticket for the American ship. There weren't even marks of where they had once been, so well had their cabins been levelled. Up in the hills, Mullan pulled the horses over and tethered them, and let down the steps and came into the carriage, where she lay already soft with desire. He helped her – a hazy, golden sunlight filled the autumn morning – to the little meadow that had once been the garden of a cottage. He rode above her, blotting out the sun. He had the outline of a giant to her bedazzled eyes.

Afterwards, he had had to spend a long time on his knees in front of her as she lay naked on her corsets and skirts in the carriage, picking out the sheep ticks that had begun to burrow into her skin when she was pressed into the grass. The tiny black heads glistened in her white skin, and his nails were thick and horny, and left red semicircles where he dug the ticks out.

For nights afterwards, as soon as Maria and Margaret had filled her bath and left her, she pinched those red marks herself, to stop them from fading away. As her hands made the soft hurts on her own body, she saw him again as he had been then – a quiet man on his knees before her. The shafts of light that came in under the canopy and hit the planes of his face. His intent head, bent close to her skin.

Sometime around the New Year of 1850, there was an event that for William Mullan marked the end of the big hunger.

A few emigrants had come back from America already. One fellow from beyond the lake told William that the Indians would eat you in America and that he was going to try Australia now. Money was coming in the post, regularly, now, and there were shops in the square selling bread made in a bakery in Athlone and the people bought it with the American money. But there was no specific moment that he thought of as the end of the bad time until he got a message from some men that he knew. They were respectable men of his own kind who had had resources to help them through the bad years but now were leaving their homes in the long valley, and giving up the attempt to go on living on Talbot land. They had taken tickets for New Orleans. They sent a message to Mullan, to meet them at his mother's place.

When he got there, on a rainy evening, five or six men in ragged trousers and worn boots, with water running off the brims of their hats, were sheltering as best they could under the overhang of the thatch. They were starting next day for Dublin to board the boat to Liverpool where they would embark for the New World. They were waiting for Mullan to come out from Mount Talbot so as to tell him who they had buried over the last years in the soft soil of his mother's garden, so that anyone who came back trying to find news of their people would be able to get it from him. They did not hear the horse on the muddy causeway because of the rain. But the dog ran up to them and capered in greeting in front of them, her white muzzle moving in the dusk. A minute later Mullan dismounted.

'*An bhfuil cead againn . . .?*' one of the men began quietly –

'*O! A chairde.*' Mullan could hardly speak. 'My dear friends –' he began again.

'You will be here when we are gone,' someone murmured. 'So remember –'

'*Máire Mhicil Eoin,*' someone said.

'*Seán an Chóta.*'

'*Leanaí Uí Choileáin.*'

'The deaf boy.'

'*Seán Ó Muirthile.*'

'Padraig O'Connor . . .'

They crossed themselves at each name.

William took the *Northwestern Herald*, when it came down from Richard's office, to his friend the parish priest.

'The Tide of Emigration flows on in this part of the county with a rapidity almost incredible,' he read out. 'On Monday last, no less than eighty-seven men and women left this locality. Two villages where the better class of peasants resided are quite deserted, except here and there where an old man or woman may be found. Their destination is New Orleans. These parties had kind and indulgent landlords but nothing could induce them to remain in Ireland . . .'

'*Kind*,' the priest said, and laughed to himself.

Sometimes Richard read the newspaper to Marianne. Towards the end of 1851, with one foot on the fender of the fire grate in their bedroom, he read out in a most bitter tone, '"Mr Baron Richards sat in the chamber of the Incumbered Estates Court at two o'clock pursuant to arrangement, to consider and decide upon the proposal which had been made by the Law Life Assurance Company of London, to purchase the Coby Estate for a sum of £186,000. The claim of the society on these estates amounted to £240,000 . . ."'

'Coby had sixty thousand acres, Marianne!' Richard shook his head. 'Finished! The care of this whole district is left to me.'

He brought the paper to his office to look at again. His occupation that morning was making out orders of eviction as a landlord which he, as magistrate, would sign. It was boring because it was ridiculous, like everything else about being an Irish landlord in these times. He was so bored he fell asleep all the time.

Even after a year, a year and a half, two years, two and a half years, the lovers had not tired of each other. They met less often than in the beginning, and sometimes they simply sat beside each other in the hidden hollow among the piled grain sacks in the small buttery. They had a home there, with a bed William made from thick layers of sacking. For a long time their home had been an unused stall at the back of the big stable. Marianne loved it there especially because there was no smell of the house. But they had several times been almost surprised. Only the dog had saved them, barking so vociferously that the visitor did not dare unlatch the wooden door. The buttery was dangerous, too, of course. But she never had enough of him. Her physical desire for him was now, almost always, satisfied. But she still longed for something she could not have, because now she wanted his company.

She said, 'My husband has gone away to Dublin.'

'I know it,' Mullan said. 'I drove him to the turnpike. There were several other gentlemen there.'

'I want you in my bed.'

'No.'

'Yes.'

'No. That is pure folly.'

'Yes.'

She moved her head slowly down his throat, then down his chest, then down his stomach. Her loose lips, that she pouted out to their full fatness, left trails of wet and little puckered marks all down his body. She came to the coarse hair. She suddenly straightened back up, her plump body moving with the suppleness that came to it when they were together. She stretched out beside William Mullan, her nose touching his.

'You know the word the Irish people say when they are begging?' she said. 'Ukrish?'

'*Ocras*,' Mullan said. 'Hunger.'

'Well, I am ukrish for a night in a bed with you. I want you to come to my bed when Richard is away. No one will know.'

The days were still painfully long to Marianne, though now she would not have left this place. Her morning room was often cold, and the hangings and so on were shabby, and even, as she remarked petulantly to Mrs Benn, torn. From her windows she could see nothing but the marshy hill that rose to the horizon behind the demesne. She did not write letters much, now – she received few that needed answer. Her father was ailing and had moved to a small house on the seafront at Hove. She had no relations closer than her father's cousins, the Pagets, and they had no links with Ireland. When cousin Letitia went back to London, invitations to social events in the district became sparse indeed. Mab needed instruction, but Mab was frail and could not endure more than one or two hours of her mother's tuition a day. Then Marianne and her daughter lay together on a chaise longue under the thick fur cloak that Richard's great-uncle had brought back to Ireland from Russia.

A volume of poetry might lie on the table at Marianne's side but she scarcely read. She lived a good deal of the time in a light dream that was made out of the memory of what she and Mullan had done last, and the anticipation of what they might do when next they were together. But the dream was not enough. Now, there were many moments when an angry restlessness rose in her.

She thought of getting one of the maids to pull the boots onto her feet. But what visits could a lady make? Richard had told her they would not be calling on the new people who had moved in around the county. She paced her room. She sent for Halloran, who had come as butler, to ask him when the party from Mount Talbot would be back from the steeplechases at Boyle. She had wanted to go herself, because Mullan was with them, but Richard said there was still a lot of Molly Maguirism over in Roscommon, and that anyway, it was only a rough, country meeting, because no gentleman had come forward to be steward. She feared Halloran might guess that she wanted to know when Mullan would be back, because he had seen the two of them coming out of the orchard together one evening, and she had had to call him and remark that the child needed sweet apples to eat.

Halloran said the master would be back the next evening, probably, but they were travelling only by day because of the Molly Maguires. She sent for the child and took out the playing cards and played a game of hearts with her. She imagined a different life with the child. She and the child would take their places in the box of a theatre, and a tall escort in starched evening dress would be standing behind her chair, holding her fan for her; or she and the child would be in a London emporium like, say, Whiteley's, and their escort, leaning gloved hands on an ebony walking stick, would be waiting on one of the chairs at the entrance, while she and Mab looked at the things. In these daydreams, Mab was always happy. The escort had no face.

The vicar, Mr McClelland, remarked, when he breakfasted at Mount Talbot, that the native people set such store by coffining their dead that only now were coffins to be got again.

'In the end, at the worst,' he said, 'they used to knock a few stones out of the bank at the side of the road, and push the corpse into that declivity, and then replace the stones.'

The only companion Marianne had was her body. She petted and stroked it, and palpated herself, and turned herself this way and that in front of the mirror, kneading herself, and slapping herself. She looked at her hands, looked at her nails, gripped the white underside of a forearm to watch the site blanch and then redden. She had little use for the hours of the day, but to wait for them to pass.

On big evictions, there was often trouble, and there was always loud lamentation.

'And it is not the native people only,' Richard said to the lieutenant who commanded the soldiers who escorted the bailiffs. 'Our own people are in a bad way of things. The Partingtons, to the north of my land, went without even trying to sell. They walked out the front door and down the steps into the two carriages and they drove away. Themselves in the first car, the English servants and the luggage in the other car. They did not even stop to close the door behind them. Their cottiers were over the house like locusts by the time the carriage had turned out of the driveway, my steward Finnerty told me. But they found no food. The Partingtons must have taken all their stores with them.'

Dr Madden was allowed to visit Mount Talbot again, now that disease was on the wane. He examined Mab each time, and then he took some refreshment and told Marianne the news of the district. Old Mrs Treadwell had taken him, for instance, down the dark and crumbling corridors underneath the drawing rooms of Treadwell Lodge.

'There were rats there, too,' he told Marianne, 'barely kept out in the yard by the old menservants. She had some food. She showed me her stock. Enough for two to three months, I would guess.

'"But, doctor!" she said to me. "I forget my duty of hospitality completely!"

'And she told one of the old men to bring a bottle of Marsala to the drawing room.

'I tell you, Mrs Talbot, I drank that Marsala like water. I never knew the cold to get into my bones so badly. I turned back to her when I was already mounted. She was standing there on the steps without even a cloak.

'"Why do you not go to Mr Treadwell in London?" I said. "I will assist you in every way. How can you hope –" and I was pointing to those woods around the house – you know how overgrown and dark they are, Mrs Talbot? – and it was pouring rain from a grey sky, as usual. How can you hope, I was beginning to say. And she cut me off.

'"I came here as a bride fifty years ago," she said to me. "Ireland is my home."'

'You are the best of wives, my Marianne,' Richard said.

He had been so intoxicated after the first few glasses of wine at dinner that he had fallen asleep in front of her at the table, his head on his chest, snoring. She went up to Mab's room and read to her. He must have somehow instructed Halloran to get him to her bed. He'd slept by the time she had come into the room. She came in with her candle. She saw his boots beside the hearth.

He'd said to her across the room, 'Leave off your nightgown this night, Marianne.'

She blew out the candle, and before she came to the bed, she covered the glowing sods in the fireplace with their own ash. She did not want there to be light by which the bruises on her body might be seen. She had coaxed Mullan into leaving her bruised. She wanted to see the marks of his mastery of her. He did it – pinched, bit – but all his instinct was to cherish her, and he hardly ever forgot himself in the way she wanted. Still – if Richard had seen . . .

As soon as her husband slept she reached down beside the bed and felt for her nightgown in the dark and slipped it back over her head.

The priest lived in a low cottage behind the thatched church on the Fair Green. William Mullan went down to him every so often and they tried to answer the letters that came all the time now.

Tell my dear mother that Patrick her son is at present in Springfield,

261

Mass. My name is Elizabeth known always as Tetty – where is my sisters that went to Sligo to go on the boat to Quebec? Please tell my brother if it be that he is living still that there is everything here and these dollars will bring him to me signed Marcus Cody that was the head boy in Hurley's shop . . .

'I have been rebuked by the authorities, both ecclesiastical and civil,' the priest said to William Mullan, 'on account of a letter I sent at the very height of the catastrophe. A letter I had myself forgotten about. But the British civil service never forgets. I received a circular from the Relief Commissioners four years ago, when the big hunger was upon us. I opened it – certain it would contain the plan for the relief of the terrible and unmerited suffering of Her Majesty's subjects in this part of her Kingdom. This is what I replied to that circular letter.'

He cleared his throat, and read in even tones:

'Sir, I beg to acknowledge the receipt of your letter conveying to me the request of the Relief Commissioners to communicate with the Lieutenant of this county with a view to his appointing a committee of relief for this distressed district. I beg to state for the information of the Commissioners that we do not know the address of the Lieutenant of this county; we are informed that he is, at present, in some part of England. There are but three resident gentlemen for fifty miles around here. There are none but the clergy to convey the wants of the people. In the absence of most of the magistracy, in the absence of the Lieutenant of the county and with absentee landlords, we can but beg most earnestly of the Commission not to suffer all of the people here to starve. We seek not alms. We seek employment.

'The new bishop was sent, not a copy of my letter but the letter itself by the office of the Under-secretary for Education. They will not keep such insolence, it seems, even in their archive. And the bishop writes to me that I am to teach Latin in a new boys' school in Dublin. It is doubtful that I will ever see Ballygall again. Come to Dublin with me. If you come to Dublin, William, I will get you work about the school. There is nothing for you here. Come, dear William.'

'I cannot leave Mount Talbot.'

'Come with me!'

Silence.

The priest sighed. 'William, you are a man in the prime of life . . .'

Mullan shook his head without looking at the priest, and said nothing.

Mullan walked back from the priest's house through the lanes behind the square. The shops here had been for the country people. They were open sheds, where produce had been sold from baskets on the ground. They had all been closed off now, with rough planks. There was no flicker of light from the small windows above, where two and three families had once crowded into each loft. Grass already grew between the stones of the walls of the lane. The low sky, the still dusk, the empty street were all one.

'Mary, Blessed Mother!' he said under his breath. 'Help me! Help me!' As if he knew that something terrible was going to happen.

If the priest had still been there, the night that Marianne Talbot's adultery was discovered to her husband, perhaps there would have been a different outcome to the whole matter. But the men who dealt with Marianne had no one to answer to, and no wisdom to draw on. Richard Talbot and the Reverend McClelland had always been outsiders. And Halloran and Finnerty belonged nowhere. They had not been nine months in their posts at Mount Talbot when they captured her.

Marianne Talbot was being driven over to Mrs Treadwell. Richard had heard from the doctor that the old woman was now refusing to eat.

'You must bring her back here,' Richard had said. 'Marianne – offer the best of what we have to her! We will not regret it.'

Marianne stood up abruptly from the breakfast table. Richard thought it was because she was impatient to set off on the errand of mercy.

Mullan merely showed his whip to the ragged women who lived beneath the arches, as he slowed the carriage to go out through the South Gate. It was easy, now, to keep them back from the wheels. They knew there was nothing to be got from the Mount Talbot people. Marianne had the blinds of the carriage down. But though she did not have to see the women, somehow a hand, the dirt-encrusted palm bent upward to beseech alms, got in through the gap where the hood was lashed to its frame, and was there until the carriage picked up speed. She recoiled into her mantle.

She could hardly wait to get out from the town. They could stop anywhere, now, that Mullan chose, so little likely was it that they would be seen. Nothing moved in the countryside flushed with the pale green of May. She did not draw the blind up to look out, even at the lovely day. She had come to crave the dark, and the smell of the lining of the carriage that overwhelmed her nostrils whenever he pressed her face into the wide leather seat. She thought he might stop today soon after they turned off the causeway onto a track that led up through heathery turf into low hills. She took her hands out of their gloves and put them under her skirt and into her drawers, and widened her legs, and pinched the fat lips between them in delicious anticipation.

He did stop, and she felt the carriage tilt as he loosened the horse between the shafts, but he did not come to her. He knocked on the door, as a servant would.

'For heaven's sake!' she said, and she leaned over and unlatched the door. 'What game is this?'

He stood slightly below her, his face looking up into hers, unsmiling.

'I have been seeking the opportunity to speak to you,' he said.

'I have been seeking an opportunity, too.' Marianne smiled. 'Come!' She patted the seat beside her.

He bent instead, and released the steps of the carriage.

'Come you with me,' he said, 'and walk a few paces.'

'No!' she said. 'Come you here and warm me.'

He did step up into the carriage, but he sat across from her, not touching her.

He began heavily. 'I care no more to stay in these parts. My friend Tadhg Colley and I will head to Liverpool soon to get the American boat.'

'I do not want you to go!'

'We are in danger of discovery, you and I,' he said. 'There is need for us to go.'

'I have no such need,' she said. She moved in a flurry of cloth to sit beside him. She put her lips to his cold cheek, and with her hand tried to turn his mouth to hers.

'Come!' she said. 'It is foolish to spend our time at this, when we must get on to the Treadwell place.'

He took her hands.

'You are my woman,' he said. 'My wife, as I would wish to call you. I will give you my son. I will have you in my bed every night, and I will give you the rides the little landlord could never give you.'

He did not know how crude the words sounded to her. Her face darkened.

'I have no need to go to America,' she said, after a pause. 'I do not wish that you should go to America. Soon Richard will be gone away to London. You could sleep all night in my bed. All day. I shall keep the other servants away –'

'In America, there are no servants. We would be as man and wife.'

'I do not wish to speak of this further,' Marianne said. 'The disparity of condition – but, never mind! I do not care to explain to you. Let us drive on.'

He half rose. Then he fell back onto the seat and found her hands again. He brought his face close to hers and looked straight into her eyes.

'I have never said it before,' he said slowly. 'Be with me! Be my wife! We can take the little girl and go now. Nobody knows what people are from which place at the boats. In America they do not ask the people to show their marriage papers –'

'Drive on!' she said, and turned her flushed and angry face away. 'How could I do that?' she cried. 'What would become of me? Drive on!'

She went across to his room in the stable block that night because she could not endure not having had any closeness to him that day. She brought the child. Everyone saw her go out with the child. But Mab was a silent child. Marianne had often presumed that Mab did not see what the quick hands of lovers could do.

Mullan was frightened by her daring. After a while he said, 'I must go and see to the master's horse.'

She waited, standing in the bleak room which had a small iron fireplace but no fire. The child sat on the edge of the pallet which was Mullan's bed. The child could feel her mother's rising irritation. First, Mullan had been difficult – even insolent – on the journey over to Treadwell's and her body had been left restless. Then, Mrs Treadwell had declined to leave the home where she now stayed all the time in a bed the last servant had managed to bring down to the kitchen. The two of them, Mrs Treadwell in the bed and the old servant on a kitchen chair beside it, had gazed at Marianne like children, as she stood in the kitchen door and pleaded with them to come away.

'No thank you,' was all Mrs Treadwell would say.

There was a howl from the distant house, and a nearer sound of shouting, so the child and Marianne were already on their feet in fear when headlong footsteps reached the top of the steps and the door of the room crashed open.

'He knows,' Mullan said. 'Your husband has been shown the things you gave me that I had in the back stall. He is inside the house with Halloran and Finnerty. He told Halloran to tell you to go to the vicar and me to go to hell –'

'Come, Mab!' she said. 'We will go into the house!'

'Do not go to the house,' Mullan said.

Then Richard and Halloran came into the room, and Richard without looking at anybody else rushed to Mab, and pulled her out of her mother's grasp, and thrust her ahead of him out of the door.

The child's screams died away. There was no sound in the upstairs room, except Halloran's thick breathing.

*

266

There was no relenting. At the front door Richard came to the other side of the wood and with a bellow answered her knocking with, 'Whore!' She ran down the steps and around to the French doors of the morning room. 'Whore!' he roared from inside. She ran, panting and panic-stricken, along the edge of the shrubbery to the wicket door where the main house joined the east wing. He had known where she would go. 'Whore! Whore!' he raged from inside the door. 'Get away before I vomit on your whore's face!'

'Mab!' Marianne cried. 'Mab!'

'Do not pronounce my daughter's name, you whore!'

Mullan was waiting as she stumbled back to the forecourt to go around the wing to the servants' entrance.

'Everything at the back is locked fast,' he said. 'You must take shelter now with respectable people. Let me take you to the vicar.'

'Yes!' she gasped. 'The vicar will bring me back here, and then Richard will let me in! He would not shout at the vicar.'

'Go to the carriage,' Mullan said. 'I will be there presently.'

'No, no,' she said, clutching at his arm. 'Do not leave me. Come quickly!' She began to pull at him.

'Halloran says he has taken Lolly into the house and tied her beside the fire in the drawing room. I must –'

'No!' she shouted at him. 'Come with me!'

They made their way down the driveway. He had to wait for her, because she went so slowly, turning back all the time, her body dragging. Her sobbing was like an infant's. If the black sky overhead was lit by stars that night then it would have been cold. But very often the spring nights at Mount Talbot were darkened by a low cloud so thick that even the wind didn't disturb it. It was always said in the area that that was the kind of night it was when Mrs Talbot was put out – not cold, but very, very dark.

She was more and more distraught. The best Mullan could do, when she was not able to walk the length of the avenue to Ballygall, was to rest the shafts of the carriage on the stone coping of a bridge, and help her in, and wrap his greatcoat around her where she huddled in a corner. Then he took the horse through the trees and let it crop the lower lawn.

He half ran down the dark avenue and out past the sleeping squatters under the Great Gate and around the edges of the silent town to where Tadhg Colley lived in a low cottage, facing the Fair Green.

'Mrs Talbot and I are discovered,' he said.

Tadhg Colley hit the table in front of him in anger.

'What have we to do with those people, William?'

'Who will give me the price of my father's field?'

'Hurley will give you something, but he won't give you a fair price. He can get land for nothing, now.'

'When I get the money, will you help her and me to go to the boat?' Mullan said.

'What use would a woman like that be to you in America? That woman couldn't even get herself to Sligo! None of those ladies do work.' He said it with contempt. 'I'll give you money this minute, and get you away to hell out of this yourself!'

'I wish that she should have my child,' Mullan said softly.

'Your child – by such a woman!' Colley said, appalled. 'William, you can have a family in America –'

There was a tapping on the window. Colley went across and peered through the glass.

'Tracy,' he said. The three men had sat on the one bench at the travelling master's classes when they were ten years old.

'William!' Tracy said, as he came into the room, 'the master has brought up extra constables from Roscommon. Coby's men have been sent for. They have taken your clothes and your boots. They are ready to swear you into the jail at first light –'

'And my dog? Where is Lolly?'

'Your dog is –' Tracy stopped. Then he said, 'William, there are dogs galore in America.'

Mullan took Tracy's hands in his.

'Give me your word, Michael, that you will watch over Mrs Talbot! Do not let Talbot have her in the room with him by herself. She will be in terrible circumstances when morning comes –'

He broke off. There was a moment of silence, and then Tadhg Colley took a box down from a shelf and unlocked it with the key on his watch-chain, and he counted out banknotes, and William Mullan folded them carefully into the inside pocket of his jacket. The three men stood close together for a moment. The street outside and the room were completely silent, except for the harsh sound of the sobs that, as William went out the door, Tadhg Colley could not keep back.

14

I slept deeply after I finished writing. Sometime on Friday morning I woke and began to tidy the cottage by putting a bin bag in the middle of the room and throwing everything I could find into it. I'm fed up with housework, I thought, crossly – the basement in the Euston Road, and now this! All I'd done for years was leave some money for the chambermaid and pick up the towels before I walked out of a hotel room, and that was in memory of the days when I lived at Joanie's and worked with the Spanish girls – pushing our cleaning carts slowly down the corridors, like old women, and calling to each other about dances over the noise of the radios we turned on in the bedrooms. And I hadn't even faced my half of the office yet! How would I ever have the courage to clear out my desk, when Jimmy's mark was on everything?

I began to sweep around the cottage door, but I raised so much dust that I gave up. I'd leave money with Mrs PJ for a cleaner when I was settling up for the phone.

The phone. I'd better make a few calls. Start my life going again.

Alex was not in the office.

I rang Betty in Administration.

How long does Alex think he'll be gone for, Bet?

He didn't know, Kathleen. He's staying with the mother at some nursing home for the time being, anyway. I've a phone number for him that I can give you – I don't recognize the code. But there's no problem here – he left everything in apple-pie order. A whole file of stockpiled stuff, properly identified, properly subbed, contact sheets attached to the copy. He's a miracle of organization, that man is.

Hardly the most exciting male attribute I ever heard of, I said.

I've worked for exciting, Betty said. They give me a pain.

*

Alex was very quiet. He made an effort to ask me about myself and how the story in Ireland was working out now, but his voice began to break up.

She's sinking fast, Kathleen. Until this morning I thought they might still do something for her – take her back into Intensive Care, maybe. But I've just come from talking to the doctor. In the next few days, he says, short of a miracle –

Where are you? I said. Where are your friends?

And, Kathleen! he said. I'm not even sure that she knows me.

I'm so, so sorry, Alex.

The doctor said it might be best to say my goodbyes to her, Kathleen. I can hardly believe it! For the whole of my life the two of us have been together almost all the time, just the two of us, because I barely remember my father. And never, never a cross word, Kathleen! Never! Not even a raised voice –

But Alex –

I'd almost said, Is that always a healthy thing? But I stopped myself in time.

Doctors aren't always right, you know, I said.

Oh, my mother's doctor is a top expert in the geriatric field, Kathleen, he said reverently. Do you remember Father Gervase, who celebrated the funeral Mass for poor Jimmy? Well, the doctor is a personal friend of his, and that's how I was lucky enough to get Mother in here. They don't take just anybody, you know – it's a private hospice –

He broke off from talking to me, and I could hear several muffled voices at his end.

I must go, Kathleen! The doctor is on his rounds. I'll be in touch! Or you ring the office –

I hung up, miserable. He was having the worst time of his life, Alex was, and I didn't even know where exactly he was. And even if I did know I could hardly turn up there, as if I were family. *And* he was probably being taken for a ride by sundry doctors and priests – he was such a pushover for men with titles in front of their names. I wondered how much they were charging him for hospice care.

He would feel his grief so genuinely, when it came! I had no difficulty in thinking of Alex as a child, even though he was a middle-aged man. A whole well of innocence was still there to draw on in him. He would mourn for his mother, when the time came, with the complete abandon of a boy. He had hurt me, in our day; this was the first time that I had had to think of him having to bear hurt himself. He was going to be so shocked to discover what suffering is. Whereas I was an old hand. You had to develop survival mechanisms if you grew up in Shore Road.

Nora. I hesitated so long about what to say to Nora that a sparrow pecked its way in from the porch and realized where it was and fluttered its way out through the open door again, before I picked up the phone. I was in trouble already if she realized that it was three or four days since I'd gone to see Danny and Annie. She'd want to go over every single detail of Kilcrennan and Ned's place and Shore Road. She wouldn't understand why I hadn't rushed to a phone to tell her everything. On the other hand, I couldn't possibly not tell her that I'd been home.

It was six in the morning in New York.

I rang her office machine and left a cheery message about how well Danny and Annie and Lilian were and how the old place looked nearly the same but Kilcrennan was a big town now, and how everyone had been asking after her –

– I didn't bother going up to the graveyard to the parents, in the end, I finished off, knowing she'd be pleased with me about that. She'd never forgiven either of them. She said they'd put her off marriage so thoroughly that she'd never wanted a boyfriend, much less a husband. Not-an-inch Nora, I used to call her.

I got Caro, she informed me when she answered the phone out of breath, just as she was running to the library to do a crucial bit of revision – the most difficult of the week's BEd papers was that afternoon.

Long time no hear, she said lightly. I'm just admiring the lovely flowers you sent me to wish me well in these terrifying exams.

Oh, I'm *sorry*! I said. Oh, Caro – I did forget! It's been so long!

I had only to say to her – I was distracted because I met a man on a ferry and he's been with me twice and it was marvellous – and she'd be nice to me. But I couldn't. Or I could say, I was upset because I went to see my brother and his family. Or I could say, I'm trying to sort out what the Talbot thing means to me and that's preoccupying me.

I really must rush, Caroline said. And I must say I don't know what you mean by 'it's been so long'. I was talking to you last week.

Were you? I said.

Yeah, she said. You were in a hotel somewhere. You rang and gave me the number. You'd met a wonderful librarian –

God Almighty! Was that only last week?

Yes, Caroline said.

Oh.

Are you all right? she said.

I'm fine . . .

There. Calls made. Bag in car. Everything in order.

Except the Talbot project.

And except for Shay. Imagine – being Ireland for someone! That that's what I was to him – half real, and half a dream! I walked over to the bedroom door and looked at the stripped bed, the white boards of the ceiling, the low window.

No matter what happens, I said to myself – and I didn't laugh at my own solemnity – no one can ever take away those two nights with him.

One of the Russian prayers to be said on leaving a place would be appropriate now, I thought. This bedroom was blessed. The cottage in the middle of the rough field was blessed. And at the top of the hill I pulled in and wound down the window and looked across the amphitheatre to the headland and the ocean. The sea, under an almost imperceptible veil of summer rain, was as still as the land. It, too – the whole lonely, beautiful vista – was blessed.

Only the sky was alive. Far out on the horizon, dark veils of rain drifted down, yet over where the spire of Mellary church showed behind the edge of the hill, light was breaking through cloud. Then, the belt of whispering rain passed on, and the sky began to clear. I heard the noises of the bushes and grasses near me as they responded to the end of the rain. The rustlings were so small that a tractor starting up somewhere drowned them out. Then that noise abruptly stopped, and quiet came back again. The earth had settled itself. In the silence of the washed, fresh day, a blackbird began to sing.

I turned away and headed for Ballygall as fast as I could. For once, there was Dixieland jazz on the car radio instead of sad music or talking.

Caroline had sounded quite resentful, for her. She was not usually one to utter a reproach. She must be really thrown by the exams if she was starting to say things straight out. But, of course, she'd never tested herself before this BEd. Her first degree was a little thing from somewhere easy. She'd never really worked, apart from bringing up Nat, because her job at the education paper was a joke. Was she genuinely angry with me for forgetting her? I felt a little flame of gladness at the thought that she might be – it would be a rare hint that I mattered to her. I'd never known what she saw in me, that had made her befriend me the day Hugo threw me out. I'd never dared to ask. It seemed to me that I hadn't heard an unguarded word about myself from her in all the years. Even when our friendship broke down, both the parting and the reconciliation had been completely wordless, on her part. Whereas I, I would never forget, had leaned against the plastic wall of a telephone kiosk in Oslo airport, and babbled and babbled into the phone, in the hope of forgiveness . . .

When Ian turned up you'd think Caroline was Eve, and Ian was the first man she'd set eyes on after eating the apple – the only man in the whole of creation. She was as wild about him as if he were food she'd been deprived of all her life. I remember thinking, when she stopped going to her job after she met him, that I simply had not been free to be as crazy as that about Hugo; I always had to work. Even with someone as scrupulously unassuming as Caroline, money means you can indulge yourself.

As for me, when Ian happened, she all but forgot my existence. We'd been together for more than a year, and I was just beginning

274

to believe that we were comrades, but she looked through me quite absently when we bumped into each other around the mews. Ian was a divorced teacher from somewhere in the north with black eyes and hair and a wiry body and a mean smile like a fish smiling – the exact opposite of jolly, silver-and-pink Sir David. Ian and Caroline went into her bedroom where they stayed, more or less, for three months. I once heard muffled screaming, and occasionally, crying. I was passing her room one night and the door swung open and I glimpsed her sitting on the bed, naked, with her hands, in orange rubber kitchen gloves, held above her head. It must have been the configuration – a corridor, a door ajar, a bed – that reminded me of Mammy, because I never actually witnessed an intimate moment between my mother and father. But my mother, when Daddy was at home, had the bearing of a slave. To see my cool Caro becoming abject made me tremble. I used to go out to the Irish pub on the corner and sit there with my book, protected by the vigorous, foul-mouthed barmen. Sometimes, I didn't even read. I just sat staring ahead, like the other solitary people in there, though they were emigrants of the 1950s, much older than me.

One Saturday morning, Caroline came out of her room in a big T-shirt and touched my shoulder as she passed to put on a kettle, and I was just choosing in my head what subject to talk about when I realized she was crying.

She told me she was pregnant.

Make me a cup of tea, will you? she said. While you're at it – she turned her face away – you can put some poison in it. I have to make a decision. I have to get Ian to marry me. Or I have to have an abortion.

I went around the table and crouched down beside her and stroked her face.

She pulled her head away.

I have to decide soon. I think I'm nine weeks pregnant. He said to do whatever I like – that it's all the same to him. Mummy – she said it with a pale smile, because they weren't at all close – is actually coming up from the country to have lunch with me today, and Daddy is flying in tomorrow.

So she'd already told her father and mother . . .

What the hell kind of man just leaves a baby's fate to his girlfriend, as if getting pregnant had nothing to do with him, I began.

Listen, Caroline said. Don't say any of those things to me. I love him. That's all.

Love! I said. I told you what Borges said: love is a religion organized around a fallible god. I remember reading that out to you –

And I don't believe in abortion, she said.

I didn't know how far I could go. I wanted to call Ian every dirty thing in existence. I wanted to take her, now, to a clinic. All her contentment and pleasantness ruined, for nothing much of a man! But she hadn't chosen me to be her adviser. Could I even say that he never seemed to visit his two existing children? Could I say, The way you walk ahead of him into the bedroom reminds me of my mother, and she was the unhappiest person I ever knew? I could not. She'd give me a look that said, *Your* mother? Like *me*? And I couldn't bully her – she was too frail. All I could do was try to show her how much I would like to help her.

Our birthdays fall on the same date, and ages before I'd booked us into a spa for the weekend, as a treat. To have had the confidence to book us a whole weekend away together – that was the fruit of coming to believe that she really liked me. I tried now to trick her into going through with it, even though everything was different; I said I'd paid in advance, though I hadn't. No reaction. Then I said it would do Ian good to do without her for a couple of days. Let him see what that was like. That swung it.

I went into her room that Friday morning, to help her put a few things in a bag, even though I didn't want to breathe in there, in case I smelled him.

Where's your bathing suit, Caro?

Oh – I'll hardly be swimming.

You might, you know. I'll put it in anyway. Where do you keep your moisturizer? Is this make-up bag the one you want?

And so on. It was like handling someone in shock.

I saw her walk across the concourse to the gate for the Canterbury train that evening. I winced inside. She wasn't sick at all. It was the relationship with Ian that was dragging at her and making her shuffle.

It turned out that she and her parents had decided she should marry Ian, but when she'd rung him just before she left for the railway station she couldn't get an answer. There wasn't anything I could do. She didn't enjoy the spa at all, though at one point she remembered her manners and gave me a ghastly smile across the crowded jacuzzi and said, This is very relaxing, isn't it? She must have rung the house where Ian had a room ten times during the Saturday. I managed to say nothing. But when we were in our twin beds that night and the light was off, I couldn't keep quiet.

Don't! Don't go on with him! Don't! He's no good! He's a rat! Even the cruelty of not telling you where he'd be this weekend – the bastard! And whose idea was it to get you pregnant? Did the bastard not even try to protect you –

I need him, Kathleen! she cried. She was crouched under the bedclothes but she stretched her arm across and tried to touch me in the dark to make me understand.

You do not need him! I said. You have ample money and helpful parents, and I'll do anything – I'll happily babysit, or mind the baby at weekends – anything. We could get a bigger place and I could easily get a job where I'm not away as often as *The English Traveller*. Because he's no good, Caroline. I know that. I *know*. He'll make you very unhappy –

I don't care, she said. I don't care if he does make me unhappy. I'm mad about him. That's the thing you don't understand, Kathleen. It doesn't matter what he's like.

The words hung in the air.

We fell asleep, and in the morning it was our birthday. We sang 'Happy Birthday' to each other from our beds. We were twenty-five.

I must have driven more and more slowly as all the old stuff about Caroline came back to me, because when I took a minute to look around I was still about twenty miles from Ballygall. I was crossing a high pass between hills – an entirely silent place, except for a stream, fed by the water trickling down the slopes of coarse, green grasses, that rushed between mossy boulders beside the road. This road would be following the ancient path beside the stream, and the people's cabins would have been down there, on the banks, beside the foamy pools, below the path. There was no variation anywhere in the monochrome of hostile green, except for tumbled granite rocks. I longed to get down out of the hills to street lamps and traffic and modern bungalows. And to get to the warmth of Bertie's where they knew my name, and Joe and little Ollie would come running. But this upland pass was the right place for remembering how, when I was young, I learned to feel for the harshness underneath every soft appearance. I was betraying Hugo even when we seemed so loving, and Caroline's father, behind all the fatherly charm, used me like a thing. And I was more or less put out on the street when my supposed friend Caroline fell for Ian. There was no real love anywhere. There was a worm hidden in every rose.

It *was* abrupt, the end of being Caroline's girlfriend. I didn't have more than a couple of weeks to find somewhere to move to from Hampstead. That would have been enough time if I was going to settle for living like a student in a shared flat. But I wanted to be on my own. I'd run out of optimism, deep down. I was afraid of everyone. It had meant more than I would ever say to be taken up by Caroline. There was even something unbalanced about my feelings for her, though I put that down to our different nationalities. For example, Caroline's physical self more than pleased me – it delighted me. And I remember thinking to myself, I'm as bad as Sir David. He decided he could paw me, whereas he'd never paw one of Caro's English friends. And I watch every little thing about her, as I never would if she were just an American girl, or French. As if she were my opposite . . .

My feelings for her were hidden so deep that they were hidden from me, too. I walked and walked around north London, when I had to leave our flat, in a distress I could not analyse. I was desperate to find a place where I could be on my own and not get into any more trouble. Then Mr Vestey saved me. I could have kissed his hands. I would have taken the basement in Euston at the rent he was asking anyway, but when he gave me the keys to go and have a look at it, and I saw the dark, silent rooms, I recognized my ideal mausoleum.

And you'd never have known any of this to look at Caro or me! We went back and made an attempt at cleaning the Hampstead place together, the evening after we moved out. She had her shining golden hair tied up with a J-cloth, and we bopped around to the songs on *Sergeant Pepper's Lonely Hearts Club Band* that some station was playing on her little transistor. We left the rooms a bit smeary, but okay, and we slumped together on the Underground, tired and pleased with ourselves. We went our separate ways at Warren Street station, clinging to each other for a minute in the middle of the concourse, with people streaming around us. I wanted so much to say to her, I love you too, you know.

It made me feel old to realize that it had been better not to say it. Would she even have heard me? If she had, what could my declaration have meant to her? I didn't say it. I cried, going home. I didn't think we'd know each other any more.

And now I know almost every detail of her life! I can almost see her fair head bent over a textbook as she conscientiously starts her preparation for Monday's exam papers. My belongings are stored in her house in London. I'll be living with her when I go back to England. I spoke to her today. If we have almost always spoken instead of really talked, well, reticence was something we had in common from the beginning. And if I thought when I was young that her reticence was part of the courteous geniality of her personality, whereas my reticence was an outsider's furtiveness, that was my problem, not hers. She's not responsible for how much more I liked her than I liked myself.

The familiar crunch of The Talbot Arms's gravel at last. No cars. What day was this? The wedding party must have gone. The old dog slept like a heavy bundle of rags abandoned on the wide bottom step. I patted his brindled skull as I passed and was answered by an eyelid half lifted from a milky eye. The hallway was even more worn and shapely than I remembered, and again, in spite of its elegance, it reminded me of Uncle Ned's cottage kitchen. A tinny television voice seeped from behind the curtain of the den. Bertie was watching a soap.

He was in his armchair, but his face was sombre in the light from the screen. Joe was lying across his chest, half asleep.

Is something wrong, Bertie?

Kathleen! He went to pull himself to his feet.

Let me just sit with you, I said.

He subsided back into the armchair and I sat on the other chair. On the television there was downhill skiing from Slovenia. We watched various men in helmets being shoved, it seemed, out of a hut, and whooshing down a completely featureless snow-covered slope. Each time a man fell towards us out of the hut the digital read-out on the corner of the screen returned to zero.

We sat for three or four minutes. Joe had fallen back asleep. I heard a phone ringing somewhere and then Ella talking to someone in the hallway outside.

Bertie finally said, I come in here for a rest. They know to leave me alone.

I need a rest, too, I said. But I have to go and see Miss Leech.

She left you a note. It's out there on the desk. She's going up to Dublin this evening. He looked at me piteously.

She's not well, he said heavily. There's a lot of worry about her. She's been going up to St Luke's to see one of the consultants there. She thinks no one knows, except me, but the woman that does our books, her sister is on the switchboard there and she keeps an eye out for anyone from the town.

Where?

Womb.

Can that not be taken out?

Depends on whether it has spread . . .

How old is she?

She's seventy-five. She told the *Northwestern Herald* she was in her late sixties when they did a write-up about her and her Famine exhibition, but that was a fib. See, she never wanted anyone to know her age because she never wanted to retire. But I know it to the day because we were neighbours, growing up, and when I used to study my school books up at the library when I was trying to get into college, she was my idea of what a woman should be. That's how long I know Nan. I used to admire her in her little suit. They used to have long skirts then – straight, with a slit – do you remember? No. You're too young to remember. There are twelve years between Nan Leech and me, to the week. It might as well have been a hundred years when I was twenty. Don't say anything, Kathleen, about the cancer! She'd kill anyone who said anything to her! She had to tell me because I go in and feed her oul cat, and I'll be taking her to the train. And collecting her. They'll send you back from the tests in an ambulance, you know, the Health Board, but she wouldn't be caught dead in an ambulance.

I started to laugh at that and he did smile a bit, too.

A skier fell very badly and skidded down the slope, bending pole after pole flat against the snow.

Hello, little darling! I said to Joe.

The child looked at me solemnly. Spot's gone, he said. The man that ownded him took him home to his own house.

Spot'll be coming back, Bertie began to say, and then he suddenly beamed at me.

That's what we'll do! he said, with an air of satisfaction. We'll borrow Felix's place for you! Felix is going away again tomorrow, and he was going to bring the dog back here, but I was worried about that because we have teachers coming in on Sunday night and they create mayhem. And Spot loves a bit of mayhem. Spot has no sense –

He has so got sense, Granda! Joe said. Ollie crawled into the garden and he was going out the gate into the street and Spot barked and barked.

Give us over my glasses there, son, Bertie said to the boy, till I look up Felix's number.

Who's Felix? I said.

Felix is a friend of ours, but he's an architect and he's always on the go. He works in Brazil I think it is at the moment, and he's going to marry a girl there, according to him. He has a house out the road that you could stay in, and you could mind Spot. You remember Spot? The little terrier? A grand little dog, but a handful. And come in to us for your meals if you like –

C'mere, Bertie, I said. This is a hotel. This building that we're sitting in. Have you ever heard of letting your guests actually stay here, instead of posting them around the country?

Did you like Mellary? he said.

I can't tell you how much, I said.

Well, wait'll you see Felix's house. Trust me. And the teachers are only coming in for four days anyway and you can come back to us then.

I opened Miss Leech's envelope.

Dear Miss de Burca:

A document has come to the hand of my young colleague in the form of a pamphlet written by John Paget, QC, who seems to have been a connection of Mrs Richard Talbot's. I have perused it rather more rapidly than I would have chosen, but it would appear to argue most persuasively that Mrs Talbot was innocent of the charges made against her by her husband. This is an unexpected turn of events, you will agree, and I look forward to discussing it with you on Wednesday of next week when I shall have returned to Ballygall. I regret that due to personal circumstances I am not at present available on the telephone.

This pamphlet may have been circulated, but it was never published. It is, in fact, a considerable rarity, and I am very pleased to have acquired it for the Ballygall local collection. It is confined to the locked shelf here, and may not be consulted elsewhere than in our reading room. Professional advice would have to be taken from our colleagues in the conservation department of the library service in Dublin, were the question of photocopying to arise.

I have arranged that the Paget pamphlet will be available to you on Saturday from 10 a.m. onward.

I received your postcard re H. James and have to say I am in agreement with him not only about historical fiction but

fiction *per se*. Humbug is indeed the *mot juste*. I sincerely hope you have not taken to the writing of same.

N. Leech, MA (NUI), FLAI

Back in a few minutes! I said to Bertie, and I ran out through the garden into the street.

The florist was closing but I mimed urgency through the door at the woman trying to make herself invisible behind the conical tin vases of flowers.

We don't – she began when she finally opened the door.

It's just flowers for Miss Leech at the library, I said. Here – cash! I pushed the notes at her. Roses. Daisies. Anything except pink. But it's the message I want.

She gave me a little card.

I won't be able to go up with them till I lock up here.

Go up with them then! Not to the library – to her house!

Miss Leech,

I sincerely look forward to seeing you whenever you find it convenient. I will be at someone called Felix's house, which Bertie is arranging for me to borrow. I apologize for abandoning the discipline of fact. Caitlín de Búrca.

If she knew how I'd let myself go! I couldn't think of anyone who would disapprove more completely of the tale I'd woven around the facts of the Talbot divorce. I'd invented an aunt Paget in my Talbot tale because I had come across the name – it was mentioned in the *Judgment* that Marianne Talbot's only living relations, besides her father, were of the name of Paget, and that it was a Mr Paget who had tracked her down to the asylum in Windsor. The Lord Chief Justice had been commenting on the fact that when Marianne's adultery was discovered, her husband and Mr McClelland spirited her away – concealed her, in fact – first in Dublin and then Windsor. The judge remarked – mildly enough, I must say – that even if her father was ailing, her other relatives – the Pagets – should have been informed of the position she was in, so as to offer her sanctuary if they so wished. The *Judgment* did not specify how, exactly, Marianne was related to the Pagets. I'd taken a liberty in conferring an aunt Paget on her. But then, what liberties had I not taken? If Miss Leech ever discovered the fantasy I had woven on the theme of the *Judgment*, extreme disapproval would be the least I'd come in for. It was even difficult to decide from which standpoint she would object most – as a historian, as an Irish person, or as a woman. But let her rebuke me, if she ever found out! Let her be as scathing as she liked, if it meant she was well!

I said a prayer for her as I went back down the town – a prayer I'd always been easy with, because I thought of it as a woman-to-woman prayer, like phoning some woman you barely know to help in an emergency because her child is in the same kindergarten as your own.

Remember, O Most Gracious Mother, I began, but even in those few words I started to gabble, because we had always gabbled prayers. So I began again, slowly, narrowing my eyes so as to look inward. I could see in my head Miss Leech standing in a laneway beside the ruin of a cottage, her tiny hand in a red mitten pointing out the shape of a doorway in the wall of stones.

Remember, O Most Gracious Mother, that never was it known that anyone who fled to Thee for mercy, implored Thy help or sought Thy intercession was left unaided. Turn then Most Gracious Mother – no, that's wrong. Is that the Hail Holy Queen? Isn't that a different one from the Memorare? Ah, what does it matter! Turn then thine eyes of mercy towards us – all of us, but especially Miss Leech. Spare her above all any pain. Also Alex now that I remember and also Alex's mother, who is facing into death. Also – please help Caroline with her exams because it matters so much to her to do well. Help me to know what to do with myself. And after this our exile show unto us the fruit of Thy womb, Jesus. That's definitely wrong. It doesn't matter, for God's sake – they're all the same! O Clement, O Loving, O Sweet Virgin Mary, pray for us O holy Mother of God that we may be made worthy of the promises of Christ.

15

The next day I went to the library to read the Paget pamphlet.

The man at the desk of the reading room went upstairs to get it, and I stood and waited, rigid with excitement, like a child before its birthday party. I signed for it and carried it down to my table between the book stacks. It burned against my fingertips. I turned it over in my hands. I held it against my cheek. The wine-coloured board covers were dried out and discoloured, and one of them hung by coarse threads from the binding. It could never have been touched since it was bound for 'The Library of the Queen's College, Leicester, Gift of the Author' (according to a pale stamp on the margins). I couldn't get enough of moving my fingers across the thin, powdery pages. When I realized that some of these were uncut, and that I would surely be the first living person ever to read them, I went warm with pleasure.

Talbot v. Talbot, A Statement of Facts.
   'I believe her to be innocent of all charges, and I have formed that opinion and firm belief, knowing as I do, that such charges were supported by persons wholly unworthy of credit, and AS I FIRMLY BELIEVE, BEING THE RESULT OF A FOUL CONSPIRACY.'
   John Paget QC,
   London:
   Printed by C. Roworth and Sons, Bell Yard, Temple Bar. 1854

What a ringing statement! I thought, almost chuckling. Isn't family loyalty an extraordinary thing? Because I never for a moment expected to be persuaded by whatever argument John Paget was going to make. It had never even crossed my mind that Marianne and Mullan might not have been lovers. The whole matter had been through two lengthy proceedings – in the Ecclesiastical Court in

Dublin and in the Houses of Parliament in Westminster. Not only that, but Marianne had not denied the adultery to the Reverend McClelland the morning after she was confronted. That was why – when that fact was passed on to him by his own vicar – her father did not defend her. That was why no questions were asked about her disappearance.

And even if she *had* denied it, there was all the evidence. Halloran and Finnerty, butler and steward respectively, had caught her in Mullan's room. Mary Anne Benn had told about the bottle of wine Mrs Talbot gave Mullan. The two sawyers had seen the pair together in the straw of the stables. Purcell had seen them sitting affectionately on a sofa with their arms around each other's necks. Bridget Queeny had seen them going into the orchard. For heaven's sake, Maria Mooney had seen them *in bed*. I might not have believed the Law Lords, but I believed all these witnesses. Why would they lie? Why would Richard lie?

I began to read.

I began to make notes.

Within a few minutes my hand was shaking so badly that I could hardly write.

I sat back and closed my eyes and tried to calm myself, so as to fully grasp what John Paget had argued so passionately in the year – I suddenly saw the significance of the publication date – when argument was still worth trying. 1854 was the year between the end of the Ecclesiastical Court marital separation proceedings in Ireland, where Marianne was represented only by a court-appointed proctor, and the beginning of the divorce proceedings in Parliament in Westminster. There was still a chance that what Paget had found out could change things.

Why did he bother? She could not thank him. When he finally found her in the asylum in Windsor, he tells us, he was deeply affected by the spectacle of her wandering mind, and her meek and fearful demeanour. It was chivalry, above all, that had made him defend her. And that was the first shock to me, even before I attempted to follow his argument. That she was, in historical fact, mad – frail and mad –

only seven months after Richard Talbot and the Reverend McClelland put her away, changed my picture of her. My imagining of her hadn't got as far as that point. I'd liked to think of her as strong and plump – juicy with health, like Kate Winslet in *Titanic*. I'd thought of her as being brought from England to a remote and desolate spot in Ireland over which the suffering of the Famine hung like a miasma, and being sufficiently young and vital to insist, even in that place, on a sensual life. No law or rule or custom, no practical obstacle, could keep her from celebrating, with William Mullan, the life of her body. I thought of her as having shy eyes and a modest manner, but naturally red lips and a body that wanted to burst the hooks and buttons of the rich clothes that contained it.

Perhaps she had been just like that when she was a girl, and John Paget knew her then, and was moved to defend her by the pitiable spectre of what marriage and Ireland had done to her.

He begins his pamphlet solemnly:

I depose that since the month of August 1852, I have been unremitting in my exertions to obtain information regarding the monstrous accusations brought against the Impugnant [he used the old-fashioned term for a defendant, as if Marianne were standing in the dock], *the result of which exertions has been to strengthen my belief into an absolute conviction of the Impugnant's entire innocence, and to convince me that those accusations are a tissue of inventions and falsehoods, and I depose that also I believe the Impugnant to be perfectly innocent because having lived for nearly eleven months now under the same roof, in daily and hourly communication, I have never observed the slightest look, word, or action inconsistent with the most perfect purity and delicacy of mind; and which is more especially convincing to me, perceiving as I constantly do how unsound that mind continues to be. The Impugnant never told me she was innocent, and I doubt, indeed, whether she has any consciousness that anybody accuses her of being guilty.*

She was that mad – that she didn't even know who she was, or where she was!

But how did my blooming, lusty Marianne go mad?

Richard Talbot, John Paget argues, deliberately drove her mad.

*

John Paget goes back over the evidence sworn at the Ecclesiastical Court – evidence which the judges in the House of Lords had had in front of them, but much of which they had not referred to in their *Judgment*, and which I, therefore, had never seen.

I did not know that a maid called Hall, who had come to Ireland with Marianne, had sworn to this:

I well knew Richard Talbot, Esq, the Promovent, and Marianne McCausland, otherwise Talbot, the Impugnant. I lived with Mrs Talbot as lady's maid until I left Mount Talbot shortly before the child became ill. During the time I so resided at Mount Talbot I observed that the Promovent treated the Impugnant with indifference, coldness and unkindness. I have more than once seen the Promovent decline to answer questions asked him. I was engaged in London, and previous to our leaving there for Ireland the Impugnant requested me to purchase some small articles she required. I did so, and expended five shillings of my own money for her use. She promised to pay me out of the first money she would get. We left London without my being paid.

In about three months after our arrival at Mount Talbot I received 3s.6d. from her in two payments. At each occasion she expressed regret at not having the means to pay me the entire 5s. 1s.6d. remained due to me until the night previous to my leaving Mount Talbot; she then paid me by three fourpenny pieces she got from her child, and which the child seemed unwilling to part with and said she would never get them back; the remaining sixpence Mrs Talbot paid me with postage stamps. I know and depose that, to such an extent was the Impugnant deprived of the use of money that she was frequently obliged to borrow money from the servants in the house to purchase necessary articles of dress. I was discharged as appears by the discharge I received, in consequence of the Promovent's determination not to keep a lady's maid for the Impugnant in future.

I never saw the Impugnant and William Mullan in familiar conversation on any occasion. I never did on any occasion during my stay in Mount Talbot by Impugnant's desire or otherwise, take or bring meat, eggs or other articles, or wine from Mount Talbot to said William Mullan's room. I never knew the Impugnant to have the power or opportunity of sending or giving such articles to anyone; she was not allowed such matters for her own use.

I have seen and known her lunch for several days to consist of nothing more than a cut off a dry round of beef, and no drink but beer, not good enough for a decent servant to drink, and she has complained to me of the want of proper nourishment.

My God! I thought to myself. Since I came back to Ireland I've thought about the condition of hunger over and over again – about whether it goes on hurting, or whether, after a phase of desperately eating roots and berries and rotten potatoes, you lie down, and indifference comes. Never, never did I think of a lady in a big house being systematically underfed! A beggar stretching a hand to her, when she made her way from her carriage to the doorway of Mr McClelland's church – that half expiring, barefoot, ragged beggar could have had in common with her a gnawing in the stomach under her fine clothes.

John Paget went on highlighting pieces of sworn evidence, each one of which demolished another bit of the world of passion I had invented:

I did not consider the Impugnant a strong-minded woman; she was generally in low spirits, and I have observed her to have the appearance of crying.

When hiring me he [Mr Talbot] said in her presence and hearing, that he wanted a person capable of taking the entire management of his house, as, he said, Mrs Talbot was a mere child, and knew nothing . . .

That was from a housekeeper who had come to Mount Talbot about a year after Marianne did. The housekeeper ended her evidence by declaring:

. . . I depose that the conduct, demeanour and general deportment of Mrs Talbot was that of a chaste and modest lady, and of strict propriety; she was, in my opinion, one most unlikely to conduct herself in any improper manner, and I verily believe she was incapable of doing so. I do not believe the said Impugnant to have been guilty of an improper and criminal intercourse with said William Mullan.

And Paget quoted this passage from a respectable lady acquaint-ance of Marianne's – the only witness from a class higher than the servant class – who visited the couple around that time:

> Q. When you saw them, on what terms were Mr and Mrs Talbot living, as far as you observed?
>
> A. Very affectionate terms, but I consider he neglected her very much in her dress, and the whole establishment. He neglected her; he treated her with very great neglect. Her dress would strike me very much. She never had any money.
>
> Q. Mrs Talbot received, I believe, £5,000 from her father upon her marriage?
>
> A. She did. But I cannot say, to my recollection, that I ever saw her with any money in her possession.
>
> Q. At the time you observed Mrs Talbot without money, was Mr Talbot keeping hunters?
>
> A. He was; two hunters . . .

That was interesting – the 'very affectionate terms'. How did that fit with all the rest? Was Marianne so crazy about her husband that she accepted privations from him as marks of love? Did he speak to her lovingly while treating her abusively, so as to drive her mad with dissonance? But why? Why would Richard mount a veritable campaign to break Marianne down?

Because, Paget informs us, the Mount Talbot estate was bequeathed to Richard Talbot only on condition that he had a son!

He had to get rid of Marianne so that he could marry someone else. It wouldn't have been enough just to separate. He had to get a legitimate male heir. And the only way, at the time, that he could divorce an innocent woman was if he somehow made her admit to adultery, and then fleshed out the confession with testimony from suborned or hired servant witnesses.

I had thought that the *Judgment* was a summary of all the evidence in both the Irish and the English proceedings. Now I saw that each of the three Lords had been reconstructing the argument that had led him to the conclusion he had reached, and each had naturally favoured the evidence that had persuaded him towards that conclusion; therefore, they favoured the evidence that made Marianne seem guilty, and gave short shrift to the evidence that did not. What John Paget was doing was drawing attention to the evidence which favoured her innocence. The reason I had never heard this evidence was simply because, overall, the Law Lords had believed her to be guilty.

An under-housekeeper, for example, had said on oath:

> I depose that one day while I was living at Mount Talbot and on my going into the dining room for orders, I heard Mr Talbot in conversation with a gentleman then present, but who I did not know, say – 'Oh! Mrs Talbot is too delicate to have more children.' The conversation ceased on my going into the room. I depose that the Promovent was cold and indifferent in his manner to Mrs Talbot, and I know that he did not allow her any money when I was in the house.

I stood up and paced the back of the library, behind the last row of bookcases.

Why had Richard Talbot locked her up in Mrs Trueman's asylum while he was getting his divorce, after all? Why had he needed to get her off the scene, if she was *admitting* to adultery? Could it be that any well-wisher would have seen that she was too broken to know what she was admitting to?

I was beginning to believe in Marianne Talbot's innocence.

The stories, John Paget says, which the servants – Mary Anne Benn, Maria Mooney and so on – swore about their mistress were

> incredible or impossible. They had fabrication stamped on every word of them; and absolute silence had been maintained for years as to matters which, if they had existed, must have been as public as the noonday sun . . .

He brings forward the evidence of other servants – living at Mount Talbot at the same time – who swore to benign versions of the episodes the Law Lords had chosen to rely on. One Hester Keogh, for instance, testifies that she did accompany Mrs Talbot to the wine cellar *and it was raspberry vinegar, and Mrs Talbot took only one bottle, and went up to the bedroom with such vinegar; and she desired me to bring up a little of hot water, as she wanted to make a drink for the child, who was complaining . . .*

No wine? I thought. I was bewildered myself. No wine? But the wine was one of the most erotic of the details!

Another witness says:

I depose that Mrs Talbot's child told me several months before she became ill that Mrs Talbot went with her into Mullan's room to dry her stockings, which were wet.

Another one:

I depose that any persons going to said William Mullan's room must be seen by the persons in said apartments and offices. It was necessary to cross a yard which said several apartments faced, and which was a thoroughfare for servants. I depose that the said William Mullan's room was the very worst place she could go to if she had any improper object. I do not believe that any person could go or pass from the hall door of Mount Talbot through the side gate leading into the stable yard of said premises, through the harness room and upstairs to the room in which William Mullan slept without passing the windows either of the steward's office or the laundry, or some of the other servants' apartments; the harness room was seldom without men being in it, and particularly the gamekeeper and his son, there being a large box in it with ferrets in said room.

The two sawyers who said they saw Mrs Talbot with Mullan in the stable got hopelessly confused under cross-examination. The attitude of the court to them did not help their confusion. Counsel is quoted as saying:

Anything more dogged and repulsive than the looks of these men and more unsatisfactory and suspicious than the mode in which they gave their evidence, I never witnessed. I shudder to think that upon the testimony of such wretches the very issues of life and death might be dependent . . .

Their evidence was given, John Paget says, 'with the habitual cunning of their race'. No Ireland-lover he; he makes it pretty plain, with further remarks along the same lines, that Richard Talbot was able to get away with framing Marianne *because* they were in Ireland – *because* Irish witnesses were such liars that they could be got to say anything.

The sending of kisses through the child? This turns out to have been suggested by Richard Talbot's solicitor, as something she might be able to remember if she tried, to a servant who had moved on from Mount Talbot. The former servant says:

> *I depose that in the month of April last Mr Talbot's solicitor called on me at Lady Ashbrooke's at Castle Durrow where I was then residing as lady's maid. He said that Mrs Talbot had been seen in the yard sending her daughter to kiss Mullan, and that when the child had kissed Mullan, she kissed the child, and he explained that thereby Mrs Talbot sent kisses to Mullan and received them back from the child.*
>
> *I told him I never saw anything of the kind, though I was most constantly with her and the child . . .*

John Paget follows this with a good point:

> *. . . When the solicitor told Margaret Hall this he exceeded his duty, and did not exercise a sound discretion. He said what was not true. If she was seen to commit this gross and silly act, to prostitute her own child to the purposes of her own lust, why did not the prosecutors call the person who saw her? The suggestion was simply a monstrous and groundless falsehood.*

The lovemaking on Marianne's own bed which was witnessed by Maria Mooney? Again, John Paget has a certain amount of contemptuous fun with an Irish witness:

> *It appears from the evidence of a Mr Quirk that Maria Mooney did on one occasion in a public house swear to Mrs Talbot's innocence on a one-pound note (which in her estimation would doubtless be regarded as equivalent in point of solemnity to the New Testament) and that she also stated it was 'the most infernal*

wrong that ever was done and that she could prove it'. Mrs Mooney, however, though she admits having protested her mistress's innocence to almost every person except Quirk, denies that she ever had any conversation with him in her life 'and never saw the fellow in Kelly's beer shop at all'.

Paget goes on to show to his own satisfaction that Maria Mooney lied about everything. And, a heavy blow:

A most respectable lady's maid swears that she distinctly remembers the occasion to which Mooney refers and states that at the very time when the alleged act of adultery was stated to have been committed in the bedroom, 'Mrs Talbot was in the library hearing her child say a lesson, and repeating a hymn, as was her custom every night before going to bed.'

And Bridget Queeny, who said she saw Mrs Talbot go to Mullan's room alone? She *'was discharged from her service for not making butter to please her master, or because she was suspected of bringing things to her family, who lived near'*.

And Mary Anne Benn? Who had brought the glass of milk to the drawing room and seen Mullan there? She was dismissed without a character, *'for quarrelling, and talking too much . . .'*

I began to sort the different kinds of testimonies and the different tones of voice into categories relevant to a finding of guilt or innocence.

First, there was the evidence of Richard's ill-treatment of Marianne.

Second, there was evidence about the characters and credibility of the servants.

And third, there was the detail of Marianne's last day in her home in the company of her child, and the aggression and deliberate terrorizing which led to her breakdown. Having broken down in mind she failed to defend herself: thus, she was assumed to be guilty. By the time of the expulsion she was at least temporarily crazed. The story of Marianne's final twenty-four hours in Mount Talbot, as pieced together by John Paget, was important character evidence –

of Richard Talbot's character. It was so damaging to Richard Talbot that it was difficult not to believe that he had, all along, been a sadist.

I summarized the events of 19/20 May 1852.

Halloran, the recently arrived butler, seems to have been the instigator on the day. Therefore it became important to ask – who was Halloran? He was a man with a most chaotic past, it struck me, including *returning* to Ireland from America in 1847 – the year of the Big Hunger. I could not resist copying out the list of the names of his employers, even though they were in themselves of no importance to Marianne's story – though the number of them was. Most of them were redolent of a class that had disappeared – the Protestant families who had owned the land and the commerce of Ireland before independence. They were the English and Anglo-Irish names of families whose main, if not only, contact with the likes of a de Burca would have been master or employer to servant or employee.

I could almost have applauded all the trouble Halloran's erratic career must have caused these masters, and brooded on the demons that drove him, and speculated with sympathy on his curious partnership in rootlessness with Finnerty, but for his cruelty to Marianne. There is no suggestion that she ever did him any harm. Why should he, then, organize her downfall? Was he jealous of Mullan's privileges with her? Or were he and Finnerty, and perhaps Richard Talbot, utterly contemptuous of women? Richard's treatment of Marianne throughout their marriage certainly suggests that he despised her. About Finnerty we know nothing, except that when the name Halloran is mentioned, Finnerty is bound to be mentioned, too. Paget writes:

During the last five years Halloran has been in nine situations. Three months with Mr Blackburn. Three months with Mr Pollock (discharged for drink). Three months with Mr Plulgate (discharged for drink). Six months with Mr Verschoyle. Six months with Mr Gabbet. Four days with Mr Studdart. Seven days with Colonel Smith (discharged for drink). Six months with Mr Brennan. In service twenty-seven months and eleven days out of the sixty months of the five years. He refuses to answer whether he obtained Mr Gabbet's place by a forged character: he knows a man named Maginnis, but refuses to say whether he

forged discharges for him; and he refuses to say whether or not he obtained Mr
Studdart's place by a forged discharge. But he admits that he was confined in
Richmond Bridewell for three months for forgery, and he enters Mr Talbot's
service within one month from his leaving gaol . . .

   His imprisonment terminated less than a month before he entered the service
of Mr Talbot, where he had not been many weeks when Mr Talbot gave him
notice to quit for drunkenness . . .

How did Halloran get from that position, to the point where he held
Marianne Talbot's destiny in his hands?

On the May evening in question, the butler – accompanied as always
by Finnerty the steward – went to the shebeen outside the walls of
the demesne. The housekeeper testifies:

Halloran stated to me that he gave punch to Mullan and made him drunk at
Kelly's, in order to bring him back to Mount Talbot.

They deposited the drunk Mullan in his own room. Then they
followed Marianne and the child, and they saw her go into Mullan's
room. Paget says:

It is proved that Mrs Talbot had been in the constant habit of occasionally
visiting, either in company with her child or one of her servants, the rooms of all
the servants, to ascertain that they were kept in a pure and wholesome state (a
supervision which the habits of domestic servants in Ireland seem to have rendered
necessary) . . .

The two menservants locked her into Mullan's room. Then they
fetched Richard. Richard accused his wife of adultery and snatched
the child.

The housemaid testified:

Mr Talbot, before leaving Mount Talbot, left in a piece of paper a very small
(and insufficient for one meal) portion of tea for Mrs Talbot and a few lumps of

sugar. On my going upstairs into her room she was crying; she exhibited every symptom of mental agony and grief, and said she would go mad. Finnerty and Halloran locked the doors and refused to let anyone see Mrs Talbot.

John Paget continues:

Mr Talbot then packed his things and went with his child to his agent's, leaving £20 to pay the expenses of Mrs Talbot's removal, a small quantity of tea and sugar for her breakfast, and £9. 12s, the balance of wages due to Mullan.

Mr Talbot appears to have acted under the shock with singular coolness and self-possession . . .

Richard left Marianne – her child taken from her – locked up for the night in her bedroom in the main house with the two dangerous drifters and Mullan, who was presumably too drunk to help her. Paget's argument is that on top of being unjustly accused she was so terrorized that night – especially by Halloran, who was seen by a maid beside her bed, holding her feet (there is a clear suggestion of rape there) – that she went mad.

He concluded:

In the middle of the day, without the slightest warning, this weak, childish, innocent woman is suddenly and violently charged by her husband, in the presence of three menservants, with adultery; her child, who had never left her side from the hour of its birth, is torn from her; she is locked up in charge of her accuser; attempts are made to induce her to leave the house with the alleged adulterer; Halloran, Finnerty and Mullan all get drunk and Halloran offers violence to her person. She passionately protests her innocence, and struggles with violence to obtain access to her husband; she is prevented by force, she attempts to throw herself out of the window. This state of agony continues for eighteen hours when at last Mr McClelland, the rector, makes his appearance, and – as he states – at once 'upbraids her for her criminal intercourse with Mullan'.

Then McClelland arranges to take her away. And the sinister, Pinterian pair, Halloran and Finnerty, make their last appearance:

297

Peter Conboy, lodge gatekeeper at Mount Talbot, swears that in the afternoon of that day, about half an hour before Mrs Talbot left, he let in Halloran and Finnerty at the gate: they were both very tipsy, 'staggering at going in at the gate'. 'Finnerty said nothing, but he smiled; and Halloran asked me, "Has Mrs Talbot come out yet?" I said, "No." "Well," said he, "if she is not out against I get down, I will haul her out like a dog."'

John Paget also says that shortly before Marianne's departure

Halloran attempted to steal her dressing case, which was found in his pantry, after being carefully packed in the carriage by the housekeeper.

I had no problem, after all that, in agreeing with John Paget's basic thesis. Anyone might be driven out of their wits by what had been done to Marianne Talbot. Eighteen hours! With her child torn from her! No trust could be placed in her so-called confession. And little trust could be placed in those who had given evidence against her, either.

I went and stood at the high window at the back of the room and looked down on the quiet roofs and back lanes of Ballygall.

There were still odd aspects to the whole affair.

Look at the phrase slipped in, as if it weren't important, in Paget's summing-up:

... attempts are made to induce her to leave the house with the alleged adulterer ...

And earlier Paget writes:

It appears that Halloran and Finnerty understood and acted upon the understanding that they were, if possible, to get their mistress away WITH MULLAN, and that the £20 was left for this purpose.

What was going on? Obviously, it would be more than convenient for Richard Talbot if Marianne did run away with Mullan; it would save him the trouble and expense of hiding her away and going to court and dealing with the suspicions of the John Pagets of this world. But why did he believe it was possible that she would do it? Did he genuinely suspect her of infidelity? Had she had running away in mind?

No, that could not be. No one denied her great love for her child. She would never have left her child. And all the witnesses Paget quoted had said on oath that there wasn't the slightest reason to believe that Marianne had ever contemplated, much less actually had, an adulterous relationship.

But mightn't there have been some kind of innocent, wistful yearning – across all the barriers of class – for the man who looked after her horse and drove her carriage and led her child out on the donkey? Might Mullan have been moved by how she was treated? *Might he perhaps have brought her food, when her husband was keeping her short?* And would not coarse men like Richard Talbot and Halloran have misinterpreted his delicacy?

I could never know.

For the moment, at least, I could only agree to be persuaded by John Paget's robust handling of the point that most disturbed me:

> *On the terrible night when this detestable conspiracy against Mrs Talbot exploded, and her husband abandoned her to the worst outrages of lust and drunkenness – when money was supplied by him and every circumstance of horror was accumulated for eighteen hours upon her head to force her into the arms of the man for whom she is said to have entertained a frantic passion – did she go?*
>
> *No.*
>
> *That one word is a demonstration of her innocence and of the deep and monstrous guilt of her accusers.*

The lights in the library had dimmed and brightened a couple of times, but I was too absorbed to move. The elderly man from the desk had to come down to me and touch my shoulder.

I'm afraid we're closing now, he murmured. Saturday we close an hour early.

I didn't want to give up the book. I longed to have it near me while I thought and felt my way through what I was learning.

May I have this book again? I whispered to him.

You'll have to ask Miss Leech, he said. I'm afraid I am obliged to lock it in her safe now.

I looked around to make sure there was no one to see me, and I dropped a kiss on the old book. For the tragedies within it.

Then I handed it back to the man at the desk, and walked like an automaton out of the room.

The library was on the square in Ballygall. I stood on the top of the steps, breathing in the evening air, giving a few moments – as you do when you come out of a library – into putting what I'd been reading to the back of my mind while I resumed real life. The air was warm. Summer must be very near. As usual, the queue of cars for the supermarket was inching around the square, past the half-derelict Mount Talbot gates.

I came to, as if a shock had gone through me. I wasn't just standing outside a library where I'd been reading a book. This was where it had happened! This library had been the court where Richard Talbot had sat as a magistrate. He might very well have walked up these worn steps. That arch across the square – that was the very arch the carriage had come through, with the disgraced Marianne wrapped in her cloak within, and the Reverend McClelland sitting – surely – as far from her as he could. The horses would have trotted out of the gate, and the coachman checked them at the edge of the street, and then he'd have cracked the whip and the carriage would have turned up to the right, to begin the long journey to the railhead. She – a real woman – would have looked her last on this square through eyes swollen with the loss of her daughter, and of all her security, and all her happiness. Her hands would have been twisted together in her lap. And now, when I thought of her, I didn't know which would have been the more tragic – her despairing bewilderment at this nightmare turn in her life, if she was innocent, or the pain of being ripped from the man she adored beyond anything, and from her daughter, if she was guilty.

Either way, in real fact, a young woman – perfectly well in every way – had come from England into Ireland and entered this square behind the high-stepping Talbot carriage horses in 1847 or 1848. Healthy, comfortable, secure – her little daughter held firmly by the nursemaid at her side. Perhaps Marianne sighed compassionately at the beggars around the gate, too weak with hunger to lift their hands to the slowing carriage. They were her husband's beggars, after all. But probably she flinched. I did, myself, at small airports in Africa and Asia, standing around in the stifling dark outside some dimly lit terminal and just making out, maybe, a gaunt, legless figure loping towards me on his arms, or a dwarf pulling at my sleeve, or blind women with their hands outstretched, or feral children as agile as rats.

It was inconceivable, the day she arrived, that a mere four years later, she would be brought out through that same gate, a broken woman – at least as unhappy as the starving paupers around, and perhaps more desperate. They could implore her, when she passed them, Do something for us! Do something for us, my lady! But there was nowhere she could turn for compassion.

And for what was she destroyed? What did Richard Talbot gain for himself? By taking her child? Taking her freedom, when he sent her to serve a life sentence of imprisonment in Windsor? By callously, and then wickedly, step by step, terrorizing her till her mind went? The mansion and the gardens were a tumble of overgrown walls in an expanse of weeds and rubble and mud, now. The great orchards were wildernesses of barren and diseased boughs behind rusted gates. The house was gone. The land was gone. The Talbots and their kind were entirely forgotten by the Irish families laughing with the children in baseball caps who waved out the back windows of their cars as they queued for the supermarket.

Richard Talbot thought to secure his wealth and his name by driving her insane. But she was punished for nothing. The Talbots were already on their way out of the history of Ireland and the world. The sacrifice of poor Marianne did not avert his ruin. He crushed Marianne, and it turned out there was no greater meaning to it than the crushing of a butterfly. John Paget ends his pamphlet by telling the

301

reader that Marianne has been living in his household since he rescued her from Windsor, and that no trace of levity or impurity has been discovered among the ruins of her intellect, where all is pure, simple and childish . . .

Here we have no abiding city! The words from the Bible came into my mind, and I clenched my own warm hands. I hurried my step and even began to half run down the street, feeling the satchel with my notebooks bump against my hip. I wanted to be in the light and the companionship of Bertie's kitchen. And I wanted to tell everybody – Alex, Bertie, Caro, Nora – Guess! Go on – guess! She was innocent! Marianne Talbot never was a libertine. Listen to this!

But the only person I saw that night, to get a reaction from, was Bertie, and his was one I hadn't dreamed of.

My Talbot story is in a bit of a crisis, I said to him. It looks as if she didn't do it.

Didn't do what?

Didn't have an affair with the groom.

Thanks be to God! Bertie said fervently, and blessed himself.

He meant it, too.

I was shaken. It hadn't occurred to me that to a Catholic like Bertie, death would not necessarily have brought peace to Marianne. That she might still be being punished for the sins she had committed here on earth – suffering, in the afterlife, for all eternity.

That night in my room I opened my laptop to enter the day's notes. My eye was caught by the reverse images of my gestures in the wavy old mirror. When there was movement in its aquarium depths, I had often imagined that Marianne was on the other side of the glass, trying to reach me. I distributed the quotations into their categories: Servants' evidence, pro and con; Richard's behaviour to M; Events of final day in Mount T.

Now, I opened a last category: William Mullan. Then I typed in Esq, to show him a bit of respect.

When John Paget began to take an interest in the case of his disgraced cousin, he went to Ireland – not knowing that Marianne was incarcerated in Windsor – to look for her.

On the morning of the 14th August 1852, he writes:

I was in conversation in the inn yard at Athlone with a man who had driven us the day before. It came out in the course of conversation that this man, who could not by possibility have the slightest knowledge of our errand, was acquainted with Mullan, and that on the morning of the 20th May, Mullan had come into the inn yard at Athlone; that he had told him of the row at Mount Talbot, that he told him it 'was the spite and malice of the other servants', that the little girl had been out feeding the chickens, and Mr Talbot had spoken sharply to her for getting her feet wet, and that Mrs Talbot had taken her up into that room to dry her socks at the fire; that he was cleaning his things at the other end of the room; and that, to use the man's own words, he 'never thought of his mistress no more than you, Sir'.

This was the closest I had yet come to hearing Mullan say anything in his own voice.

I was brushing my teeth when it hit me.

But if there was nothing at all between Marianne and William – why did he follow her to Dominick Street? What was in the letter he sent in? Why did he stand outside waiting for an answer? Why would he go to her, of all people, if what he was doing was protesting his innocence?

I went back to the table, and back to my Mullan notes.

In the *Judgment*, the Lord Chancellor had sneered at Richard's being awarded £2,000 in his action against Mullan for damages.

The amount . . . was nominal only. The man had gone off to America, and from his position in life he could not have paid two thousand pence.

But John Paget, QC had shown that flight in a new light, too:

After his unsuccessful attempt to obtain an interview with his mistress, Mullan resorted to an attorney to defend him in the action of criminal conversation, brought against him by his master; and he made similar representations to the attorney as to his mistress's innocence and his own as those he had previously

made to the car driver, and was only induced to abandon his defence upon finding
that the whole of the money he could scrape together for the purpose would be
ridiculously inadequate to provide for the costs of his defence; and as he set his
foot on the deck of the vessel which was to remove him for ever from his native
land, he accompanied his last farewell to his relatives with an earnest and emphatic
declaration of the innocence of his mistress.

I got into bed.

How does Paget know that? I thought to myself as I lay there.
Who was he talking to? Or did he just take poetic licence at the end
of his tale? Did he not know that anything he was told by the Irish
people he interviewed was likely to be whatever they thought he
wanted to hear? Though Mullan surely emigrated. I set my foot on
a deck myself and bade farewell to my native land when I was twenty
years old. Except I didn't, really: I never noticed we were leaving the
harbour because I was so full of vodka and tears and rage –

I heard Bertie's heavy footstep go down the hall below and crash
the iron safety bar across the front door. McClelland's iron bar.
Maybe I'd be able to think more clearly when I got away from this
house where the vicar who hated her had trod the floorboards,
touched the panelling, pulled the wooden shutters of the windows
closed. It would do me good to move out. Felix was by all accounts
young and cool and international. His house would not have ghosts
in its mirrors. And I'd have Spot the terrier to be my friend and keep
me safe.

I tried to keep my mind clear, but it kept sliding back into what I
had believed since I was a girl leafing through the xerox of the
Judgment for the first time on my lover's bed – that Marianne and
Mullan were passionate lovers, like Hugo and I. I had a very exact
picture of Mullan in Dominick Street in Dublin in my head. The
windows on the ground floor and the first floor of a Georgian
building like Coffey's Hotel would be so tall and low-silled that if
Marianne had pressed herself against a window – straining towards
him, or shouting Mab's name – he would have seen all of her. Her
whole desperate body would have been framed in the window. And
she would have seen all of him, if she looked down at him standing

in the street. It made things worse, that they saw each other tip to toe – as if it were only a bit of space and a few panes of glass that separated them, and not every law that was ever made to keep a man and a woman apart, and every convention, and every possible practical consideration.

What did it say in the *Judgment*? That Mullan's note '*was put into the hand of Mr McClelland who was there as her protector, and he having read it destroyed the note, not allowing her to see it*'. Then Marianne said she wanted to see it. Then she wanted to see him. I remembered that the phrase the judge used was, that she was 'extremely anxious' to see Mullan – that she asked not only to see him but said, 'I wish to go off with him to America.' Did she wish this as a new thing, now that she had lost everything and had no future at all amongst her own people? Or had she always wanted to go away with him? Or had the bullies around her – Halloran, Richard Talbot – planted it in her addled brain that that was what she was supposed to do?

I will just have to wait, I said to myself. I'll let my mind rest in contradiction, the way Keats advised. Negative capability: 'When a man is capable of being in uncertainties, mysteries, doubts, without any irritable reaching after fact and reason . . .'

But I had to get out of bed, and type out a final quotation. I put it right at the top of my tale, before its first sentence.

In the *Judgment* it is noted that after some days in Coffey's Hotel, Marianne was taken to a lodging house in the Rathgar Road, a suburb of Dublin, where she was guarded by a nurse. I assumed she was moved from the hotel so that Mullan or anybody else looking for her would not be able to find her. The story given out to the lodging-house landlady was that she was ill.

The nurse who guarded her in the Rathgar Road was called to give evidence before the Law Lords, and so was the landlady.

The nurse explained that she tried to prevent Marianne from talking to the landlady, because the landlady was very perceptive. '*I prevented Mrs Talbot going to drink tea with the person we lodged with in Rathgar. This was a penetrating woman. . .*' But Marianne did talk to the landlady, and according to the landlady was very frank, and told the landlady she had been with – by which I suppose she meant, had been intimate with – a groom.

I typed in the question and answer.

Counsel: Did she call him a groom?

Landlady: Yes, with this groom. She said she had gone with him, and he had told her he would have a child if she was confined to himself. She said she considered his embraces more warm to her than she did that of her husband . . . Mrs Talbot said she should have something to love; and I wished to know what she meant by wishing to have something to love.

That was the sentence. That last one. The meaning was a little obscure, but even so, I understood it. I was moved by its being so nearly a direct quote from Marianne. And I was moved by the simplicity of what she said. The landlady wished to know what Marianne meant by wishing to have something to love. Therefore the real, historical Marianne Talbot – whether she was guilty or innocent, mad or sane – must once have spoken the heartfelt sentence: I wish I had something to love.

16

I woke up wondering whether Marianne Talbot had been in love with her husband. Richard, surely, was incapable of inventing the tender detail about sending the child to be kissed and then taking the kisses from the child. But what if he knew about it because Marianne had done it to him? Maybe she adored him, and sent Mab running to him to get kisses for her? It seemed to me the kind of thing a young wife might do, especially if she was being prettily feminine in the face of indifference or hostility.

I'll say that for my mother, I thought. At least she didn't simper. She was as silent with her husband as with everyone else.

But she obeyed him. And she stayed with him.

I got into the bath. The water was a bit cold but I deliberately left it like that.

Marianne would have kept to her room as much as she could, wouldn't she? Her big bedroom would have been colder than our place in Shore Road. Much colder. Those gentry houses – huge spaces in them had never been warm and never could be warm. Even in summer, under the ceilings of the grand rooms, or along the high corridors, the air would have kept its aboriginal chill. She would have had a fire, of course – the turf sods sending out erratic heat from the shallow fireplaces with their high grates. Or wet logs, spitting . . . But no – he might not have given her a fire. If he saw to it that she was kept short of food, surely he saw to it that she was kept short of fuel, too.

Maybe the poor woman was drawn into Mullan's room by the fire there.

The child has wet her stockings, Mullan – in a high voice. We shall dry them at this fire –

And then trying to cover up the shudders of relief, as she stood beside the child in front of the glow, with the flames reddening her pale cheeks, getting warm at last . . .

My mother had only her own breath to warm herself with, five nights of the week. And it wasn't as if her lair, down in the middle of the lumpy mattress, was always warm because she stayed in bed so much. Her bed went cold during the long hours of daylight, when all you could hear if you were alone in the house was the tap dripping in the kitchen sink, and Daddy's alarm clock on the shelf over the range, ticking. I know because when she was away, once, having a miscarriage or a baby that died, I tiptoed into her room and stood beside the bed, and listened to hear what she would hear. You couldn't hear the sea from her room – not on that day, anyway.

At least Mammy didn't have to talk. No outsider ever came into our house except Uncle Ned and, when there was an emergency about babies, Mrs Bates. My mother was extremely lonely: I know from the way she made human beings out of the characters in the books she read, and from the way she watched films on the television with hope and interest on her face, as if she were socially involved with the people in them. *The Philadelphia, Story*, now – I'd say she didn't breathe during that. But at least no one was looking at her. Except me, of course. But a child doesn't count.

How much did Marianne enjoy Mab? Surely Mab was everything to her? Especially as the child got older. Surely Mab was to her what I would have been to Mammy, if Mammy had had no one but me? Sharon's mother used to be nice to me – trying to sponge stains off my school uniform, and taking a bit of ham out of the salad she'd got ready for Sharon's tea to make me a sandwich. When she did things like that I'd have a spurt of bitterness about Mammy. Lying there in the bed. Driving us mad with her silence. But when Mammy did say anything it was worth listening to. She said, for instance, that Anna Karenina was right to throw herself under the train and that there was nothing else she could do, since Vronsky was obviously beginning to go off her. You'd be a long time waiting for Sharon's mother to say something like that.

I used to get up in the mornings in the basement and wander into the kitchen, naked, and make a mug of strong, milky tea, and I'd put on Radio Three to hear a bit of music and also to find out what time it was. You couldn't tell from the permanent twilight in the flat, and it was a game with me not to look at the clock. It might be any time; my nights were so agitated that sometimes I'd sleep late into the morning, or it might be only six-thirty or seven. Often, as I sat in the armchair with my tea and a cigarette, slowly coming into the day, I was glad of the fate that had led to my living alone. My place was mine. The choice of music – mine. The little cloud of smoke – there by my choice. I was sure that countless women made unhappiness bearable by relaxing with the little comforts they set up for themselves. But the married ones – bang! They had to pull themselves upright, like tired waitresses going back on duty after a break, when the husbands turned up. Richard Talbot striding into the hall at Mount Talbot with the dogs behind him, throwing his whip onto a table. My father puttering up to the house on Shore Road on Friday nights at seven o'clock, taking his things out of the back of the car fussily and carefully, before he greeted anyone. Then, later, the shared bed . . .

Once, Nora said to me, Do you know something, Kathleen?

What?

She must like him.

What?

It's the only explanation.

This was on a Sunday afternoon when they were in their bedroom and we were cleaning up the kitchen.

I looked at him closely when he came out around five o'clock. His forehead glistened. He was in his stocking feet.

Daddy, Nora began. She was sitting at the table doing homework.

Don't Daddy me, he said mildly. I'm busy. And he turned on the radio and put his four black shoes on a newspaper and started polishing them for the next week.

Caroline didn't stay in contact once we left the mews. I knew that the baby was called Nat and that the three of them lived somewhere south of the river. She did come back to me, but not for more than four years.

She wasn't so much aged as bleached and drained.

He's left me, she said on my doorstep. Her eyes were sunken from crying.

Not a word about me, or how I'd been. Straight into bloody Ian.

He said we'd go out to dinner. It was three months ago yesterday. No – the day before yesterday. I was thrilled, because we never go out. He doesn't like me leaving Nat at night. And in the middle of dinner he just stood up and said, I'm leaving you.

But it's not that, Kathleen. I could bear that. It's that he didn't say anything else, except that when he was walking away from the table he turned back and said, I never loved you. Never.

I listened to her, as well as I could, for many months. I even tried not to take on jobs abroad. I'd sit at the table in my flat and Caroline would sit in the armchair, so near that our knees almost touched.

She was in so much pain that it almost made me sick to look at her.

It's as if my heart has been put into acid, Caroline said. That acid is gnawing at it.

And it was true that the whole of her had become suffering. She had been taken over by the same force that had filled her with passion for Ian in the first place.

All I could say, over and over, was that the pain would go away, the pain would pass.

When? When?

I can't make it take less time than it has to take, Caroline. Oh – I wish I could!

Nat placed himself between his mother's knees when she slumped back into the armchair. His mouth drooped in discontent, and his big, fringed eyes looked at me with pure resentment. He played as well as he could in the space he had. He clung to one of his mother's thighs, then the other, then he tried to swing from them.

The park, Mummy! he'd say. We'll go to the park!

She would eventually summon up some response to him.

You get ready and we'll go to the park in a minute. But what do you think, Kathleen? Do you think he did love me, and maybe if –

Jesus, Caroline, I don't know. But I do think that saying 'I never loved you' at least shows that the vile creep has some feelings.

Some remnant of her training as a wife still clung to Caroline. She looked at me with exactly the same limpid reproachfulness as Nat. Simple abuse of Ian wasn't allowed.

Come along, Nat, she'd say, as if it had been the child who had kept her waiting. What time is it, Kathleen? I have an appointment . . .

I was in Australia for a while that autumn. The day I came back, she phoned.

Kathleen, I came home from doing a Sainsbury's shop and he was waiting for me, and the first thing he said was why had I let Daddy change the car without consulting him? I thought he'd come back! Anyway he came to the house and he told Nat to watch the cartoons and he practically hunted me up the stairs and threw me into bed and – oh Kathleen, I can't tell you how blissful it was!

Isn't marriage interesting? I said. Wherever he was, he sensed that you were getting a bit better. So he turned up to drag you down again.

Oh, and Kathleen – afterwards he jumped up and said he had to be going and I ran out onto the stairs after him, pulling at him, terrified that Nat would come out and see us. I said to him, How can you go after what we've just shared?

He said, What? What have we just shared? And I said – I was really embarrassed, but I said it anyway – well, lovemaking. We just shared great sex.

It wasn't sex by my standards, he said. It was like a fairly satisfying sneeze.

She went completely quiet after that episode. It must have frightened her mother, because eventually she astonished Caroline by offering to have Nat stay at her house in the country while Caro had a rest.

Isn't that marvellous, Kathleen? Caroline said to me. Mummy said that all her friends know how to entertain children even if she doesn't. She even said she'd come up to town for him, if I didn't want the long drive.

Then she smiled properly for the first time in months.

Oh, Kathleen! That Nat would have a proper Granny! It would be so good for him! Nat, my pet, you're going to have a Gran!

I swung Nat up myself and twirled him around and said, Happy days are here again, kiddo.

It was one of the things I meant to ask the psychiatrist, that time I arranged to go and see one – not at the first session, of course, but later, when we understood each other. What makes a woman into a doormat? What makes her see some quite ordinary other person as a looming Goliath? And where does the awful pain of losing the oppressor come from? And are not these relationships such an outrage to reality that they cannot last a lifetime? My mother was the emotional equivalent of an extinct volcano . . . She couldn't leave him, of course, with the pregnancies and the poverty and Ireland, and anyway she had nowhere to go. If she could have left, or if he had left her, would she have eventually recovered, like Caroline?

But Caroline didn't get better for years. You could even say she never got better, because she retreated behind a perfect imitation of a mannerly, shallow, woman of her class. Lately, she'd gone to the opera in Verona and so on with a barrister from her dinner-party circle. But she'd never slept with him, as far as I knew. You couldn't imagine her ever sleeping with anyone again. And such a lovely girl, she'd been! So shining and golden . . . I'd have wanted to ask the psychiatrist whether it is some immeasurable loss, back there in infancy, that lays a person open to such hurt. Or does the imagination transform the other's hostility into some kind of biological challenge? Or is all this excess of feeling a form of narcissism?

Now, I wouldn't expect a psychiatrist to have the answers. And not just because of the trainee-behind-the-screen fiasco. Now – thinking about it all as I put my clothes on and brushed my hair in the sunlight in Bertie's old green bedroom – I saw it as a mistake on the same spectrum as infatuation, to confer the power of explanation on another person. I simply wouldn't privilege a psychiatrist's version of the world, now. There was something about even the short time with Shay that had made me sturdy. I felt quite grounded in common sense. I could see a few things clearly. For example, that time is the third party to every relationship, and that if Marianne and Mullan *were* together then the important thing is that they were together for three years, and such a duration suggests love more than it suggests passion. Or, for example, that Mammy and Daddy never chatted and laughed the way Shay and I did, and that though silence must add intensity to your intimate moments, it must also shrivel your soul to lie beside someone who doesn't talk to you. Or, for example, that if we are loved as babies we learn how to love. And that we go on needing to be loved. There was no doubt, for instance, that her mother coming back to her was the thing that began to heal Caro.

She never noticed that, and I never said it to her. I used to think at the time that a little love in childhood – which is what she got from her mother – leaves you completely vulnerable as you try to add to it, whereas none at all is good for you. When you grow up and realize you were never loved at all you're reassured, in a way, that you never got what by then you believe you don't deserve. I never made the demands on anyone that Caro made on me. I didn't ask anyone to listen to me while I writhed and wept for Hugo; I just stepped back from the whole love thing, as if there'd been a terrible event that happened once, when I'd fallen into a snake pit, and then realized that the snake pit was inside me.

If I had a child myself, I used to think, I would know the mistakes not to make. I would love it so wholly that it would go through life smiling and calm. But something was wrong inside me. I saw an artefact once in a display in one of the Smithsonian museums in Washington – a baby garment, made from a single, soft animal skin. The Inuit people, up around the Arctic Circle, keep their babies in it – a minute, all-in-one suit, like a Babygro, with arms and legs that end in pouches for the hands and feet. You put the baby in, and then you close the opening with thongs of the same suede. Where the baby's bottom would rest there was a clump of moss. You threw that out when the baby dirtied it, and put in fresh moss. It was a thing that evoked an actual baby – its delicate limbs flailing, its head rolling and chuckling. The little round halves of its bottom would be silky. I stood looking at the display case and I accepted that a baby called Kathleen's baby would never exist – that the words didn't sound right. I wasn't, then, particularly upset. I had come out of my mother's house not liking babies.

It was as I got older that I began to be moved by the beauty of new creatures. By the miracle of their creation. By their smallness, and helplessness, and their amiability in the face of the world. Once, in the Shedd Oceanarium in Chicago, I even cried with delight at a newborn beluga whale cavorting like a lone dancer in the great tank of murky water. Its white body was marked with deep wrinkles, still, where it had been folded like a telescopic umbrella in the mother whale's womb. It swam up to the glass wall and looked at me with innocent blackcurrant eyes . . .

The older I got the more I asked questions about the purpose of my existence, if it was not to have a baby. And, of course, I asked myself why it had been that not one of all the billions of men on the planet had ever *wanted* me to have their baby. Maybe I'm infertile, I thought, because of that – because no one out there *wanted* to fertilize me.

I didn't tell Jimmy when I went into hospital for a few days to have fertility tests. I hadn't tried to become pregnant by anyone in particular, but I had a growing feeling of uneasiness.

The elderly consultant called me into his office the day I was leaving.

We think there's old scarring there. He pointed to an X-ray of my ovaries. Is it possible that you could have had a tubercular infection in childhood that went undiagnosed?

You could have had leprosy in my childhood home, I said, and no one would have noticed.

There was a silence.

Will I ever have a child? I asked.

We don't like to say never, he said.

I walked out of the hospital and dumped the holdall with the things for my hospital stay in a litter bin, and got a taxi straight to the office. If I had had nowhere to go but back to the basement I would have broken down. When I got up to the office – and it wasn't easy to move, because I was sore from the probes – Roxy was sulking, because Alex was sitting across from her giving her an embarrassed but brave talking-to about the importance of spelling and commas and full stops and how she was screwing up copy that Jimmy and Kathy had written with great care and that he, Alex, had edited with the same care. As I was passing, Alex without getting up handed me a sheaf of signed expenses and smiled up at me. It's just a matter of reading over what you've typed, he went back to saying, because you're a very intelligent girl, Roxanne, only you're careless . . . The room was warm, and clouds sailed by our half-moon window and there was the smell of cloves from something. Roxy, seeing an escape from being rebuked, said, Will I put the kettle on? The geraniums on the sill were the clearest of coral reds. Jimmy lifted his shapely head and looked at me. My face must have been very pale, because his smile suddenly became alert and knowing. He thought I'd taken the few days off to be with a man.

Not long afterwards, I was at a party on the deck of someone's yacht and I went home with the pleasant man I'd been talking to. It was obvious that this was about as important to him as a visit to the gym, but I was so lonely. In his apartment, in the airless bedroom with a steel security grille across the sealed window, he had sex with me on a water bed. The bed had a hospital feel of flesh sticking on polythene. He was an athlete, and he leaned back from my body and rested on his arms above me and thrust and thrust.

But – this is ridiculous, I thought. You do this to make babies . . .

That was maybe the worst thing, as a matter of fact. Being always in danger of perceiving the act of love as a pantomime.

I never cried about all that side of things when I was with children. But once, I was in Berlin, doing a piece on the new museums, and I was stopped in my tracks, passing a newsagent's shop at the Ku'damm station, by the covers on a shelf of pornographic magazines. Huge breast after huge breast. One magazine had a photo of a blonde holding up weighty breasts with her hands, so that the nipples pointed straight out. Big Tits! the caption said. Suck Them and See! In front of this picture, gazing at it, immobile, stood a Turkish labourer, shivering with cold.

I looked at her, and at him. Then I looked at myself looking.

I wanted – an intense, incoherent, sexual longing surged up through my body – to both feed, and be fed. And there was no chance.

I did cry. It must have been February or March, because I remember the metallic sky behind the leafless trees, and how I could cry with abandon, walking along, because it was so cold that everyone's eyes were watering.

I am motherless in every direction, I mourned.

I wanted to have sex there and then. The vast breasts turned me on, too. But then I thought of my mother having breasts and feeding me – which Mammy did – and I was repelled. I didn't know how men managed to keep the breast erotic and distinct from their mothers' actual breasts. In Berlin I arrived back at the perennial question: how did my mother hold us tiny beings to her skin and fill us with herself, and yet look at us indifferently three or four years later, as we sat at the table doing our homework and waiting, without the courage to say anything, for her to cook some food? It seemed the biggest of ironies that maternity killed her. But look how the womb shapes lives! Marianne Talbot would not have been degraded and driven insane if she had had a healthy womb and borne Richard a fine boy, and secured the inheritance of Mount Talbot. Caroline might not have surrendered so explicitly to Ian if the skin around her eyes hadn't been blueish and taut from pregnancy when he said to her that it was nothing to him, either way, what she did.

And me. I forced the zip of my jeans up my stomach. Somewhere buried deep behind that soft flesh, I imagined, there was a shrivelled organ.

Tear-shaped. Wombs are tear-shaped.

In real life, in May 1852, Marianne Talbot must have realized more clearly with each passing hour that her little girl had been taken from her for ever. That's pain. That's what I'd call pain. She would have been plunged into a living hell. If she was in hell – her frantic mind must have reckoned – she was being punished for sin. And if she was being punished, she must be guilty. And so she never denied a thing. Just as, in a show trial, you finally say to your tormentors, You are correct, sir. Yes, sir. Whatever you say.

I had written out on the back page of my notebook a passage from John Paget's pamphlet. It was about guilt and madness. When Paget had Marianne examined by his doctors, they all found her to be mad. And they weren't surprised – they knew lots of madwomen. The passage that I had copied out was from the most eminent of the doctors who reported on Marianne:

> *I have known, in the course of my practice, a lady of unexceptionable character, but who eventually destroyed herself during an attack of mania, declare that she had been repeatedly guilty of criminal connexion with a medical man, whom she had only seen once or twice. Another case of a young lady about to be married, who became insane, and declared she had been seduced by her expected husband and was pregnant by him. She recovered and it was discovered that such a statement was all delusion on her part. A third case of a young lady living with her uncle and aunt, who had many delusions, and among others, declared that the manservant in the same house seduced her, and slept with her frequently. She recovered, and it was well known that all her statements were mere delusion. I am consulting physician to the Hanwell Lunatic Asylum, where there are 500 insane women confined; and I have known many married women, inmates of said asylum, declare that the night previous to their making the statement, men, sometimes naming them, came into their rooms at night, and had connexion with them . . .*

Pitiful sisters!

The women in the lunatic asylum claiming imaginary sex, and Marianne, claiming imaginary guilt, seemed to me to deserve a special kind of pity. Something real in them was trying to get out – some life force was still trying to express itself through them. They parodied the impossible ideal of women they had learned as girls – to be lascivious at night, but keep their sexuality in line in daylight through shame and self-loathing.

And, of course, the fact that the women in the Hanwell asylum, and Marianne, creeping around John Paget's villa in England, were defined as mad didn't make the rest of us sane. Their actions, and mine, and those of many women I had known in my life were variations on the one theme. The ravings about love, the going onto beds in locked rooms with men picked up in bars, the exposing of bodies, the marriage vows spoken against reason to cruel men, the days made bearable by tranquillisers, the kisses delivered with eyes tight shut. It is not a great distance from the poor madwoman in Hanwell Asylum babbling about being fucked by the gardener, to the old lady who sheds one tear, in her neat, nursing-home bed, at Madame Butterfly singing ecstatically on a distant radio about the fine day when Pinkerton will come back to her. Even when we seem to be gathered safe into the fold of marriage, we can be driven by a dream of fulfilment and completion that leads us – like sheep hunted over a cliff by a wild dog – into a terrible fall.

I went down to the kitchen for breakfast. Ollie was heading across the rug like a land crab, making for – Spot! Spot was back!

The terrier came up to me and did a bit of prancing and rubbing his muzzle against my calf. He had a white tail in the middle of black curls, and he wagged it with generous enthusiasm.

Felix is gone again, Bertie said, and he says you're welcome to stay in his place. I'll take you and Spot out there later on, if that suits you. The teachers will be coming in around teatime. They have the first of their workshops as they call them tonight. Work, my arse in parsley! Playschools, they'd a right to call those yokes.

There were two ducks who lived under the trees down at the end of the hotel garden in a weedy enclosure made of an old gate and the planks from a shed. I hoisted Ollie on my arm and took him and Joe to see the ducks. The sunshine today was very warm and so steady that you could feel it healing the grass and the bushes still roughened and muddy from the spring. We stood under a willow shimmering with new leaves of the palest green, and the ducks stood in front of us in profile and quacked busily. Everything around was soft. The light, the willow leaves, the children's round arms, the slight give of the black earth under my feet. The light dappled on us, and Ollie crooned to the ducks. I knew how pretty the scene must look.

And suddenly, I hated the whole thing. I didn't want to belong to it. Rejection of it surged up in me and I plopped the child onto the path. What was I doing in this soggy, quiet place, with these people who moved so slowly? And getting sentimental about children and dogs and so on. Give me something with a bit of style! I needed a few of Jimmy's smart remarks. Or just – smartness. The tiles at the back door of the kitchen had reminded me just now of the floor of the Palm Court of the Ritz in Madrid, and of a moment when I walked across it, perfumed and made-up and dressed in a wisp of a dress, towards a man who stood up from behind the glass and candles of the restaurant table to greet me. Jasper Conran, that dress was. The details didn't matter – that the man was quite an autocrat, or that he kept breaking into Catalan when he knew perfectly well I couldn't follow him. What mattered was his perfect evening dress and the perfumed air of the wonderful room and that moment of walking towards him in my Rita Hayworth slingbacks when I was all artifice – a crisp person, brightly coloured, metropolitan, light. Oh – I *missed* all that!

I picked Ollie up again and we began to make our way back to the house. The thing was – if I could have that night in the Ritz back, would I want it? And, no – I wouldn't particularly want it. Tens of countries, hundreds of restaurants, thousands of meals – how many of them did I remember with joy? I began to think about breakfasts on balconies, picnics in forests, thimblefuls of aromatic coffee in bright bars . . . Meals I had liked.

And then my heart warmed before, even, my mind identified the memory. A few tables outside a quayside building on a hot night, behind a little box hedge, the lights from the moored yachts bobbing, the tablecloth held down with little clips against the warm breeze that came in from the Adriatic. The three of us there. My dear friends. My dear Jimmy and my dear Alex. The dinner we shared in Trieste on a night of wonderful silly happiness, two years ago. Even if, the next morning, I had to run away.

Jimmy must have gone up to my room in the hotel to collect me for breakfast, and seen that I'd gone. He followed me, anyway, to the train station. That's where I had to be. He saw me. He pressed his face comically to the outside of the window against which mine was slumped, unseeing. He passed a magazine in over the top of the window. And a bottle of water, and a box of crystallized fruits.

Are you going to Venice? he mouthed.

I nodded. All the trains out of Trieste seemed to go to Venice.

I was holding back a flood of grateful tears. That he should run through the streets, and in and out of the shops at the station! The train creaked and clanged and began to move along the platform. He mouthed one last thing. Look after yourself, I thought it was.

The three of us from *TravelWrite* had been summoned to an international NewsWrite think-in at the Hotel Colomba D'Oro in Trieste, even though we were usually left to do our own thing in the attic in the City of London for years on end. Why should they interfere? Alex used to say: we're very successful as we are. Jimmy always said that the reason he stayed with *TravelWrite* was because we never saw the bosses.

But the Human Resources people had made us go to this 'Preparing for the Millennium' seminar. It was an odd enough venue – there wasn't even a health centre in the hotel behind all the plush and gilt. But the New York boss was keen on 'the Opening to the East', and Trieste was a gesture to his Hungarian and Slovenian contacts. Some of the Germans had come down the motorways in four-wheel-drives and were going on up to the Kajarska plateau to shoot. They were big, sonorous men who crunched in and out of the foyer of the hotel in brown shoes and complex leisurewear of suede and corduroy. They laughed at each other's witticisms in deep, slow tones. They were as confident as huge two-year-olds.

It's not fair that poor, anxious Alex has to speak in front of men like those, I said to Jimmy.

I know, Jimmy said. I hope he doesn't collapse from nervous tension.

We were in the ballroom, Jimmy and I, rehearsing Alex. There was a row of long windows with gold trim and lavish purple velvet drapes. Through the frosted glass the silhouettes of people on the street hurried past, and every few minutes the room was darkened by a passing tram. We made Alex walk out from behind one of the curtains, count out six paces, and then turn and smile and say, Good evening, friends, colleagues and above all, fellow architects of the project of Writing this Wonderful World. He got it wrong over and over. We would have fallen around laughing but for his white face.

At first, I said to Jimmy when we gave Alex a coffee break, I thought that he couldn't say the words because they're such balls. But then I saw that he couldn't say them because they mean so much to him.

He had to speak for five minutes, in the last hour of the day. We had printed a précis of his main points on big sheets of paper. New travellers will bring from travel riches the same as old-time travellers. Respect for cultural heritage bridge between new and old. Alex tried and tried. He stood out on the parquet. I could see his reflection in the floor. The trams groaned outside. We coaxed him through.

All right then, Alex, try it again.

He'd look at us desperately. But in the end he got it right: And so, friends, as we enter a millennium where the business of the planet is more and more consigned to the abstract realm of electronics, the project of Writing the Reality of the World looks forward, not backward. We celebrate what is: above all we welcome what will be. Thank you.

Jesus Christ Almighty! I said to Jimmy. How in the name of God did he come up with such rubbish?

Ssshh, Jimmy said. He's very proud of it.

Come up to the room with me, Alex said to us when there was about half an hour to go. Jimmy went into the bathroom with him to go over the speech one last time while he shaved. That had always been something I loved about Alex's looks – that black shadow that came up through his matte skin by late afternoon, as if there were more life going on in him than you'd guess from his slight frame and his thin dark hair.

I was disturbed to be in his room. I didn't want to see any of his secrets, even though I'd been trying to get to know him for a long time. I'd asked him time and again to come with me to previews or to brochure launches in posh restaurants, or to industry cocktail parties, or just to have a drink with me and Jimmy – a cold beer on a summer evening, or a hot whisky when the streets outside were dark and wet when we left the office. He never accepted. We knew nothing about him except that he lived with his mother. He never mentioned a woman or a man friend or a pet animal. Amazingly enough, given Roxy's booking skills, which everyone in the building used, no one knew where Alex went on holiday. He'd come back from leave in the same slightly-too-big business suit, not looking any different.

In the hotel room, I sat on a sofa opposite the bed. On my right, in the window alcove, there was an ornate table. A small leather travelling folder, with photos in it, was propped on the table. Two or three small books were beside it. I couldn't make out the details across the room. I could hear him in the bathroom intoning the phrases Jimmy was reading out. I knew I could easily walk over to the window and look at the clues on the table. But I didn't. It was superstition. I wanted this day to go right for Alex. I wanted to be nothing but his friend, wishing him well. I stayed where I was, and trailed behind the two of them when they went back down to the conference room.

Well, he didn't disgrace himself, Jimmy said to me when Alex – in his best suit, which Jimmy said was even more of a mistake than his usual suits – sat down to a respectable amount of applause. For a shy man, he did a good job.

Yeah, I said. Funnily enough, you could see that he was absolutely sincere.

When Alex was settling back into his seat the biggest boss of all made a point of getting up and threading his way across the room, and leaning down to say a few congratulatory sentences. He might as well have put explosives under Alex. By the time we caught up with him, at the reception before dinner, he had a flushed face and shining eyes, and he was talking to one of the big Germans and flourishing his sherry glass as if there were no tomorrow.

Darlings! he cried, and he put down his glass and embraced Jimmy and then me, smacking kisses on our cheeks. The German looked at him as if he were mad. We'd all been together, after all, only an hour or so before.

Oh – however badly it ended, that was a night I loved!

Alex – Alex, the dutiful! – said, Let's get out of here and eat on our own!

It was June, and the evening air was hot, and we ran down a flight of steps and under a great baroque archway and came out onto a square that opened to the waterfront. We went along past ferryboats and yachts and freighters on rocking green water, skipping over the ropes that crossed the worn slabs of the old quay.

Jules et Jim, I laughed at them. With me as Jeanne Moreau.

I don't think I ever felt as happy. I think that was the one time I got it right – the balance between thinking of myself as smart and competent in the world, and also as having warmth in my heart and serenity in my veins. I didn't just love the other two. I loved myself, and my hair in the breeze off the sea, and my long waist and my red sandals that matched my nail varnish. They each took my hands to help me skip over the ropes. I must have been something to look at, laughing there in the summer dusk, beside the water. A man passing paused to look at me, and said something like *carina* to himself, under his breath, as if he were savouring my joy.

Then we dodged the traffic to cross the road, and settled at a table behind a box hedge outside a restaurant.

Wine! Alex commanded. *Vino!*

We didn't eat much of the bony fish, but we drank a lot of wine, and kept asking the waiter for more grissini, and then we each had a crème caramel so that at least we'd have eaten an egg for nourishment, and then we had little glasses of sambuca.

Con la mosca? The waiter said. *Zzz, zzz.* He made a floating, nipping gesture with his hand.

Jimmy was studying him.

He's talking about a fly. I think it's a fly, not a mosquito.

Yez, the waiter said, nodding and smiling. Fuly!

He put a coffee bean on the surface of the sambuca.

Fuly! he said, pointing at it.

It does look like a fly, Alex said, beaming.

Oh! I said, delighted. The villain in *Volpone*. Isn't he called Mosca? Oh, what a great name for a villain!

The men looked at me. *My* men, I was thinking fondly, by then.

Then the waiter set fire to the surface of the liqueur, and the coffee bean roasted in the momentary flame. Then we blew the flames out, and drank our sambucas with their hint of coffee.

We discussed Alex's speech from every possible angle. His triumph grew greater and greater. We toasted it in sambucas we soon got too impatient to set on fire. Several times.

I don't know what happened next. I could have asked Jimmy, at least about the bit between the restaurant and the hotel, but the whole thing was too painful to talk about. It wasn't the waking up in the dark, mouth dry and dirty, bladder bursting, beside Alex in his bed, with my skirt twisted around my waist, though that was very bad. It was realizing that Alex was wide awake – that he was lying motionless with his head on his pillow, looking up at the ceiling. Eventually I said, Oh, dear – lightly, in the hope that we could make a joke of it. But he didn't speak or move. I got out of bed as if I had been beaten.

My blouse and bra and pants were in a tangle on the chair. I pulled them on. I couldn't get it right – I was hurrying too much, and shaking too much. It took ages. And all the time there was nothing but silence from the bed. I found my bag and went out of the room. The man from the front desk brought me back to my own room. I didn't know where my key was. He was wonderfully polite to me.

When I heard the hotel stirring I stood under the shower for a long time and then put on a lot of make-up with trembling hands. I had taken all the aspirin I had, but I could still feel the sick headache at the back of my neck. A bottle of wine, maybe, I'd drunk. Before the liqueurs . . .

I was nervous to the pit of my stomach at having to face Alex again. But I did it because I had to. I walked into the breakfast room. There was a long queue at the buffet. I saw Alex, standing on his own. I did what would have been natural the day before: I walked over to join him, keeping my hands down, because of the trembling.

He recoiled. He actually, physically, jumped back when I approached, as if I were a devil. He looked at me with a horrified face. The way he looked at me was much nearer hatred than embarrassment.

My mouth had been opening to say some ordinary morning thing to him, but I couldn't speak with shock. I turned and hurried out. I'd found the seat on the Venice train before I breathed normally again.

Jimmy's running after me to the station helped me to cry, at least. By the time I'd travelled as far as I could go – to Venice and then past Venice to the Lido and then across to the other side of the Lido – I was able to open the casements of the high, pale hotel room and sit with my face up to the sun.

He's known me for years and years! I cried out to myself. Couldn't he have been friendly? What's so terrible about a tumble into bed? A bit of a roll in the hay, for God's sake, between middle-aged people?

He blamed me: I felt it in his rigidity in the bed. Not himself. Not us. Me. But even if it was me who made all the running –

Well, it was me, of course. He'd never even wanted to have a drink with me, so he'd hardly wanted to go to bed with me all of a sudden.

Ah, hell! What is the big deal here? I didn't mean to get drunk. I didn't mean any of this to happen. What harm did I do him, anyway? What kind of mean little man is he that he couldn't have said a word to me, or maybe just given my hand a squeeze and left it at that?

Then I thought to myself, But would I have left it at that? No. I'd have been encouraged. And it *is* a big deal. We've worked together for eighteen years. It *is* a big deal, us in a bed in half our clothes, even if nothing else happened . . .

My body, as well as my heart, felt shocked. I couldn't tell from it whether there had been any physical intercourse. I felt so sick, still, and stiff and sore everywhere.

I bet I did make all the running.

But even if I did . . .

And so on. Round and round.

*

Venice in early June is at the point of perfection. I had been in the city once before, when I was starting out in travel writing, visiting it by myself, when Caroline had gone to Hong Kong for Christmas. I'd sat, then, hunched over the one tepid radiator in a cheap, stone-floored back room. I'm as poor as Mary McCarthy when she was writing about Italy, I remember thinking in a welter of self-pity: I only wish I was as brilliant as she was, too. Concentrating on what I hadn't got, as usual, instead of what I had: the low silvery light through the chill mist on the lagoon, and getting off the ferry on the island of Torcello, the only visitor, and walking along through the frost-bound vegetable gardens and across the little canal, flowing black under shards of ice, into the basilica where I could hardly see the marvellous Last Judgment mosaic through the cloud of my own freezing breath.

Now I was in one of the grand hotels, in a room of faded mirrors and old carpets and long muslin curtains, where the balcony was level with the feathery tops of the tamarisk trees that lined the terrace. Below the terrace, the water barely lapped against the beach. Tonight, I would come back from the city in the hotel launch and dine on the terrace, the lagoon a dark presence beyond the clean, raked sand. The candles on my table would be golden in their squat glass jars. There'd be time today to look at something. The Carpaccios, maybe, that were so full of life and fun. Or I could wander the alleyways, going into each church I passed, moving across the island to the quarter of the ghetto, where the tall tenement buildings are still as bleak as when the Jews of Venice were shut in there at night. I could sit in the big piazza and put coffee and cake at Florian's on the *TravelWrite* credit card, and watch the people and the pigeons and the light playing on the façade of St Mark's. I could buy *The Wings of the Dove* in a bookshop and find a quiet piazzetta and read the Venice chapters sitting on worn old steps to the sound of a fountain trickling and children playing and the warning shouts of boatmen on the canals somewhere out of sight. I needn't do any of those things. I could swim right here. I could walk up through the quiet villas behind the hotel to the shopping street and buy something to swim in, and when I came out of the water I could splay out in a wicker chair and feel the droplets dry on my body in the bright, fresh heat of early summer.

And all these glories were nothing, just because a man had hurt me. Well, I'd hurt myself, through a man. Well, an inappropriate thing had happened with a man. Oh, I didn't know what the hell to call the thing that had happened! I didn't even know what had happened.

I tried to reach Jimmy at the Trieste hotel.

All the NewsWrite guests, madame, are gone to the reception of the City Council, and they will go on to dinner at the Miramar Castle. Yes, I will take a message . . .

Miramar! Rilke lived in the Miramar Castle! I hunched up on the sumptuous bed. Oh, to have been a poet like him! To have been grand! To think in sweeps! To see life and death and love in deep and beautiful forms – not to be suburban, a nobody with a drab little imagination, just enough to have a crush on the boss and to snivel at humiliation, but not enough to see into the mystery of existence, like Rilke. I memorized a remark in an article I read about him once – that 'he had a bitter self-knowledge of the weaknesses from which his strength came'. Well, why couldn't I hope to be like that –

Then I started to laugh, even though I was still crying. I'm used to your whining at the least opportunity, I said to myself. But to start crying because you aren't a genius takes the goddamn biscuit!

That's what I'll do, all the same, I thought, sitting up on the bed. I'll read him. I haven't in years. I'll go over to the bookshop in Venice, and see whether they have a Rilke in English.

I jumped off the bed and went into the bathroom and washed the tears off my face. I was glad to have the Rilke project. Rilke would probably be a better resource for me, when I was an old woman, than any man. I would bounce across the green lagoon towards the splendour of Venice in the hotel speedboat.

I got myself going again, and left it to another day to figure out how to face the office.

I made excuses so as to stay away for a long time. A bit of illness. A few weeks' leave to get over the illness. A fraught stay with Nora in New York. A trip to California to do a few pieces on the Getty Museum. Eventually, from a dim sum restaurant in Los Angeles I rang Jimmy for the second time that day, and he said wearily, Come back, Kathleen. You're as lonely for us, as we are for you.

We? I said. Us?

Once and for all, Kathleen, listen to me, properly. You're being selfish as well as ridiculous. Things don't just happen to you, you know – you have an effect on things, too. You seem to think you have no effect on people, but you do.

Do you swear on your oath you'll meet me in the hall and be with me when I go up to the office? Just the first day?

You're being *silly*, he said.

I'm going to improve! I said. I'm going to take steps –

Me too, he said. I'm going to take steps to improve you.

Alex was perfect. He behaved as if nothing at all had happened – so much so that I began to ask myself whether I had overdramatized the whole thing. From time to time I'd remember his face in the darkened bedroom beside me, looking, open-eyed, at the ceiling, but his present self was so much the same as it had always been that the memory started to seem unreal. He was what he had always been in the office – helpful, fussy, bad-tempered, reliable. But if Jimmy hadn't died, and we hadn't become close the evening of his funeral, I would never have heard Alex's side of things. I would have gone on, like many another woman, baffled, and even frightened, by the distance there can be between the instinctive generosity of the body, and any good coming of it.

I followed Bertie's car, brushing against the hawthorn hedges, up through winding boreens and across what looked like a featureless bog. Then he turned a corner, and I was looking down on an oval, reed-fringed lake. It lay in its hollow of green like a perfect thing. His car disappeared. Then I saw that there were no gates or driveway; he'd driven into Felix's house through a gap in the bank and across a plateau of short, springy grass.

Below, in a fold in the ground, a few yards from the water, what looked like a tumbledown stone farm building was the house. The small fields around the lake were streaked with the glowing mustard-yellow of gorse and, leaning over the house and shedding their ivory petals on the slate and the rough grass around, and even on the still water, were two wild cherry trees. Spot flung himself, barking with joy, down the slope of the field. We walked in through the stone wall and onto a platform of wood which looked through glass and a wide balcony over the water and the rushes and the fields. We went down wide wooden steps to see the bedrooms and bathrooms on the ground level, and then we went back up an outside staircase to the main room and its deck.

Now! Bertie said, with immense satisfaction. Didn't I tell you! Isn't it gorgeous?

God, Bertie! I said, talk about a change! In Mellary, I felt as if I had been there for ever, you know? Those thick walls of the cottage? You could sit anything out behind them. Storms. Landlords. The Black and Tans. And it was hard work just living there. Every time I went out for a bucket of turf I had to pity the man who saved it and the woman who had to cook on it. But this place is from another planet.

He did it himself with a few local fellas, Bertie said. There's great craftsmen around here if they could be bothered to get off their bums.

I walked back with him to his car up a path of worn flagstones.

Felix got them down at the edge of the lake, Bertie said. There was a whole village there before the Famine. There were people there when there were dinosaurs, nearly. He found a wooden bowl there once that was a thousand years old.

Do you think they'll be digging up Alessi lemon-squeezers a hundred years from now? I said. Will anyone care about what we were like?

Cheer up, Kathleen, Bertie said. And if you can't cheer up, you've only to lift the phone and I'll rescue you. And the teachers will be gone in a few days, bad luck to them anyway.

Thank you for everything, Bertie, I said. But especially, for letting me mind the dog.

The valley was so full of light that I imagined the people from it as if they were in the negatives of photos – grey, with white features – coming around the lake with their bundles. Coming down the slope of the hill. Coming out from their abandoned dwelling places with cakes of new-baked bread in their shawls, and leaving their native place to sunlit silence. The starvation was over by the time they left; they weren't, any more, like the children in the concentration camps who were so hungry that they ate their cardboard identity tags – ate their own names. But the Irish people, too, were losing their names, because they were walking away from their own language as they filed up the field behind the house, on their way to wherever their journey would end.

Light flooded the house. I hadn't noticed at first that, besides the wall onto the lake being made of glass, the roof was ribbed with glass.

First, panic rose within me. How would I get through the time?

I could leave a few pounds on the table and make phone calls. Though – not to Nora, anyway: it was midday in Manhattan, and on Sundays the women in Nora's circle threw seriously competitive brunches after Mass. I nearly went back on cigarettes from the tension, the last time I was there for Nora's brunch, a couple of years ago, after the debacle with Alex in Trieste. Nora served bagels from some special place only she knew on the Lower East Side, and juice from organic oranges and big steaks with eggs on them to the portly Irish-American men who were busily getting high. She'd put plastic covers over her sofas, for fear of spills, and all the surfaces were strewn with coasters and doilies and little table runners with NB embroidered on them.

Her living room was the exact opposite of the simple spaces in Felix's place. It was an expanse of tan plush and enormous terracotta lamps.

This place is worth three-quarters of a million, she said. I gasped obediently.

Yup, she said. Maybe more. That's America for you. Anyone can make money here.

I don't think I could, I said.

You could of course, she said, if you weren't such a snob.

She shot me an impersonal look. I'd completely forgotten that she could be formidable.

You know you could, she said. You're much smarter than me. But most people aren't good enough for you, are they? And you can't have that in business.

I'm not in business, I said huffily.

I know, she said. That's why.

I got my composure back a little while later, when she showed me to the guest suite. It was a rampant jungle of florals and frills.

I did it myself, she said happily. It's the old-style look. More European than they usually do here. It's kind of a hearkening back to the old country.

What old country? I said.

Ireland, she said.

There's no chintz in Ireland, I said.

Oh, it's not exact, she said. More of an interpretation.

I loved this remark. I needed to tell it to Jimmy straight away. But at the same time, I did admire her. She unconsciously narrowed her eyes and pursed her mouth when she contemplated her surroundings.

Shrewd, she looked. Self-satisfied. But then – what did we come from but a long line of small farmers? Wasn't her apartment her field and her flock? Why wouldn't she look like a peasant who'd done well at the fair?

Who else could I talk to? Alex was out of touch unless he chose to ring Bertie's place and get my new number: or Betty in Administration might have news of him when the office opened tomorrow. I'd leave Caro till the morning to send her out to the exam with my good wishes ringing in her ears. If only Miss Leech was back so I could talk to her about the Paget book. If only Miss Leech came back well. . . .

I set up my laptop and looked at the last note I'd made. It was Marianne's exclamation in Rathgar – that she wished she had something to love. The next step for her in real life was the Reverend McClelland taking her across the sea to England and locking her in the asylum in Windsor. When I thought of that long, silent journey I said to Marianne in my mind, Run away! Run! But she was just a poor mad lady in huge crinoline skirts by then. Or if not mad, going mad. Perhaps she didn't lose her reason altogether until she found herself locked up – as far as she knew, for the rest of her life. But I'd leave Marianne until I could talk to Miss Leech. I began looking through Felix's bookshelves to see whether he had any interesting books.

But in the end, I didn't read. This is a very special place, I finally admitted to myself, and a special time. For half a day and then a whole day and then another day I did what I could hardly ever remember doing before: nothing. That first evening I showered looking down through the glass wall onto a moorhen guiding her flotilla of tiny chicks through the reeds, in the wonderful bathroom lined with tiles of the exact blue-green of the hill across the lake. There was a marble chair to sit on and nozzles and sprays that came from every direction. I washed my hair with Felix's seaweed shampoo from a classy gents' hairdresser in Milan. Then I opened a tin of tuna. I spread half of it on bread and butter, for myself, and put half on a tin plate on the flagstones outside the French doors of the kitchen. The three meagre smoky-grey wildcats had vibrated with fear at first, but after they devoured the tuna, they played in the long grass underneath the outside staircase, nipping and then chasing each other, rolling lightly in and out of the evening sun and the lengthening shadows like skeins of silk. As my hair dried in the mild dusk I brushed every single tangle out, and it floated around me. I woke up once during the night to check that Spot was beside the bed, and I was lying on my hair, and even to me it seemed to smell beautifully of the air of the valley.

And next day, different weathers came and went, and the house was immersed in sun, then darkened by cloud, then freed into sunlight again as the cloud was scoured away by wind. In the afternoon, a settled spell came. The wind died away to the lightest breeze, and the house was translucent, and held me quietly. I sat out on the wooden deck with Spot asleep at my feet. When I crouched down beside him to hold him for a minute, his coat was hot from the sun. The sky was a great arc of the most perfect blue. There are tiles on the roofs of old mosques in Iran that are a blue that has no hint of any other colour in it, and the blue blazes like a horizon between a sky white with heat and the dun-coloured concrete houses in the desert dust. Here, the sky was one of those domes turned inside out, and the azure made everything in the green fold beneath it, pure. It seemed to hold under its span the very essence of early summer. I felt each move I made – my foot stepping onto the springy grass of the field, the warm breeze lifting my hair and laying it back on my smooth neck. I breathed with delight air so fresh that it might have been newly made. I heard each layer of sound, from the liquid squealing of the larks up under the sky, to the susurrus of the reeds in the lake and the tiny lap of water against the brown crescent of beach.

The sun sank in a riot of pink and purple along the horizon, and I made a nest of cushions on the outside steps and watched the cats hunt up and down the hedge. Then, after it got dark, I lay on the sofa with Spot in front of the television. A woman in Texas had murdered her golf instructor. A Taiwanese opera. A long discussion of the economic implications of the weak yen.

That night I pulled the mattress out onto the deck and went to bed when it was still twilight. The darkening lake seemed to sway, but not move, a few feet away. I would have been frightened anywhere else at being so vulnerable to night creatures. But here, after so many hours in the quiet presence of the water and the fields, I felt a part of the valley. A swan drifted past out on the black water as I lay among the pillows, waiting for the end of the Schubert piano sonata I'd put on – the last one, the one that Schubert was writing when he knew he was dying. I'd brought this CD everywhere since Jimmy's death, like a fetish. I never got tired of playing it. I listened to it to see whether I could hear the shape of death. Or hear Schubert accepting death, on behalf of all mortal beings as well as himself. I used to try to talk to Jimmy about music, but he didn't really care. I'd played this piece to him, never dreaming that I would lose him. I said to him, The music is describing the experience of dying, as if it had already happened and was understood, and at the same time it is experiencing dying. That's what's so consoling about music, I think – it evokes experience far beyond our understanding, and yet it controls it. What do you think, Jim?

Jimmy said, When my father died they played 'You'll Never Walk Alone' on the harmonium, and when my mother died, she'd left instructions for a selection from *The Three Tenors in Rome*. So don't expect a son of Scottsbluff, Nebraska, to know what you're talking about.

I said, Shore Road, Kilcrennan, wasn't exactly Vienna, you know . . .

Without expecting to, I started to cry. I cried and cried, soaking the pillow and the sheet under my neck. Tears poured from me, like blood from an artery. The little moorhens and the bony wildcats are busy with living now, I thought, exactly as they have always been. But humans have to deal with the past and the future. I felt the luxury of my nest of sheets and pillows and I was so sorry for my poor mother, trying to start the old stove with sticks from the tideline on the beach that were too salty to catch light. Even my father, I was sorry for. This house – so beautiful and confident! And Daddy with his old-style Irish stuff, going along in his worn, navy-blue suit, greeting the neighbours like a potentate, and at home, shouting 'Get out to hell out of that', to get us off to Mass. He never lived in a bright place in his life. He turned himself out, pin-neat and shiny clean, from our cold bathroom at home with its stained bath and its torn lino. Imagine how he would have whistled in Felix's gorgeous shower room! The Ireland of my parents' time wasted its people as if people were valueless. And as for their grandparents, like the people who lived beside the lake . . . They had their Jimmies, too, and lost them. Their Jimíns. Their thousand-times-beloveds. Driving out from Ballygall a man on the radio sang a love song made by the people whose ghosts were rustling in the reeds below me. *I would wed you if you hadn't a cow, a pound note, any bit of a dowry, love of my heart. It is my bitter sadness that you and I, love of my heart, are not in Cashel, and for a bed beneath us, a plank of deal from the bog* . . . And Marianne – her limbs trapped under layer upon layer of horsehair and whalebone and starched muslin – never to know the feel of a cotton shirt and shorts and the soft wood of a deck under bare, brown feet. I could have lived somewhere like this myself, I wailed, most of my life, and instead I lived down that hole in London – when I was twenty-five, thirty, forty, forty-five. The older I got, the heavier my burden of not having been happy yet.

This is going to be an awful night, I thought. But that's not what happened. My eyelashes were stuck together with tears, but gradually, only an occasional one broke through and slid down into the fold of my neck. And the next thing, I was ravenously hungry. I woke up Spot who was stretched beside me and put on my sweater, and we went into the kitchen and I made cheese on toast for me and sardines on toast for him and played some forties chanteuse singing 'Begin the Beguine' and drank a glass of delicious wine from a whole cabinet of chilled bottles. I felt extraordinarily well. I tidied up, and the two of us went back out to our alfresco bed. We're as snug as bugs in a rug, I said to Spot.

I'd like a Cole Porter medley at my own funeral as well as the Schubert. If I could still hear, so to speak. It amazed me that I couldn't remember what music there had been at Jimmy's funeral in the fake-medieval chapel in the crematorium. But then, Alex did all the arrangements. I left everything to him. After the morning when we found out Jim was dead and I drank a lot of gin in a pub near the office with Roxy and Betty, I just went home and read. Alex rang me all the time to tell me what he was finding out and what he was arranging. Heart attack. Cremation. Jimmy turned out to have had a recent lover, but he was in an Aids clinic in Miami and had been for a year, and the director of the clinic said he was not well enough to be told about Jimmy's death, but that he and all the staff would miss Señor Jimmy terribly. I just said yes, yes, to everything. I didn't see anyone for a few days. Three or four.

Another reason I couldn't remember the details of Jimmy's funeral service was that I was in shock.

When Alex called for me and I realized we were both dressed completely in black, I said, We were more than just people who worked with him. Well, after Mr and Mrs Beck passed on, we were his family.

Well, you really were his family, Alex said. Going to America with him for Christmas and so forth. I was never his *pal*. But I think he knew I thought the world of him. He did know – Alex turned and looked into my face – didn't he?

He did, I said. Of course he did.

The car beat its way up the Holloway Road through the heavy traffic towards Highgate in streaming rain. Alex said that it always rained at funerals and I said that I didn't know that, because I'd never been to a funeral before.

You've never been to a funeral!

No. Not of anyone I knew myself. I've seen funerals, of course. In Egypt, they run past, the men, carrying the corpse and shouting.

You're a Catholic, and you've never been to a funeral!

What's Catholic got to do with it? The thing is that I didn't go back to Ireland for my mother's funeral and my father died there a few years ago and I hardly knew the man.

I'd better explain to you, then, he said. Today's service will be pretty High Church. Incense and so on, and Communion under both kinds – bread and wine. I think Jimmy would like that.

Oh, yes! I said. He liked a bit of camp.

I won't be able to sit with you, Kathleen, he said. Actually – and then he seemed to run out of words – actually, I'll be assisting Father Gervase.

I was dumbstruck. After a while I said, Do Protestants have altar boys, too, then?

Not really, he said.

When did you practise what to do? I said.

Well, I've always known, really, he said. There was a small Anglican foundation near our house when I was a boy. I would have joined the monks but my father died . . . But I have been a lay brother since I was eighteen. It's kind of a breakaway foundation. We call ourselves the Brothers of the Annunciation. I took vows when I was twenty-one. That's where I go on my holidays, actually. The very same monastery.

Vows of what?

Poverty. Chastity. Obedience. The usual . . .

If only Jimmy had been there! I talked to him when Alex, in a surplice, stood beside the priest and held the brass bowl of holy water that he was sprinkling on the coffin.

How about *that!* Jimmy my darling. Who'd have thought in a million years that *that* was the story. A *priest*, Jimbo. Our boss was a *priest!*

There was a buffet lunch in a hotel in Muswell Hill. Jimmy's friends, who looked so heartless when they flitted around the bar of the Salisbury at night, blinked with sadness and unease. They'd get talkative among themselves for a moment and then go silent again. The big boss, Alex's superior at NewsWrite, kept buying rounds of drinks, trying to impress Caroline. Roxy's mother in a pink pudding-bowl hat sat beside Roxy like an illustration of what Roxy would become.

Alex bent down to whisper to me, I'll take you home whenever you want to leave.

He came into the basement. I put the fan heater up to high and opened a bottle of the champagne that was the only thing I had in the fridge and we sat at the table in the kitchen. During the evening both of us at different times bent our heads onto the white table and wept. All kinds of things came out. The Becks in Scottsbluff at Christmas, and the way the four of us shouted the answers at the quiz shows, and the way Jimmy used to get obscurely angry at his father, but was heartbroken when the old man died. Alex's mother: still making his breakfast every morning at the age of eighty. My mother's death, and how I had never been home since. The funeral today, and how the rain had stopped while we were in the chapel, and it had become a real spring afternoon by the time we came out. How there had been no young people or children at Jimmy's funeral, or even talk of them.

There won't be at mine, either, Alex said.

He said it so simply. It was the saddest thing, to hear him.

Much, much later the subject of the night in Trieste came up. I think Alex brought it up himself.

That night in Trieste, Kathleen. That was the only time in my life. I couldn't explain to you. It was such a surprise. And I was so sick from all the wine we'd drunk. And then you didn't come back to the office for nearly two months and I didn't have the courage to talk to you . . . And I wanted to say to you, What we did was so nice! It was so lovely! I said it to God as soon as I got over my hangover – I never knew the sacrifice I was making for You until now.

It was news to me that we'd done something lovely, but I wasn't going to tell him that. I just smiled in a mysterious kind of way.

Then – blowing it, as ever – I said, Well, if ever you'd like to try again, Alex . . .

But Alex just kissed me on both cheeks, holding my chin, the way Jimmy used to.

God really exists, he said. Did you not feel His grace on all of us today? I'm nothing like as smart as you are, Kathy. It takes me all my time just to love Him.

I heard the rain before I felt it. The stars disappeared, and the whole valley seemed to take an enormous, sighing breath in the dark, and then I heard the phalanx of raindrops sweep towards me across the lake. I just got my mattress in across the threshold in time. Spot did a lot of growling at being woken up so suddenly but we settled down again just inside the sliding door, a few inches from where the rain was hitting the deck. It was a wonderfully hypnotic sound, and I began to feel the first swirls of unconsciousness in my head. But before I went asleep, I remembered one last thing from the day of Jimmy's funeral.

I'd been standing a little way away from the chapel after the service, while Alex got everyone organized into cars. I was looking at two bright birds tumbling in a bush beside the path. The twigs of the bush, still covered in raindrops, sparkled in the sun. Father Gervase walked down the path towards me on his way to the gate. He stopped, and stood beside me.

Chaffinches! he said. His voice was full of pleasure. The one with the colours is the male, and the plain one is his lady wife.

Odd, isn't it, I said, that it's the other way around in the human world? Except for bishops and cardinals and priests like yourself, Father, in your vestments. You display your colours. But you don't want lady wives.

Oh, we may want them all right, the old man said, but we may want something else more.

People were calling to each other, and a radio was playing a cheerful pop song in a van someone had left with the door open, on the other side of the railings.

Well, he said amiably, beginning to move on, God bless you!

Thank you very much, I said. I mean it, and I don't even believe in God.

You know the old saying? he said. It doesn't matter whether you believe in Him, it's whether He believes in you.

I don't know what to do, I astonished myself by saying to him. I'm sick of my job and my best friend is dead. I don't know whether to go on with what I know I can do, or whether there's something new I could try even at this late stage . . .

I wouldn't dream of advising you, he said. A fine woman like you. And one that doesn't believe in God and all –

Ah, Father! I laughed at him. Don't be putting me down.

I was only having a joke! Just a joke! Listen to me, he said gently. One thing. This is just something I found out for myself one time. Do the thing that's less passive. Do the active thing. There's more of the human in that.

Does the Church of England pay you to stand around outside churches giving out advice? I laughed.

That's it! he said. It's a great way to make a living.

It's like Barbados here, I said to Caro when I phoned her the next morning. This is the best holiday I've ever had. And in Ireland! Spot is panting with the heat already and it's only breakfast time.

Oh, don't, she said. When I've nearly another week of sitting at a desk like a schoolgirl.

We'll go on the razzle-dazzle when I come back, I said. We'll drink cocktails in the Savoy and try to pick up men –

Now, *Kathleen*! she said, in her most decorous voice.

I was thoroughly pleased with myself after this call. At least I'd mentioned men. I'd been censoring every reference to the fact that there are two sexes since Caroline and I had got back together.

Towards the end of the afternoon I tore myself away from lying on the deck in the sun listening to Felix's Fred Astaire CDs, and I drove into Ballygall to get some emergency clothes for the heatwave. In the Drapery Hall on the square a murmuring lady sold me two cotton skirts from a cardboard box that had 'Skirts – Ladies – Various' written on it in black marker. Then she moved a few feet down the wooden counter, to the stretch which on some conceptual level constituted the teenage boys' department, and sold me two T-shirts from a box marked 'Boys – V. Large'. I left the bag in the car and went down the street and in the back gate of the hotel, to see whether there was any news of Miss Leech and to say hello to everyone.

Kathleen – get the baby!

Oliver was moving at speed, on his bottom, but using his arms and legs like paddles, towards the door out into the yard. His mother dropped the kettle she'd started filling at the sink and ran and scooped up the infant from behind. At first he wriggled and chortled in her arms, but then he began to wail.

Poor little fella! Bertie crooned down into his cross face. Is your Mammy bold? Did your Mammy make you cry?

He's getting too heavy to carry around, Da, Ella said.

Sure he'll be carrying himself around soon, Bertie said. Won't you, son? Here, give him here. Get a biscuit out of the tin, Kathleen. A nice iced one. We'll teach him to walk. Your mother taught you – he was smiling at his daughter – in this very kitchen, and you were off out that door and up the garden. Like Tarzan you were. I'll never forget it.

We all went out onto the grass. I sat on the garden bench with Spot at my feet, and when I narrowed my eyes the shape the three of them made with the hedge behind them – two big pinkish blocks on each side of the pink block of the child – was like a classic frieze. Or a passage in a Poussin, or a Cézanne . . . Their voices faded away for a moment as I closed my eyes to feel the sun. I remembered – yes, being beside a swimming pool, in some hot place. I know that under my parasol I'd been typing a piece. It must have been long ago, because I was using a portable typewriter. A man and two nut-brown children were playing in the pool, and the mother lay on her sunbed like a sleek otter, reading a magazine. The children kept calling, Mama, watch me! and Mama, look what I can do! and my stomach got more and more tense with fear that the father would get annoyed at them for wanting her attention more than his, and that he'd do something nasty to her or to the children. I'd had to get up and go.

Ella held Ollie upright in front of her, by his plump upper arms. He fitted perfectly against her skirt. She walked him in front of her, steering him to put his wavering bare foot forward – first this one, then the other one – by nudges from her wide thighs. He must have felt very safe – held so firmly in the shelter of her legs. But his round face was frowning, the lips pursed with effort. He looked at his grandfather crouched on a level with him, a few feet away from him on the lawn. He looked at the outstretched arms, and the piece of yellow biscuit in each hand.

There's a good Ollie! they were saying. There's a good little boy!

I laid my hand on Spot's silky head, to keep him from moving.

We were immobile, us spectators, but Ella and Bertie were as pliant as reeds, bending into the little boy with no thought but of him. Ollie strained forward, and his mother let his arms go, and for a few seconds he teetered, there in the sunlight, upright for the first time. It seemed, for a split second, that everything waited for him. Even the ducks in the tin bath under the apple tree stopped squawking. Then he plopped down, hard, on his padded behind. He didn't have time to cry, because Ella scooped him up again.

There's a good boy! Bertie called to him lovingly. There's the best little boy in the world!

His shorts and his nappy had fallen around his ankles. He looked down at them, in bewilderment, and then lifted his face to his mother, expecting her to do something about it. She slipped his legs free with one smooth movement.

She moved him forward again in front of her, her hands big and red on the white skin of his shoulders. His thin torso and the pink cheeks of his bottom and his tiny penis looked new to the world, naked below the little shirt. But he was more confident now. She let him go again, and he wobbled again, and she caught him. But he hadn't fallen down. She let go again. The chubby legs held under him.

The mother arched up over him, and steadied him, and let him go again, and this time he did it – he stumbled across the grass into the welcoming grasp of his grandfather. Maybe five or six headlong steps was all he'd done, but he had moved from one set of arms to the other without falling.

Well! Aren't you the great little fellow!

The praise was beginning –

I threw myself back on the garden seat, a tension I hadn't known I felt flowing out of me. These were the moments of the end of Ollie's infancy and the beginning of a long life of walking. And I felt as if I had crossed a threshold, too. To be absorbed by watching a child learning to walk! Me! To have arrived somewhere where I knew people who taught children to walk!

Attly! Ollie cried, in a confusion of falling down and getting up and trying to run towards me.

Leave Kathleen alone, son, Bertie said. Kathleen has to come and have her tea now, to celebrate.

We went for a walk along the lane at sundown, the dog and I. The scene in the garden had entered into my heart, and I thought about it as I walked between hawthorn hedges embossed with creamy-white blossom. Wagtails skittered ahead of us down the grassy track.

The people I know who are very well – this is what must have happened to them. Their mothers must have led them forward into the world. The mother stands behind the child, and lets him move forward on his shaky, bandy legs, and he knows that there is a mass of love behind and above him – so attentive to him that even when he falls, he is safe. In fact – when he falls, he is loved the more. That must be what gives the healthy people the gift of unselfconsciousness. They can let go of themselves, without panic. They can peer at things, or listen to things wholly, without keeping something back to guard themselves with – their mouths slightly open, their eyes bright, their heads moving from speaker to speaker. They can look with perfect candour into the faces of the people they love, their selves forgotten. They are not afraid to forget themselves. They do not have to labour to tell the truth. They are themselves through and through. The shelter of love made them honest.

I can walk, I said to myself. But that was as far as my learning to walk went. But if I'm not what I wish I was, what can I do? There are no loving arms to go back to.

I was stopped for a moment, leaving the lane, by an idea. Suppose my mother was raised in an institution? One of those brutal orphan-ages, maybe, where they whipped you if you wet your cot? That would explain why she didn't know that mothers are supposed to love their children –

Ah! I said to myself, as we came back across the field to the house in the gathering dusk, Leave it, now! Just do your best. Do the best you can.

18

I'd just woken the next morning when I heard the noise of a car driving in through the gap in the bank behind the house.

Spot flung himself down the outside stairs.

I waited, without anxiety.

A voice called softly from the bottom of the steps.

Kathleen? Wake up, Kathleen! Kathleen, where are you?

Shay's voice.

The bedclothes were covered with a light dew. There were drops of dew on the hair on my forearm, where it had lain outside the duvet. When I half knelt up out of the nest of duvet and pillows, I had to shake the wet from my hair and the drops sprayed onto the deck like sequins.

He smiled across at me from the top of the steps.

Don't get up, he said. Sure I'm getting used to making you your morning cup of tea. Where's the kettle? I'm parched. The old gentleman in the hotel gave me currant bread he was taking out of the oven when I called there just now, looking for you. I hope there's butter. Did anyone ever tell you that you look like a little girl when you're lying down?

He's not that old, I said. Bertie isn't. He's sixty-three. You're no chicken yourself.

None of your impudence, he said. You're supposed to say, Darling, how wonderful to see you!

Darling, how wonderful to see you, I said. What are you doing here, anyway? I thought you only came to Ireland once a month?

What do you think I'm doing here?

I actually dozed when he went back in to make the tea. That's how easy the whole thing was.

*

A seagull came down out of the blue and stalked across the deck towards us with a glittering, pinhole eye.

Imagine, Shay said. Seagulls! This far inland! He threw a crust down in front of the bird.

He thinks this house is a boat, I said.

It feels like a boat, he said.

When I crawled out of the covers and stood up to go to the bathroom he caught me around the hips and pressed his head against my belly and held it there.

I'll shower, I began.

Don't, he said in a low voice. I love the smell of you in the morning. Do you hear me? Don't.

Tristan and Isolde, I thought, when I was brushing my teeth. They went mad with love on the boat to Cornwall. And in *Brideshead Revisited* didn't Whatshisname make love to Julia for the first time on an ocean liner?

When I came back he held the bedclothes up for me to slip in face-to-face with him, and he was ready to enfold me, and I was ready to be folded into him. My feet were cold against his for only a moment.

Oh – and *us*! I thought, delighted. *We* met on a boat! The ferry to Mallery Harbour!

My beautiful girl. My little girl. My little vixen.

He said those endearments over and over again. Once he pulled my head down and whispered in my ear, Will I spoil you? Will I spoil you, Kathleen, till it hurts? Say yes! Go on, say it!

I dimly heard Spot's breathing become more and more agitated as the noises we were making became faster and louder. And when I eventually opened my eyes, still blurred by wave after wave of ecstasy, the poor dog was standing right beside me, scanning my face with his black eyes, to see whether I needed him to protect me.

It's all right! I murmured to him. This is my friend, Mr Shay.

All the same, you know? I said to Shay when we were back to normal. Even though that – you know, what we were doing – is an animal thing, I don't feel right that an innocent animal was watching.

Well, I feel right, he said. I never felt as right in all my life.

*

Will we go for a swim? he said, sometime around midday, when we were tired of playing with each other.

A *swim?* In *Ireland?* In *April?*

Those lakes are only a couple of feet deep, he said. They only need a day or two of sun to warm up. Sure didn't I grow up beside the twin of that lake there?

So we went down to the lake. I wondered whether he was telling me something – quite unconsciously – about how fit and macho he was, and that it was my remark about his age that had brought this on. I liked him very much, that minute. I'd have done something far harder for him than flap across the grass in my unlaced sneakers to the beach at the end of the lake. But the water there was almost warm, so maybe he was simply right. He left his boxer shorts on a boulder beside my slip, and holding hands, we inched across the fine gravel of the beach onto mossy stones and through mud that squelched up between our toes. The water was cold, underneath the top layer, but not unpleasantly cold. We were the exact opposite of the beautiful young couples in ads who hold hands and run into the ocean. He was less white than me, maybe, because his arms and head were weathered from working outside, but between us there was a lot of pallid flesh. And we made our way forward on middle-aged feet, wincing loudly. We had to break apart and splash forward to swim when the water was only up to our knees, just to get off our tender soles. There was an instant of teeth-grinding shock. But then – the reward! This was bog water – brownish and velvety and softer than any other water. Shay smiled at me, victorious, as he swam away, his face streaming with drops, and his eyes seemed to flash the blue of his youth. Then I dog-paddled out to the middle, and turned over on my back to float in the warm top inch of the water, the sun beaming down on me and the water stroking me. It was thickened by particles of turf, and I could feel my hair move heavily and slowly, like fronds of weed.

Kathleen! His voice called across the water. A blackbird went squawking and whistling up the field. Kathleen! I'm going in to look at the golf . . .

Floating was like being held in a hammock of satin. I lifted a languid hand in front of my face. Drops of water clung to it as if the skin had been oiled. My fingers had gone an ivory colour from the water. Then I began to get cold and I swam, overarm, up and down, as far as I could go in each direction, exuberant, feeling the mild surface break apart and release the chill beneath. And then I picked my way out again on blanched feet. The last people to swim here, I thought, if anyone ever swam here, would have been children. *A Phádraig, fan orm! Tar isteach, a Mháire!* The children might still be alive in some facility for senior citizens in Florida or Michigan, nodding on a veranda, nobody around them ever thinking that they had once sported and played . . .

Afterwards, when I was curled up on Shay's lap, watching the last few holes of the golf with him, he ran his hand, in a leisurely way, all over me. I flinched when I felt the hand going under my slip, and moving towards my pubic hair – I disliked touching it myself, it was so dry and wiry. But today, the water of the lake had softened everything. Shay absent-mindedly stroked the soft fur over and over, as he lectured me on the finer points of Tiger Woods's play.

He moved his hand up to my head and smoothed my hair back from my forehead. He sang, *I'll take you home again, Kathleen, across the waters wild and wide to where your heart has ever been* . . .

That was written by an American, I said. From Illinois, I think. Professional songwriter. Nothing to do with Ireland. Not many people know that.

He sat upright. No! 'I'll Take You Home Again, Kathleen'? By an American?

'Fraid so, I said. With a name like Westender. Westendorf. That's right – Westendorf.

Why did you have to tell me? he said. Ruining my illusions.

That's me, I said, and he lay back and laughed at me.

Which would you rather, I said to him when the golf was over and we'd even watched an expert analysis of some of the play. Would you rather be in bed with me for ever, or play golf like Tiger Woods?

He looked at me, and then he looked down at his hands and laughed shamefacedly. He looked up with a mischievous face.

If I could play like him, he said, they'd give me everything else I want, too.

It was still only early afternoon, but he said, I'll have to go at four o'clock, Kathleen.

And when I turned away, disgusted, he said, I could only get away for a day. No one even knows I'm in Ireland. And I wasted time waiting at the hotel for someone to wake up.

What did you expect me to do? I said. Sit on the front steps indefinitely in the hope you'd pass by?

Stop it, he said. You know it isn't like that.

Well, what's it like, then? I tried to snap, but it came out more like a whisper. What's the position, then?

Now Kathleen, he said, and he reached for me and kissed me tenderly. You're a grown-up woman. You know the situation. My wife – you just couldn't get a better mother – she lives for our girls –

I bet your wife knows about me already, I said coldly.

She couldn't, he said.

Bet she does, I said.

He gave me a haughty look, as if to say, My wife is none of your business.

Yes, he said, I think she does have a smell of something in the air.

I took him down to a place one field away, on the edge of the lake, where a thorn tree twisted out of the grassy bank in a knot of thick roots. The lichen-covered stones from some old building were tumbled in the ditch beneath. I had left the garden trowel there, among the primroses.

I was looking for chaneys, I said. Felix has a collection and I'd like to leave him some good ones. I'm looking here because these stones mean there was a dwelling here.

Shay knew what they were.

There were loads of them around our place at home, he said happily, as he began to dig. No one put any value on them and then a Swedish woman opened a craft shop and started threading them on silver chains. They looked lovely. I bought three of her first necklaces.

His big fingers were laying out fragments of delph on the grass. Pieces of blue-and-white willow-ware.

Dudeen I'm looking for, too, I said. The little clay pipes. The kind all the women smoked their tobacco in.

Oh, there's a few of those in my father's house! he said. I could bring you one.

Where? I said. Bring me one where? And when did you have in mind?

I heard my own whine.

I'll tell you when I'm ready, he said.

He'd stopped turning over the earth and leaned back, to gaze at me. And I gazed at him. He looked very tired, and overweight, and not graceful. But he had the build of a strong man, and a candid face quite unconscious of the expressions that came and went on it. I'd tied my hair back with a ribbon. He smiled when he noticed it.

I love that song, he said. '*Take the ribbon from your hair.*' Somehow it makes you imagine all the rest. Do you have anything that you think is really, you know . . .

Sexy? I asked him.

Well, he said.

Do you remember the old Spice Girl – Geri something?

Geri Halliwell, he said. Of course I remember her.

Well, she said to a crowd of photographers once, What do you want me to be, boys? I can be anything you want. I can be a ten-year-old with big tits . . . I think that's very exciting.

He glared at me, speechless, and then he stood up and began brushing himself down.

Well, I said. Do you want to know what I'm really like or not? Or do you want me to pretend that I'm all fluffy and sweet?

After a minute or so, he hunkered down opposite me again. His voice was much harder than it had been before I shocked him.

He said, I've been thinking about you night and day. That's no exaggeration. Sometimes I can hardly believe you're real, and that's the only thing that stops me. A woman like you – what would she be doing with a man like me? Tell me the truth. What do you want with someone like me?

I said the easy thing.

I don't know, I said.

No, seriously, Kathleen. Why me?

I'm not so great . . . I began.

Don't, Kathleen. You know what I mean. What are you doing with me?

Why do you keep asking me that? What are *you* doing with *me*?

Ah, for God's sake, he said. Who *wouldn't* be with you if they got a chance? There's no mystery about that. But me – I'm not even much of a gardener.

I mean it, I said. I haven't been close to anyone for a long time . . . I hate talking about it. I wish I'd been more successful. Luckier, you know? But anyway, I haven't felt the way I feel about you since I was young. That's the truth.

He looked at me shrewdly for a long moment, and then he made an impatient *tsk*.

He didn't believe me.

I pretended to go on calmly scraping my trowel into the square of earth in front of me. It was a deep reassurance that he evidently thought I was so marvellous that I *must* have had a great love life.

But what I had said was the truth. The only dishonesty was that I was hiding the bitter regret and shame that went through me when I thought of all those wasted years.

Something made me ready for Shay, I thought. But I'll never figure out exactly what. It has something to do with being in Ireland and going back into the past and remembering the boys Sharon and I used to do hot, slow waltzes with, and with him being a happy husband and a loving father, and with me being free now because I live nowhere and I have no job, and Jimmy being dead and never able to make love again, and all the passion buried with people like Marianne and Mullan, but which of all those things, I'll never know.

The only thing I'm certain about, I said looking down, is that I want to be in bed with you. That's all. But that's an important thing to want.

I think about you every morning when I'm shaving, he said. That's just when I begin. I want to put my mouth around – and he held his hands out and put a palm under each breast – these, he said. I could kiss these for ever . . .

Oh, *do*, I laughed up at him, and I covered his hands with my own.

Can I say something serious? he said.

Yes.

You are a really beautiful woman.

That was the fourth time in my life that I believed it. I walked ahead of him back to the house, with the walk of a queen.

When we were sitting at the table drinking a last cup of coffee he startled me by beginning to talk to me in an impersonal way, with a more English pronunciation than usual. I imagine this was his business voice and manner.

Are you writing the story you mentioned, he said, about the divorce case?

Well, I said. I have a lot of figuring out about that to do yet. I'd planned to go over it all in my mind today.

But you are writing something about it?

Well, I'm not sure.

But you are a writer? Like – that is how you earn your living?

Yes.

And can you write anywhere?

I laughed at his seriousness. Anywhere there's a power point, I said.

He began to speak to me slowly, his face frowning with earnestness.

There is something I want to ask you, he said. I want to ask you whether there's any chance you could live somewhere between Shannon airport and where I go in Sligo? I think I could persuade my wife that it would be a good idea to try to run my father's business as well as my own; it will be ours someday, anyway. I could be in Ireland every month. If I fix things up right I could be with you one or two nights, maybe three. I wouldn't know which ones exactly till the last minute, because there's only me in my landscaping business and I can't foresee when a job might come in. But I could always manage a couple of nights. And a good bit of the daytime . . .

My skin flushed with shock. I looked at him as if to see him for the first time again.

He looked straight into my searching face. I would be able to help you financially, if you want, he said. No problem there.

He looked into my face again. He said, I don't know how long the whole thing would last, but a few years, we might get out of it. That is – if it appeals to you. I could help you around your house, too, wherever you live. You know? The gutters and that. Cutting the grass.

By now his face was red with embarrassment.

I don't know what else to say, he burst out. I've practised saying that much. I don't want to go on just meeting you hit and miss like this. And I want there to be something promised between us. And if you do this for me – he took my two hands in his and closed his eyes, and his voice was as clear as a bell – I swear, I really swear, that I won't let you down.

Then he held my hands to his heart. This isn't a good enough deal for a person like you, Kathleen – do you think I don't know that? But it is all that I can think of that won't ruin a whole lot of lives. And if you do this for me, I will never, never let you down. You would be the only one.

At first I couldn't speak. I thought of the way men I met would show me photos of their children and dogs, and of how men I went out with would call and say, sorry, but they'd met someone they really liked – as if I could never be the person that someone really liked, or the person whose photo was shown around. And now, I was being implored . . .

But Shay, I said sadly, what's the name for what I'd be the only one of?

Please, he said, almost under his breath. Please, love.

We held hands on the table in absolute silence. My wide hand made delicate by his. Hands show age more than anywhere.

I just *have* to go, he said.

I could not move. What day is it today? I whispered.

Tuesday, he said.

Friday, I said. I could decide by Friday. Ring me here.

He looked around for the phone, and took a little notebook and a stub of pencil out of his jacket on the back of the chair. He put on his glasses and wrote the number down. When he was passing behind my chair he lifted my ponytail and put his lips to the nape of my neck for a long time. Then he dropped the hair back into place and kissed the top of my head. I sat unmoving. I heard his solid footsteps on the outside stairs and, after a few moments, his car starting. The noise of the engine died away. The dog, who had slept through all this under the table, sighed as if he heard it, too, but he did not wake.

I didn't want to think about Shay's offer. This was only Tuesday. Wednesday, Thursday, Friday. There was ample time to think things out. Stay cool and collected, I said to myself. Pretend you're in danger. You're in a room in a hotel in a town at the edge of the jungle, and you know that down at the desk the manager is drunk and you hear a furtive noise out on your balcony . . . Be alert in every pore – No! Eat some food. Tidy up. Make phone calls.

I did take the phone out onto the deck but it was getting cold out there. Clouds were massing with silent speed on the horizon behind the hill. I tried to follow just one of them in its career from a first drift of vapour to a huge puffball that lost itself in the widening canopy, but the movements in the sky were too mysterious and fast. I went back in. The pathetic fallacy, it's called – the idea that nature sympathizes with our human dramas. That at the hour of the Crucifixion the sky went black. That just because Shay had gone again, the light went out of the day.

My skin felt extraordinarily fine. I moved the thoughts in my head around with care. Shay's offer sat just behind my consciousness like the light and music and excitement of an opera. I'd peek in around the curtain . . .

Oh, I could have it all! I could see it! A new computer on a table in a sunny room, and the grass outside the window, and old trees all around – beech, I think. I love beech trees. I'd have any number of cats and two dogs to keep each other company. And birds! Not caged birds, but birds that came to my kitchen window to be fed. Robin redbreasts. I wouldn't care that people saw me as a pet-mad old spinster – my body from the wrinkled throat down would be pink and soft with loving, where no one saw it but Shay. I'd be always melting for him. At such-and-such a time in each month my body would begin to turn towards his arrival like a sunflower, and I would have a gate, just for the pleasure of hearing the car stop at the gate and the man get out, leaving the engine idling, and my hands would begin to shake at the sound of the gate.

> To have a clock with weights and chains
> And pendulum swinging up and down,
> A dresser filled with sparkling delph,
> Speckled and white and blue and brown.
>
> I could be busy all the day
> Clearing and sweeping hearth and floor,
> And fixing on their shelf again
> My white and blue and speckled store . . .

I'd save up all my news for him. Look, Shay! I have a dozen chicks in a packing case. Look – the magnolia in the corner behind the barn bloomed. That blue mark, Shay, on my calf – is that a varicose vein? Come here, darling, he'd say. I'll kiss you better.

For an intelligent woman, I said to myself crossly, you sure have soppy fantasies!

Do I care? Did anyone ever hear of an intelligent fantasy?

Who could I talk to?

I knew that I was sitting in a deep chair in a room in a silent house and that I could see through the skylights that the clouds were clotting together at the beginning of evening. My body was more alive than ever, as if Shay had woken the underside of my flesh as well as the skin he had clutched and grasped. My limbs were tired with new use, and I was conscious of the whole of myself – even my insteps, that he had knelt and kissed, even the back of my neck and my head, sensitive from where they had been pressed down into the pillow when he reared back and roughly pulled my legs up around him.

Jimmy. I thought about the lucid tone of voice he used when we talked about serious things. There wasn't the slightest doubt that the first thing he would have said about Shay's proposal was, *Nearly sixty*? A happily married grandfather? You sit in some goddamn Irish field and you *wait* for this guy?

But I didn't want to have that conversation yet.

I should sleep. I should think about other things. I should live my ordinary life and wait for the answer to Shay to form itself inside me. I should go back to the Talbot story. If there were no more documents, then I'd have to make a decision about what really happened based on the *Judgment* and the Paget pamphlet. Soon. At least I'd have Miss Leech to talk to about that. There was no one, except the ghost of Jimmy, to talk to about Shay —

That stopped me. Why? Why was there no one to talk to about it?

Well, take Alex. I could trust Alex with my life. But I was hardly going to tell Alex about this. He'd think it was – well, there were any number of things wrong with telling him. First of all, I didn't want him to know the side of me that went to bed with complete strangers. It would hurt him. Of course, it had hurt me, too, and I always knew it, and that would bewilder him. Alex would say, If this man wants to be with you that much, why doesn't he ask his wife for a divorce? And if I said, But we don't want to cause anyone any pain – he'll only be with me one weekend a month and the wife will never know, Alex would look at me dubiously. He mightn't know how to put it, but he'd be feeling that there's something dodgy about an action that is only not wrong as long as nobody knows about it. I'd spent years and years sitting opposite him trying to persuade him of this and that and I well knew his dubious look. Actually, I was very fond of his dubious look, when he wrinkled his forehead and peered at me with his melancholy brown eyes without seeing me. Such as the time I promised a Hindu taxi driver that *TravelWrite* would pay for him and me to take his father's body from the undertaker's in London to the burning ghats of Varanasi and cremate it. And the time I arranged for Jimmy and me to pose as newlyweds and try out the all-inclusive honeymoon deals in the Caribbean. I couldn't imagine a man like Alex offering a woman the deal Shay had offered me. Yet I knew Shay was trying to keep as many people as he could as happy as he could. And himself, of course.

I'd need to be careful when I spoke to Caroline, too. She knew me very well. There might be the echo of joy in my voice if I'd been thinking how things might be – how there might be nights in the cottage in the beechwoods with me beside the fire with my Labrador asleep against my knee and the room full of the scent of hyacinths and narcissi from my bowls of spring bulbs, and the sound of the engine of Shay's car coming nearer and nearer as it drove up to the gate. When I allowed myself a peek at that beautiful future a lilt worked its way into my voice. She'd hear it. She was very clever that way. And there was really no question of discussing Shay's offer with her. Well, there was. But she'd be very, very cold about it. She'd automatically imagine that she was Mrs Shay and that Shay was Ian, carefully arranging to cheat on her. She wouldn't say that or even admit it to herself. Instead, she'd throw every little argument she could think of at me. Why do you have to live in Ireland for him? she'd say. What about your own life? Yes, you do so have a life of your own! You live in London. We're supposed to be learning bridge, you and me. What about Alex? What about travelling . . . In other words, I said to myself, she'd be hurt. And that stopped my train of thought again. It was so long since I had decided that I was the supplicant in our relationship, that until now I hadn't admitted to myself that I could hurt Caroline. I can hurt her, I said to myself, wonderingly. She would be hurt if I went off and did this.

And I needn't bother thinking about Annie. Annie believed in the marriage vows. Simple as that. She'd dislike and disapprove of Shay very much. She'd dislike me for liking a man like that. Oh – she must never know! I'd have to say I'd simply decided to retire to Ireland. But she'd feel free to drive over to Sligo and drop in to see me any time. I'd have to tell her that she'd have to give me notice. But you couldn't do that to family. I'd have to live secretly. But you couldn't keep a secret in Ireland . . . Not to mention that the idea of organizing your whole existence around sex would dumbfound her. But it isn't *sex*, I'd say, it's *passion*. Huh! is the least of what she'd say.

Bertie would look on the thing as sinful. He'd say something that didn't seem seriously critical, something like, Why don't you do something useful with yourself instead, Kathleen? Sheepdog trials, now there's an interest. Or teach Ella and the kids a few things. Look at all the things you know. But he would put me in the prayers that he said last thing every night beside the kitchen range. He believed that there was sin, and there was punishment for sin, and he'd fear for my soul and pray fervently for me.

Well, what of my soul, now that the word had come into my head? Would I be spiritually well – even by my own standards – in that life?

I thought you said you weren't going to think about the offer yet! I answered myself. It's far too early. You haven't even slept on it.

But my mind rolled on.

Nora would have a field day, mocking me. Boy! What a lucky man! she'd say. I take my hat off to any man who can fix things up for himself like that! The little wife, and the adoring daughters, and the woman who's so terrified she'll never get laid again that she's willing to be tucked away in a cottage. Not going to cost him a penny, either! *Save* him money, probably, fitting in a visit to the old father at the same time!

I'd have to keep it a secret from Nora.

Think about something else! I commanded myself.

What will I think about?

My mind's a blank.

It is not a blank. You just don't want to think about what you've just discovered. This is not a decision separate from everything else, that you can make privately. You always thought you were solitary, except for Jimmy. But, see? No man is an island.

I opened a bottle of wine, and drank the first glass in three minutes flat. Then I looked through all Felix's CDs. He didn't have any of the music I felt like listening to. The Tristan overture, to celebrate the boat we'd loved on. Or Mahler. *Big* Mahler. Or I'd even like one of the old crash-bang piano concertos that Mammy stood still to listen to, when they came on Radio Éireann. Rachmaninoff. Tchaikovsky. The piano solo hurling itself against the orchestra, climbing to heroic heights, tumbling thrillingly back down into the bass. Her pale cheeks would tinge with pink. She really was a romantic. Now, my mother – she'd say, Do you adore this man? Does he adore you? *Do it*.

Why turn to your miserable mother for guidance? Since when is she a role model? She was dead before she was the age you are now. What about thinking what Mother Teresa of Calcutta would do? Or Germaine Greer? Or Jane Eyre? Or Colette? Colette was seventy-nine years old when she wrote down her three wishes. To begin again. To begin again. To begin again.

See? I said to myself. Do what you'll least bitterly regret. You're free to handle this any way you want.

Of course, Shay is not. Not free.

Yes, but his marriage is his business. It's up to him to decide what to do about his people.

Does that mean everyone I don't know is none of my business? Does that mean that like some Polish villager I'd let my Jewish neighbours be loaded onto a cart for Treblinka, saying, It's none of my business?

Oh, don't be so melodramatic! Maybe she *wants* him to have an affair.

When did you last meet a wife who *wanted* her husband to have an affair?

I pulled my exhausted body up out of the chair and went to run a bath. I loved the way moving reminded me of him, physically. How long would I be able to relive his caresses? Two days? Three?

Whatever I do, I said to myself, I'm not going to be sad. Tragic, maybe, but I've had it with sad.

I smiled at myself in the mirror like a crazed Doris Day to emphasize this good resolution. I was amazed that it had come into my head, as a matter of fact. There was a rhythm in my previous life that I was attuned to: I was so primed for enduring grief that I could hardly imagine anything important happening to me that wasn't going to make me unhappy. I became unhappy; then I was sorry for myself for being unhappy; then I despised myself for my self-pity. Why should I suddenly be able to break that rhythm now? How could it be that now – in this situation of all situations, so full of feeling, and of intimations of profound misery – I saw the possibility of bringing zest to whatever I decided? Probably it was the love-making itself that had made me so positive. In which case, what seemed like a new perspective was really something hormonal, that would wear off . . .

These thoughts jostled on one layer of my mind. But on another, dread accumulated.

Jimmy, I began, as I lay in the bath, you know that neither you nor I would have cared for a moment about family or friends or work or even each other, if the perfect lover had come along.

I all but heard his voice, quiet and clear, say, That is true.

Jimmy, I want to make love with this man all day every day for ever, and he feels the same about me.

There was silence from Jimmy.

Jimmy, I'm fifty. Two of my bottom teeth are wobbling. Coffee gives me heartburn. I dye my hair. Even if a few men want me when I'm going through my fifties, and maybe even my sixties, I won't want them. I'll sleep with anyone who asks me the same as always, but you know yourself how it was – it was ashes, Jimmy. It was lonely as hell. This is my only chance to be kept soft and warm by a true lover, and to stay with him until we know each other so well that we wake and roll over to the other and slot in as easy as an oyster slides into a mouth, and then fall back asleep, the two of us become one. This way, we'll get older, but we'll have the confidence to go up to bed after lunch on Sunday pinching each other and giggling and able to laugh about weak bladders and impotence and flabby stomachs because we know the wealth in the bank of pleasure we are drawing on. Twenty-three I was, when I lost Hugo, and forty-nine when I opened up again. A quarter of a century between! Like those flowers deep in the jungle that only blossom twice in a human lifetime. All that time that I can never have back again, Jimmy! And maybe nothing, nothing till I die, if I can't have this!

Jimmy? I called to him. Did you ever see the Hockney drawings of his dachshund dogs? Sausage dogs? Wrapped around each other, asleep? How lovingly he drew the shape of their innocent and comic embrace! We would be like that, Shay and me . . . Jimmy?

I may even have called to him out loud.

But there was no sound anywhere except the dripping and ticking of bathroom noises.

After a while I came back to composure. But as I reached for towels, I caught a glimpse of my bottom in a mirrored wall. A soft yellow bruise was beginning to develop across one cheek. And my breasts? I spun around. Yes. The mark of his mouth, and on the white flesh, fading pink lines where his fingers had clung. Deep down where nobody knew me and I hardly knew myself, I was as gratified as an animal standing over a kill. I could have growled under my breath, I'm his, these are his marks on me, he owns me, I am his woman . . . Then my ordinary consciousness came back to me. What makes me feel *pride* in these stigmata? I asked myself. What makes me feel smug, as if these were decorations that I *won* fair and square? There is nothing honourable about them. I can say that our lovemaking was as honest as it can get, that we were as honest as animals. But not that we are honest people. His lies. His fooled wife. My secrets.

Years and years ago, when I was just becoming a girl, when I won the essay competition on 'The Beauty of this World hath Made Me Sad', and Mammy came with me to Dublin, we spent the money in Clery's of O'Connell Street. I bought tights with glitter in them for Nora and football socks for Danny on the ground floor. Then we went up the stairs to Ladies' Apparel for Ma to try on a few cheapish frocks. I could remember very clearly the cubicle with its sagging curtain, and the chipped gilt chair outside it that I sat on to wait after the old saleswoman had ushered Mam in and hung the frocks she'd chosen from a hook and pulled the curtain across behind her.

Mammy came out onto the scuffed carpet to show me herself in a frock that was made of dark blue cotton with a pattern of little blackberries and pink flowers. It had a square neck and three-quarter-length sleeves, and she liked it. But the lady made her try on a few others. Mam wouldn't let me or the saleslady in behind the curtain with her. I thought she was probably ashamed of her underwear. But there was one dress she tried on that she must have liked very much, because she came out from behind the curtain preening herself a bit and held out the skirt in front of me and the shop assistant, like an old-fashioned model. This frock had short sleeves. She hadn't noticed that.

I saw the marks on Mammy's upper arms. Livid bruises. Yellow and purple and black. She followed my gaze and saw where I was looking, and immediately turned in behind the curtain.

She bought the dress with the long sleeves, though it took all her money.

I looked at my own marks again, discolouring so quickly. I stood rapt, remembering the grip of him. My head bowed of its own accord as if in obeisance.

Then I threw down the towels and hurried out into the living room calling, Spot! Spot! Food! Quick!

A grotesque picture had presented itself to me, and I wanted to make it go away. My mother silently held out her bruised arms to me, and I, with my arms by my side, mutely matched her with bruises of my own.

19

I was suffused with happiness from some dream which had melted in my head when I was woken next morning by the phone ringing. I stood on Spot's tail in my hurry to answer.

It was Betty from *TravelWrite*.

You're there! she said. I've tracked you down! Alex is in a phonebox somewhere waiting for me to ring him back with a number for you. And the poor old boy sounds as if he's in a terrible state. Don't move, Kathleen.

When Alex got through a few minutes later the heavy rumble of traffic behind him was what struck me first. I'd forgotten about noise.

I've only a few units left on this card, he said. He was speaking so slowly that his voice dragged. We've lost her, Kathleen! Yesterday. The most beautiful death they ever saw, the Brothers said.

Oh, I'm so sorry, dear Alex. You sound exhausted. Where are you, my poor darling?

I'm at the monastery –

Pip. Pip Pip. There were only seconds left. I shouted over them, May I come to the funeral, Alex? Where are you? Do you want me to come over?

The Brothers don't really like outsiders in the place . . .

You mean women! But your mother was a –

Then the line went dead. I waited beside the phone but he didn't ring again.

I was glad that the old lady had finally passed on. She'd kept Alex from living, the selfish old bat. He wouldn't even eat the delicious things Roxy and Jimmy used to bring into the office at lunchtime, out of loyalty to her horrible Hovis sandwiches. But that just showed how completely lost he was going to be without her. He would be quite as lost as an orphaned child. The Brothers would get him, now.

Namby-pamby idiots. The ones at Jimmy's funeral were probably nerds called Sid and Les in real life, but they called themselves Father this and Father that. Father Edward the Confessor one whey-faced little tick called himself. And they swished around in robes they'd designed for themselves straight out of Cecil B. De Mille. Imagine a decent man like Alex falling for all that faux-gay, sub-Iris Murdoch stuff! Woman-haters, the lot of them. Woman-fearers, anyway. When he'd never had his chance – never, as I knew from the night he talked to me at the kitchen table, had a girlfriend, or been to Paris, or drunk a glass of cold wine on a hot day in bare, sandy feet. The reason he couldn't swim in the sea, he'd told me then, was that though he and his mother went on seaside holidays when he was a boy, it made her nervous if he went into the water.

I wouldn't mind if they were real monks, I was saying to myself indignantly, when I heard myself, and started to laugh. Talk about Catholic prejudice! Frightening, how knee-jerk attitudes stayed with you long after every other bit of your native religion had departed! Of course there were Anglican orders I would take seriously. Only these self-invented Brothers of the Annunciation weren't one of them. Father Gervase, the chief witch-doctor at Jimmy's funeral, was a lovely old man, I thought at the time. Watching the chaffinches with me, and giving me advice. But this morning I was so agitated that I turned against him, too. A parody of a twinkling old sage he was. I bet his real name was Cecil. They'd take dear Alex, who hadn't a phony bone in his body, and they'd screw him up . . .

I was pacing up and down. Spot's head moved with me like a spectator at a tennis match. I couldn't stay in the house. Anyway, I was getting tired of the house. In dull weather, like today's, there was something very depressing about all that glass.

But I did pray for Alex. I buried my head in the calfskin sofa and prayed that whatever there might be would watch over him and not let him grieve too badly or be too lonely for his mother, and protect him from evil . . . I remembered that the last prayer I said was for Miss Leech on her way to Dublin for the cancer tests. I said the same prayer again, for Alex and for her. This was Wednesday. She should be back in Ballygall.

Remember, O Most Gracious Mother, that never was it known that anyone who fled to Thee for mercy, implored Thy help or sought Thy intercession was left unaided . . . I included Shay in the prayer. Turn then, Most Gracious Mother, Thine eyes . . . I included myself. I needed help, too. It was as if nothing at all had moved in me for decades, and now the permafrost had thawed and I had to do something about the corpses its melting ice was uncovering.

I went out on deck. The wildcats were playing at the edge of the field, above the lake. The grass was succulent from the rain that had come down at dawn, silent and sudden, as if the day briefly wept before beginning. I had named the cats after the elves in *A Midsummer Night's Dream* even though they were scrawny, determined cats, not at all pretty. The only one I could definitely identify was the smallest one, Moth. Amazingly, it crept up the stairs towards me as I drank my coffee, and stayed near, its beautiful tortoiseshell fur streaked black from the wet grass, and after a while, it rolled into a ball and slept.

Once, when I was very unhappy, I was awake early in the morning in Tel Aviv. I'd been standing at the window of someone's hotel room as the dawn came up, waiting for them to settle more deeply into sleep so I could creep out. I was parched with thirst. I didn't want to think about the night just past and its various fumblings and reproaches. Down below, light was beginning to flood the stocky white buildings along the curve of the bay. Set back from the road there was a big swimming pool, and already, although it was in the shadow of the hotel, swimmers were steadily shuttling up and down each lane. The stiff way they held their heads in rubber caps showed that they were old people. Determined old people.

The sun reached the waste ground outside the back wall of the swimming pool. A small cat was making its cautious way along beside the wall through the dry weeds. It came to open ground. Suddenly, it succumbed to the glorious morning. It came out into the dusty clearing and tumbled luxuriously onto its back. Then it stretched itself, slowly, perfectly, and lay in the golden sun, and slept.

That's how I want to be, I cried inside myself. Let me be that way, too!

It was thinking about Alex that had reminded me of that. Alex was always himself, like cats are. He was Alex through and through.

I have always appreciated the good in other people, I said to myself, as if to recommend myself to an invisible judge.

I didn't know how to pass the time till I could ring the library. And what if they'd kept Miss Leech at the hospital in Dublin? Bertie had said that she wasn't well, but his face had been far more grim than his words. I'd go into town to the hotel and scrutinize his face again.

I was so full of apprehension that after I got petrol in the garage behind the supermarket I left the car and walked up the lane to the high wall that had once been a wall of the workhouse. When the lane was empty for a moment of its usual queue of cars, I pressed my hands until they hurt against the flinty stones. God knows there were tragedies bigger than I could even grasp. Huge, collective griefs, as well as millions and millions of personal ones. But tragedies end. These walls had been touched by the bony fingers of the starving and the dying. But they ended, the terrible years of famine.

Bad things end, I said to myself.

And in fact, it was cheerful at Bertie's place. Ollie, his face and hands covered with mud, was careening around on the grass outside the open back door, and Spot, who'd jumped elatedly across me as I opened the car door, joined him. The two ducks huffed away into the hedge. Ella was sitting at the kitchen table writing a letter. And Bertie came down from his den behind the reception desk in a good enough humour.

Who was your man who came looking for you at the crack of dawn? he greeted me.

Daddy! Ella said. That's none of your business!

An old friend, I said firmly. If you'd let me stay in this so-called hotel instead of boarding me out all over the country you wouldn't be bothered with people looking for me.

That plague of teachers will be gone tomorrow, if you just hold on, Kathleen. Have a bit of my apple tart, he said. Go on, it'll sweeten your tongue. I brought half of it up to Nan Leech last night but there's a nice bit left.

How is she?

Well, she seemed a bit fragile to me when I got her off the train. But I didn't go into the house so I didn't get much of a look at her. All she said was that they've advised her to retire from work completely, to save her strength. And that she was glad she was home, because she couldn't sleep unless the cat was on the end of the bed. But she was delighted with the present I had for her.

What? Ella and I said, simultaneously.

A mobile phone! he said. I got one for myself, too. The fella in the shop explained the whole system to me. Now she can get on to me anytime she wants to.

He beamed at us, delighted with himself.

So I was not adequately prepared for the shock of Miss Leech's frail voice when I rang her from the den at two o'clock on the dot. I said the first thing that came into my head – a leftover from thinking about Alex's English monks.

Have you ever read Iris Murdoch, Miss Leech?

I read her husband's book about caring for her in her declining years. I must say I envied her. I envied her both the Alzheimer's and the caring husband until I realized that if she had the one she didn't know she had the other.

You're the first person I ever met who envied someone with Alzheimer's, I said.

Oh no, Miss de Burca, she said earnestly. I think any reasonable person would envy those who lose their memory as they approach the end.

Miss Leech, I said, I don't know at all what you feel up to at the moment, and I know how busy you must be, but would you allow me to take you out today? It's a bit late for lunch, but if you felt like dinner tonight? Or, we could have tea somewhere? We don't have to talk about the Talbot affair, of course, but it is really a matter for talking over now, isn't it? Rather than formally meeting about. Now that John Paget has upset the applecart.

Certainly! she said. Excellent idea. I shall be at the bottom of the library steps at half past two, precisely. I had in fact been going to ask you to take me, in so far as it is possible, up to Mount Talbot. Bertie tells me there are only outbuildings left. But I have never been there. I never wanted to go there, even when the really daring children went up to the demesne and roamed the house, every summer. It hadn't been long abandoned by the last Talbot, then.

You've never been there!

My family were Republicans, she said sternly. We had no time for ogling the ill-gotten gains of the oppressors. What's more, the Leeches were the last word in respectability. I always had neat boots and a bow in my hair.

Well, I'll do my best. I could drive you up the back avenue. There is one thing I could show you –

Half past two, she said. And remember, punctuality is the courtesy of kings.

She came down the steps uncertainly, holding onto the railing. She had her little red pea-jacket on and her cap, and the wisps of hair stuck out from under the cap as always. Her face was taut – a polished and fleshless white – but she smiled around at the square and the cloudy, warm day and at me.

I rang Cecil Coby at the Lodge to ask him what time tea is served at the Coby Castle Hotel, she said when she was settled. He was furious! He knows that I know perfectly well that the family have nothing to do with the hotel.

I thought adversity was supposed to make us nicer people? I said.

Not me, she said. Not you, either, I'd lay money.

Did you ever ask Mr Coby about the Talbots?

He's not a mister. He's an Honourable. Though I can't bring myself to use these ludicrous titles. He said the Talbots were a mess – that was the word he used. They always behaved like Catholics, he said. They weren't really one of us.

The hell with him anyway! I said, bouncing away from the last traffic light, and out on the road to the west. Him and the rest of the Anglo-Irish gentry. Any gentry, anywhere, if it comes to that!

Don't be wilfully simple-minded, she said. It ill becomes you. Though I must say all you feminist types are very weak on class politics. You're well able to analyse the carry-on between men and women in great detail, but you never seem to move on from that. You never seem half as acute about power in public life as power in private life –

Oh, Miss Leech, I cried. Explain!

I can't be bothered, she said.

We were driving along past the fine stone wall of the demesne. After a minute or two I brought out the question that I somehow expected her to settle.

You had a fairly good look at the Paget pamphlet, I think? I said. Extraordinarily convincing, didn't you think?

There was a pause before she said, Extraordinarily.

Yet I was absolutely sure when I came here, I said, that Marianne and Mullan had known a great passion.

Quite, Miss Leech said shortly.

I tried to make out her expression, but she was looking straight ahead, her face pale above the jaunty little jacket.

I've always hated this, she said, pointing at the stone wall. Built by our people in their captivity.

Are you changing the subject? I said suspiciously.

Later, she said. We'll have a word about the Talbot imbroglio later.

Oh, Miss Leech! I wailed. Stop tormenting me!

I have a – no doubt – final Talbot document to show you, she said. Which I will do over our tea. Declan found it. It is the front page of a short-lived London newspaper of the early 1850s. A tabloid, in today's parlance.

And? I said. *And?* Guilty or innocent?

Later, she said.

We turned in at the Great West Gate of Mount Talbot. Someone had pulled back the rusted iron gates, and as we slowed to start up the avenue, a Garda stepped out from behind them and waved us to a stop. He walked slowly around the car, and was taking out his notebook to write down the number when Miss Leech lowered her window with a whoosh and snapped, Brendan Buckley! What do you think you're doing!

Oh, Miss Leech! How are you! He fumbled to put his notebook away as if she shouldn't have caught him with it. Sorry about that,

Miss Leech. The sergeant told me to get the particulars of any vehicle I didn't know personally and this is a hired car. But if I'd seen *you* –

What's going on?

It was a few days ago we got a tip-off. The wine cellar of the old house – you can still get down to it by a tunnel. Some kind of IRA fellows were using it as a shooting gallery. They were training down there, apparently. There were targets up on the walls, and shells and so on –

And what's happening now? she asked.

Well, the four lads are in custody in Dublin. And myself and another officer are preserving the scene, like.

We're just going to the stable yard, I said. Is that all right?

Oh, Miss Leech – you go anywhere you like. Sure Chris up at the house knows you well. Chris Byrne, you know?

And how is Mrs Byrne? And how is your aunt, Brendan?

They chatted for a few minutes, and then we made our way up the dark avenue, where overgrown laurels met above our heads.

When I got the car as close to the arch into the stable yard as I could, I stopped on the grass-covered cobbles and opened the passenger door.

The stables are through this arch, I said.

Are the stables what you brought me here to see? She was looking up at me from the passenger seat, leaning back on the headrest. I realized with a pang that she simply had not the energy to get out, at that moment.

Look! I said, turning away from her and going in under the arch to hide my distress. Look!

I pulled aside a mat of ivy.

She gazed from the car at the graceful little statue of the boy with his arrow.

Cupid, she said. And she gave a tired laugh.

I sat in the doorway of the driving seat with my feet on the cobbles, looking fixedly at the faded brick wall of the stables and the slate roof that moss had colonized, and I talked to her over my shoulder.

Miss Leech, I said, there's something I'd like to ask you if you didn't mind, even if it doesn't really strike you as having anything to do with the kind of thing we usually talk about. But of course you can just tell me to stop any time you feel like it.

She said nothing.

It's just a theoretical discussion, in a way, I said.

Still silence.

What I was going to ask you, if you didn't mind, well, not so much ask you as talk over with you, maybe . . . Well, I could put the situation like this, perhaps. Miss Leech, if an independent, competent, lonely woman of fifty met a man of fifty-seven – a happily married man – and they discovered that as lovers, they were born for each other; and if the man asked the woman to locate herself near a place he visits in the course of his work so that they might be together, discreetly, two or three nights a month – a thing she could very easily arrange to do – would you advise her to accept the offer?

She was silent for a time. But when she spoke, the only change in her was that she called me by the most intimate version of my name.

That is a very important question, Cait, she said. After a moment she went on, That question contains a number of other important questions.

There was nothing she could have said that would have comforted me more.

I wonder what's it like to live in waiting? I said. Because even if I busied myself with bits of writing and gardening and travelling, that's what I'd be doing – waiting.

I was perfectly well aware that I'd said *I*.

If this man were free, would he marry you? she said.

Oh, I don't think so, I said. He has daughters and grandchildren and a business in England. I don't see him wanting to bring a woman in . . . And he'd be heartbroken if his wife died. And I don't want to be married. What would I want to be married for? Why would I want to go goo goo at his grandchildren? And I hardly know this man, but I don't think we'd have much to say to each other on a day-to-day basis.

So, what if one of you gets sick, say?

I know, I said. The deal would be off, wouldn't it? It would be basically a very crude deal – ignoble, as a matter of fact. But I'm stuck with the values of the world I've been alive in! They're inside me. I want a lover! I don't want to be noble. Even though, you know, I really believe that Western civilization is going to have to grow out of this thing about romantic love. I'm always meeting hurt children who've lost one or other of their parents to it. And it's making women too lonely. Men, too, I suppose, but women – millions of women would jump at what Shay has offered me, they feel so wasted as women. But there must be something better –

Bertie has looked after me for years with a devotion I can still hardly credit, Miss Leech said. The small things of each day – I could tell him about every one of them. And I put up with his depressions, and he put up with my bad temper. There's a lot to be said for humdrum companionship.

But would you have chosen devotion? I said. Or would you have swapped Bertie for a lover who made you feel – I don't know how to describe it . . . radiantly womanly, to be perfectly frank with you . . .

I would, Miss Leech said. Yes, I would have swapped him for a lover such as you describe.

For a moment, neither of us spoke.

These arrangements, she began again, like the one you and this man are thinking about, no one ever really believes that they're going to have to abide by the rules that are agreed on. They always believe they're eventually going to get more.

I genuinely don't want more, I said. Or – not more than a day or two more. You just can't feel as extremely as I feel when I'm with him for very long.

Well, that seems to me a very important point, she said. It means the whole relationship is artificial.

Or, I said, magical.

You said yourself your life would consist of waiting.

I know, I said. But it does now! I'm waiting in the hope of seeing him again now! I gave up cigarettes a couple of years ago, and I had to train myself not to keep imagining time stretching away into the future when for ever I'd never be able to have a smoke. I could try to extend that to his visits . . .

Your life would be more about waiting than his life would, she said. He seems to be much busier than you. More productive, if I may say so. On the other hand, I daresay he's less imaginative.

All the same, I said, there's a wife. Even if she never found out, we'd be doing her a great injury, by abstracting him – literally – from their daily life. And distracting him. I mean, I don't think it's very important whether he makes love to someone who is not his wife a few times a month. But to undermine their daily life . . . My father used to come home full of his own thoughts on Friday nights and even though we didn't like him, it still hurt. Everyone does infallibly know when the other person isn't really with them. And she would never be able to put her finger on what's wrong with him.

If you were his wife you might think it's important who he makes love to, she said. And Cait – the gratification of lust, I think you should admit to yourself, would be the reason for all the other disloyalties.

Even if his wife didn't exist, I said, I'd be hesitant. The thing is, Miss Leech, I told you when I met you that I wanted to change. And I do! I long to! I want to be better at living than I have been in the past. And I wonder whether if you live for passion you can improve your everyday life? Or whether you're always living forwards, towards the future? Whether you keep life on hold until the moment when he arrives, and so you're never in the here and now?

Yes, she said. That's it. The bit with him would be more intense, but all the rest would be waste.

Do you know what I see now, Miss Leech? I see why there is marriage. It is the only arrangement designed to include the whole of the person and the whole of a life.

Yes, she said. You might as well have been a good Catholic from the beginning. The solutions the great religions propose to the dilemmas of human existence are basically very *sensible*.

But you said you'd do it! You said you'd accept the deal!

Yes, she said again. If it were offered to me, at your age, I would accept without hesitation. I'd read and write while I waited for him. And let me tell you, I believe I would be very, very happy.

Let's go! I said, getting up. Let's go and have our tea! I'm dizzy trying to think out the pros and cons of it. And I want to know what

372

Marianne Talbot did or didn't do. I can't wait to hear what the newspaper Declan found has to say.

We drove out of Mount Talbot and up across the high bog towards the Coby Castle Hotel. I realized Miss Leech was asleep when I heard a tiny snore. Asleep, holding herself as upright as ever. But just as we came down beside a conifer plantation and turned in to Castle Coby, through woods of beech and chestnut newly in leaf where bright saplings lit the vistas between sombre trunks, she spoke again.

You are in very good company, Cait, if that's any consolation. It was the great poet John Keats's bitter regret, when he lay dying in the little ship that brought him to Italy at the end, that he had not made love to Fanny Brawne. He said it to his friend: 'I should have had her when I was well.' Not – I should have written better poems, or been a better man, or made a lot of money. *I should have had her when I was well.* And W. B. Yeats – you'd think that Yeats was so grand he'd be above all that. He got injected with monkey glands and told one of the mistresses of his old age that he – and I quote – was 'going to be a sinful man to the end'. 'I will think upon my deathbed,' he said, 'of all the nights I wasted in my youth.' And there's Marvell, of course: 'The grave's a fine and private place, but none, I think, do there embrace.'

We came to a stop on the gravel outside the hotel before she could survey the rest of English poetry.

It was a redbrick pile with turrets and battlements.

Battlements, for God's sake, I said as I helped her across the huge hall. Who did they think they'd be battling?

I felt her small body sag. To cover up, I went on, Imagine, Richard and Marianne Talbot would have walked across these very tiles when they came to a ball, or supper.

She hadn't the breath to say anything. After a minute we started off again, at a snail's pace.

Twenty miles from the nearest neighbour! I chattered determinedly on. What was Marianne supposed to do for pleasure? How could the way of life of an English lady of the manor have been reconstructed here, even in good times? Fox-hunting, for instance, wouldn't have been possible over terrain like these bogs.

We passed through a dark dining room, where the tables were laid with linen and glasses, but with tomato ketchup bottles, too, and sugar bowls. The lounge beyond had a semicircle of tall windows showing a lawn sweeping down to a lake, and a grubby temple on an island in the middle of the lake. In the middle of the lounge a small boy was making a barricade of upturned chairs around a family group who were knocking back their drinks in silent concentration. A baby with a large pink face was asleep in a stroller beside them. Otherwise, the whole place was empty.

A young waitress gestured weakly at the room. Anywhere you like, she said.

Then a manager in morning dress came in, almost running.

Miss Leech! he said. Nan Leech! Of all people! Why didn't you tell me you were coming! Oh, it's so nice to see you. This is an honour!

Cait, she said with a smile, this is Paddy. He used to be in the pub beside the library, but he went on to better things.

Here, he said. Or here? Here? Where would you like? Bring the wine list, Noeleen. Or would you like a pot of tea, Miss Leech? Or a sherry? Would your friend like a drop of gin and tonic? Let me help you with your jacket. You're too small, it's ridiculous. We have a good filter coffee that we're trying out. Noeleen, get one of those footstools from the drawing room for Miss Leech and a cushion for her back. Now, ladies, could I tempt you to a sandwich? There's a very nice bit of chicken in the kitchen. Or salmon. Right out of the river yesterday but don't tell anyone. You might prefer a slice of cake . . .?

In the end, we had the room all to ourselves, and Miss Leech was as comfortable as she could be. She ordered smoked trout, but she didn't even pretend to eat. She took a sip of wine from time to time. But she seemed content. She took her mobile phone out of the pocket of the red jacket at one point, but she couldn't work it. Noeleen the waitress had to ring Bertie to tell him where Miss Leech was and that she'd be fine for another half an hour.

He worries, she said. I don't like to see him worried.

Then she said, I don't like to see you worried, either, Cait. You're the age a daughter of mine would have been, so I'll tell you what I've been thinking. I do value physical love very highly – maybe too highly, because I have never known it. But I'd want more than that for a daughter. I mean, I'd like a companion for you, not a visitor. Someone you could rely on to care for you if you needed care. Someone you could respond to with the best in you. Because you are a good girl. A feeling girl.

I bent over my plate as if I were eating, to hide how moved I was.

Shay's is the best offer I have, I said. It's the only one. I'm terrified that I'll never get another one.

These things must be connected with childhood, she said. They are so vast. They are oceanic. It is a bone I intend to pick with God, that I had a happy childhood and it seems to have left me boringly undramatic. But you know, there's one simple thing I see absolutely clearly, now that I am so very old.

I looked at her. The Albert Einstein hairstyle, and the bright black eyes and the sharp nose. That pallor on her face.

She put her small hand on mine.

The world is wonderful, she said. All its little things. It is *wonderful*.

Excuse me, I said. I'll be back in a minute.

I went out to the Ladies' Room and sat at a dressing table and wept.

When I came back, Paddy the manager was fixing a portable heater beside Miss Leech's legs.

Coffee, ladies? Made on milk for you, Miss Leech – of course I remember. A tiny liqueur? For your blood-sugar level. Well, a finger-nail of cognac?

I knew I only had a little more time with her. Half of me was longing to get to the subject of the Talbot piece Declan had found, but the other half strained to hear everything she might say about Shay and me – especially about me.

I hadn't for a moment guessed what was coming next.

You wouldn't by any chance know someone who wants a cat,

would you? she said. I have to find a home for my cat and Bertie won't have her because of that wretched old dog of his. Put the dog down, I told him, but he won't.

But I thought you were very fond of the cat, Miss Leech? I thought you could only sleep if the cat was on the bed?

I hadn't wanted to mention it, she said, but I'm going into the hospice in Galway tomorrow. That's why I'm on this spree today. They're rather good at pain control in Galway.

I was shaken, but I tried to match her conversational tone.

But the hospice will let you have the cat! I said. They're very keen on pets –

No, she said.

Why not? I said, but my heart had gone cold with understanding.

It won't be long enough, she said. It wouldn't be fair to the cat.

After a while I whispered, I can get an excellent home for the cat.

She smiled at me in a most beautiful way. Well, Miss de Burca, she said. It was an unusually benign providence that brought you to Ballygall Library!

I saw Bertie come in from the hallway and look around.

Apropos my coming to Ballygall Library, I said – by a great effort in an ordinary tone of voice – when are you going to unveil the piece about Mrs Talbot from the newspaper?

The journalist, whoever he was, she said, actually came to these parts, after Mrs Talbot was found guilty and her husband's divorce bill was passed. Hello, Bertie! Kathleen and I are on the razzle-dazzle. Have a brandy! Noeleen – could you bring us three brandies? Though we could have done without his visit. Do you think in the next world the Irish get away from English condescension? Listen to this! She took a folded page from her pocket. Read it for us, Bertie. Read it out there in your best London accent.

Bertie did it with gusto, reading the piece in a tone of outraged contempt.

He read:

Mount Talbot stands on the road leading from nowhere to nowhere. The broad waters of Lough Aree compel the traveller to diverge southward or northward and it is difficult to conceive how anyone but a drover bringing sheep or cattle from the pastures in the north to the great fair at Ballynasloe should ever find himself upon the bridge at Mount Talbot, under which the waters of the Aree river, roused from their habitual torpor by the unwonted obstruction, flow for a few minutes with a perceptible current. Bogs, which appear interminable, and in which human beings burrow, and live like prairie dogs or rabbits, low hills checked over with stone walls, valleys which are lakes in winter and swamps in summer, extend for miles on every side, and the sense of dull desolation is only broken by the recurrence of the neat dwellings of the constabulary, and the presence of the smart, well-mounted policeman, with his military bearing, which remind one that though in a land of crime and outrage, law and civilization exist somewhere.

Passing through Ballygall (perhaps the most desolate, melancholy and poverty-stricken of Irish towns) the parish church of Mount Talbot which recognizes the Rev. Wm. McClelland as its rector, comes in sight. After an Irish mile, a whisky shop [the memorable Kelly's, where Finnerty and Halloran made Mullan drunk] is on the left and on the right is the long high wall which surrounds, and the massive iron gate which opens into, the domain of Mount Talbot House, a gloomy castle of modern Gothic, whose dark grey walls echoed on the night of the 19th May to shrieks more agonizing than those which 'rang through Berkeley's walls' – shrieks of a mother torn from her child, a wife outraged by her husband's menial –

This chap certainly didn't think much of the place, Bertie broke off to say.

What is 'Berkeley's walls', I wonder? Miss Leech said.

Well! I said, furiously. The people living 'like prairie dogs', did he say? Living in burrows out in the bog? *After* the Famine, this was! *Five* years after the worst of it. But imagine them! Out in the bog, he said, in burrows like rabbits! It must have been the evicted people.

And do you hear the sneer of him? That's how much compassion there was! No wonder we were left to starve.

Now, Cait, Miss Leech said. Calm yourself. You are about to get a rather large shock. Read the rest of the page.

She handed the photocopy to me.

This must have been suppressed at the time, because it is a passage from the House of Lords *Judgment*, but it doesn't seem to have been printed by anyone except this muckraking journalist . . .

I read, in an imitation of Bertie's imitation English accent:

My Lords, the Rev. Mr Sargent, who was assisting the Rev. McClelland at that time, saw Mr Talbot going away from Mount Talbot and he took that opportunity of calling. Now what he says is this. He came to the hall and having entered it, he opened the door on the right hand which opened into the drawing room, and what he describes is, that he was shocked by seeing that of which I need not go into the detail, except he says he saw Mrs Talbot lying on her back on the floor; her heels towards him, her head from him, rather on one side; and a man kneeling down with his clothes loose, apparently between her legs, her person being partly exposed, and that this person was dressed apparently in a shooting jacket, and he saw that his clothes were loose or down.

I looked up at Miss Leech. It is a bit close to the bone, I said. But it's not much more explicit than what the two sawyers said they saw when they looked in the stable window and Marianne and Mullan were lying in the straw. I'm surprised they suppressed this passage.

Read on, she said.

Lord Chancellor: That the Rev. Mr Sargent saw Mrs Talbot upon the floor in the way described, I am perfectly satisfied. He is pressed in the strongest way and asked if he is quite certain that it was Mrs Talbot. 'I am exceedingly sorry,' he replies, 'to be obliged to say that I have no doubt the woman on the floor was Mrs Talbot.' Again he says, 'I have not the slightest doubt upon the subject, and I regret to be obliged to say so. Mullan, in my opinion, was not upon the floor.'

I read that again.

. . . Mullan, in my opinion, was not upon the floor.

I looked at Miss Leech, bewildered. She gave me no help. If anything, she looked grimly satisfied, and gestured to me to continue reading.

I went on in a faltering voice.

. . . Mullan, in my opinion, was not upon the floor. But as far as regards Mrs Talbot, the Rev. Sargent distinctly saw her, and it is impossible that he should make a mistake. This gentleman saw Mrs Talbot; he knew her, and he believes he knows who was the other party, but he would not disclose who it was.

I looked at Miss Leech again, beseechingly. The other party? I said, and I could hardly form the words. There was another man?

Bertie said, How do you mean, another man? I thought there was no man at all. She was innocent, wasn't she?

The Reverend Mr Sargent, I went slowly on,

believes he knows who was the other party, but he would not disclose who it was.

Good Lord! Bertie said.

It appears that on going up to the house he was threatened by a dog, and was seeking refuge in the house, and hastily opened the door of this room, without any introduction, and there he witnessed a sight which might well appal any man. It was but an instant, but in such an instant a century passes, while it only occupies a single glance, a single moment to ascertain what is taking place. It is impossible for any man to have seen what he saw, and not be satisfied as to the party. He says he is not satisfied that the man was Mullan. Indeed, Mr Sargent was perfectly satisfied that it was not Mullan.

I read that sentence to myself several times.

Mr Sargent having witnessed this, he went to Mr McClelland, the clergyman of the parish, and communicated the fact to him. Mr McClelland had a communica-

tion with Mrs Talbot and then he saw Mr Sargent again and he communicated his opinion that it was better not to stir any further in the matter.

The vicar knew this all along? I said. Knew it when Richard came to him about Mullan? No wonder he assumed she was guilty and took her away to Coffey's Hotel! No wonder he collaborated with locking her up in Windsor!

The passage ended:

I cannot but come to the conclusion that Mr McClelland had satisfied himself as to who was the adulterer in that case, and that the adulterer was not the groom Mullan, and that being communicated to Mr Sargent, he received subsequent information which led him to believe that he knew who the person was. I for one feel perfectly satisfied that William Mullan was not the actor upon that occasion.

He knew who the person was! I said to Miss Leech. Who? A passing army officer? A gentleman come over from the next county to an emergency meeting? Lord Coby? A judge visiting for the assizes?

He must have been from her own kind, anyway, Miss Leech said. She got away with this lover. Obviously, it was all kept from Richard. This one must have been of her own class, or she would have got the punishment for being with him that she got when she went with an Irish servant.

I read the last sentence of the passage:

Here is a clear case of adultery, of which there is ocular demonstration, taking place in Mount Talbot, and it shows the unhappy state of sin into which this lady had fallen, at a time when she already showed affection and regard for Mullan.

Oh no, I cried. At the same time! She was with this person when she was going with Mullan, too!

Take the photocopy with you, Cait, Miss Leech said. I'm tired. It opens up a lot, doesn't it? For some reason I believe in this episode completely.

So do I, I said. The only question is – did Mullan know about this man? And if he did, did it hurt him?

He'd have known, Bertie said. Servants always know everything.

But maybe she never was a lover of Mullan's, I began. But then, why did he follow her to Dublin –

I'm amused, Miss Leech said in a voice that had become sleepy, at the story being so modern in the end. Because this story does exactly what a lot of the highbrow fiction coming into the library these days does – it keeps changing as you look at it. You don't know what to believe. Our readers hate that, of course. They're forever complaining about it, as if the library service is responsible for literary fashion. But there is something odd going on here. For example, why did the Reverend Sargent call at Mount Talbot when he knew Richard would be out? And since when do hostile dogs – you'd know from that mongrel of yours, Bertie – chase a man *into* a house instead of keep him away from it?

Both Bertie and I opened our mouths to speak but she suddenly cried out, Not that I care! I don't care! I'm *tired*. Take me home, please, Bertie – I'm so tired.

We began to get up.

They must have been watching from the kitchen, because just when Bertie had carefully put Miss Leech's cap on her head, Paddy the manager and a boy in chef's whites and the waitress burst through the serving door, the boy carrying aloft a small sponge cake with some lit but crooked candles. They paraded to our table, and Paddy popped the bottle of champagne he was carrying. *Miss Leech* was written in wobbly pink on icing liberally dotted with drops of candle wax.

What's this for? Miss Leech said.

Ah, for nothing! Paddy said. To celebrate your visit to Coby Castle.

The five of us drank a toast to her – Three cheers for Miss Leech! Paddy, who looked terribly upset, and the boy, and Bertie and myself. We all knew what we were doing, except the little waitress, who thought this was a party.

A birthday celebration! Miss Leech said with an attempt at a smile, in all but the essentials.

Then she leaned up to Bertie on her tiptoes and dabbed the tears off his cheeks with the table napkin.

I said I'd ring her the next day about collecting the cat.

Her last words to me were not a farewell. They were, as we recrossed the hall: By the way, Cait, I think you should brush up your architectural history. This house is rather obviously from the 1880s or '90s. So Mr and Mrs Talbot cannot, as you imagined, have walked across these tiles.

I was grateful to her for her forethought. She had saved up the little rebuke, so that we could part on an unemotional note.

20

I started the drive home with the phrase 'he saw Mrs Talbot lying on her back on the floor', still reverberating in me. It was as if it had been in wait for me. There was a picture of myself I'd managed not to look at for many years – tumbled on my back on the tiles of the floor of the kitchen in Bloomsbury, with my sweater and bra up around my neck, and my face red and slack . . . the man's face above me full of contempt and revulsion . . .

I never got a chance to explain, because Caroline and I never spoke about it. But my excuse to myself was that I'd had a bad shock that day.

I'd collected the travel documents for a trip to Lapland and walked back to the office even though it was a dour December day with a cutting wind. I took a short cut past the Old Bailey, where a big IRA trial was going on. And I thought I saw my father.

There he was! Either him, or somebody very like him. He'd propped his placard against the wall. For some reason, he was the only demonstrator outside the court at that particular moment. The street was nearly empty. I wasn't more than twenty feet from him as I passed, walking stiffly, shocked.

The man advanced towards me, but he held his placard in front of his face as if it were a big mask. The old gabardine raincoat beneath it looked like Da's coat. The worn black shoes were like his.

The man proffered his slogans.

STOP ENGLISH LIES ABOUT IRELAND!
RELEASE THESE INNOCENT MEN!

After a moment of complete stillness there in the middle of the street, I hurried on.

I don't know whether the man was my father. Maybe I thought he was because I was already thinking that afternoon about Mammy.

I'd deliberately walked a certain route so as to pass through the streets and laneways named in a novel she and I read once, about young people hiding in the bombed ruins of the City of London just after the war. *The World My Wilderness*, it was called, by Rose Macaulay. It was high-minded and intensely romantic. Mammy said when she finished it that she'd have loved to be in London during the Blitz. Or any time. There was almost nothing left now of the devastation the novel described. But when I stopped and pressed my face into a rectangle cut in a wooden hoarding – the viewing point above a deep building site – and looked down, demolition had uncovered the basement of a Victorian building and I saw a fireplace sliced in two and a wall with a palimpsest of wallpapers, and half a stairwell hanging in mid-air. It might have been a scene out of the book.

I am the only person on earth who knows what this would have meant to my mother, I thought. She might as well be standing here beside me in Nora's old coat.

And twenty minutes later I thought I saw my father.

I rang Danny as soon as I got home and Danny said it couldn't have been the Da – he was sure. The stepmother would never have given him the fare. Well, he was nearly sure.

I'd just put down the phone from talking to Danny, when it rang.

Who? I said, not believing what I was hearing.

Ian Arbuthnot, he said. At least he didn't say Caroline's husband.

I'm in town, he said – I hadn't known he was out of it, or where he was – and I'd like to see you. I understand Caroline is seeing a lot of you. And I'm worried about her mental health.

I almost choked. If Caroline had ever been in a worrying state it was only because he'd put her there. What badness was he trying to get me mixed up in? I'd never exchanged more than a few words with him in my life.

Where did you get my number? I asked him.

I copied it out of her address book, as a matter of fact.

And what made you do that?

I happened to note down a few numbers when we were splitting up. As I said – I worry about her. And I am entitled to know whether my son is in the hands of a sick person or not.

Would that be Caroline you're calling sick? I said. Because if so –

Oh, for God's sake, Kathleen! All I want is a quiet chat about a person who both you and I are fond of, and both you and I know isn't very strong. With an old man like David she never had a chance.

He went on for a while along those lines. I noticed he liked the familiarity of saying David instead of Sir David. I'd have told him to stuff his fake concern, but that I knew she'd never forgive me if I didn't follow this up.

I can meet you for an hour at nine o'clock, I said, in a pub near the British Museum. Otherwise I won't be available.

It was true – I was going to Lapland the next morning to check out the various Santa Clauses.

In which case you'll just have to cope with the mess you've made of your marriage yourself, I added, in case he didn't know where I stood. I'll listen to what you have to say, I said, but only because I'm Caroline's friend.

I could hear the undischarged energy in that marriage in the gasps from Caroline when I rang and told her this amazing news. At first she didn't want me to turn up for him. Then she changed her mind and made me promise to remember every word he said, and every gesture he made and what he was wearing, and she wanted me to let him know without telling him directly that she was blissfully happy and looking better than she ever did in her life. He still brought out the child in her, although otherwise she became more cool with each passing month.

I'm suddenly really important to her, I thought, just because I'm meeting him.

Ian was a skilled combatant, I knew. I remember Caroline telling me, for example, that once when she asked him for a small sum – ten pounds maybe, or twenty – he'd held the notes out in front of him, telling her to kneel down to get them. And she did. But he brought out his most charming manner for me, and after a while I relaxed. I liked being in the pub. The gas fire brightening the wall and the warm, lustrous air, and my arm in front of me on the glossy table reaching for the glass of wine. It's nice here, I thought to myself.

Let me get us another drink, Ian said, before it gets too busy.

I liked that, too.

The sequence of events was accidental. Surely? I did have two large glasses of wine very quickly, but that need not have mattered. Then, he was going on about Caro never wanting to let him out of her sight and how difficult it is being married to the daughter of a millionaire who is in love with her father, and at that moment the barman swept the empty glasses off the table in front of us and we were crushed into each other as a group of girls shouting Push up! Push up! tried to fit themselves onto the end of our seat.

Let's get out of here, Ian said. Isn't there anywhere quiet we could go? This is your neighbourhood, isn't it?

So I said we could go to my place for half an hour or so, but that then I'd have to throw him out because a car was coming to take me to the airport very early in the morning. I thought at the time that I made that offer for Caroline's sake – so as to go on listening to him talking about her. But then, the night we went out into was icy cold.

God! What a shock! I turned down the alley beside the pub that led to my street, and I began to run, half backwards, to keep the wind out of my face.

How far have we to go? he gasped beside me. I'm freezing to death!

And the two of us ran the hundred yards to my front door laughing excitedly at the cold.

He put his arms around me from behind as I fitted the key in the door, snuggling me for a moment between the wide sleeves of his tweedy coat. Like a friend would.

Everything was still manageable until he touched me. But I shuddered at being touched. I couldn't help it – I shuddered as a woman who hadn't been touched by a man for a long time, not as me being touched by Caroline's Ian. I shuddered with longing. And he felt it.

I'd left the lamp on. I reached into the fridge and brought out a bottle of wine. When I turned round to say something he was standing close behind me. He took the bottle and put it on the table without looking at it. He just looked at me. He unbuttoned my coat.

He didn't kiss me. He put his hands under my sweater, one on each side of my waist. He waited for a second or two while they warmed. Then he moved his hands upwards and pushed my bra up over my breasts. Then he sat back into the armchair behind him, bringing me gently with him. He settled me across his knees, both of us still in our coats. He pulled my coat around us both, as if to shield us from the outside world. Then he pulled my sweater up with one hand and with the other he readied the breast an inch from his mouth. The nipple swelled towards his mouth. His warm lips closed around it. The room was absolutely quiet.

Then he dropped me on the floor. My head hit the tiles and I could feel my nipple sticking up absurdly from my twisted torso. I felt the warm saliva going cold on it as I tried to pull my sweater down quickly.

You're some friend! he said, bending down and sticking his face grotesquely close to mine. Then he slammed out the door.

I had never, in all the years since then, allowed the whole of this episode back into my mind. Now I let it come, all the way across the bog and past Mount Talbot to Ballygall and then around Ballygall and out to Felix's place. I half knew what the agile thing inside me that knew about survival was doing: it had jumped in, the instant I visualized Marianne Talbot splayed on the floor, so as to gain time for me before I would have to think about Miss Leech.

But also, to let this memory escape from where I had had it caged. Because it was still full of power, the power that events take on if you bury them – fast! fast! – when they are still unexamined. I know that my life – which had been nothing much anyway, except for work and the office – went into its emptiest phase after that night when Ian was in my kitchen. I felt myself settle into being an unpleasant person. I always felt that, no matter how vivacious or confident I might have seemed. I got some relief, when I was in bed with somebody, from the company I disliked – my own company. But I only got the lightened feeling for maybe a day. And the malaise was still there long after I'd managed to forget Ian. It was there, I might almost say, until I started on the road to change by deciding to do something about the story of Marianne Talbot and William Mullan.

And now an idea struck me.

Perhaps it was not its erotic promise that had made the Marianne story so meaningful to me, any more than what I hoped for that night from Ian was an erotic experience. Or rather – sex was only a gateway to the state I really craved. The state I knew as intimately as my own breathing, and could not live without, was the state of punishment – of paying for wrongs that I did indeed commit, but despairingly, as if I had been sent into the world flawed. I'd known from the beginning that being locked up for the rest of her life in a madhouse in Windsor was how Marianne Talbot's passion was rewarded. And I must have known, when I told Ian he could come back to my place, underneath my chatter to myself, that nothing good could come of it. But I had to drive towards locking myself in my own Windsor. Because that was where my innermost self felt I should be. Just as I pulled the happy house of my life with Hugo down around my own head. Because I should live among ruins. I was meant to.

I clung to Spot that night. He lay beside the bed and I stretched my arm down and stroked and stroked him. I couldn't eat or drink. Miss Leech would die soon. And Marianne's perfidy – I didn't even know how to think about that. And I had so much to forgive in myself, if I could forgive. And Shay knew nothing about the Kathleen who could not bear happiness, and Miss Leech had advised me in such contradictory ways that I'd have to make the decision about being his lover by myself.

There was a waterfowl out on the dark lake who had a cry exactly like the first, helpless exclamation at the beginning of a woman's orgasm. What worlds had been lost, so as to make that sound happen! From my restless bed I could see one star. Miss Leech had quoted Keats, and now I did, too. *Bright star! Make me steadfast as thou art!*

I jumped out of bed. There was something I had forgotten to do.

Please, Annie, I pleaded down the phone. Please. Your Furriskey is ancient. This one could be Lilian's cat. If the cats don't get on or you hate it I promise I'll come back and find somewhere else for it. Please, Annie. I may be able to take the cat myself – I might settle in Ireland. No, I don't know yet. Somewhere near Sligo, maybe. But I want you to take the cat now, because I want to be able to tell her tomorrow. She doesn't have long . . .

In the end, Annie said that tomorrow was Holy Thursday and the beginning of the Easter break and Lil didn't have school, so she'd get the woman who owned the shop to mind it, and she and Lil would come over to Ballygall to see me and collect the cat.

And to see this house, Annie. I've never lived in such a marvellous house!

Yes, Annie said, but it's only borrowed.

Oh, I said, surprised. What does that matter?

It would be no good to me, she said, if it wasn't *my* house.

I lay down again. My bright star had been covered by cloud. In a few minutes I heard, like furtive footsteps, the first drops of rain. Soon, the whole air was filled with the sound of plump, copious rain. Tonight the rain seemed to have an aftersound of the most subtle kind. I imagined, as I listened, that what was making that sound was the drops, when they hit the surface of the lake, rebounding a little, and then falling onto the water for a second time.

First thing next morning I answered the phone to a gruff, male voice with a London accent.

Are you the girl who works with old Alex? it asked.

Is he all right? Is Alex all right?

Well, the voice said, he is and he isn't. I'm Ron from next door. He asked me to give you a ring. His mother passed on a couple of days ago, not before time if I may say so. He was awfully good to the old lady, but she was a bit of a trial. She was gaga, actually, not to put too fine a point on it.

I know, I said. He rang and told me she was gone himself. Why isn't he ringing me now himself instead of you?

I've just passed him leaving his own house, Ron said. He was going down his front path and I was going up mine. Those Harry Krishny types he goes around with were just ahead of him – they were getting into their minibus thing. So he leaned over and gave me a bit of paper with your number on it and he just said to give you a ring to tell you the funeral was beautiful.

But – that doesn't make sense, I said.

Well, you'd know that better than me, he said. But I got the distinct impression he didn't want the Harry Krishnys to see.

They're not Hare Krishna, I said. They're English monks.

They *dress up*, he said. I don't think they're English.

Well, maybe they're a comfort to him now, I said.

They're the only life he had! Ron said. I've lived here for the last thirty years. Raised a family. And I doubt that Alex has gone out at night more than ten or twelve times a year. Even at Christmas, himself and herself were in there by themselves with a bit of a roast chicken. But that shower of nancy boys want the house as an extension to their convent or whatever you call it – the old lady told me so herself, a year or so ago. So maybe he's under a lot of pressure.

But what can I do about it? I cried. How can I help? I don't even know where the monastery is. And I can't stand that particular lot – dreadful people, they are.

Good girl! Ron said. The fighting Irish, begorra! A girl with a bit of spirit is just what old Alex needs. Will you be at that number if I see him again? Or – here, I'll give you my number, if that's any good to you.

I'll give you my friend Caroline's number, I said. I'll keep in touch with her, and you contact her or tell Alex to contact her if he surfaces again. And – thank you, Ron. Thank you very much.

Then I rang Caro, to tell her all about this. And to check, of course, that she was still there. I dragged the phone out onto the deck and chatted to her in the fitful sunlight, and as we talked, I saw a plump hare lollop up the field beside the hedge. That would bring me luck.

Everything was fine. It was a normal conversation, such as we'd had every week or so since we got back together. She'd survived the exams. Would she sign us up for the next beginners' bridge lessons? How was the Talbot book coming along? Oh. No book, maybe? Never mind – you'll never be short of an idea, Kathleen! Nat was cycling in Spain. She was waiting for the new kind of tulip in the pots around her front door to come up. It was called black but it was really the darkest purple. She was going down to Cornwall for Easter to help her mother with a village fête.

It was absolutely impossible to mention that the Ian episode had come back to haunt me. She would not let me into her confidence about what it meant to her. She never had, even at the time.

I'd rung her from Oslo airport on my way to the Santa Claus place. I might not have owned up at all, but that I knew Ian would tell her. Was there any chance that he wouldn't tell her? No. No chance. It sank in – that he'd never wanted me. That he'd coaxed me along till he had me where I opened out to him, to mock me and to tell Caroline he had mocked me, and to tell her that she had no friends.

You're some friend!

The thought of my father – of all things – kept me going. Or the man who was maybe my father. I discovered in my turmoil that every time I thought of him and his placard and his big stupid obsession with England – which had heroism in it, all the same – I toughened up.

It isn't the end of the world, I tried saying to myself.

If anything, I said to Caroline, bent in against the plastic wall of the airport lounge so no one would hear me pleading, it will make me a better friend to you.

I understand better now, I cried down the phone, desperate at her silence. I see his power. I see that he'd do anything. I don't know how you survived him, Caroline!

But I could feel Caroline's instincts fasten on the flaw in what I was saying. Why would I have brought him home to the basement, but that I hoped for something from him?

As it was, all I had said was that Ian had made a pass.

When she still said nothing, I said, We never kissed! There were no clothes taken off or anything like that. It was the drinks! I was upset because I thought I saw my father in the street!

I tried again.

I didn't need to phone you to tell you I was meeting him in the first place, I said. If I'd had any bad intentions, I could have met him without you ever knowing.

I heard Caroline's breathing change. That was a good point. But she hung up.

Fuck the lot of them! I thought. Bloody fucking English people!

She never even said that she didn't want to know me any more. I made that assumption. I cut her out of my life – which didn't leave me much in the line of friends, except for Jimmy. At first I missed her very much. Then time passed, and I forgot her almost completely. I felt not so much that I was going downhill as that I was desiccating. I was so empty that I blew this way and that. Happiness keeps you poised, and you do the right thing without effort, whereas you get things wrong when you're struggling with lack of life.

It was about two years ago that I gave in to an impulse to contact her. I surprised myself by the decision to dial her number, which I did the day I arrived back in London after several months in America, in flight from the fool I'd made of myself with Alex in Trieste. I was extremely lonely after so long without the companionship of the office, but that wasn't why I rang Caroline. The truth was that staying away from Alex had involved living in California for a while, and I had a terrific tan and that gave me confidence. The evening of the day I got back I had bad jet lag and by six o'clock I was so disoriented that I couldn't think straight. And that did it – the combination of a hazy detachment in my head and a tan. I rang her: I wasn't even trembling. I was ready to be so out of it that even the worst snub wouldn't hurt.

Kathleen! she said, and she sounded delighted – admittedly the way she always did, whenever anyone at all rang her. I'm just poaching a superb wild salmon for a few people. Do you like sorrel sauce? Do jump in a cab.

So I did. It was ideal, that she was having a dinner party. I sat there in her gorgeous kitchen drinking very good wine the others had brought and listening, in between nodding off, to a conversation about the awfulness of au pairs, left-wing councils and house prices. One fairly drunk woman even started on a tirade about her Irish cleaning woman, but I just smiled and said nothing.

I'm so sorry about that frightful woman, Caroline began, when she rang the next day.

I said, And they're *Labour*, those people. Remind me not to come to dinner when you're having Tories.

And that was that. She'd been the one to ring, so it wasn't as if I chased her. We talked about her training to be a teacher, now that Nat was at college, and there was no mention then or since of my encounter with Ian when she still adored him. Ian himself hadn't been around for years. But Caroline was so opaque that I did not know whether she had actually forgotten the whole thing, or whether she remembered but had decided to forgive me. If she had decided to forgive me, what I wanted to know was *why* she had forgiven me. I wanted to know whether, if I had not rung her the night I got back from California, she would ever have rung me. My punishment was that I did not dare ask, and she never said. I had known her now for the better part of my life, and I still did not understand her. Or, I often understood her, but I still didn't know why she had me for a friend. As for what I thought of her . . . When I began – just recently – to look back over the shape of my life, I placed the decisive moment at turning against travel writing, when I was so shaken by Manila. But what made me sensitive to Manila, when I'd seen abject poverty and exploitation tens of times before, and gone on churning out my cheery copy? Mustn't some process have been happening inside me, to change my perception of things? And mightn't that process have begun when Caroline, as if it were the most natural thing in the world, took me back? Maybe there was more of the angel to her than just her looks.

Spot and I watched an origami demonstration on morning television. I'd turned the volume down and I had a Fred Astaire CD playing at the same time. Picture and sound didn't suit each other at all. But load every rift with ore, I said to the dog – that's what Keats advised Shelley to do. Try to pack everything in. And Felix has the best collection of 1940s songs we'll ever see.

Bertie rang.

I have the cat, he said. But I'm afraid Nan wasn't able to stay to see you. She told me on the way home yesterday that she was going into the hospice, but I thought that was months away! Then she rang me this morning to say that she had a hangover from all that drinking with you yesterday – and I'm not surprised, because I never knew her to take more than a sip of sherry in her life before – and that she'd rung the hospice people to collect her straight away so she could be put out of her misery with sedation. So. She left in their ambulance about half an hour ago. I can't get over it – I didn't even get the chance to drive her.

She's a wonderful woman, I said. She set that up. She saw how to get away without saying goodbye to anyone.

Do you think so, Kathleen? She just walked out of the house as if she might be back tomorrow. She never even took the milk off the table.

The last I saw of my mother, I said. Her bed – it was the way it always was when she got out of it. It looked as if she'd be getting back in at any minute. Her coat was on the hook in the hall. The pockets were baggy. You could see the outline of her fists . . .

The cat, he said, when he realized I had finished talking. The bloody thing is in a box in the back of the car and it's making an awful noise and the box is moving around.

Well, I have a rendezvous with my sister-in-law and my niece in the square at midday, and then I'll be down to the hotel to collect it.

Sister-in-law! he said. Niece! I never thought of you as having family, Kathleen. You're the real I-walk-alone type.

Put it in the shed beside the back door until we take it away, Bertie. And give it something nice to eat. Pretend the cat has a tiny bit of Miss Leech in it. Because after all their years together, I'm sure it has.

He did manage a laugh at that.

Bertie, I said – and it only came into my head as I said it – Bertie, now that Miss Leech has gone, I think I'll move on, too. Tomorrow, maybe. Maybe head over to the Sligo area and look around. Or maybe go back to England. I've had enough of being on holidays, to tell you the truth. I'm used to work. My boss is away, otherwise I'd talk to him. And I don't know how to go forward with the Talbot stuff. So I think this'll be my last day in Ballygall – for the time being, anyhow. Would there be any problem if I took my visitors up to Mount Talbot?

No problem in the world! he said. I'll take you myself if you like. I'd rather you had someone with you because there's bad drops in those old ruins.

I hate to be thinking of leaving, I said, without settling in my own mind whether Marianne Talbot was or was not unfaithful to her husband. But I just don't know how to decide.

There's a very old fellow out the back of the demesne – Curly Flannery by name – who knew all the people round here who were young when the Talbot scandal happened. He's ninety-something, Curly is, but he might be worth going to see. I could ring the niece he lives with.

Oh, Bertie! That'd be wonderful. Thank you.

But are you sure about leaving, Kathleen? Should you not wait till Nan's back?

Do you think she'll be coming back? I said, after a moment.

He didn't answer that question at all.

I went up and down and in and out of Felix's house, tidying, and collecting my belongings. Sunshine and light showers were following each other so quickly that my eye would fall on the wood of a deck dark with wet, and when I passed it again, it would have dried. Wherever I went, Spot came, too. I had to apologize to him several times, because he would settle with deliberation onto his paws and find the rhythm of his breathing and half close his eyes, and then I'd move on, and he would have to get up and pad after me and settle all over again. I was using Felix's sound system to play the last Schubert piece again. The notes made a crystalline pattern as they fell through the air – on the grass, and on the wildcats asleep under the outside stairs, and on the reeds, and on the water. Today I was convinced that I could hear *acceptance* of death in the piece – a rich acceptance, if that was possible.

Spot reminded me of the day we heard that Jimmy was dead.

There'd been a dog in the pub, that awful morning, that peered at me exactly as Spot was doing now. Roxy and Betty and I had gone to the pub when it was opening and started drinking gin. I don't know why gin. Roxy got very upset after a while. The dog, a little Jack Russell, was sitting quietly under a table beside the door and his owner was sitting with his pint in a patch of winter sunshine. Roxy got it into her head that the man was mistreating the dog – that you could tell by its eyes. We had to ring her mother to say she was on her way home in a bad state, and then get her past the man and the dog into the cab.

Jimmy? I said. What will I do? What will I say when Shay rings me tomorrow? I thought I'd spend most of these days thinking about him and weighing up what to do, but so much else is happening . . . And the real meaning of never is never. If I turn Shay down, I may never make love again. But I know for certain that I will never see Miss Leech again.

I went across the grass to collect the trowel from under the thorn tree. One of the wildcats didn't skitter back the way they usually did. Oh – she was pregnant. I could see her heavy belly, under her thin frame, weighing her down. She dragged up the slope, keeping in under the hawthorn hedge. The leaf buds on the hedge were so tiny that the bushes seemed to stand naked in air tinged green, rather than be beginning to go green themselves.

I would remember this valley for ever, though it itself had made me ready to move on. It was all the light and space in Felix's house that showed up how little I had to do. I'd just been hanging around, waiting for Miss Leech to see me –

Hanging around. Waiting. Were these the words I would always be using with Shay? Mean words, and discontented, when the whole taste of what I'd known with him was generous and happy . . .

But it wouldn't be hanging around if I were busy on a task. I would have to write. That was the only profession I was capable of following, that could be followed no matter where I lived.

But write what? What was the right ending to the Marianne Talbot story? I couldn't imagine how John Paget handled the Sargent allegation. Paget had based his case on the evidence given in the

Ecclesiastical Court in Ireland. He would not have heard the Reverend Sargent's story until the House of Lords divorce hearing, two or three years later. What if he was persuaded by it? As well he might have been, since he couldn't explain it away as part of Richard's conspiracy against his wife – Richard, apparently, never having been told about it. And Paget could hardly argue, either, that there'd been a case of mistaken identity – that the man on the drawing-room floor was really Mullan – since he firmly believed there had been no amorous dealings with Mullan. If Paget, her one protector, turned against her, the situation for Marianne was appalling – even if he only turned against her in his heart, and still pretended to stand by her. With any luck, she really was mad. But even mad, wouldn't she have known if his belief in her turned to scepticism?

I was plagued by questions to which there could never be definite answers. For example, if Paget's account of Marianne's married life was accurate, she might have been so broken by years of humiliation and underfeeding that she was like the victim child in a trash family: everyone abused her. In that case, what Sargent saw would be closer to a rape than anything else. But maybe not. Maybe she did indeed have a passionate affair with Mullan, and – like me when I was with Hugo – her sense of her own sexual power made her reckless, and the man kneeling between her legs was the equivalent of my Sasha. Or maybe some of the gentry in the big houses of Ireland after the Famine – growing more impoverished with each day they stayed on in a country where hatred for them was only kept in check by weakness – were becoming bizarre. Like in an Almodóvar movie. Anything might happen – this man with that woman, in this stable or on that floor – as the landlord class responded to the violent death of the world it had constructed. Could Marianne have had an affair with someone of her own kind and a completely innocent Mullan been made the scapegoat?

But there was the curious detail that when the Reverend Sargent told the Reverend McClelland about what he had seen, McClelland went back and had a word with Marianne herself, and that was that.

It couldn't have been *McClelland* on the floor, could it? If McClelland was making love with her, and *then* was told about Mullan, that might explain his extraordinary vengefulness towards her. Taking her guilt for granted; taking her to Dublin straightaway; reading and destroying her letter from Mullan. Watching the poor woman go mad – searching for her child behind the curtains and under the bed and in the wardrobe of the room in Coffey's Hotel. Hiding her in the Rathgar Road, and then bringing her across to Windsor and dumping her there with a keeper. Then allowing Marianne's father to understand that she had admitted guilt, and that the proceedings in the Ecclesiastical Court could go ahead without a defence. Even if McClelland did not have sexual relations with her, his behaviour was so excessively punitive that it suggested that he desired her. Another enemy for poor Marianne, created by nothing but her sex.

Whatever had happened, there was one definite, true fact.

She ended up with nothing.

I went for a last walk along the edge of the lake. The weather had settled into a sunny, early summer – not exceptional, like the flawless hot spell when I first came to the house, but sweet. The stone walls of the old fields were now low banks covered in grass. Below each bank, like a rim of surf, there was a wash of creamy primroses.

I imagined the mean house in Windsor and the woman who was the keeper of the lunatics there clawing at Marianne's fingers. And Marianne, who did not remember her own name, or anything except the face of a laughing child, looking in bewilderment at this strange woman who was being so rough with her.

Where are your rings? the woman said.

Rings? Marianne said.

Richard had perhaps instructed the Reverend McClelland to get back his wedding rings from Marianne while she was in the hotel in Dublin. Perhaps the vicar had wanted at first to demur. But when he thought about the sin that Mrs Talbot had committed – when he imagined her groaning in the arms of an animal who no doubt stank of animals – he was happy to do it.

So the vicar looked across at her swollen face one morning in the parlour of Coffey's Hotel.

Your husband has requested you return the rings which he presented to you when he wed you, when they represented with a most sacred symbolism all that he expected and had every right to expect of the marriage bond, and of which you have proved unworthy.

When she did not respond, he walked over to her, pulling with him, abruptly, a small, ornamental table. He laid her plump white hands on the table and slowly pulled the heavy gold band, and then the diamond band, from the left hand, and an intricate cameo ring with the Talbot crest in intaglio from the middle finger of her right hand. When he was finished he stood up, but Marianne did not move her hands.

You may take your hands down from the table now, he said to her.

When she did not respond, he bent down and pushed her hands back into her lap, and returned the occasional table to its own place . . .

I turned back along the lake to the house. I couldn't see any way of writing about Marianne Talbot that wouldn't be like bad costume drama. Even though real life was more melodramatic than melodrama. Consider, for instance, the possibility that Marianne Talbot was not mad, but had had to pretend to be mad, since otherwise she would have been cast out of society completely. Madness was her only defence, once she had not denied adultery with Mullan. She could only be innocent if she was mad. If she was not mad, who would feed her and clothe her? John Paget would never have befriended her if he had not been honestly satisfied that she was mad. Where could she have gone if she was not mad? An utterly disgraced and fallen wife and mother? A woman who, as far as her peers were concerned, had mated with an Irish menial – a thing more like a prairie dog than a human being.

And once she started pretending to be mad, she had to keep it up as long as she lived.

It's probably quite easy, I thought. It's probably like sex. Well, one kind of sex. You just let your mind go slack and babyish. The discipline of being a person falls away. But at night, in her room in the Pagets' villa in Leicester, did she allow her sanity out of hiding?

The truth was that I did not know. I could not know.

I called Spot, and we went up to the car, and set out for Ballygall. I drove very slowly, trying to be calm. The thing about my life during all the dry years in the Euston Road was that nothing much ever happened. If I dropped a tissue on the floor, it was still exactly where I had dropped it when I came back from a trip. There might be three or four messages on the machine, but there would be no letters; I used to scoop the mail into the bin without even looking at it. It may have been the quiet of a living grave, I thought to myself, but at least it was quiet. Now . . . Shay would ring tomorrow. Miss Leech was facing death. Alex was grief-stricken and out of touch. And I was on my way to see Annie. Family – twice in one month, for God's sake!

The sheer excess of the whole thing made me facetious.

Maybe I could make it seem that I was moving to Sligo to write one of those best-selling books about buying an old place and fixing it up and having funny things happen with the lovable local plumbers? No. No one wants to move to melancholy Ireland the way they want to move to Tuscany or Provence. And there is no local cuisine. And the natives are not necessarily lovable at all. Anyway, the people who write those settling-down-in-a-lovable-foreign-country books lead sunny, blameless lives, full of little humorous scenes with their spouses. You wouldn't catch them living semi-secretly, waiting to spend a couple of days a month in bed with another woman's husband.

It was a relief to see the spires of Ballygall. Towns are where things get decided.

Annie and little Lilian fitted with perfect ease into Bertie's place – much more so than Miss Leech's cat, an enormous, suspicious-looking tabby called Rita, who everyone kept looking at because she hadn't eaten for twenty-four hours. We had a cup of tea in the kitchen. Spot sat under the table, staring up, transfixed, at the budgie, who'd been let out of its cage and was flouncing up and down the curtain rail. Bertie was rolling out pastry and Annie was peeling apples.

Bertie kept giving me little approving nods, as if to congratulate me for having turned up with normal people. I was feeling, myself, the mixture of anxiety and reassurance that I associated with family. I'd noticed that when I'd been hugging Lil and asking after Danny, Annie hadn't answered. I knew there was something wrong. But I didn't follow it up because I didn't want to hear bad news at the start of the visit.

Ollie came bumping down the stairs on his bottom and ran into the kitchen, and when he saw me he shouted *Attly!* But when I held out my arms to him he staggered past me over to the sofa under the high window, and started talking into a toy telephone to someone also called Attly. The room was so nice – shabby and warm and smelling of Bertie's baking.

Lilikins! I said. Come here – I want you!

Just to feel her. Just to see her running towards me saying, What? I picked her up for a minute to ask her which was bigger – Furriskey or Rita.

Are you not supposed to be more the sophisticated Palm Court type? I said to myself, sarcastically.

We barely fitted into Bertie's bockety old Toyota – Annie and me, Lilian and little Joe, and Spot. But at least we were going up the front way to Mount Talbot in a car. Where Bertie and I had struggled across gates and tussocky fields, a muddy track had been cut out by a bulldozer.

The Guards did that, Bertie said. The Dublin ones. When they came to catch the IRA fellas that were practising their shooting in the cellars above. Our local lads walked up the same as you and me, Kathleen, in their Wellington boots. But when the big boys from the Special Branch in Dublin came, they sent in a bulldozer first and then they drove right up to the steps.

But I thought the IRA was having a ceasefire! Annie said. God Almighty!

They weren't the usual IRA – some other crowd. I forget the name. They don't approve of the ceasefire.

In Ballygall! Annie said. Dear Jesus.

They were from the north. The only one from around here – his father grew up in the demesne. The grandfather was the herd on these fields here and he and the wife took over a couple of upstairs rooms that didn't leak too badly in the stable yard. Anyway, when the young fella was caught with the guns, he gave Mount Talbot House as his address. The judge said, Is post delivered there? and the Garda said, No way, so the judge wouldn't take that address.

When *was* post last delivered here? I asked.

There was one more Talbot after Richard, Bertie said. A woman. I don't know whether she was Richard's by a second marriage, or who she was. But she was living like a rat down a hole by the end, I always heard. There was just her and an old butler, and they were both as odd as two left feet, and the butler used to have to stand behind the old lady's chair when she was having her dinner – even if they were eating nothing but potatoes. She walked out without as much as a travelling bag in 1922, on March the thirty-first, the day the Anglo-Irish Treaty became law. She said, That's it – I'm going back to England. But she died in the Shelbourne Hotel in Dublin that night. And the old butler was taken away to the county home.

Auntie Kathleen? Lilian was tapping on my shoulder. Auntie Kathleen? Joe wants to know can we go and see the guns?

I hear you, Missy, Annie said. And the answer is no.

We arrived at the gap in the wall where ornate gates would have led to the inner demesne and the lawns around the house. Bright yellow police tape was draped across this gap, and when Bertie stopped the car and we got out, we saw that tape had been stretched from wooden post to wooden post in a huge circle all around where the house had been. KEEP OUT! KEEP OUT! It was such a formidable display that when Spot bounded past it, Annie and Bertie shouted simultaneously, Come back here, Spot! Come back!

They came running up from Ballygall the minute the old Talbot lady was out the gate, Bertie said, and they took the glass out of the greenhouses in the orchards. There were plums and grapes and orchids in them at the time. And they smashed up the big wardrobes and carried them down the stairs and then they began smashing the stairs. My uncle saw the pigman and his brothers carrying out the billiard table. What did they want with a billiard table? But the place was still sound for a long time. The people used to come in and fill their kettles at the taps when they were making hay in this vicinity.

We were walking along the slope above the river, towards the bell tower and the back of the stables. Lil and Joe and the dog were running ahead of us. As they ran, you could see bright drops splash up from their shoes. There were clumps of primroses under the wall, and a thin haze of blue at the edge of the woods, where the bluebells were beginning. The first cuckoo I'd heard this year called imperiously from the woods. The children shouted back: Cuckoo! Cuckoo! For an instant it was possible to imagine happy days in the history of Mount Talbot House, with the young mistress frolicking under the eyes of the nursemaids, and the happy servants singing as they went about their work below stairs.

No. Never.

I'll show them the statue in the ivy, Bertie said.

I'll go on to the church – I haven't seen it, I said, and I walked on until I came out through a wicket gate at the derelict Protestant church. A new sign on the broken gate said that the cleaning of the graveyard was a Fás project for the long-term unemployed, and you could see where workmen had slashed back a tangle of twisted thorns and laurels and overgrown yew, and put the top slab back on the mausoleum with an Egyptian-style door that was the Talbot family grave. Its iron entrance plate looked as if it had been rusted shut for ever.

Beside it, a newly cleaned cross of the simplest kind read:

Wm. McClelland
Rector of this Parish
Died 1857
As for me I will behold Thy face in righteousness

She entreated of me to allow said W. Mullan to come upstairs to see her, which I having refused to do, she was deterred from seeing W. Mullan . . .

That's what this man said in court.

Why had Mullan followed Marianne, if she was nothing to him? John Paget faced that problem head-on.

The earnest petition, John Paget wrote,

so ruthlessly refused, that the witness of her innocence might be admitted to an interview IN THE PRESENCE OF THE RECTOR OF THE PARISH, was the last rally of the forces of reason, before they were finally broken, scattered and routed!

That could be true. Mullan may have wanted or needed her to stand with him against the conspiracy that accused them of adultery, and it may have been that when McClelland would not allow even a meeting, Marianne's sanity gave way. John Paget's capital letters were certainly impressive.

McClelland died very soon after the Talbot scandal. I wandered into imagining the where and how of his death.

Perhaps the Reverend McClelland had been feverish throughout the disturbance caused by Mrs Talbot's disgrace. Perhaps that whole time was a nightmare of confusion to him. He signed a statement for Richard Talbot's solicitor, saying that Mrs Talbot had confessed her guilt to him, but he may have had to add that he could not remember where exactly she had done this. He thought it was in a closed carriage. But – what closed carriage? Perhaps his head was never really clear again after he helped Richard destroy Marianne. Perhaps he picked up some parasite on the journey to Windsor – the quaysides he forced his way along, her veiled figure behind him holding onto his sleeve, were thronged, after all, by people in various stages of privation. So, though he had the satisfaction of seeing Marianne securely locked away, perhaps his health was never the better for his journey. He obviously managed to testify against her, but then . . . Then what?

Where would I place him, to die? I decided that the Church of Ireland would have had an infirmary in Dublin, where the staff were accustomed to mysterious fevers. Many missionary vicars and missionary wives and children had succumbed in those low, white rooms to diseases incurred while doing the labour of the Lord in foreign parts. They were used to the ravings of the dying. Nobody who knew him visited McClelland, because he was in strict isolation, and nobody tending him knew what he was shouting. He was shouting someone's name . . .

Kathleen! We were calling you!

They looked so innocent. Bertie in a woollen bobble hat, and Annie in Ella's wellies that were too big for her, and the kids in bright little sweaters.

Sorry, Bertie, I said. I was wandering. You know, it says in the Paget book that McClelland told some local gentleman that 'he hoped it was not a conspiracy got up against Mrs Talbot'. And he told someone Paget interviewed that 'the servants at Mount Talbot were a very bad set and combined, he thought, against her'. So he must have had awful doubts. But Bertie, why would the servants gang up on Marianne?

Why not? Bertie said. Sure what was she to them? Come on, we'll go out the back gate to Curly Flannery's. They're expecting us.

They moved on. I stayed for a few minutes as silence settled again on the graveyard, looking into the unwinking eye of a glossy blackbird that was nesting in an angle of the lichened statue of an angel. There was no silence. There was the constant rustle of the trees around, and wood pigeons crooning. And again, from back down the valley – Cuckoo! Cuckoo!

We walked out of the demesne through the enormous mock-Gothic archway.

These could be grand little houses, Annie said, pointing at the gate lodges half covered with nettles and ivy. Why does no one fix them up?

Ah, no! Bertie said. There was no luck in this place after all that went on. Nobody'd live up here.

Across from the gate lodges, a site had been cleared between the road and the bog, and a pin-neat white bungalow sat in a rectangle of emerald lawn.

A woman opened the door eagerly before we even knocked.

Sure you're welcome! she said to us. Sit down and have a cup of tea! And I have lemonade and all for the children, by a miracle! Sure you'll be company for him. He's a wonderful man, God bless him. Not so much as an aspirin does he take and he ninety-two years old. Just a drop of whisky last thing at night. Isn't that right, Uncle Curly? she bellowed into his ear.

Curly Flannery was as bald as an egg. He was blind, too, and the hearing wasn't too good, apparently. But he was propped up behind his walking frame in the neat parlour, in front of a two-bar electric fire, as tidy and clean and smiling as could be.

Who's here, Maisie? he asked her. Who's the company?

It's Bertie from the hotel! she shouted. And two ladies from America! And two lovely children, God bless them. They want to hear your stories about the old days.

We're not from – I began.

Bang! Bang! Mr Flannery unexpectedly shouted. Bang! Bang! He was making unmistakable shooting gestures with his little right arm.

We couldn't sleep in our own beds! he said. We were on the run! Michael Collins for ever!

Curly was a great man, Bertie explained, in the War of Independence. Him and his brother raided all the explosives out of the County Council's stores and they blew up bridges galore.

What about before that, Mr Flannery, when there was the trouble at the Talbots'? Bertie said.

Is it Talbot you're talking about? Mr Flannery cried. Didn't he bring all his troubles on himself? The greatest bastard unhung he was that ever trod shoe leather!

Ask him did anyone around here remember the divorce, I said to Bertie. Miss Flannery had brought in a tray of tea, and she was attempting to settle her uncle into an armchair with a cup. But the old man heard me.

Certainly they do! Mr Flannery said, and his saucer slid to the floor. There was a man over at the demesne be the name of Quirke and didn't Quirke go over to London to give evidence for the wife, and he got the price of a cow out of it from Mr Bennett the barrister. And the name of the cow for ever after was Bennetteen! And do you know, Bertie, that a man called Molloy from around here gave evidence for Talbot, and when Johnny Molloy that was the grandson of that one went for election to the Dáil – there after the Second War – didn't they all shout at him at the meeting and he asking them to vote, You shut your mouth! Talbot's lapdog! Talbot's lapdog!

He laughed contentedly at the memory of it.

What about Mullan? I asked. The coachman?

Mr Flannery either didn't want to talk about that or had nothing to say. He had eaten a slice of fruitcake with his tea and the niece was brushing the crumbs off the neat waistcoat he wore under his jacket.

They had a single carriage and a double carriage, he rambled on happily, and a phaeton with a hood, and the sidecars, and then there was the float with two horses on it and the market cart that went to the town once or twice a week. My own grandfather was the boy they had specially to drive that.

Mr Flannery, I said, I'm sorry if we're tiring you –

Divil the bit! the niece said. Sure he never gets tired!

But could you tell me whether there was much Irish around when you were a boy? Would the servants have spoken Irish?

I didn't have it meself, he said, till I learned a bit of it when we were fighting for our freedom. When the British were here we used to be beat for using it. But all the old people still had it. At that time when I was a gossoon there was up to thirty houses in Cloonacurrig alone – they're all gone now – and there were a lot of old people there and they'd four miles to go to Mass and no way to get there, so they'd collect in my grandfather's house and say their prayers. The Rosary, it was. In Irish, the whole lot of it. Maisie! Did you offer Bertie a drop?

Did they ever talk about the Famine?

There was a pause. Then Mr Flannery said after half a minute, There was no famine in these parts.

Another pause.

Mr Flannery seemed to have gone asleep.

We were just getting up to tiptoe out when he suddenly shouted, Maisie! Get the medal to show the American ladies.

We admired the silver medal he'd got from the government for his exploits in the War of Independence, and turning down repeated, pressing offers of a drop of something, we backed out of the house.

Annie walked on quickly with the children through the derelict, ornate gate.

They often deny there was a famine, the old people, Bertie said softly. They don't want it talked about. It's better to stay silent about misfortune. I heard my own mother whispering one time. She was talking with a neighbour woman. Apparently, there was a maid at the time that they forced to go over to London to give evidence against Mrs Talbot, and she had to leave her baby with the neighbours, and she was away for a few months and the whole time she was away the baby cried. Day and night. And the minute she came back it stopped crying. And that night it died.

We were passing the bottom of a cobbled yard. A chilly breeze stirred the nettles around a heap of rusted farm tools and rotting wooden carts.

They knew at the time that a curse had been brought on the place, he went on. It was always known that the night Mrs Talbot was put out, the old nurse that lived in the house that was a bit of a witch said, The crows will fly through the rooms of this house yet! And there you are –

He pointed up the slope. The lone bell tower from the Mount Talbot stable yard stood gaunt against the sky.

The crows do fly through it, he said.

We ate Bertie's apple tart for tea. Joe and Lilian sat on the sofa in the kitchen and watched a video of *The Lion King* and Rita the cat sat between them.

Where *are* you going next, anyway, Kathleen? Annie said. Do you ever stay in the one place long enough to catch your breath? Though, I haven't known where you are for the last thirty years, so there isn't much point in trying to keep track of you now. Mind you, none of us are getting any younger. Which reminds me – we should be going! Danny's on his own all day. Lilian! Come on! We have to go. Get the cat's box and its food.

Aw, *Annie*! I said. What about Felix's house? I wanted to show it to you.

No, Kathleen, we really must get going.

Mammy, we're just getting to the good part –

No, love. I'm sorry, but I don't want to do the whole drive in the dark. Maybe Joe could ring you up tomorrow and tell you what happens to the lion in the end. Go and put the cat's belongings into the car.

Mammy, Joe is going to cry.

He's not going to cry, I said, because Spot is staying here now because I'm going away, and Spot wouldn't like him to cry.

Bertie and the children went out, and I smiled up at Annie, who had closed the door after them.

Thank you again for taking the cat, darling, I said to her. And tell my brother I was asking for him.

He's only out of the hospital, she said flatly. She was looking down at me.

I began to be nervous. It wasn't a neutral intentness – she was looking at me sternly.

He hadn't had a drink for a year, but with the money you gave him –

What!

On the money you gave him, Kathleen, he landed himself in hospital within three days. He drinks, by himself, out the back, in the shed. He won't talk to me. It only happens maybe once or twice a year but it's terrible. Then he gets sick and they come out from the hospital for him. They know him of old. That's the only good thing – the binges don't last long, now. He's getting past it. You should have asked me for a bit of advice, you know. I could have told you.

Told me what? I said.

Danny's got a lot of problems, Kathleen. The last thing he needed was you turning up with your thousand pounds. Himself and improving the stock! Even I don't know how many loans he has out on the place, but I know we have a hard time keeping going. And he never wanted you to know! He has his pride. And he's the best man on earth when he's well. We love him, so we do. Everyone loves him. You know yourself, Kathleen, there's no one as nice as him –

It's not his fault, Annie! He had no childhood –

You don't need to tell *me* that. Your mother – a more selfish, lazy woman I have never known! You children should have been taken off her. You know, to this day Danny has so little confidence he can't sign a cheque with his own name. The girls are the survivors in your family, which I'm glad about because Lilian is a girl. But even if you've done well for yourself, Kathleen, you can't just waltz in after God knows how many years, and throw money around before you know the half of what's going on!

You're right, I whispered.

Sure I know you meant it for the best, Kathleen, she said, though her face had not softened. And you have a good, kind heart. And when he starts drinking he keeps going whether he has money or not. But it was *thoughtless*, Kathleen. You're *thoughtless*.

I – But I couldn't think of any words. My mouth was dry with shock. What she said was true: I hadn't listened when I went home. But I'm not used to people! I said to myself. The way I lived all these years – I didn't get any practice at thinking about other people! I was going to say that, but I saw that her face was full of conflict. Then she sat down on the kitchen chair next to me and leaned towards me so that our faces almost touched. And she gave one long, tired sigh. She was telling me that she'd run out of wanting to rebuke me, that we were in this together. We sat there quietly and the racing of my heart began to slow. I was glad I hadn't given the excuses about myself. They sounded ridiculous, compared to this tragedy.

I said to her, stumbling on the words, If I harmed him, I cannot tell you how sorry I am.

Kathleen, she said, he was harmed before he could walk. And he was only sixteen when your mother died and he was left to mind Sean – do you remember Sean? – and Sean was always sick. I wasn't even sixteen myself and I'd no patience with the unfortunate child, God forgive me. And Dan never really got over finding your mother, you know. To this day he has nightmares –

Mammy!

Coming, chicken –

Mammy, could we not stay here? Because Uncle Bertie was saying –

No.

But Uncle Bertie said –

He's not your uncle –

But –

No. Go and say goodbye to Ollie and Joe.

Annie lifted her head, and she looked at me with the full candour of her face.

I meant it when I said to you, she said, that I have had a happy life, thank God. I wouldn't have it different. I wouldn't change Danny for any man on earth. So don't be cross that I spoke out, pet. We have to get it all out in the open. Because I want you to start coming home. It would help Danny, Kathleen, to have a sister like you around. Full of life. And I'd love you to be an auntie to Lil. Both of us would, Danny and me – we said it after you came over. There's no one like you in Kilcrennan.

Soon, I said. If you'll always tell me when I'm wrong? Promise?

Promise!

I went out with her to see them off. Then I ran back in for my camera, and made Lil get out of the car again and hold Rita while I took a photo for Miss Leech. The child smiled into the camera, and the cat, clutched to Lilian's front, displayed an enormous tummy and long back legs, like turkey legs covered in fur.

Back at Felix's house it was extraordinary how hard all the surfaces seemed and how harsh the space without Spot living his busy dog life down at knee level. I went to put on some music, but I didn't want any of Felix's 1940s songs, and I was far too shaken for the Schubert. It even, with its great beauty and intelligence, mocked my mother's death. It made an ordinary person like her seem inferior – a human being who was as obscure and clumsy in death as she'd been in life.

I saw now that Danny did bear the brunt of her dying. Of her collapse, first, and then of trying to keep things going. And he was only a boy himself, and a dreadfully neglected one.

He'd never tried to leave home, even though he saw Nora doing it and me doing it. It was as if he couldn't leave until our father noticed him. He dropped out of school at fifteen and went to work in the garage on the edge of Kilcrennan. But he had status because he was on the town soccer team. That's what he lived for. Other boys' fathers sang Tony Bennett numbers in the aisle of the coach going to away games, and roared themselves hoarse and ran onto the pitch, and cried with pride on the local radio station. The mothers all went to the same pubs and did a line-dancing routine to the team song at fund-raising events, falling around laughing. Danny's gift was ignored at home. Daddy was actively hostile to soccer. He believed so strongly that Gaelic football was the real, native football, and that soccer was an English imposition that when the soccer club needed the loan of the Gaelic pitch for a charity match, he brought pressure through Irish-language circles in Dublin to stop the pitch being lent.

But Danny still lived at home. He didn't have to – Annie was his steady girlfriend and he could have lived with her people. Or, his boss's wife at the garage who washed his football gear because she had a washing machine would have taken him. But he stubbornly went on living at home, getting his own meals and often making food for Sean, too. Mammy was very withdrawn at the time. I know I rang the Shore Road pub from Trinity a few times at one o'clock on a Sunday, and Mrs Bates said she hadn't come in – that my father was there, but Mammy wasn't. I thought, if she's not going to the pub she's really depressed.

If she had ever come to the phone and asked me to come home, I would have done. But I loved being a student. I didn't want the old misery dragging me down. And I had to earn my keep. In London at Christmastime I got quadruple the going rate in any hotel for working Christmas Day. And even now, as I moved restlessly around Felix's studio, hardly seeing the blue-black evening and the silver lake, I thought – I was right. I was right to start living. But Danny was left with too much to handle, and I turned my back on him.

He found our mother on the kitchen floor. He told me about it when I met him on the second night of the two nights I spent in Kilcrennan when she was in the hospital there. He got off early from the garage and met me in the lounge bar across from the hospital. It was Friday, but it was still only four or five. I know it was Friday, because I knew that my father would be back from his week's work and be going in to see my mother later.

There was no one in the pub except a barman heaving crates of bottles around. It was so cold Danny and I were in our coats.

She was on the floor, Danny said. Sean must have been asleep in the other room. I went into the kitchen and she was there . . .

What was she wearing?

He lifted his head and looked at me.

It was quite hard for him to tell me about it: he usually hardly spoke at all. He had sideburns, and he was trying to comb his hair forward into a Beatles fringe, but his fine brown hair sprang back from his forehead in a parallel with the arch of the eyebrows, like some piece of decoration on a butterfly, the same as Mammy's.

She was just out of the bed, he said. She was in that old dressing gown with the flowers on it. She was on her face on the ground, and the whole back of it, the whole skirt, was sopping with blood. When

413

I turned her over, the front was wringing wet, too. Her face was a weird colour.

Were her eyes open?

Yeah, they were open, but she wasn't looking at anything.

He ran up the road to the shop, and Tommy Bates got on the phone, and Mrs Bates came back down with Danny. Mrs Bates got the blanket off Danny's bed and wrapped her in it. She started packing things in a carrier bag to go with Mammy in the ambulance. She put Mammy's big handbag in, and a toothbrush from the shelf over the sink.

Where does your mother keep her clothes? she'd asked, and Danny said just anywhere around.

Was your mother expecting a baby?

He said, How would I know?

The wardrobe in their room was full of Daddy's suits. Mrs Bates disentangled some woman's things from the heap of clothes in the cupboard beside the range. Danny put in the detective story that was on the bedside table. The broken-down court shoes went in.

Her shoes always upset me. When she went to the pub she had lipstick on and she combed her hair and she had a good black jumper with a scoop neck that we always told her she looked great in. But the shoes . . .

She wasn't unconscious when they were putting her onto the stretcher, Danny said. She was crying. I think she could have talked, but she didn't. I went to work. Mrs Bates took Sean.

It was Nora who had told me about Mam. She called from New York and by a miracle, she got me on the public phone in the Trinity Students' Union.

Mam is in the Regina Coeli hospital in Kilcrennan. Uncle Ned called me. I've talked to the head nun there, and she said not to quote her but we'd better come home.

How will I get home? I said. I've no money.

That was just the shock talking. I was already deciding which of my jobs I could get advance wages from, and Kilcrennan was only an hour and a half away on the train.

414

I'm not going home, Nora said slowly. What's different about her, just because she's dying? She's still no good to me. That woman never did or said one thing in her life that was of any use to me. And she put up with that old pig. I'd have to see him, too. Why should I pay a thousand dollars to go all the way to Ireland to puke my guts up at the sight of him?

What if she asks for you? I said.

Oh well, Nora said. If she asked for me I'd go.

I borrowed a whole month's wages, so I had a lot of cash. The railway station is on a hill, and on the way down into the town, I left my bag in a bed-and-breakfast. The woman said, Didn't you pal around with Sharon Malone one time?

I told her I hadn't seen Sharon in a good while.

She married the Moran twins' brother.

I knew that.

She was a sight to behold, on the day.

I'd say she was, I said.

Make yourself a cup of tea any time, the woman said. And don't bother with the pay phone – come in and use ours. And don't worry – your ma will be all right. I'm going into town now to light a candle for her.

It took a while to piece it together. But by the time I met Danny in the pub opposite the hospital, on my second day, I knew enough to explain the whole situation to him. He hadn't a clue what was going on, himself, and he'd never have asked anybody.

Our mother, who had caught my hand in her grey hand when I touched her face, and bent her lips to it and kissed and kissed my fingers – that woman was five months pregnant, and she had cancer of the womb. I learned through and through that she had cancer, because I was just beginning to talk to her, murmuring to her about bringing in a brush to do her hair, when she twisted up in the bed and a terrible shriek tore out of her. Her face was mud-coloured and her eyes were staring with fear, and there was sweat all along her hairline. I began to suspect that something awful was going on when the nurse hurried in, but gave her nothing for the pain. I said to my mother, Wait, love – just wait till I get this sorted out, and I ran down the corridor after the nurse.

I didn't sort it out, though. I tried. All that first evening, I could not be stopped. I got to see the matron, the chaplain, the pharmacist up the street who was the head of the hospital's ethics committee. I ran around the town. I ended up in the pub opposite Malone's, having drink after drink by myself, and someone got Sharon's father and he brought me back to the bed-and-breakfast and told the woman not to let me use the phone, and I sat at the kitchen table with her and I raved and shouted.

I explained it all to Danny. The hospital was Catholic. It would not do anything that might harm the baby. It would not terminate the pregnancy. It would not give radiation therapy. It would not administer morphine in a volume that might have an adverse effect on the foetus. The baby must thrive, even though the cancer would thrive with the baby.

Why? Danny asked innocently.

Because the Pope says so, I said.

But – why? he said.

Because old men like him say it's the same as taking a gun and killing someone. It would be a kind of abortion if the treatment for Mammy killed the baby that's growing inside her.

Danny blushed brick-red. No one said that word in Ireland in 1970.

But, Danny said, the baby isn't even a baby yet, and this way they could both die.

But they'll both go to heaven, I said.

Even Danny saw I was being sarcastic.

The consultant had refused to let me into his office.

Your father is the relevant person here, he'd said on the phone. If you want a discussion, have a discussion with your father.

But I'd stood at his door, my face against the wood, banging on it, indifferent to the people waiting in the room, and the secretary, outraged, at her desk.

How long will it take her to die? I shouted through the door.

416

Come on, Mr Daly! I'm a busy person. How long will it take? Mr Daly? How long?

Now, I admired that girl, Kathleen. Well, not a girl, perhaps; I was twenty. But still, it was admirable that I was so unafraid, even though I was the child of two people who in their different ways feared authority. The only person I was afraid of was my father. I'd seen him lash Danny with a leather belt when Danny was only nine. I walked all the way to Uncle Ned's and complained. But much as I always loved Uncle Ned, I learned then that he wouldn't confront his brother. A man's family is his own business, Ned said to me. No one has the right to interfere between a man and his wife and children.

So who was there who could help? Other women? Mam had no friends. The nuns from school wouldn't help. Mrs Bates couldn't. What exactly, even, could I ask for? How did I know what my mother wanted herself? On the evidence of her life, and how she'd sat there passively as long as I'd known her while my father bullied her, she would endure this, too. Except – I kept remembering the scream –

Mrs O'Connor in the B&B sat with me that first night at the kitchen table. She made pot after pot of tea. She let me shout. She let me bang the table with my fists. I remember her face: she was nearly as desperate as I was, out of pure sympathy. She had family trying to sleep upstairs, and work to do in the morning, but she never lost patience with me. I tried to explain that Mammy had never got a break, that she'd always been pushed around, that she was dying for no reason, dying young, leaving her kids before she'd got anything back from them, for no better reason than she was a woman in a country run by bad old men.

Them and their unborn babies! I choked. Them and their rules for the womb! I could accept that she's dying, if she wasn't screaming in pain . . .

All night.

The woman was dropping with tiredness when at last I dragged myself up to the bedroom. She'd said maybe it was part of God's plan, and at that I had nothing more to say.

I was very shaky the next day when I finally managed to get going. I went out to the house in Shore Road and made the driver wait in the car till I was sure Daddy wasn't there. But he never varied his routine. He hadn't other times, either, when the Ma was in hospital with miscarriages and so on. Danny was in the kitchen with Sean. For the last few days he'd been getting everything he felt like on the bill at Bates's shop.

Jesus! he said. About time, Kathleen. I thought no one was going to show up! I have to go to the garage. We're busy.

My name is Sean, Sean said. He was going on five. His sandals were on the wrong feet. He hadn't seen me for nearly two years.

Is Mammy gone to heaven? he said.

I said nothing.

Is she your Mammy, too? he said.

She is not gone to heaven, I said. I was talking to her yesterday.

That was a lie, though I didn't realize it till afterwards. She never spoke to me. Her actual last words to me were what she said when she gave me the crystal necklace the day I left for college – the ones about not getting into trouble whatever I did. For a long time I believed that she did say something to me in the hospital that time, but now I think that it was her whole face and body mutely crying Help me! that I remembered as speech.

I didn't know where to begin. I had an awful hangover. I took Sean's sandals off and put them back on the correct feet. What was he doing in sandals in the winter anyway? He was a grand little boy and very good-tempered, but what the hell was I supposed to do with him? I took him along the terrace to Bates's shop. There must have been a high tide, because I could hear the waves rolling the rocks and the shingle at the top of the shore. I had passed the open door of Mammy's bedroom going in and out, and glimpsed the bed. She had always been there. Even if she wasn't much good as a mother, she was always there, since first I looked on the earth. Like a soldier, dumbly hanging on at his post.

Sean clung to Mrs Bates's leg. He must have been only pretending to trust me. She made sugary bread and milk for him in the kitchen and I talked to her from the door.

She said, But even if your father did ask them to discharge her, where could he take her? Sure she's on a drip.

He could take her to the nursing home.

The nursing home can't give cancer treatment.

Well then, he'll just have to take her to Dublin to a Protestant hospital.

But there's no abortions in Protestant hospitals, either. And anyway, maybe an abortion would just kill her quicker.

But they'd give her the morphine, Mrs Bates, I said. If you'd heard her shrieking!

Mrs Bates tried to put her arms around me. But I felt sick. I just made it up to her bathroom to retch and retch. Then I washed my face.

Does he go to see her? I asked Mrs Bates when I went down. I mean – other times, when she had the miscarriages and that?

Oh, indeed he does, she said.

What do they talk about? I asked.

Oh, I don't think they talk, she said, embarrassed. My own fellow never said a word, either.

Through the window behind her I saw the bus from Kilcrennan go past on its way to the circle of tarmacadam above the shore where it turned around. It only waited a minute or two at the stop there before it started back to the town, though the conductor usually lit a cigarette at this furthest point from civilization.

She saw that I was going to run for it.

But Kathleen, she began. And then she stopped. We looked at each other and everything must have been said on our faces. I hope, anyway, that she did see that I was saying that I could not stay. I could not. I thought – on the bus going away – that the main thing on her face had been pity. She had always pitied us, Mrs Bates had.

When we were in the lounge bar and I was explaining everything to Danny I didn't tell him what I was going to do, though I was shaking all over. It wasn't generosity on my part; I thought I'd have a better chance of getting Daddy to talk to me if I was on my own. I asked Dan to stay in the pub till I came back and I went over to the hospital.

It was just after seven. I only had to wait a few minutes. My father came in the swing door, his big red face as shiny as ever, his glasses halfway down his nose. He had a beige raincoat on over his dark suit and he was carrying a briefcase and a small paper bag.

A few plums for your mother, he said, gesturing at the bag, when I stood up in front of him.

I want to talk to you, I said.

So I believe. So certain parties have intimated to me, though I'm only half an hour in the town. I understand that you're not satisfied with the treatment this hospital offers? He was moving off already.

I'm not satisfied with *you*, I said. It wasn't easy to talk up at him, moving along the corridor with people passing. I think he said, Oh, *are* you not, madam.

She's suffering terribly, I began.

I can see that myself, he said.

If you could get her to somewhere that isn't Catholic, I began again.

He stopped abruptly, and bent his heavy face down into my upturned one.

Why would I do that? he said.

It's the Catholic thing that says the baby has to be protected –

Listen, he cut across me – I'll say it just once. That's my child, the same as you are. That child has as many rights as you have. Your mother is my wife. Your mother and I were married in a Catholic church and please God we'll be buried in a Catholic graveyard –

I'll take you to court, I said.

Do, he said. Give us all a laugh.

Then he nodded to the security guard they'd put outside the door of Mammy's room.

That's her, he said, pointing to me. She's not to be let in any time.

When I went back to Danny I told him the end of the story. I'd waited outside and I followed my father out to the car park, and I jumped at him beside the car. I kneed his big belly. I kicked his legs. I punched my hand into his mouth when he was gasping and I pulled out his upper denture and threw it on the ground. He nearly went mad. I was disgusted at having touched him so intimately. I stood off and spat at him, and then I ran away into the dark.

You're as white as a sheet, Danny said.

Are you going home? I said.

Sure, I have to, he said miserably. I can't just leave Sean with Mrs Bates.

When are you going to see Mammy? I asked him.

I'll go on Monday, as soon as he's gone away.

I got a brown envelope from the barman and wrote to her in block letters. MAM – IF YOU WANT ME TO GET YOU OUT I WILL, JUST TELL DANNY. NORA HAS MONEY. I WAS OUT AT THE HOUSE AND ALL IS FINE. I AM GETTING ON GREAT IN DUBLIN. PLEASE GET BETTER SOON.

I didn't want to sign it love. My feelings about her were different from love. I signed it:

YOUR KATHLEEN.

He looked at me with Mammy's big grey eyes.

Is there no chance at all you'd stay? he asked with what now strikes me as heartbreaking humility.

And I said no.

The next morning, Mrs O'Connor actually brought me my breakfast up to the room. It was the first time in my life I had breakfast in bed. I went down the hallway to the bathroom and washed my face so as to enjoy it properly and in a way I did love having a tray and the little thing of salt and pepper for my egg. I read *Mansfield Park*, which was the only book I had with me, while I was eating. Fanny Price had had a black time, too, but Edmund always loved her. I didn't have a boyfriend. I wanted someone to hold me tight. And I wanted someone to back me up against the system that made Mammy, who'd always been so quiet, cry out. And I wanted distraction from how guilty I felt – eating off a tray in a nice, pink room, and Danny left at home with Daddy, and stuck with Sean. I was always sure – since long before I started mooching after boys with Sharon, even – that there was a lover for me somewhere who'd help me with everything.

And instead, I have to be like a man! I thought, resentfully, because it seemed to me, looking at the world, that, like a man, I was on my own. I wasn't like a woman. Women usually had someone to look after them.

I took the tray down to the kitchen when I had my bag packed and my money counted.

I need all the money I have, I said to Mrs O'Connor. Could I pay you what I owe you another time? I'm going to England tonight.

I thought you were at college in Dublin?

I'm not going back, I said.

But aren't you on a scholarship! she said. You must be. And you're nearly finished!

I don't want to live in Ireland, I said. I don't ever want to set foot on Irish soil again.

Ah, for God's sake! she said. If the rest of us can put up with it, why can't you?

But then she saw my face and she said she was sorry.

And there's no problem with the money, she said. You can give it to me again.

She made me ham sandwiches for the boat. Her own soda bread, cut as thin as she could, swiped with bright mustard and folded carefully into greaseproof paper. She was nearly as upset as I was when I left to go up to the train. She said, over and over again, She'll be all right. She'll be all right. God is good . . .

I was running away. But I could think of nothing else to do. At least I still had the deep mark from my father's denture across my thumb. But then again, who would have guessed that he'd bring her in plums? For a while outside Kilcrennan the railway line goes along beside the sea, and it was pock-marked with rain that afternoon, but then the train picked up speed and the thick raindrops on the windows flattened and spread, and sealed us into the carriage, blinded.

When the train pulled, squealing and clanking, into the cavern of the station in Dublin, I let everyone else get off ahead of me. I walked down the long ramp from the station to get the bus to the ferryport to go to England. It wasn't really clear to me what I was doing, because I couldn't completely believe that she was going to die. To hell with them all! I thought. To hell with this whole fucking place!

I had deliberately left the ham sandwiches behind on my seat. Even now, I don't understand why I did that. Maybe I had some idea of sloughing off tenderness of any kind, and being as self-sufficient as I could from then on.

And it worked, for a long time. I did put Kilcrennan and Shore Road behind me. I was back at Joanie's, a month later, when my father rang to ask whether I was coming home for my mother's funeral. I wouldn't go to the phone. I moved out of Joanie's the next day into a staff room at the hotel I worked in, so no one would talk to me about it.

I didn't keep in touch with anyone. And Danny was very bad on the phone.

But he rang me about a year later to tell me Daddy was getting married to a woman who had been a nurse in the hospital Mammy died in. I was speechless.

And I don't blame him, Danny said. Sean is always sick. Someone has to mind him. And I'm going to live in Annie's until we save up enough to get married.

Nora was on Daddy's side, too.

If whatever her name is is willing to marry him, Kathleen, that's her business. Sure – our mother – it was like living with a corpse anyway.

I burned with anger when she talked like that about Mammy. But I wouldn't let her know that. She'd have been twice as delighted.

It didn't work, anyway, if that's why Daddy got married. Sean died when he was six and a half. When I heard, I thought with keen pain about the child's fat feet that he had so laboriously stuffed into the wrong sandals. Eventually I remembered Mrs O'Connor in the B&B, and sent her twenty pounds, with my apologies. Then I got annoyed with myself, because when I did that I had to go the whole hog so I sent back the wages I'd borrowed at my waitress job, too. I left myself broke.

*

I worked at my cleaning and waitressing jobs, and I talked my way into the London City Poly to do journalism, and I made friends there. I lived nowhere in particular, but I was young and it didn't worry me. My policy was never to think about home at all, and never to think about Ireland. And never to think or talk about politics or religion, or even read newspapers, because if killing poor sick women like Mammy was how church and state ended up two thousand years after Christ, I didn't want to know. I meant those resolutions with all my heart. I chose travel writing because it was the only kind of journalism I could think of that didn't involve believing in anything at all. The women's movement was the nearest I ever came to being an activist for social justice, but I was the most confused and wayward feminist you could imagine. I did take note of injustice, of course, but I would not allow my own life to respond to it. Instead, I went back to my basement and unpacked and opened a bottle of wine and tidied my notes. Until Manila. Maybe because the two kids and the baby under the dusty hedge in the middle of the highway reminded me at some deep level of myself and Danny and Sean.

When Danny and Annie got married they came to London on a weekend honeymoon trip. I went to see them at their hotel. Annie stayed up in the room at first, to give my brother and me a chance together.

Did you give Ma my note? I asked. This was three years after she died.

No. I never saw her again, either, he said. She was put in some kind of isolation place.

After a pause I asked him, Did the Da go to your wedding?

Of course he did. Made a speech.

Then Danny looked at me with a kind of grin.

He's having a hard time, he said. She's a terror, that wife of his. And what good did it do poor Sean?

Here, I said, and I put the present I'd bought for them on the counter in front of Danny. Tell Annie I couldn't wait, tell her it was too much –

He slipped down from his bar stool and folded me into his arms.

Mind how you go, he said.

I went back to where I lived at the time, which was south of the river, with Hugo, but I didn't mention to him where I'd been. It was the worst pain I have ever known – to think that since she did not get my note, she may have believed, in the three weeks she had left to live, that I abandoned her.

I never told anyone all the details surrounding Mammy's death, all my life. I didn't tell Jimmy, for instance, about Sean. I didn't know how to stop him thinking, for one split second, that Sean's death was like something out of Dickens. I made my father into a kind of comic, stage-Irish figure. I sealed my mother away in my heart. I didn't feel at ease when I did talk about her. It was out of all proportion, the pity the memory of her aroused in me. But I clung to it, as I would have clung to her love if she had loved me. I led a secret life, from her death on.

No! I said to myself, now. That's not true! You did forget her. And anyway – let it be, now.

The room where I was sitting in Felix's house was like a glowing, empty stage. The black night sealed off the world beyond the skylight and the glass wall. The place was like a setting of which I was the centrepiece, and I was a setting for the centrepiece of me – my heart.

Let it end here.

You thought you were the only one who knew about suffering, I said to myself. Well, late and all as it is, you know better now.

I left Mrs O'Connor's ham sandwiches on the seat of the train from Kilcrennan, and got the bus to Dun Laoghaire. I was early for the mail boat to Holyhead. The boat was in, but they weren't going to let us board for an hour. I walked up to the nearest pub. My heart lightened as soon as I went through the door into the roar of noise in the big lounge bar. It was a scene of near-abandon, almost a happy scene. The place was as big as a barn and it was packed with people – people in groups and lone people like me. Each bay of banquettes all down the hot, smoky lounge had its tribe of men and women and children and luggage, the tables laden with pint glasses and crisp packets and bags and sweet wrappers and Coke bottles, all swimming in spilled drink. At the bar, men called above the babble to the barmen who were literally running to try to serve everybody before the boat went. I took up a place at the back of the scrum of men nearest the door.

What're you having, darling? a man said back to me over his shoulder.

A vodka.

Men passed the drink back to me, and then a big bottle of lime cordial for a mixer. A few minutes later, when someone else must have stood their round, another drink came back. The men weren't trying to talk to me; they were urgently talking to each other, and drinking deep and fast. It was just that there was a camaraderie to the whole place. You could feel the recklessness.

I didn't see those men again. We all walked down the street to the boat at the last minute. It was dark, and children were crying, and someone was bellowing a song.

Then there was a long trudge along narrow walkways, where the wind off the harbour blew coldly through the wooden partitions, out to the gangplank. More families, everywhere on the boat, sitting on the floors, settling down in corners, the children running from side to side of the central lobby, and playing on the iron stairs, and coming back to their mothers propped against piles of luggage, the infants beside them askew in their buggies. Some people were already asleep on the carpet, their naked faces offered up to strangers, and latecomers picked their way across the bodies. In the bar, the men waited quietly at the counter. The metal lattice was down, though the barmen were working behind it in half-dark, getting ready for the night. The boat shuddered, and the siren gave a long wail, and the lights on the quayside began to slide past the windows of the bar. The crowd was quiet. There was no reaction to the last of Ireland. But when we were out of the harbour, and the boat started to buck a bit in the open sea, the metal lattice was thrown up, and the bar started serving. A cheer went up at that.

22

The sky was thick with pearly clouds on my last morning in the glass house beside the lake. But sparrows were chirruping in the thorn hedge, and behind me, on the highest point of the roof, starlings were pouring out the swooning cries that seemed the very sound of spring. The air was full of calls and trills and abrupt melodies. The birds owned this place, not Felix. That was something I would like to know about – birds. I would never have known that the coloured bird and the plain bird, outside the chapel after Jimmy's funeral, were chaffinches, if the old priest hadn't stopped and told me. There were probably lots of birds in his monastery. Though maybe it wasn't in the country – I had the impression it might be quite near Alex's mother's house . . .

I didn't want to tie up the phone, because this was the day Shay was going to call me. But I thought I should just let Ron next door to Alex know that I was moving on from this number.

I stood up from the top step of the outside stairs where I'd been drinking my coffee, and as I did, the same chubby hare I'd seen before lolloped out from beneath me and hopped in a leisurely way up the field. I was delighted. Hares are as lucky as seals. Seeing the hare was the next best thing to being blessed, going into this momentous day.

God! Am I glad to hear from you! Ron said. The person in question is here! Yes – Alex! My wife is making the poor old chap some breakfast. I went and got him this morning. We knew he was back at his house, you see, because I saw him going in the door on Wednesday evening, and we knew no milk had been delivered and that he'd done no shopping. So when he wouldn't answer the bell I got through the hedge at the back, and I saw him, sitting at the table in the kitchen.

His voice dropped to a whisper.

He's very, very down, old Alex is. Very.

When Alex came to the phone, he would hardly talk at first. I had to say several times – This is Kathleen, Alex! Kathleen!

Then he started talking non-stop.

Did I ever tell you about the time we were in Broadstairs? No? Isn't that extraordinary – that I didn't tell you that! Well, Mother had a small, leatherette purse. No – not leatherette, Kath – what do you call that stuff that's like plastic but it flakes off where it has been used too much and there is a kind of coarse fabric behind? With three ten-shilling notes. She said to me, Alexander, when we pay the landlady we will have enough for tea every day on the front, and supper every other day. She used to dig the fish out of the batter and pass it over to me and just eat the batter herself. Then the landlady gave me a shilling one day for bringing in the sacks of coal the coalman had left at the back gate, and I spent it on two fish suppers and I saw her wolfing her fish, and I realized what she had been doing . . .

Alex! I said. Have you slept?

She said to me the day I left school, when I was doing interviews for office work – Alexander, she said, your father was a thorough gentleman, but he did have a weakness, and a great deal of suffering was caused as a result, and I want you to promise me that you will never walk through that door with the smell of drink on your breath. And she understood me so well! She knew everything! When I came home from Trieste she didn't ask me how my talk had gone. She said, Alex, I fear you have been drinking! She said afterwards that all my success at work would mean nothing to her if I went the way of my father. Of course I didn't tell her that I wasn't a success at all. Even in Trieste, in the workshop, someone was talking about compiling e-mail address books, and Bobby Pick from Human Resources said, Oh, old Alex won't want to give up his quill and his parchment! and everyone looked at me, but I never told her things like that. She really lived for me, after God of course. She used to tell me a story when I was a little boy about a heart that walked along the road by itself. It was like a big, red hot-water bottle but it was

428

bleeding. She said, That heart can't find anyone to live in because it is a mother's heart – it is too big for just one woman!

Then he started to cry.

Alex! I said. Stop that!

And another time, she –

Shut up! I shouted. *I want you to stay in Ron's house.*

In Ron's house? he said. But I'm in Ron's house.

I know, I said. Stay there till I come for you.

I can't, Alex said, in something like his normal voice. What day is it today? I have to go to the monastery for Easter.

Oh, please, Alex, I said. Please, my dear. Don't go until I can see you. Please wait in Ron's for me. I can be there tonight. Please – I want to talk to you about you and me going on a little holiday –

But, Kathleen –

Put Ron on now. And wait for me till tonight, or I'll never forgive you!

Then I asked Ron to hang on to him.

Give him a sleeping pill if you can, Ron. I can come and get him tonight sometime. And then I'm going to take him somewhere and see that he eats properly and take him for walks until he's well enough to make decisions.

Roger! Ron said.

Don't tell those creepy monks anything if they turn up. Hide Alex from them.

Roger! Ron said. Over and out!

The boy at the car-hire desk in Shannon read me out the London schedule and I booked myself on the six o'clock to Heathrow. Then I picked up the phone again to ask Caroline for beds for myself and Alex. Then I reproached myself for not having rung Caroline before I did anything else.

Alex is in bits, I told her. He's probably terribly run-down as well as everything else. If he wants to be a monk, Caro, I can't stop him, but at least I can help him to get well first.

You're more than welcome to bring him here, she said. And I'm sure you'll be just the friend he needs. There's nothing like a holiday, is there? I would have loved a few days away after the exams but Nat wasn't available, as usual.

Oh, *Caroline* –

But what could I say? It had never crossed my mind to suggest a holiday to her. I laughed, but not very happily, when I put down the phone, at the familiarity of the situation. I was in the wrong with Caro already.

Then I stopped using the phone. But I was aware of it. I knew the instrument was squatting there, even when I was out of the studio packing my bag and breaking leftover bread into small pieces and scattering the pieces on the grass for whatever animal would come. I filled the tin plate with milk and a can of tuna. But the cats were nowhere to be seen. It was the middle of the morning; they always disappeared around then.

I'll use it again very quickly, I said to myself, and I rang Bertie to say I was heading back to London.

I was onto the hospice, he said heavily. It's not looking good for Nan.

I'll pray, I said, because I couldn't think of anything else to say. That it will be painless, above all.

She could easily go into remission yet! he said. It could be a long while yet before we have to give up hope. Couldn't it, Kathleen?

You might be right, I said lightly. He'd know what I was saying by the wrongness of the tone. But Bertie – do you think you'd have time to make up my bill for me? I have to go back to England today. A friend of mine isn't well –

The man who was here the other morning?

What man?

The one that was looking for you that I gave the currant bread to –

Oh! No. Not him.

I'm glad it wasn't him. He looked married.

For God's sake, Bertie! Even if it was him I was going to, it's none of your bloody business.

It is so, he said imperturbably. I'm nearly old enough to be your father. And I've been around. I know the way of the world.

The one I'm going to see is a monk! An Anglican monk! Is that good enough for you?

They're not proper monks, he said.

You're a bigot, I said. You ought to be ashamed of yourself, giving bad example to Ollie.

I waited another half an hour. Shay didn't ring. And of course, it would always be like that – that I couldn't phone him, that I couldn't act, that I would always be the one who was waiting for him to act. And I would always be ignorant of his circumstances. There was a story by Alice Munro about a man and woman meeting and spending a miraculous short time together. He indicates that he'll be back, and she buys lovely new sheets and delicious food. And he doesn't come back. And she walks out and drives all the way across Canada to get away from the pain, and starts a new life. And eventually she hears that he was very ill for a long time before he died. Shay could be dying or dead, and there'd be no way I'd know.

If I was going to catch the flight I'd have to leave now. Time was running out.

Time.

I will be dead for ever when I die. I am fifty years old. Well past the middle of the journey.

I'd hurt my fingernail pushing open a derelict stable door the first day I was up at Mount Talbot. I'd watched the black blemish move up my nail slowly. Soon, I would be able to cut it away. That movement was time working on my body. And there were two young girls at the edge of the square in Mellary the afternoon of the 1798 commemoration. Thin, laughing girls, looking around for boys. They had sticks of legs in absurd shoes – platform high heels, with just a curl of narrow strap. I'll never wear shoes like that again. I couldn't walk the length of a room in them.

What will become of me? I'll hate myself. Rotting on a bench, Henry James said, like a spinster in a hat. But Shay would want me even as I aged. His hands would stroke my thickening flesh. I could forget the onward rush into the dark. He would lift my foot, when he was crouching above me on the bed making an inventory of me, and he would kiss it, tenderly. He would help me to get old, because he would cherish my wrinkles and swellings and my tired toes.

Yet my decision was made. It had made itself in me. I hadn't been persuaded by one argument or another; it was simply that more weight had settled in one part of me than in another. When I recognized what I was going to do, I knew it with my mind because I already knew with my spirit. When Annie said to me that I was full of life – that Danny needed a sister who was full of life, like me – I involuntarily said to myself, Oh, I'm glad I didn't throw my life away! And in the Mount Talbot graveyard yesterday, when the others had moved on and I was standing on the path, I watched – tucked behind the green-stained wing of a stone angel – a blackbird, sitting quietly on its nest. Its head was bent onto its soft breast and it returned my look with a jewel-bright eye. Without any effort – like a ship sailing majestically into my head – the memory of standing outside the chapel after Jimmy's cremation came to me, and the tumbling birds I'd been looking at then. The pair of chaffinches. And the improbably twinkly old priest who had stopped beside me to look at them, and the advice he'd given me. Do the thing that's less passive, he had said. Do the active thing. There's more of the human in that.

That was it.

I would have to do the more active thing. I could not live in waiting. Waiting was too little to spend precious life on.

And I *would* always be waiting. No matter where I was, no matter what I was doing. I'd be like Marianne. As she begged her husband for tea and sugar, I would have to beg my lover to go on wiping out time for me. Because I would be living for him. Living on the meetings with him. Not living, for good or bad, on myself. My needy flesh would have walked me into another trap. I would have manipulated my life until it mimed my mother's, as exactly as Danny's hairline mimed the spring of her hair. We would never be out in the world together, Shay and I, any more than my mother and father had been. We would hardly need to speak. We would have made our own Windsor, our own Shore Road. We would die to time, yes, when we reached for each other. But time would get in through the lock

432

of the door. We would get old, anyway. We were not Tristan and Isolde. We would not die of passion. Passion, domesticated, would die on us, and what would be left would be life lived wrong.

No. The answer was no.

I didn't know what to do about telling him. Half past twelve, and Bertie's place still to call at. Maybe I could miss the flight and get a later one?

No. Either turn up for supper in Caro's when you said you would, or don't use Caro at all. Either collect Alex like you promised, or stop interfering. Either take account of other people from now on, or go back to the bad old days.

I knew that there was an answering machine on Felix's phone. I didn't want to leave a message for Shay that anyone at all who happened to ring the number would understand. And I didn't want to leave a businesslike message, as if what he'd asked of me and offered me was a practical thing. He had been shaking with sincerity, out there in the field, under the thorn tree, when he asked me to fit my life to his. But I would leave a private message. If Shay didn't grasp what I was trying to say . . . But he would. He would.

I found the right CD from Felix's collection – *Hit Songs of 1946* – and I scanned it till I found the few lines I wanted. I played them – they took about fifteen seconds – and then I went back to their start point and set them up to play again. Then I held the Record microphone slot of the answering machine to the speaker of the CD player. I pressed Play on the CD player and Record on the answering machine simultaneously. Then I checked the answering machine: it had recorded the few lines from the song perfectly.

I looked around the house, to say goodbye to it. I touched the handle of the kettle lightly, because the human being, Shay, had touched it, too. I closed my eyes and ran my hands down my body. I swallowed the panic and misery that wanted to rise in me. I walked through each room and I paused in each, to feel them. I locked up, and with one last, loving look at the valley and the lake, and one wistful call for the wildcats to come to me, I walked up to the car. In only the few days I'd been at the house, bright daisies had appeared in the grass. Under the greening hedge, where the boulders were covered in moss, the first bluebells had opened. If only he had rung! I would have heard, to take away as a comfort, the way his voice warmed the word Kathleen. And maybe, if he insisted, there could have been one more time. But now – I'd never even know whether he did ring, or not. He had been thinking, too, these last few days, after all.

It was only a mile and a bit to Ballygall – empty countryside all the way. Yet halfway along, the lane became a road as wide and straight as a motorway. I knew from my paperbacks about the Famine what that meant: a famine relief road – a purposeless fragment of highway – built to make the starving work for their welfare shilling. There was no traffic, so I could do what I had a sudden whim to do. I drove that sorrowful stretch of the road as far in beside the verge as I could, at 10 miles an hour – the pace of a hearse at the head of a funeral procession. I did it deliberately. I imagined I was dragging below me a line that went down from myself, through the steel of the car, and the tarmacadam of the road surface, into the skim of stones and earth that cadaverous hands and arms had spread along this ridgetop. There was only work for some of the hungry, so others, desperate, worked breaking stones beside the chosen ones all day, in the hope that someone would pay them. This happened often; but they never were paid. That was the only detail of all I had read about the Famine that had made me break down.

Take this with you, I thought to myself. This happens now. This happens anywhere people are demeaned by hunger.

I pulled out and brought the car up to normal speed. I had a long drive ahead of me.

The emigrants who had walked out of this landscape with their bundles would have walked past the men at work on the famine relief road. They all knew each other, of course. The ones who were going must have stopped for a word, a reassurance, a blessing. That would have been the very last occasion when the whole society was present, before it split into those who left and those who stayed. But William Mullan began to pay his dues for knowing Marianne when he had to go to America on the run, without farewell or blessing.

It said, in the Lords *Judgment*:

Mr Talbot succeeded in obtaining a verdict for damages, however, Mullan had gone off to America, and from his position in life he could not have paid two thousand pence . . .

That was a fact. It was fact that Richard had won a case for damages against William Mullan, and that Mullan, penniless, went to America. What frame of mind he went in, however, and what he did in America, were matters for speculation.

I didn't *know* the truth of what happened at Mount Talbot and I would never know it. There were too many contexts missing. When I remembered turning the key in my door to let Caro's Ian in, and the feel of his cold hands on my warm skin, I could fit those details into a framework of the wine I'd drunk, and the way we ran through the icy night, and my stomach turning over that day when I saw the man who might be my father. But without flesh like that on their bare bones, the reported actions of Marianne and Richard and William Mullan were surreal – literally detached from reality.

I could *choose* what to believe about the Talbot scandal. I *would* choose what to believe.

And what else could I believe, on the day I was tearing myself away from my dearest lover – feeling, gaping within me, a gulf of cold fear that I would never know physical bliss again – but that Mullan had adored her, and she had adored him? And in truth, I didn't see any explanation for his following Marianne to Coffey's Hotel and sending in the note, but that it asked her to come to America with him. And I didn't believe he had gone to America in any other frame of mind but the one I was in myself when I let myself think about what I was losing in Shay – longing, and uncertainty, and bitter regret, and desire still so vivid that at the sound of the lover's approaching voice the body would have curled back to present its interior.

From Bertie's den behind the desk in the hotel I dialled the number of Felix's house. Yes – the answering machine kicked in perfectly. And there was my message to Shay – the gravelly voice of Walter

Huston singing the few lines I'd chosen from 'September Song' –

. . . But the days grow short,
When you reach September.
When the autumn weather
Turns the leaves to flame,
And I haven't got time,
For the waiting game . . .

Then the beep came.

Tired, the singer sounded. Hoarse with experience. Dragging his voice up to the word *time*. The ironic tune in its minor key told Shay what he and I had no choice but to accept: that we were grown-up.

I kissed the children and Ella goodbye in the kitchen, and I promised to come back soon – maybe for Joe's First Communion. Bertie hurried heavily up the path behind me as I made my way blindly to the car.

They're not worth it, my dear girl, he said, holding me in his big woollen arms and patting my back as if I were a child. I'm one of them, so I know.

This man was lovely, I said. I was so happy when I was with him –

Sure, how do you think I'm going to manage without Nan? he said. And Ella's fella will be home soon and they'll be all over the house mooning at each other. And I never as much as held Nan Leech's hand. Not once.

You have the little boys . . . I began.

He said nothing for a long moment, and then, Yes.

I drove through the afternoon in a trance. When my hands moved on the wheel, or my thighs shifted a tiny bit, or my foot came up or down, my consciousness would drift, slow and heavy, up towards the surface, and before I could divert it, the lament inside me would begin again. I'd lift a hand from the wheel and touch my cheek and I'd feel its skin under my fingertips. I put my hand on my leg under my cotton skirt. Silky skin on the inside of a thigh. The soft skin on the swell of my stomach. The rough skin of my knee. The warmth of the skin. Life coursed underneath my skin. Where my fingers rested – where skin made a small pressure on skin – vibrancy collected. Oh! and how much more if these were another's fingers, not my own, if they were broad-tipped and hard, if they pressed into me, moved on me. If they were intent. If they were feeling me out, like a minesweeper moving across terrain. If someone was touching me who desired to know the make of me.

If I were William Mullan I would have stayed with horses. Not just because horses were what I knew, and that there was a lot of work available – Irishmen brought horses to both sides in the Civil War and provisioned them and shod them and tended them when they were injured. But because you can lean your head against a horse's flank. You can plait a horse's mane. You can use your hands to gentle a horse. You can use your thighs and knees and heels to send a horse flying. I hope he worked at a racetrack – the Saratoga track opened a few years after he got to the States, and it isn't too far inland from the immigrant ports – because racehorses are maybe the most beautiful of all horses, when they hit their stride, and their ears go back, and they do, perfectly, the thing they can do. He could easily have got up to Saratoga, and been allocated a bed in one of the clapboard dormitories there, behind the exercise yards and the stables.

When he left Ireland, he had nothing. He owned what he stood up in. The same as me, when I went straight to London after leaving Danny and Sean in Shore Road and my mother in the hospital in Kilcrennan. He and I left Ireland on our own, like Irish men and girls usually did. Maybe there was a better chance, statistically speaking, of finding someone to lie entwined with in the New World than in the old. But they didn't know that as they walked up the gangways of the emigrant ships. They were like me today – unable to imagine anything about the future except how difficult it would be. Conscious only of what they had lost.

Once Marianne disappeared from Coffey's Hotel, Mullan must have been completely lost. He cannot have known that she was locked up in an asylum in Windsor. That was the terrible thought – that she was an Englishwoman. He could not believe that she had

437

merely been amusing herself with him, but he knew nothing about her life before Mount Talbot. For all he knew, she was comfortable, now, somewhere in England, in some big house of the class of people she belonged to. He did not even know whether, among those people, she was seriously disgraced. He was not quite disgraced, among his own. But it would never be forgotten to him, all the same, that the scandal between himself and the Englishwoman happened at the time it did. They were still burying people in pits because there were no coffins left in that part of the country, at the time that he and she were first seen to go along the corridor behind the wood store towards the small buttery, a candle half shaded in his hand.

He cannot have known what happened to the note he sent in to the hotel. He must have suspected, while he waited for the reply to the note that did not come, that she read it but would not answer it.

I was preparing to leave my characters, now, where the historical record had left them. The Reverend McClelland dead in the graveyard at Mount Talbot. Marianne, feebleminded, dependent on the charity of the Pagets in their villa in Leicester. And William Mullan in America. I'd allow myself, as I drove along, when I was trying not to think about myself, the invention of this detail or that to embellish the record. Then I'd risk coming back to myself. I'd rearrange myself in the driver's seat, lean forward, drive with great precision. The country I was driving through was only a green space. I didn't care any more what was outside. What would become of me? Dread flushed through me. I'd flex myself a moment against the seat of the car, and the consciousness of my physical self would turn, like a wave falling down into its underside, into an ache.

It was all physical, my regret. I had known Shay the way Marianne had known Mullan. Flesh on flesh. We had had to, all four of us, leave the memory and the promise of passion behind in Ireland.

In America, at that time, every Irish person looked at every other to see whether they had known each other at home, before the exodus. Some years after Mullan began to work at the racetrack, a woman from Ballygall came as head barmaid to one of the big taverns near the springs at Saratoga. It was packed with trippers in the summer, and it was where the workers from the track drank in the fall. One night Mullan came in on his own, and went up to the bar for a beer. The barmaid said to him, over her shoulder, as she moved away, *Bhfuil fhois agat – tá aithne agam ortsa!* She said it coldly, not flirtatiously.

Where do you know me from? he asked, when she was next in earshot.

I was a maid in the demesne for a while when you were carrying on with the mistress. She leaned into him, and they spoke in Irish and in low voices. My mother was told about it and she took me out.

He looked at his feet. But he was still, then, a man a woman might think of. And the scandal associated with him lent him attraction.

They said things that weren't true, he said.

Ah – I'm not sorry that I left that place, she said. I have a house of my own here. My little girls are receiving the best of education here. If we had stayed at home, what would there have been for them?

What news does your mother send? Mullan asked.

The big house is gone to hell. And they closed down the National School as soon as they opened it – there's no children for it.

Why are there no children? Mullan said, bewildered.

None of the women had any children for years after, she said. The women didn't get enough food! I was the same – my bleeding stopped for two years after the hunger.

I never knew that, he said.

It was a punishment on all of us, she said. Was there ever any other people that such a thing happened to as the potatoes failing and then the fever and then the exterminations?

But what was it a punishment for?

Oh, for everything! she said. I don't know what for!

Is Mrs Talbot dead? he said in a casual way, his voice muffled as he finished the last of his drink.

Why would she be dead? the barmaid snapped. What would someone that never did a tap of work in her life die of?

*

He did well for a while. He had a steady job in the Whitney yard, in charge of exercise for the thoroughbreds. A small house came with the job – the first house of his own he had ever had. The house was in the middle of a wood of birch and pine. Now that he had good money and a good place, he thought about her more than ever. But then, he thought of her when the hot food was dished out to him in the canteen, and he thought of her when he slid into his bed at night, and he thought of her whenever he smelled smoke, and at many other times. The way it is, he said to himself, once, when a woman in a tavern ran her hands over him, I think about her all the time, but sometimes I think about other things.

He lived neatly. He cleared a plot of earth beside the deck of his house and planted potatoes in tidy ridges. He planted a row of cabbages and two rows of carrots. Inside the house, he had a rocking chair beside the stove, and a paraffin lamp that he won at a carnival that had red roses on its opaque globe. He had a concertina. He could only pick out a few of the tunes his mother had played. Still, he would spend hours over it, on winter nights, his big fingers splayed on the tiny keys. Mrs Talbot used to say that there was magic in his fingers, but that was only true when he was with her. The only thing was, that he had no dog. That was remarked of him – that he was the only man who lived in the woods who had no dog.

There was some bird in the belt of pinewoods that gave a feminine cry that tormented him. Because of the bird he wrote to her at last:

Dear Madam. I entreat you to write me a letter. I think of you every hour. I have touched no other woman, and if you had it in mind to journey over here I would provide for you in every way. Also, there would be a child. If you come to me here at Saratoga Springs, State of New York, I will give you every proof of the love and attachment I have for you.

He sent the letter enclosed in another one to Tadhg Colley, asking him to do his utmost to find an address for Marianne Talbot and to forward it.

After five months his letter came back, with a note wrapped around it.

Tadhg wrote:

We are all well here. Your mother's place is gone but Hurley has a few beasts on that field behind and they say he is draining all that end for drystock. The big house is going to ruin and Mrs Benn and the Finnertys are living in it below stairs. Halloran never came back. There was talk of the Bishop buying the big house to give it to the nuns that are at present in the old courthouse, but there is trouble as to who is the legal owner now the master is reputedly dead.

I did not know where to send the enclosed, nor do I believe that any good would come of it. Your friend.

After that, William Mullan did occasionally drink a lot with the other men from the track. He used to sing a song when he was drunk – standing up on the bench and shouting at the rowdy company to hush and listen to him. It was a song called 'The Emigrant's Farewell', he would say, that he learned from a Scotsman.

The same Scotsman was a bastard! he'd shout. He came into our place and he asked the tenants there to slink down to day men and to be called by the ring of his bell and be cuffed and cursed by a Scottish steward – men who were wont to ride a good horse to market . . .

The other Irishmen would cheer and bang their tankards. They knew Willie Mullan always said that and that also, he always cried, when he tried to sing the end of the song –

. . . *Our ship she is ready to sail away, and it's come my sweet comrades o'er the stormy sea.*
Her snow-white wings are all unfurled, and soon shall swim in a watery world.
Don't forget, love, do not grieve, for my heart is true and cannot deceive.
My hand and heart I will give to thee
So farewell my love, and remember me.

The barmaid from Ballygall married again, and opened a lodging house in Philadelphia, and forgot him.

But many years later, when she was folding sheets on the table in her dining room, she heard his name mentioned among a group of men playing cards outside the window, on her veranda.

Yes – William Mullan, she heard. The fellow that rode the arse off the Englishwoman.

What about him?

He's after dying, Lord have mercy on him. It was in a list in the paper.

And the group of men murmured, Lord have mercy on him, and went on with the game.

He had died on the path through the birchwoods, where it crossed a glade. When men came looking for him from the stables, he lay across the path with his face looking up into the stormy autumn sky, and his arms flung out, and his hands splayed – the sensitive fingers making small impressions in the soft leaf mould. Light autumn leaves blew through the clearing. He looked as lonely lying there as he had indeed been, since he left his home.

And so William Mullan departed from me, after keeping me company halfway down Ireland. I was finished with them all, now. I left the hired car in its compound and gave the keys to the boy there. The seed that had been planted in me when I was young, when Hugo threw the xerox of the *Judgment* onto the bed, that had somehow germinated in the darkness of my life, had now bloomed and died. It didn't matter that there wouldn't be a book.

I walked into the terminal lightly. If I had no plans left – if I was naked – I was perfectly free, too. Newborn, even. I looked at the people in the terminal as if I had been away from humankind, like Rip Van Winkle, and they were a species I was going to have to learn again. I liked them. I felt my own face soften in sympathy with people who smiled, and laughed, and frowned at their watches, and looked tensely at the sliding doors, their faces changing beautifully as the person they'd been waiting for came through and towards them. This hall was full of feeling, and it wasn't necessarily full of lovers at all. Where would I take Alex, if he'd let me take him anywhere?

I got a sheet of paper at the car-hire desk to leave a note for the woman I'd met the evening I arrived. The radio behind the desk was playing softly. A tenor, singing the Flower Song. *La fleur que tu m'avais jetée . . . Carmen, je t'aime.* Oh Jesus! Like a knife in me, the longing. I'd have to box my way forward – guarding myself here, feinting there; I'd have to manage the longing and the regret. Had Shay rung the house yet? What did he think about the way I left the message for him? Oh, if he walked towards me now, and tucked my arm in his and led me over to the hotel! But no – I said I'd be in London tonight. I scribbled:

Hello. Sorry to miss you. But back soon, I think, unfortunately for funeral of great old lady but otherwise looking forward already. Audi reverse sticky. I have sometimes been in heaven this trip thank you like the song says for being an angel just when I thought that heaven was not for me.
Kathleen.

Then I went into the shop and bought a map of Europe and spread it out while I waited in the departure lounge.

They were boarding the American flights. I heard the names over and over: New York. Boston. Chicago. New York . . .

Nora was a gallant woman. I now had exactly one, short-term commitment – to help Alex get better – otherwise, my life was as bare as a room. But Nora – Nora could have won prizes for networking. She and her friends were always organizing Irish-American receptions at places like the Waldorf, or sponsored races at race meetings, or golf classics with comedians and bishops, or testimonial dinners at midtown hotels or in vast steak houses in Brooklyn for politicians called Pat and Aloysius and Declan and Mike. Nora Burke was hon. secretary of this or hon. treasurer of that on the circuit of the biggest Irish-American chieftains. She was in a network of building-contractor millionaires, lawyers, CEOs of breweries, feedstuff purveyors, administrators of wealthy dioceses. She'd tell me complicated stories about how Chuck had called at the last minute to say he wasn't enthusiastic about meeting Dan after the problem with the shopping mall in Rockaway and how she'd called Al, who was the biggest shareholder in Dan's bank, at his club and said to him, Al, you know you owe me one, and how then Monsignor Horgan had heard what she'd done, and he'd said to Adele at the Sacred Heart Banquet for the Bangalore Mission, I hear Nora has been interfering in my parish again . . .

Boston. Gate 4 for Chicago. JFK now boarding . . .

I couldn't live like her any more than with her. But I would have to take note from now on of the energy – the *work* – she put into making a life. Because that was what Henry James said: we need never fear not to be good enough, if we are only social enough. See, if I *tried* I would not end up in a basement again. Not that her dizzy social life does much for Nora's moral sensibility, if that's what James meant – it barely covers up the savage self she carried into adulthood. Oh, dear. That's what Jimmy used to say – that no matter how hard I tried to be nice about Nora, I started bitching about her within three sentences.

I spread out the map of Europe. Where would I take Alex? It would have to be somewhere quiet and with good food. Maybe the weather would be nicest in Italy. If we flew to Bologna, say, and got a car and drove south . . . We could make something out of the journey, even – moving slowly, and looking around at everything – the way I did when I was on my way to Greece long ago. And we could stay at the beautiful old farm on the slope of a meadow, if we went to that *agriturismo* place in the foothills of the Apennines. We could walk into the village before dinner and sit in the little piazza drinking Campari and watching the *passeggiata* as the snow-topped mountains across the valley gradually faded into the dark blue of the night. Oh, if it were Shay I was with! In late spring, just about to topple into hot summer. Everything will be filled with glistening juice and sap – the young leaves will be bursting from the vines, the plum blossom tumbling wild through the trees, the grasses, the banks of violets and emerald moss, the red poppies in the weeds, the artichokes and onions and young spinach in the black earth – they'll all be vibrant with life. Doves will flutter from the roofs. At night, we'll hear owls in the apple orchards.

Alex did not get a proper chance at life. I'll name things for him, from the little I know: sparrow, swallow, clover, frog spawn. One of the reasons he's so involved with his monks is that he's never even looked at the natural world. And I'll teach him about food. Chilled wine and asparagus and crostini and roast lamb and almond tart and creamy cheeses. Bats will dart almost invisibly beneath the feathery trees as we walk home down the glimmering road. And we'll talk about work, but not about death, or religion. And I will listen with as much respect as I can to his memories of his mother. Which won't be easy. Only this morning, when he was going on about her on the phone, I'd had to bite back the words – already clearly formed in my mind – But Alex! She was only your mother, for God's sake! She wasn't Marie Curie, you know. She wasn't St Teresa of Avila –

I jumped up. That was Ireland talking in me! I almost ran over to the phones. Yes – Nora picked up in the apartment.

We never honoured Mammy, Nora! I said. I see that now. We should have gone to her funeral. We showed no respect for her. We didn't go because we hated Daddy, but that made Daddy more important than paying our respects to her.

But I didn't respect her, Nora said. I despise her to this day.

No you don't! I said. You know it wasn't her fault. Trapped there with no contraception and no money and no education and bad health and nothing in her head but romance –

She could have stood up to him! Nora said. She could have got off her ass and made us a bit of breakfast! She was no good –

Even if she was no good, we should have treated her properly! We should have gone home for her funeral. We should have talked about her with people who knew her. We should have, Nora! We should have! We're middle-aged women now and we have to forgive the past – for our own sakes, Nora. And the way to do that is to see the parents – and to see ourselves – as *precious*. Just for having existed!

I could hear her making spluttering noises but I ploughed on.

Alex's mother was a terrible old bag, Nora, but he's doing the right thing, mourning for her. It's the right thing to do, that's all, when the person who has given you life moves on into death –

. . . Now boarding Flight EI65 to London Heathrow, at gate 10 . . .

Kathleen? Give me a break! Lay off. I'm sick of her. I'm sick of your hang-up about her.

It's not just her, Nora. Daddy, too! He *made* us. We should have gone to *his* funeral, too. We are only links in a chain –

. . . Final call now, gate 10 . . .

I have to go, I said. I'll call you again.

Kathy – she was beginning, but I hung up.

Who knows what people are ever thinking? I looked at the blank backs of the people in front of me as we shuffled towards the gate where they were collecting boarding passes. No one looking at me would guess that I was praying. Let there be a heaven. Let Mammy be in heaven. Let there be something for her because she had such a hard life. She never went anywhere and she'd have loved it. Hotels, she'd have loved. Please make up to her for being in that house. The cold water tap and the sugar crunching on the floor and the low window and the rain. Mammy, please if you still exist, please be somewhere where you are loved, and the cold circle of neglect that was around you in life, please let it be burned away.

And, I forgive you. See, we have to part company. I have to get old, which you never had to. I have to watch the Marianne in me dying from now on. This is the hardest thing: and no one warned me.

Take-off. I huddled over at my window, peering down as if, this time, not to lose a second of my leaving. On my way to England. Like Marianne. No home, like Marianne. No child, like Marianne. No lover. No occupation. I was sitting beside a man with a very nice smile. I smiled back, easily. I must have been mad, in the old days. Oh Most Gracious Mother! Let me remember Shay as long as I can and let this surge of life in me – so strong that it could lift the plane by itself – survive into the time without him.

Such a lovely little country, all the same! Didn't one of the early astronauts say that from space, Ireland was the greenest thing on all the planet? The plane was rising over hills cross-hatched with fields.

446

Small, secret lakes were cradled on their summits. The land was green as jade from horizon to horizon as we angled up and away. Then we broke into the cloud, and were lost in pure grey radiance for a few moments, and then we were born again into the perfect blue of the high sky. Between places.

Up in those birchwoods that surround the racetracks at Saratoga there are herds of white-tail deer. Mullan used to get up at dawn to go down to the stables. And as he walked down the path through the clearing, he would see from the corner of his eye the deer startle and turn, to crash away through the flickering green-and-silver undergrowth between the ranks of trees. And the deer turned their flanks to him as they rolled and jumped away – white flanks, dun flanks. When they did, he saw in his mind's eye her naked side, as she turned languidly beneath him, on a bed of her dress and her petticoats.

Back at Mount Talbot, the old woman who was the last of the Talbots left, and the butler was taken away, and people came up from Ballygall and looted even what they had no use for from the house. The windows began to crack after years and years in wind and sun, and then split and splintered, unheard, in winter storms, and the curtains rotted on the top floors, and then the dereliction moved down the house and broken glass and leaves were scattered over the window seats and the oaken boards. Then, the smell of turf ash and lamp oil went out of the house. When the air in the house was fresh and sweet, the house had died, too.

William Mullan was not alone when he died. He did fall back onto the path through the clearing, very early one autumn morning. But the deer came to feed where he had fallen, as the morning mists dissolved slowly in the low sun. They were all around him, and he knew it, when life was draining from him. When the men from the stable found his body, it did look lonely. But he had seen her dolphin body above him – the white torso twisting and turning in a most beautiful way – at the very end. And the deer did not move away until he was dead.

Acknowledgements

My heartfelt thanks are due to the writer Anthony Glavin, who in editing *Are You Somebody?* brought me to writing.

Also to Mrs Patsey Duignan of Strokestown, County Roscommon, whose copy of the Talbot *Judgment* I brought to Yaddo, where I began this book: I thank the Corporation of Yaddo for its hospitality.

My sister, Grainne O'Broin, read an early draft of *My Dream of You* and somehow, after that, I had turned a corner.

Colm Tóibín gave me splendidly energetic advice, and Sydelle Kramer and Julie Grau helped me in every way and at any time.

Above all, writing this was never lonely, because I knew all the time that dear friends cared about me and it – on one side of the Atlantic, Mary Parvin, and on the other, Luke Dodd.

What I know of Ireland around the time of the Famine I learned from teachers at the Merriman Summer School; from the work of Professor Robert Scally; from the *Famine Diary* Brendan O'Cathaoir contributed to the *Irish Times*; and from the eloquent remains of those terrible times on the hill of Knockfierna, County Limerick.

refresh yourself at penguin.co.uk

Visit penguin.co.uk for exclusive information and interviews with
bestselling authors, fantastic give-aways and the
inside track on all our books, from the Penguin Classics
to the latest bestsellers.

BE FIRST ▼

first chapters, first editions, first novels

EXCLUSIVES ▼

author chats, video interviews, biographies, special
features

EVERYONE'S A WINNER ▼

give-aways, competitions, quizzes, ecards

READERS GROUPS ▼

exciting features to support existing groups and
create new ones

NEWS ▼

author events, bestsellers, awards, what's new

EBOOKS ▼

books that click – download an ePenguin today

BROWSE AND BUY ▼

thousands of books to investigate – search, try
and buy the perfect gift online – or treat yourself!

ABOUT US ▼

job vacancies, advice for writers and company
history

Get Closer To Penguin . . . www.penguin.co.uk